BY WRIGHT MORRIS

Novels

Three Easy Pieces (1993)
Plains Song (1980)
The Fork River Space Project (1977)
A Life (1973)
War Games (1972)
Fire Sermon (1971)
In Orbit (1967)
One Day (1965)
Cause for Wonder (1963)
What a Way to Go (1962)
Ceremony in Lone Tree (1960)
Love Among the Cannibals (1957)
The Field of Vision (1956)
The Huge Season (1954)
The Deep Sleep (1953)
The Works of Love (1952)
Man and Boy (1951)
The World in the Attic (1949)
The Man Who Was There (1945)
My Uncle Dudley (1942)

Photo-Text

Photographs & Words (1982)
Love Affair: A Venetian Journal (1972)
God's Country and My People (1968)
The Home Place (1948)
The Inhabitants (1946)

Essays

Earthly Delights, Unearthly Adornments (1978)
About Fiction (1975)
A Bill of Rites, A Bill of Wrongs, A Bill of Goods (1968)
The Territory Ahead (1958)

Anthology

Wright Morris: A Reader (1970)

Short Stories

Collected Stories 1948–1986 (1986)
Real Losses, Imaginary Gains (1976)
The Cat's Meow (1975)
Here Is Einbaum (1973)
Green Grass, Blue Sky, White House (1970)

Memoir

Writing My Life: An Autobiography (1993)
A Cloak of Light: Writing My Life (1985)
Solo (1983)
Will's Boy (1981)

WRIGHT MORRIS

THREE
EASY
PIECES

Black Sparrow Press   Santa Rosa   1993

THREE EASY PIECES. Copyright © 1971, 1973 and 1977 by Wright Morris.

Black Sparrow Press books are printed on acid-free paper.

LIBRARY OF CONGRESS CATALOGING-IN-PUBLICATION DATA

Morris, Wright, 1910–
    Three easy pieces / Wright Morris.
      p.   cm.
    Contents: The Fork River Space Project — Fire sermon — A life.
    ISBN 0-87685-924-4 : $25.00. — ISBN 0-87685-925-2 (hard : signed) : $35.00. — ISBN 0-87685-923-6 (pbk.) : $15.00
    1. Conflict of generations—West (U.S.)—Fiction. 2. Aged men—Travel—West (U.S.)—Fiction. 3. Ghost towns—Kansas—Fiction.
I. Morris, Wright, 1910–   Fork River Space Project. 1993.   II. Morris, Wright, 1910–   Fire sermon. 1993.   III. Morris, Wright, 1910–   Life. 1993.
IV. Title.   V. Title: 3 easy pieces.
PS3525.O7475A6   1993
813'.54—dc20   93-35699
                                        CIP

TABLE OF CONTENTS

THREE EASY PIECES

THE FORK RIVER SPACE PROJECT

For Jo

1

I HAVE JUST DISCOVERED I CAN MAGNIFY
objects by a slight pressure on the lids of my eyes. My head lies
on the pillow, a fold on the bedspread touches my nose. The
weave is coarse. If I press lightly on the lids of my eyelids the
material of the spread looks like a fishnet. If I lid my eyes and
turn to face the light, I see a color glowing like heated metal.
Across it motes flick, like water insects. The color changes to
a smog-filtered sunset. If I give myself over to this impression,
I am free-falling in space (that is my sensation), and only by an
effort do I recover my bearings. I owe this to Harry Lorbeer. He
started me thinking—or should I say seeing? On the mind's eye,
or on the balls of the eyes, or wherever it is we see what we imagine, or imagine what we see.

   If you browse in magazines sold on supermarket counters
you may have remarked the name Serenus Vogel. That is my pen
name. I do humorous, fantasy-type pieces. Prior to my meeting
with Harry Lorbeer I did not take people seriously. In the
checkout line at the market this morning the clerk said to me,
"Could you recommend an agent?" He had seen my face on a
book jacket. I confess I was slow to make the connection. "I've
got this story," he went on, "about my father. I need help with
the Cuban background." This young man is tall, sandy-haired,
and free of what I would describe as Cuban characteristics. His
name is Carl. I read it on the name tag that said he was eager
to serve me. People do have their place if we can just determine
what it is.

   Prior to my meeting with Harry Lorbeer I was researching
a piece of an historical nature. Not far from our house wagon
tracks wind across a field in a westerly direction, but you can't
perceive them at ground level. They turn up in aerial photographs

made in a government survey during the depression. You have to know what you're seeing. The pressure on the eyeball must be just right.

I have a fire-blackened penny, dated 1851, found in an ashpit with human bones, two sardine tins, musket balls, and arrowheads. Would you say that is history or science fiction? My wife and I live on the eastern rim of the plains, near the southerly fringe of the last great ice sheet. From the air you can see where the ice scoured the surface, rolling up balls of turf from the ancient sea's bottom. Some are petrified. My friend Rainey refers to them as dinosaur turds. Eleven miles due west a man-made mini-crater seats sixty thousand rabid football fans in season. They wear red hats and jackets and in a period of excitement might suggest that the crater is in eruption. What you see out here is from where you see it, and what you know. I see wagon tracks, covered wagons, hounded Indians, horse thieves, fur trappers, and plagues of grasshoppers. My neighbor on the south sees only the weather. His eyes are faded and creased from sky gazing. His wife's people see corn, soybeans, and beef cattle, with the exception of her brother, an engineer, who sees freeways. I have an uncle who is big in center pivot irrigation. He flies an airplane and takes his own pictures. From a few miles in space the pivot system leaves a pattern of circles like a target. An orbiting satellite might read them as a warning, or as a welcome. My friend Rainey, the weather man, sees prehistoric creatures waddling in a vast inland sea. He prefers what he sees to the missile silos that are actually there. My wife Alice sees the frost that will kill her garden. On my way to the market I often note a woman gazing over the half curtain at her kitchen window. Before her, westward, roll the endless plains, but it is not what she sees. It could be that this is the right place for her, as it is for me. I sit here for hours with my fire-blackened penny, my fingers resting on my eyelids. In the blackness of space I see a cloud-wreathed object with jade green seas, smooth as marble, splattered with sable-colored islands. Here and there patches of land, like wrinkled skin, or sweeps of sand fine as talcum, but no sign of life, or death for that matter.

12

Am I a member of the first landing party? Knowing what I know, dare I risk it? The continents corrupted, the seas polluted, every living thing converted into pet food? I wake up with dry lips, filmed with perspiration. To get back to where I sit I need a decompression chamber. And there's the crux of the matter— at least according to Harry. Why should we come back? There's a knack to it, of course, and you'd better believe it. I am now in touch with people who are working on it. In one of the recent movies I've seen primates huddled in terror at a cave's mouth. What I seem to see is a single, many-eyed monster, paralyzed with fear. The primates look alike, but that's misleading. One of them has the idea he is *human*. Just an idea, no way to prove it. What he had to be was crazy enough to believe it. In no time at all, historically speaking, he had the whole tribe of apes believing as he did, covering the walls of their caves with pictures. It's contagious. Nobody knows where such an idea will lead to. Nor am I sure Harry Lorbeer has given it much thought.

It occurs to me that I have never heard Harry raise his voice. He is calm. He looks at me as he would a wayward child. Harry is short, getting a little paunchy, with a somewhat vacant, disinterested manner. Uncertain that I'm getting his full attention, I raise my voice. He has asked Alice if I'm hard of hearing. He brings along with him, when he works, a pair of the blue overalls worn by farmers, with the shoulder straps, the bib, and the whine when his thighs rub. He often wears a white carpenter's apron to carry his tools. He uses a hippie-type van to dress in, and sits in the cab to eat his lunch from a paper bag. It's my business to note these little details. If there's going to be a change, people like Harry will make it. All he needs, as I see it, is someone to believe in him. He already has Dahlberg. If I am any judge of the matter, he's getting to me.

Harry Lorbeer is not the sort of person who would catch your eye in the street. I am. Just yesterday morning, picking up the laundry, which I carry in a candy-striped bag with a noose, I was stopped by a stranger who asked me if I cut my own hair. It just so happens I do. I've cut it since the price went up in the sixties. I also live in a community where people feel free to ask their neighbors pertinent questions. My point is, he asked *me,* and he wouldn't have asked Harry. To that extent, at least, I stand out from the crowd. Without his carpenter's apron Harry wouldn't. Alice also tells me he is slow to blink his eyes.

Four or five weeks ago—it seems longer—I called the local hardware for the name of a handyman or a plumber. We've got a plumber, but he can no longer afford to work for us. For a small-time job, say opening a sink drain, he has to come on the weekend and charge me overtime. It hurts him to do that. On my time we've discussed it at length. The hardware people recommended Harry Lorbeer, and when I called I got an answering service. Three or four days later he called me back.

"What's your problem?" he asked me. I explained we had a clogged drain in the bathroom washbowl. "Tell your wife not to wash her hair in it," he said. I explained that Alice washed her hair in the tub, and took every possible precaution.

"Take a wire coat hanger, mister, untwist it at the neck until you got one long wire, then crook a hook on one end of it and stick it down the drain, fish for the hair with it." I explained that I doubted it was hair, since I'm the one who uses the bowl and I've little hair to lose. "I'm twenty-eight miles southeast," he said, "and you'd like me to drive fifty-six miles to fish a little hair out of your drain?"

Thinking fast I said, "We've got a deck that needs painting. Do you paint?"

"I don't paint," he replied. "Dahlberg paints."

"I've had a union estimate," I said. "I'd appreciate a non-union estimate."

"He gets three dollars an hour. You supply the paint."

That was so good I didn't believe it. "Where you people located?" I said.

He replied, "Heber County. We're in Kansas."

Heber County is south of the east-west freeway, and people who live in the north see little of it. I assumed they were farmers who did odd jobs on the side. "What I'll do," he went on, "I'll stop by when I'm in the neighborhood, right?"

Before I could say yes or no, he hung up. During the week

14

or ten days we didn't hear from him I took a wire coat hanger, untwisted it the way he said, hooked a crook on the end, and fished around in the bowl drain. What I came up with you wouldn't believe. I refused to let Alice see it. Gobs of sludge with the density of axle grease skillfully blended with wadded bits of Kleenex. Alice uses bits of tissue to wipe out the bowl. I hauled out a cup of it. I called Alice in to watch the water running and make a few tactful suggestions about tissues. The banging on the door startled us both. Not familiar with a man who said his name was Harry my wife delayed opening the door for him. I ran down the bathroom window to check on him. Two men were at the door.

"I'm Harry Lorbeer," said the short one. "This is Dahlberg."

Lorbeer had left his car in the street, and walked in with his box of plumber's tools. He wore his overalls and his carpenter's apron. I thought he looked pale and sallow for a farmer. The fellow with him was tall, his hair clipped so short I could see his scrubbed suntanned scalp. Copper-colored wiry hairs glistened on his forearms, the backs of his hands. Alice would have said he looked squeaky clean.

After I opened the door I had the problem of explaining that I had taken his advice, about the coat hanger, and just that moment had opened the drain. Harry seemed pleased. "Watch the hair," he said, glancing at mine, and checked two of the faucets for drips. "While I'm here," he said, "I'll change the washers."

"Great!" I said.

"Show him your deck," he said to me, and I walked ahead of Dahlberg to the door to the deck, off the living room. He walked out on it as if he doubted it would hold his weight. He had the gangly spread-legged walk you see in stiff-jointed old men. From the back his head was knobby, the flesh of his neck lumpy and pockmarked. He showed less interest in the deck than the view we've got, and Alice's garden.

"Nice place," he said. He was one of these big fellows with a small, high-pitched voice.

"We like it," I said, "but it's a lot of work."

He used his nail to fleck scaling paint off the deck rail.

"I see the trim's the same color, want me to paint the trim?"

"I would," I said, "if you can find the time."

"You don't find time, Mr. Kelcey, you make it. If you'd like me to make the time, I'll do it." He talked looking away, squint-ing at our view, as if he was forcing the words through his teeth.

"When can you make it?"

In the door at my back Harry Lorbeer said, "That's what we don't know. We go from day to day."

I wondered what he meant to be saying. Either his humor was so dry I didn't catch it, or I failed to follow his thinking. He looked at me without blinking, his lips puckered as if he might whistle.

"Don't you find people need to know when to expect you?"

"Not us," he said, "it can't be helped. We might be here and we might be in orbit."

Had I heard him correctly? His expression had not changed. Dahlberg stood with his back to me. In my boyhood I heard stories of how the smell of the paint made boozers out of house painters. I thought it highly likely. "What do we do," I said, "just wait for you to turn up?"

"We're all just waiting," said Harry, "isn't that right?"

It's been my experience that the really funny people are those you just stumble on, like Harry. He had the role down pat. As Alice later remarked, his eyes were slow to blink.

"Well," I said, "if it's the deck, it hardly matters. You can work on it whether we're here or not."

Harry nodded. He and Dahlberg had a way of passing signals that only comes with years living together. They both left the deck and walked back through the house to where Harry had left his tool box. Harry was bald on the top, but he let his hair grow long at the back. I was thinking what an odd couple they made, but how well they had worked out their own problems. Back in some farmhouse, out of sight and off the highway, they uncorked the bottle and went into orbit.

"Let me pay you for the plumbing work," I said.

Harry said, "Twenty-four dollars plus parts."

"For washers? That's as much as my plumber."

"I *am* your plumber. Good plumbers aren't cheap."

Alice runs the finances in our family. She wrote him out a check. "Before we go on," I said, "let's have a clear understanding. How much are you charging me to paint the deck?"

Harry said, "Three dollars an hour, plus the paint."

"Two days is about fifty dollars," I said, "not including the paint." They both nodded. "How come one of you works for three dollars an hour, and the other one for forty bucks an hour?"

"A good plumber is not cheap," Harry repeated.

There was no point in my arguing about it if I ever hoped to get the deck painted. "What town you people live near?"

"We live in Fork River," said Dahlberg, "We don't live near it."

Harry puckered his lips, but said nothing.

"I don't think I know it," I said.

They did not say that I should.

"Well, I hope you can make it soon," I said, and followed them down the drive for a look at their car. They had a hippie-type van, with a Kansas license, the hood and sides ornamented with blue and yellow flower paintings. "Fork River's in Kansas?"

"Was when we left," said Dahlberg, which I took to be up-to-date Kansas humor.

On the top of the van were two paint-splattered metal ladders. Dahlberg took the wheel. While I stood watching them drive off he either didn't shift to high, or the car didn't have one.

"I'd just as soon not see *that* pair again," I said to Alice, but Dahlberg was back the following morning, before we got up. I could hear the van groaning up the street, and the rattle of the ladders when he turned in the driveway. It hardly seemed to matter whether we were home or not. He managed to find the outside socket that I had always looked for, and plugged in his sander. That just about took care of my morning's work, but he had parked so I couldn't back out of the garage. When the sanding stopped I could hear the country music on the transistor radio in one of his coveralls pockets. He did not appear to loaf. I clocked him in less than thirty minutes for lunch, including two beers and a chat with Alice about the trellis she wanted him to

17

build for her tomatoes. At four o'clock he quit, cleaned his brushes, and took off. I was ready for him the following morning, early, but he didn't show up.

2

YOUR MOTHER AND I HAVE OUR EXPEC-
tations," my father often said, whenever he wanted to express
their concern for me. I'm not sure it is possible to say more than
that, in so few words. Their expectations were that I would
amount to something, which is both explicit and hard to define.

Since I was not in the best frame of mind for work, I took
the morning off. I drove out the freeway, about twelve miles east,
to Ansel Burger's gas station. The east-west freeway bisects the
county and cuts Burger off from about half of his clients. His
loyal customers have to drive six miles west to cross it, and those
not so loyal buy their gas elsewhere. Burger has plenty of time
to think, and he saves up his thoughts for his loyal customers.
From the freeway I can see the colorful display of patchwork quilts
his wife makes, and hopes to sell to the tourists. The next freeway
exit, if they decide to buy a quilt, is eleven miles east. Burger
will check the oil, if I ask him, or smear the windshield with a
wad of newspaper. If I say, "Fill it up!" he always double-checks
to see if I mean it. In the old days a dollar's worth of gas would
last several weeks.

"How do I get to Fork River?" I asked him.

Burger has a squint that almost closes his eyes. He wears
a brakeman's hat of blue and white denim, with a high squashed
crown. He squinted into the glare of the sun. "How would I know
that?"

"I think it's just across the line, in Kansas."

"You're asking me about Kansas?"

"Have you got a map?"

"It wouldn't be on it. The maps don't show anything with
less than forty people."

You have to remember, as I do, that Burger is often lacking

for conversation. I thanked him, and bought two of the pump-
kins he had stacked in a pyramid between his gas pumps, a bit
of local color for Alice. He took pride in saying, he said in closing, that he did not take credit cards, and passed mine back to me.

Ten miles to the south I made another stop, where I was
shown a map with the Fork River on it, but no town. If it had
been on the map, I might have looked no further for it. As it
was, I stopped off to see Miss Ingalls, the local librarian. She
dates from a time when writers were important people, and wears
the paisley shawls that once draped grand pianos. She comes alive
if I ask her questions. So many books that are useless prove to
be useful. In one of them she found it: Fork River, a town in
Kansas. In 1940 it had numbered more than seven hundred people. Where had those people gone?

Miss Ingalls assured me that it was not at all unusual, during the depression, for both the town and its people to disappear.

Not all of them, I said. I had met two of them. Harry
Lorbeer, a plumber, and his friend Dahlberg.

"Dahlberg?" she echoed.

"He's the painter. He's doing some work for us."

Miss Ingalls had turned to the card file at her back. She took
out one of the drawers, flicked through the cards.

"Dahlberg, O. P.," she read aloud. "*A Hole in Space and
Other Stories.* I just knew we had a Dahlberg."

"He writes?"

"He once did. It's 1962."

Should I read the fiction of our new deck painter? "Is there
something by Lorbeer, Harry?" I inquired. Plumbers would not
be lacking in raw material. There were several Lorbeers, but no
Harry. I could see that the prospect aroused Miss Ingalls; she
visibly nibbled the bait.

"Why don't I check on the Dahlberg," she said. In a moment she was back with a well-thumbed paperback, a picture
of the author on the glossy jacket. He had not changed. He stood
with his fingers poised at his hips, as if his stance had been determined by calculation. In his pose there was longing, hankering,
and contempt.

20

"That's him," I said.

"Born in Provo, Utah," Miss Ingalls read from the jacket, "of a Swedish immigrant father and a Mormon mother."

"That makes for a hole in something," I said. "I'll take it." Miss Ingalls was pleased.

"I just knew I'd heard of a Dahlberg," she said, which I thought would be a nice thing to tell him. Nothing equals being heard of, to an author. But the moment I saw his van parked in the drive, where I couldn't get around it, I thought better of it. He was at work on the deck.

"I see you made it," I said.

"I had to drop Harry off in Seward," he replied. Seward is about twenty miles to the west. I didn't think it was the time to mention the book to Alice, so I went back to my study to read it. The opening story was titled *The Taste of Blood*. It concerned a youth who lived in Provo, Utah, the only child of Mormon parents. His mother took in washing to support his invalid father. That doesn't sound very encouraging, but you have to let him tell it.

> Would his life have been different if he had let his hair grow? On his hands and chest, where one saw more of it, it was honey-colored with a golden glisten, like that on a singed chicken. His whining high-pitched voice was made for country music, his smile like a string of pearls in his pockmarked face. Along with this, his muffled sizzling laugh was like the sound of a fuse burning. An inch taller than Lincoln, some found him ugly enough to be handsome. Of all the Mormons in Provo, what had led him to think he should write? Quite by accident he had stumbled on *The Grapes of Wrath*. He liked the turtle. He couldn't get the turtle out of his mind. Actually he didn't get much beyond the turtle, but that was far enough to do the damage.

That's on page two, and by page five he has left Provo, Utah, for a religious school in Walla Walla, Washington. Uninstructed in the school's religious doctrine, he was puzzled by the prevailing customs. There was a large gymnasium, but it sat empty. The students seemed to be ignorant of basketball, football, and such sports. Being a good basketball player, thanks to his height, he persuaded students in his dormitory to come out and "shoot baskets" with him. After a little of that, he had them choosing up sides, playing games. Not one of them breathed a word to him that "competitive" sports were forbidden. They almost went crazy with excitement. Nothing like this had ever happened to them. They played barefoot, not having the shoes they needed, and tore their clothes pretty badly in the heated scuffles. It amused the young man to see these grown young men scuffling like kids. They pushed, shoved, tore each other's clothes, but it didn't cross their minds to take offense, and get into a fight. One afternoon three of the boys were scrapping for the ball and Dahlberg moved in to try to separate them. He got an elbow in the mouth that cut his lip and loosened one of his teeth. This put him in such a rage he began to swing blindly, and they all began to fight like a pack of animals. By the time it was stopped all of the boys were bloody, and the teacher who had intervened had an injured eye, his shirt torn off his back. A taste of blood was all that was needed to turn decent young men into wild animals. Naturally, Dahlberg was asked to leave, but he had been too ashamed to go back to Provo. He became a sort of tramp, hitching rides on the highway, working at odd jobs for his meals. He worked in a logging camp in California. It gave him all the time in the world to think. He came to the conclusion that competition, not money, was the root of most evil. Men were passive enough to begin with, but they learned to be brutes. Wherever competition was encouraged, the only goal in life was winning. The ultimate winner was a killer. The ultimate contest was war. When he had thought it all out he sat down and wrote his story, *The Taste of Blood*, which won a prize of fifty dollars in a short story contest. That made him a winner. Otherwise nothing in the world had changed.

The idea behind the story was not so unusual, but I must say I liked the way Dahlberg told it. For the first few minutes after I read it I really *believed* it, the way he did. If the goddam competition would stop, wouldn't we all be better for it? The ultimate winner *is* a killer, and the ultimate killer *is* war. But a lot of men know that. Not a one of them has been able to do more than round up a few women, or give up eating meat and start drinking Postum. Sooner or later some barbarian will give them all the taste of blood.

I glanced up to see Dahlberg, right below my window, pulling off the green coveralls he wears when he paints. They fit him tight at the ankles and cuffs, and have chest-high zipper pockets. He was awkward as a gangly kid trying to put on a turtleneck sweater. It made him flustered. I could hear him muttering to himself. But what a different picture you get of a person when you catch a glimpse of what they are thinking. This dour, almost sullen, phlegmatic Swede, with his vision of a brotherhood of brutes. I felt warmly fraternal toward him. Cranking open my study window I said, "Will we see you tomorrow, Dahlberg?"

"Who knows?" he replied. Why do men with virtually no hair to comb dote on combing their hair? He raked the comb through his brush cut, then blew on the teeth, like a barber.

"It would help if we knew," I said. "We'd like to be able to make our plans—"

"Go ahead and make your plans. Just don't make me part of them."

That's the fellow who had just, almost, moved me to a gesture of fellowship. It was three o'clock. Why was he quitting so early? "I've got to pick up Harry in Seward," he said, reading my mind. I could have shattered his calm by just casually mentioning, "I've been reading a little story here," and waving it at him, "with the title of *The Taste of Blood*. I think you might find it of interest." I didn't of course. It would lose me my point of vantage. Once he was free of the coveralls he dusted them off, stuffed in the pockets, and hung them on a slope-shouldered wooden coat hanger. That's your experienced, neat-type bachelor, silent member of an odd couple. I would say he did the cooking. Harry swept up and made the beds.

"Well, have a nice day," I said, then shut the window. I walked through the house to where Alice stood at the door to the deck, checking his work. "At this rate," I said, "it will take him a week. Why don't I ever learn?"

"He's shy," she said. "He's so shy he blushes, his ears turn red."

"That could be his cooling system." She is now long accustomed to my type of humor. "Would you say he was bright?"

"What an odd question."

"Why is it odd?" I asked.

One of the things I admire about Alice is the way she never ruffles. It doesn't occur to her to take offense because our opinions differ. As she thinks her eyes dart around as if she might see the answer somewhere. "He's sweet," she said. "He is a very gentle person."

"Would you say he has talent?"

"As a house painter?"

"No, no, just talent. A gift for something or other."

"I think he's a person who might surprise you," she said, and closed the door to the deck.

"He has already. Miss Ingalls at the library tells me he's a writer."

That surprised her. "A poet?" Alice had come a bit early for the flower children, and would always feel she had missed something.

"Stories," I said, "some sort of science fiction."

"He's imaginative. When he smiles his homely face is simply radiant. I've never seen such white teeth."

"There's nothing like a pockmarked complexion to bring out the fine points," I said.

Alice has a sure sense of when a topic should be dropped. "I'm going to pick some fresh chard," she said, and slipped on her gardening gloves, with the green leather thumbs. She filled her watering can at the patio spigot and carefully overwatered the fuchsias. With my study window open I could hear the water drip on the bricks. In my typewriter was a yellow sheet of paper with these lines across the top.

> In my boyhood it was rumored that the center of this country was in a town just forty miles to the west. To have been born so close to the heart of this great nation often gave me cause for wonder.

What was the wonder? It seemed to have slipped my mind. From the morning Harry Lorbeer said to me, "Take a wire coat hanger, untwist it at the neck until you got a long wire, then crook a hook on one end and stick it down the drain and fish for the hair with it," I have been subject to distractions. This morning I drove out to chat with Ansel Burger. An hour ago I sat here reading one of Dahlberg's stories. I have the book here on my desk. *A Hole in Space and Other Stories.* The book has illustrations, black and white pen drawings, and one of them shows a wide stretch of the prairie with a small round hole, like an eye, in the overcast sky. Right beneath the hole a piece of the highway and part of a filling station, including sections of roadside motel cabins, have disappeared. Tiny ant-like figures stand peering up at the hole in the sky. That would be one of his sci-fi pieces, and I liked the way he got right down to business.

> On a warm October day, of the sort that alerts weather watchers, a man from the state light and power people drove over to Fork River to turn off the lights. No payments had been received since the first of July. He found the school bus as usual, at the highway turnoff, but it had been stripped to a hulk. From the highway there was little to be seen of Fork River since it sat in the arroyo cut by the river.

It occurred to me, reading the story, that I was faced with something you don't see at eye level: you have to see it from space, like a mini-crater, or the tracks covered wagons had left crossing the plains. Oddly enough, the overview from space was more common to early man than it is to us. They were not limited to their own view. You can see that in the cave paintings, and the Easter Island sculptures. They are not propped up there for people to see, but for avenging gods. They look in the direction that gods might come from. The best example of this is Stonehenge. From the dwarfed level of man it's a scattered pile of rocks: you have to see it from space to get the message, and that's from where the gods see it. I'm not suggesting that an airview of Fork River will spell out a new and wondrous revelation, but I know that if I mentioned it to Harry or Dahlberg they would not be surprised.

3

THIS MORNING I TOLD ALICE THAT I
would check with Miss Ingalls as to what books they had by
Dahlberg. *The Taste of Blood* would shock and delight her, but
I felt uneasy about *A Hole in Space*. Winds of any kind disturb
her. Cyclones terrify her. She would rather be taken by surprise,
she says, than cower waiting in a corner of the basement, if she
could remember the right corner. She might not want to read
about a piece of the earth, more than three acres of it, along with
the highway, a gas station, several buildings, and an undeter-
mined number of people, just whooshing off through a hole in
the sky. It's implausible, of course. But would you say it was impossible? If some trickster neutralized a cone of gravity, like the
column of a twister but without the disorder, the raging inferno
around the vacuum, anything within the cone, not battened down,
would zoom off into space like a rocket. Loose topsoil, houses,
cars, cattle, and people, along with strips of highway dangling
like Band-Aids. I can already see it as a movie. A cone like that,
without gravity, might slurp up a good-sized body of water, as
if sucked through a straw. We're accustomed to things disappear-
ing. How about lakes? This seems pretty remarkable, if we're
earthbound, and gaze upward to see it happening, but it's not
an unusual event if seen from space. A tiny puff of debris, like
seeds blown on the winds of space. My friend Rainey says the
remarkable thing is not what disappears, but all that stays put.
He says that any day now some smart aleck will come up with
a do-it-yourself anti-gravity kit. You just rub it on, like suntan
oil, then paddle around in the air like a fish. It's not a new idea.
The old masters filled their paintings with unidentified flying objects. What is it, he asks me, that man has imagined that hasn't
come to pass?

The horseshoe bend in the Fork River, Miss Ingalls tells me, was once the location of Devil's Nest, a rendezvous point for fur traders, trappers, cattle rustlers, thieves, and desperados. What the frontiersman saw from the bluffs of the Missouri was the uneven floor of an extinct sea, but luckily he didn't know it. He might have thought twice about trying to cross it. Had the wagon trains and gold seekers known it, some would have surely turned back, their doomed lives saved. Not once, I guess, but many times the wall of ice advanced and receded. Between the seasons of ice dinosaurs waddled and huge bat-like birds, the size of gliders, flapped their wings in air thick enough to swim in. For someone with a dinosaur's point of view, it must have been a place of great expectations. In a twist of fortune that appeals to me, that is also how the early settlers saw it. Man and beast found it appealing, wet or dry. The one notable exception was the women. Could we say they saw it for what it was? Not a tree for shade. No place for either creatures or humans to hide. The one departure was the occasional river that cut ravines deep enough to camp in. The Fork River was one, the tops of the willows looking like bushes if seen from the plain. That's how one pioneer described it. I loved the elevated, oratorical style that came natural to the writer.

> As my mind reaches back to the long ago, and once familiar faces cluster round, my eye dwells upon the treeless plain that rolled and swelled like the open sea.

I doubt this fellow knew what the sea looked like, until he saw the great plains.

> The reader must not expect these memories to be free [he writes] of an occasional dip into the vulgar, because I write of characters more uncouth than those we see in Heber County today.

That was dated 1887. He believed that uncouthness was about to be banished. I can be as distracted by a line like that as by the sepia photograph that goes along with it, showing the author, dressed for Sunday, on the buckboard seat of a wagon. The horse, the wagon, and the bearded writer now gone. All gone.

28

I'm so affected by reports of that type of uncouthness that I pick up the writer's voice and manner. Alice has often remarked it. In something I am doing, or something I am saying, I'll slip in a passage that I appear to have received from a departed spirit, in a seance. Miss Ingalls, who may be ten years my senior, is so close in spirit to this past she has not actually departed from it. She is dry as a twig, and there's little juice in her, but she can crackle like a brush fire when her "dander's stirred up" as she says. She felt that Fork River, given my interest, might very well repay a visit, since some of these out-of-the-way little ghost towns were very well preserved in the dry climate.

Why had such a village, of more than seven hundred people, suddenly died off? Miss Ingalls said there was always information about things that were growing, towns that were rising, but it was usually lacking about places that were declining. There had been the depression, for one thing, and the surrounding dust bowl for another. It must have crossed one of their minds that the jig was up. A compact community, of one ethnic group, would share that opinion like a family. Once one of the respected members pulled up stakes, the rest would soon follow. If I was interested, Miss Ingalls suggested, why didn't I pay the town a visit and see for myself.

She also passed on to me a Xerox copy of a story called *Waiting*. The author's name is Bergdahl, but she doubts it. She feels the internal evidence is all for Dahlberg. It's the plain, unvarnished tale of a small town on its last legs. Most of the people have left or died. The others just sit around waiting. For what? For something to happen. They sit around on the porch of the general store looking at the sky, discussing the weather. Nothing happens. That would make a better title for the story up to that point than *Waiting*. But the waiting builds up. You get a wonderful sense of what is on their minds just from the way they don't talk about it, the way you get a sense of great expectations from people who say the least about it. It seemed to be a straightforward, realistic type of story, touching on an experience common to many people. Who wasn't *waiting*? Even the reader was waiting for the story to end. All of this was done so skillfully, so

29

matter-of-factly, that when the UFO came skimming in like a Frisbee, and hovered over the square like a silent helicopter, I accepted it the way they did. Why not? Something had to happen. Why not something unusual? This big saucer just hovered—it didn't have to land, and made no more noise than a musical top— and through a green glow in its belly it sucked up the people who approached it. No hoodlum-type Martians, or beetle-legged space midgets, just this fairly commonplace but well-oiled flying saucer incorporating the improvements of the latest models. Not everybody left. The author didn't spell it out, but he seemed to imply that unless there was someone to go on *waiting,* there was no reason to assume things would go on happening.

On reflection I didn't mention this story to Alice, knowing what she would say.

In the morning Harry's van pulled up just after seven o'clock, turned in the drive, then took off. When I peered out the window I saw Dahlberg seated on the curb, reading our morning paper. He had his lunch in a bag, his coveralls in a roll bound up with a belt. He waited till about twenty minutes to eight, then he walked up the drive and around to the deck. I could hear him prying the lids off his cans, stirring up the paint. Like many painters I've observed, he keeps a cigarette dangling from one corner of his mouth, but seldom puffs it. The smoke creases his eyes. When he looks up the ashes sprinkle his face. Down to the butt, he gives it a pinch, with his thumbnail, so the tobacco crumbles as he rolls the paper in a tight little wad. I have twice seen him flick it with his fingernail at the birds in the deck feed-box, just like a kid.

I'm not an early riser, but I cannot lie in bed while I pay someone to work. I made coffee, and walked to the deck door to ask Dahlberg if he would join me. If Alice had asked him he would have. "I don't hear your radio this morning," I said.

"I thought the missus might be sleeping," he replied.

This is what a woman means when she judges a hired hand as "sensitive."

"I see you don't have the van?"

"Harry has a job in Crete," he replied.

30

"You fellows don't lack work, I'll say that."

"If we want it," he replied, "we don't lack it."

"People don't mind this day-to-day, 'who knows what tomorrow will bring' business?"

"So long as we get the job done," he replied. Have you noticed the way a house painter has of thinning his brush against the lip of the can, first one side then the other? Dahlberg could do this in a way had something subtly insolent about it, as if he took forever wiping his hands, while you stood and watched. On the other hand, I didn't feel that it was personal. He dispenses his insolence impartially. Alice would say that the way he dipped his brush, and thinned it on the can lip, was sensuous rather than insolent. I think that's true, and it might be why I felt its insolence.

Actually, I would like to have had a talk with Dahlberg about *A Hole in Space*. I don't read science fiction, if I can help it, and I wondered what his readers might have thought about it. Was it just a fantasy, or did some of them think it might have taken place? Dahlberg's touchy manner, as far as I was concerned, made it difficult for me to bring the matter up. He might think me nosy. He might think I was trying to "butter him up." I happened to be a writer myself but he showed no interest in what I might be. A more curious, observant person would wonder why I wasn't off somewhere, working. We've always had that trouble with housemaids. "What is it Mr. Kelcey *does*?" they ask Alice. Until they *know* what it is I do they are out of their minds. Dahlberg simply didn't seem to give a damn, which I find to be part of his normal stance. It's perfectly expressed in the way he stands, even with one hand holding a paintbrush. It's not so much a chip on his shoulder, as a chip that is all of one piece. My guess would be that he had had something more than just a taste of blood. I knew that if I asked him about Fork River he would clam up. Harry Lorbeer was a different type of person and would not think such a question personal, but Harry Lorbeer was a plumber spending the day in Crete. Why didn't I drive over and see for myself? Both Lorbeer and Dahlberg would be away, and I could snoop around. As a rule I work in the morning, but in one way or another I found Dahlberg distracting. I can't stand country music. But it would be worse if I asked him to turn it off. I left a note for Alice that I had a few errands, and would be back for lunch.

I drove south ten miles, then east to Millard, which proved to be a few over twenty. At a station in Millard I asked how to get to Fork River, and the kid cleaning my windshield had never heard of it. "I'm new around here," he said, "but I'll ask Jake." Jake was down in one of the oil pits they used to have before they raised the cars on hoists. He walked back to where he could get a look at me, smears of grease on his bearded face. They talked for some time, while he rubbed at his hands with a rag. He wore a hat made out of the want ad section of a newspaper, folded so it was square, fit snug like a skullcap. Grease dripped on his ears and his face. The only concern he seemed to feel was for the top of his head. The kid came back and said did I know Fork River was a dead town? I said I knew that. How did I get there? He went back to Jake, who thought that over, then climbed out of the pit and walked to get a look at me.

"Howdy, mister," he said.

"Howdy," I said.

"What you want in Fork River?"

"I want to see if it's there," I said. That seemed to stump him. He rubbed at his hands with the rag he was clutching.

"The road's closed," he said. "They got sawbucks up to close it. But there's room on the ditch side to drive around them."

"Where is this road?"

"You go four miles east. It's not much of a road."

"Why is it closed?"

"Costs money to keep it up."

"Nobody lives there?"

"How would I know that, mister?" He saw I was crazy. If I asked him one more question, and got one more answer, I would think so myself. I thanked him, and drove six or seven miles east before I realized I must have gone by it. Two miles back I found this turnoff overgrown with weeds, without a sign or road marker. Two battered sawbucks were in the ditch to one side, one with a sign stating ROAD CLOSED. The road was gravel, with weeds growing at the center, the tops lopped off about knee-cap high. In the ditch along the east side the sunflowers were coated with road dust. Just up ahead the road dipped into a gully, and in the gulch on the right, twenty yards off the road, the battered hulk of a yellow school bus sat axle deep in the soft field loam. All the windows were shattered. The radiator and the seat frames were gone, the near side and the rear of the body had been riddled with bullet holes. A common enough roadside eyesore. Why did it seem familiar? It occurred to me that it resembled the bus Dahlberg had described in his story, given twenty years' time and looting. Less than a mile to the north, up a slow incline, the road crested on the horizon. What I took to be the dead branches of scrub brushes proved to be the tops of poplars and cottonwoods in the arroyo. They looked dead. Right at the summit of the crest, without warning, the road jogged right and dropped steeply. The wrecked bodies of eight or ten cars were strewn about on the slope, where they had stopped rolling. The narrow one-way road was so gutted with runoffs the car scraped on the ridges, and I stopped to think it over. To get in and out of here one needed a jeep, or a van with high clearance. To the south and east the arroyo spread wide and I could see the distinct branches of the river, one bone dry, the other with a ripple at the center channel. Clumps of pale green willows grew thick on the islands. I had the curious impression of having stumbled on something lost. A flight of crows dipped to caw at me, then wing off to report their findings. I was less then ten miles off the freeway yet it seemed like another country. Hugging the cliff side of the road, where the ruts were shallow, I took it very slowly on the steep decline. On a curve I saw a park-like cluster of trees, and the first of several boarded-up frame houses. It was May, but most of the trees were leafless. The square buildings, once white, had the air of resort houses closed up for a season. They were not in bad shape. Heavy planks were nailed to the doors and the windows, and here and there I saw a porch swing drawn up to the ceiling, a once popular way to store them over the winter. What struck me was the absence of TV aerials. Not much remained of the lawns but sparse clumps of dead grass, the earth eroded and blown away from the roots. The houses had been patterned on the same simple design, with a porch at the front, a cellar door at the side, and either one or two gables, depending on the number of rooms. All these structures and trees were on the west side of the river, and got the morning sun. By four o'clock— early in the winter—they would be in the shade of the arroyo wall. I was so taken with this park-like setting I stopped the car and looked at it. How the kids must have loved it. In the spring they had a river right there at their feet. The hard smoothness of the road indicated that in the rainy season the street was flooded. On up the ravine, where it narrowed, was probably what they referred to as Devil's Nest, a perfect hideout for thieves and cattle rustlers. Wondering where it was the natives had done their shopping I went along slowly, into a sudden clearing. The houses on my left were larger and closer together and faced the open area like a stage. Until that moment, because of the angle of the sun, I had not been able to see the solid row of structures, many with high false fronts, set up off the bed of the river on piers. My first impression was that the earth had been washed away beneath them. At the front a boardwalk, about waist high, ran the full length of the row to the steps at each end. The long deep shadow cast by these buildings seemed to open up a hole in the street. I had never seen a ghost town so compact and spare, so well preserved. It had the appearance of a movie set put together elsewhere, and brought in on flatcars and wagons. Everything perfect. No doors or windows broken. The pale shadow of let- ters on faded blinds and curtains. Under peeling paint I saw the ghostly name of a merchant, the date 1892. Backed up to the south end of the boardwalk were two railroad coaches the dusty color of Confederate uniforms. The coach blinds were drawn, as if the passengers were asleep. At nine thirty in the morning I couldn't say that what I felt was an eerie, unearthly feeling, but insofar as the time of day would allow I had never experienced an emotion quite like it. A lost world? But nothing had been lost. Less than seven miles away was the town of Millard, and three crowded supermarkets. The block of stores were of a single piece, but a wide variety of fading colors. All the false fronts tilted

34

rearward, as if they had felt the pressure of the afternoon sun. A barber pole, surmounted by an eagle, stood to the left of a door that set in slantwise to the barber shop. Several curling posters leaned on the window, hung with the usual half curtain. In the spring water rippled and splashed under the boardwalk, but I found it hard to imagine. What had it been like? A lake village, hovering over the water, or a frontier-type Noah's ark? How explain that the country hoodlums, the souvenir collectors, hadn't ransacked it? I had forgotten that I knew two people who lived here. Were there others? No dogs barked. In lonely places of this sort people usually kept dogs. At the north end of the street, where the ravine narrowed, a school or meeting hall, with a peaked roof and a cupola at the front, with a bell, faced the open square. In the shaded yard at the side were swings, a teeter-totter, and wooden benches. The roof of the building had been repaired with sheets of galvanized metal, glinting like mirrors. I left my car and walked toward the school, the cupola crowded with cooing pigeons. A trash barrel at one side of the street was stuffed with frozen food cartons and supermarket bags. The ground was higher here, with enough topsoil to get rutted and muddy in the rainy season. A car, or cars, someone coming and going, had chewed up a large piece of it. I thought I caught a whiff, when the breeze stirred, of the pungent smell of manure and fodder. But there were no barns. A woodpecker hammered high in one of the trees. From the steps to the school, recently painted, I could see a small card pinned to the door. It read

---

FORK RIVER SPACE PROJECT
Harry Lorbeer, Prop.
OPEN 2-5 Sat. & Sundays

The heavy doors had been bolted from the inside—I could see a plank at waist level—with a slit about a quarter inch wide giving me a peek at the interior. What I could see up the center looked empty, but full of light. At the far end a platform, with

35

a portable blackboard, and in the gable behind it, high up, a window or opening on the sky. I could see the moon through it—or what looked like the moon. I walked around to the back of the building to check on what it was I was seeing but it was not the moon. Whatever it was I had seen was on the window itself, and not seen through it.

Behind a fence of wooden planks I had to rise on my toes to see over, I saw a round, level plot of ground, as sanded and smooth as a bullring, without an object or shadow of any kind to rest the eyes on. It looked as if it had just been swept with a broom. A playground? There was nothing to play with. I felt kids might feel they were penned up in it. A prison exercise yard would not have been so vacant. I find it hard to describe what held my attention. A perfectly clean slate? A new and uncharted beginning? Gazing at it I felt a surge of great expectations, but I've no idea for what. Crowds that wait in a piazza for someone to arrive must gather to share the same feeling. Their faces upturned, their eyes creased by the light. What holds them is the ceremony of waiting.

Perhaps that fence had been built to keep the children from the excavation behind it? What had they had in mind? The earth had been scooped out down to bedrock. Both the school and the playground could have been put into it, with room to spare. Perfectly round, from what I could judge, the earth had crumbled inward around the edges and there was a film of caked mud at the bottom. I turned away from it before I wondered what they had done with the dirt they excavated. Tons and tons of it. But there was no sign of it. It would be like Dahlberg, it seemed to me, or some other Swede, to get the idea there was a treasure buried in this canyon. So they had dug and dug. When nothing turned up they decided to leave. As I walked back toward the car I thought there might well be a story in a town that wore itself out digging for treasure and just gave up.

I had my head down, to keep the sun out of my eyes, not glancing up until I noticed the shimmering shadow of a man on the hard baked streets. It gave me a jolt. The figure stood between

36

me and the light, a dark profile, holding the gun at a slant across his waist, the barrel pointed up.

"Howdy," he said. I couldn't speak. He looked taller than he was, thin in the shanks, with a hulking stoop to his shoulders. "You looking for someone?" A querulous, high-pitched voice. Nothing threatening. I was able to note that he wore tennis sneakers, without socks.

"Mr. Lorbeer," I said, "I thought I might catch him."

"You know Harry?"

"He's done some work for me."

"Well, he's not here. He's not often here daytimes. He keeps himself pretty busy daytimes."

"I was afraid of that," I said.

"What's your name?"

"Kelcey."

"I'll tell him you was by, Mr. Kelcey."

"Mr. Dahlberg's painting our deck," I said, aware that I was already saying too much. It was none of his business, whoever he was. The fright he had given me loosened my tongue. "You're a native?" I asked.

"I come up here"—he turned, showing his Adam's apple, wagging his finger down the river—"on the first trainload from Bixby. That's the Junction. We had a trainload to ourselves, just local people. I was nine years of age."

"There many of you?" I asked him.

He looked at me, cagily. "If I didn't patrol, we'd have the hoodlums in here. They'd haul it away like pack rats, the way they did Cheney. All they left of Cheney was the concrete around the filling stations." He had not answered my question.

"Well, I can believe that," I said.

"You better believe it," he said, and shifted his rifle from the left arm to the right arm. I thought he might be a relation of Dahlberg's. He might have straddled a rail fence without his thighs rubbing. In spite of his suspicious, vigilante manner I could see he welcomed a visitor, a change to talk. "Yes sirree," he said, "you better believe it."

"Why would people leave a nice little town like this?" I peered up at a flight of big crows, their cawing echoed in the narrow canyon.

"They used to have wild turkeys in here. Anyhow, that's what they told us kids."

"I can guess why the turkeys took off—" I said.

"Back behind these trees we used to dig in the ash heaps left by Indians, fur trappers, horse rustlers. There used to be wild horses in this canyon. They set traps for wolves."

"And now there's just you, Mr. Lorbeer, and Mr. Dahlberg."

"More or less," he replied. I could see by the sidelong flick of his eyes that that question had been a mistake. He puckered his lips tight, as if he meant to spit.

"I want to tell you I envy you," I said. "I don't believe there's another place quite like it. You don't have the turkeys or the wild horses, but otherwise it's just like it used to be."

"Well, not *just*. We had seven hundred people, and as many as a thousand in here on some weekends. Those who moved away liked to come back. All summer long folks had family reunions. I guess I grew up thinking every place would be like it, the way you do."

"What happened?"

"Well, I suppose you would say it dated from the incident." I didn't want to push him. I let my gaze settle on the two railroad coaches backed up to the south end of the boardwalk. By accident or design the walk was at the same level as the floor of the coaches. You could step from one to the other. Topsoil and sand deposited by the river had settled in around the coach wheels, and concealed the tracks, so that it looked like a big double diner, closed down for the offseason.

"Someone could have made a diner out of that," I said.

"For who? Folks were leaving. Every train that come up had a flatcar attached to haul stuff away."

"It happened that fast?"

"You bet. One summer we had it crowded with people: the next summer it was almost like this. Not quite of course. Older people inclined to hang around until they died off."

"That's amazing," I said, "just because of one little incident."

38

"Oh, it wasn't so little. I didn't see it. I was in Fort Riley, taking basic training." He thought a moment. "I suppose I should let one of them tell it. Harry was here. He's the one to tell it."

"Too bad he isn't here," I said. "I see him so seldom."

"You go back to the war years and you'll find it reported. But with the war on it didn't arouse much interest. With so many people dead, so many missing, who cared about a handful here in Fork River?"

"How many is a handful?"

"They don't really know. There was so much confusion, when it was over, they don't know if they disappeared or just took off. Quite a few took off." What little he saw, he saw before him, wetting his lips. "The way they tell it is jumbled. Some say there was nothing but a roar like a jet, followed by a big whoosh. Others say it was one of these big funnels, bigger than any ever seen, that got its nose caught in the river canyon and just followed it along, sucking up all the water, to where it broke into the clearing right there behind the schoolhouse and sucked up the whole acre of the Victory garden, with the ten or twenty people who were working in it. Maybe more. You seen the hole?"

"It's like a crater."

"Well that's where everybody had their own piece of garden. They'd filled it all in with topsoil they found along the river, and used the river water to irrigate it."

"*That's* the story?"

"You can check it with Harry. He was here in town, but he wasn't near the garden. Some people ran around looking for people. Others just took off. The one certain thing, when it was all over, was that they had this hole in the ground and as many as ten or twenty people missing. Could be twice that number."

In the trees behind us a woodpecker hammered. It seemed so quiet in the street I could hear the heat rising. What I probably heard were bees thronging.

"You don't believe it?"

"That's a crater," I said, "not just a hole. All the dirt is removed down to bedrock. Tons and tons of dirt."

"Dahlberg's got the figures on it. It's a whale of a lot of dirt."

"It doesn't seem plausible," I said. "A twister just doesn't stop and drill a hole, like an auger."

"Most don't," he said, "but this one did. It came along to that point and just settled on it. People said they could hear it, like a big vacuum."

I tried to visualize it. "A big whoosh, right—?" I threw up my arms. "And then it all went through this hole in space?"

"Something like that. I didn't personally see it, but it's hard to believe the power in a big twister. You get one big enough it would suck you up a good-sized town, with all the people in it. I think what got people in a tizzy was that it might happen again, because of the river canyon. Like a vacuum nozzle stuck in a groove. The next time it might just suck up the whole town."

"It makes a good story."

"A body has yet to contradict it," he replied. I thought he was about to say, "and you can better believe it," but he held it back.

"I thank you for telling me. I might never have got it all out of Lorbeer. He seems to like his work."

"He keeps things shipshape around here. If somebody busts a window, he repairs it. There's nothing that you'd call run-down about it."

That there was not. Nor was there much run-down about him. I had the feeling he'd been waiting for me to arrive—I mean for years. As solid and suspicious as he seemed to be, I felt he might disappear if I took my eyes off him. "This Space Project," I said, "it's open on Sundays?"

"Yes sireeee, except in the winter. People find it hard to get in and out in the winter, but Harry likes to keep it open for interested people. They walk in from the highway"—he gestured toward it—"or they hike in from Bixby, along the river. He seems to get a lot of the younger-type people. After the meeting they sit around in the grove, having a picnic." He said "in the grove" as if we were both standing in its shade. I understood that was just a way of speaking, since most of these trees were dead. The only leaves clung to the lower branches.

"What sort of meeting?" I asked. I found it hard to visualize.

40

"Oh, they just loll around, listening to the music, or they sit around looking at the pictures."

"He paints *pictures*?" I thought he might. I can't say that hearing that surprised me.

"Paints?" he replied. "I suppose he could. If it comes to his mind, he does it. They're big—" He spread his arms wide. "He gets them from the space and the weather people."

For a brief moment I thought I heard music: flocking birds spilled their shadows around us. "I've got to run along," I said, unmoving.

"I'll tell Harry you was here."

"I'll give him a call. We've got some work for him."

He watched me climb into and start the car. Thinking over what it was he had said to me, or I had said to him, he didn't wave. You may have noticed how people off the beaten path will stand and look at a stranger until he's out of sight, as if they doubted his existence. I went off slow. I thought he might fire over my head. To change my line of thought I wondered what Alice would say when I told her about the Space Project. Her eyes would dart about, as usual, then she would say, "It could be a tax shelter these days." That's the real world for you, as distinct from the one I had just left.

4

MY FIRST WIFE OFTEN SAID OF ME,
"Kelcey is a tease," without expanding on her meaning. If we
happen to meet her somewhere she says to Alice, "Is he still a
tease?" I should tell you we had known each other as children.
Alice does not feel as I do about it since she considers the word
a term of endearment. I have found that the phrase is favored
by people who are guarded in their choice of words.

Alice is not guarded. She is small, but not petite. If she stands
at my side my arms rests easily on her shoulders: with her right
hand she often grips my thumb. Her eyes are brown, and so widely spaced they seem small. The dry summers out here chap her
lips, which are usually slightly parted. Her hair is dark brown
with bands of white at the temples her mother told me she was
born with. She combines a rabbit-like, lettuce-nibbling shyness
with inflexible assurance. In her absence, if I call her to mind,
I usually see her crouched in the garden, wearing her green-thumb
gloves, an indoor-outdoor houseplant. She likes to be rained on.
The plight of the ladybugs is her study. On leaving the house
to do her shopping I have heard her say, "Goodbye house!"
There's a side to her nature it takes time to appreciate. All in
all, I am not a bad judge of her feelings, but I would hesitate
to say I know what she thinks. If the word "tease" can be applied to me, the word for Alice is *firm*.

In the early sixties I was a member of Seminars Afloat, summer cruises combining college-level courses. I had classes in history
and journalism. Alice was one of the young teaching assistants
who did most of the work. We sailed out of Barcelona at the
end of June, and made stops at the less expensive places, Mallorca,
Palermo, Corfu, Dubrovnik. Most of the time, of course, we were
on the boat, and it was a long time. Alice seemed to be at ease

with an older-type person, and I liked her independence and reserve. I remember wondering why such a pretty young thing so seldom smiled. Over the first winter she wrote me several letters, and the following summer she was back with the cruise. It seemed to me that I handled it all pretty well, considering. As a rule it is the young who arouse our expectations, but Alice, for one reason or another, associated hers with me. I was flattered. We were both concerned to avoid misunderstandings. She didn't write to me, over the second winter, but in June she was back in Barcelona, waiting for the boat. I detected in her manner a new assurance. For myself, I had been more or less alone for eight years, after a marriage that had lasted too long. The early sixties were still too early for "shacking up," a phrase that pretty well described such an arrangement, so we both had to face a difficult decision. With the summer over we stopped off in southern Indiana to see her mother. I had never heard Alice refer to her father. Mrs. Calley lived in the outskirts of New Albany, in a dense grove of trees overlooking the Ohio. On the plains you forget about the primeval forest, and cease to believe in it. It seemed to me as peaceful and pastoral as heaven. I felt like Hiawatha. Leaves luminous as fire lit up the floor of the woods, the sky veiled with blue streamers of fragrant leaf and wood smoke. I helped split a few logs. The sound went on ringing after I had stopped. Mrs. Calley was a tall, stooped woman, her steel gray hair drawn back so tight on her scalp it made her skin transparent. She wore a smock-like gray garment that hung to her ankles, lived in the older of the two frame buildings on the property. A wood-burning stove, but no lights. Shadeless oil lamps, with wicks curled in the oil, sat around the house smoking like votive candles. No rugs. No bureaus or bric-a-brac. Time moved sideways, ticking, or rose in circles. What she had in the way of possessions she left in the other house. My feeling is that neither house had ever been painted. The clapboards had the color of old barrel staves. One window in each of the three lower rooms. A door at the front and back. She sat in an armless, wicker-seated rocker, her arms folded at her front like braces, rocking without lifting her feet from the floor. She talked easily with her daughter, as if I wasn't there. Had the summer been hot? Were the foreign people friendly? In the Bible she had read that they all lived on fish.

The nights I lay awake on the cot upstairs had about them, for me, something unearthly. Bird cries. A deafening drone of insects. Pre-DDT in the planetary perspective. Something in my nature is unduly impressed with what has been sheared off, with the ultimately simple. It seemed to me the air I breathed was holy, like a loon's cry at Walden. Mrs. Calley kept a garden, she had friendly neighbors who often looked in on her, and chopped wood for her. Her busy work seemed to consist of the quilts and afghans she made over the winter to sell to the passing tourists over the summer. Some of them were spread out on a split rail fence that ran along the highway at her entrance. Fearing the worst about plains winters she insisted that Alice take one. It still smells of lamp oil.

Either Alice had several older brothers, or one older brother who had led several lives. Three or four of his abandoned and wrecked cars were back in the woods, half buried under leaves. He had driven a dog sled in Alaska, worked at mining in Australia, sailed out of New Orleans on freighters, explored caves in Kentucky, and tried his hand at mountain climbing, which he liked. Alice seemed reticent to talk about him. I sometimes wonder if he actually existed. As a youth he made a raft, right here on the farm, that he rode down the Ohio to the Mississippi, and down the Mississippi to New Orleans. As a big brother he impressed on her all the advantages of being a man. Her mother said to me, "Why, you're as tall as Leland," a seldom mentioned name. He seemed to be a tireless practical joker. Behind his ceaseless moving around was some intangible expectation. On that point brother and sister were much the same. Alice went to local schools, then to Chicago where she studied commercial art: she didn't know, at the time, there was any other kind. Her first job was to put in the handcolored touches in a line of convalescent Get Well cards. Choosing the text for a line of cards in French and Spanish got her interested in languages. From there she made her way to the summer college cruises, and to me.

45

Does that seem a downward path of expectations? For three summers, I'm afraid, drifting at sea, with some legendary island on the horizon, I filled her ears with the fiction of the westward course of empire. It's quite a story, you know. The adventures of the Greeks were waterborne, as well as the Vikings and Columbus. They make tales suitable for growing boys. From the bluffs of the Missouri, looking west, the plains had once been an inland sea. Somehow they looked inviting. An illusion. All of that waving grass was nothing but a beachhead to the towering Rockies, and beyond the Rockies the infernos of sea-level valleys. Hell on earth. Why do so many dreams come out of such places? Is there one now hovering over Fork River? Think of it in 1840, unmapped and unknown, mountains alternating with burning deserts, month after month of danger and exhaustion, up ahead the maddening ripple of mirages, delirium cooling to cannibalism, the heat and sand to snow-clogged passes, amateurs, thieves, cranks, and visionaries making their lemming-like way to the goldfields. At once incredible and dismaying. The excursions of Alexander the Great, comparatively speaking, were like local raiding parties. The sea! the sea! was always there before them, off to one side, or behind them. To these demented land-bound travelers the sea became an hallucination, a fevered state of mind. And yet in the time span of a childhood that vast territory had been *subjugated,* a word they loved. Translated that means: The dreamer has awakened. On the surface of the shrinking planet there would never again be a dream quite like it. Beneath it, perhaps, or above it. Next on the agenda loomed the sky. It had always been there, an inexhaustible fiction, a blackboard for speculation, mapped and remapped, made and unmade, but never explored. Conceivably, I said, in closing, man might set his foot on the moon.

"Not woman?" she asked. How well I remember that! A small correction in space tactics. We were huddled in the shelter of a lifeboat, to get out of the wind. Overhead the Mediterranean sky, strange to me, brought to mind none of my star maps. For all my talk I was an earthbound voyager. "Not woman?" she repeated.

46

"Why not?" I said, as if I might personally arrange it. My feeling was that she looked to me for something, but I'm not sure what. That fall, in Indiana, I had the impression that in this union I was contributing less than I would be receiving. Forest people have long spells of hibernation, interspersed with a passion for open spaces. I suppose you could say that Alice's early training—especially mine—seemed to look ahead, or sort of set her up, for Harry and Dahlberg. That's speculation, of course, as so much of my life increasingly seems to be.

We were watching the news when the phone rang, which usually means it's for Alice. She has a friend who calls her to make sure she doesn't miss anything.

"It's *her*," Alice said. She's not on the best of terms with Miss Ingalls.

"I hope I didn't disturb you," Miss Ingalls said. "I've uncovered something." She makes a nice distinction between uncover and discover. Uncover is touched with conspiracy. "You remember P. O. Bergdahl?" I did not. "I don't know how you writers solve anything," she said. "P. O. Bergdahl, the author of *Waiting*."

"Oh! *That* Bergdahl!"

"That Bergdahl," she repeated. "I've uncovered this picture—"

"Of Dahlberg?"

"—of this old soddy, Mr. Kelcey. It's out near Burwell. Mr. Bergdahl and his family are in front of it. I believe a man from Topeka took it. I don't know why they would let him. It's appalling. It's not the sort of picture you would show *any*-body. He has this child on his lap, with two women standing in the yard behind him."

"I'll be right over," I said. She took the time to assure me she would be there until nine o'clock. "She's turned up something," I said to Alice, "would you like me to drop you off at the Bergman movie?" It surprised me that she didn't.

"I'll just read," she replied.

I found Miss Ingalls at the checkout counter. She gave me a conspiratorial glance, then let me wait. On the desk in her office she had this file of early clippings and photographs. Miss Ingalls tells me that people now bring her pictures of the thirties, like old Bibles. They collect them like arrowheads or old flour sacks. They seem to have forgotten that Miss Ingalls had actually been there, a young woman in her twenties attending Teacher's College. The flour sack and the photograph are antiques. Neither Miss Ingalls nor I draw the obvious deduction.

The picture she handed me, the color of old newsprint, was mounted on gray board. It had the usual sepia tone of old photographs except for an object at the front, gleaming like false teeth. A big gross fellow sat there, wearing a collarless shirt, a doll-size child seated on his right ham. His weathered face and hands looked fire-blackened, his black tangled hair like a pelt. The impression I had had of gleaming false teeth was the keyboard of a portable house organ, the wind supplied by foot pedals. A blurred sheet of music was propped up on the rack. In the middle ground behind him, to his left and his right, two women dressed in black stood erect as columns. No visible features, brown hair drawn back to a tight knot at the nape of the neck, the hands crossed at the front as if covering an exposure. A trim of faded lace at the cuffs and throat. Behind them, set into a low mound, with a pile of manure heaped to the left, a sod house with a single black window, weeds or grain sprouting on the roof. The door stood ajar like the mouth of a cave. I can't explain what it was that riveted my attention. Was it the women, standing like icons, as if rejecting the connection between them, or the faceless, spread-legged hulk of the man exhibiting his valued possessions, a portable house organ, a frail, slightly blurred, tow-headed child.

"Good God!" I said.

"That's Ansell Bergdahl. One is Mrs. Bergdahl." She turned the picture over to check the names on the back. "The child on his knee is Peter O. Bergdahl. That would have been his father. I really don't blame him a bit. If I had people like that I'd change my name too."

The child appeared to take after the women, thin as a stick. In the blowing grass on the soddy roof I could see a pair of antlers and the horns of steers. I understood that this picture held a meaning that escaped me.

"He dreamed the whole thing up," I said. "I should have known it."

"Dreamed what up?"

I wagged my head in disbelief. "About his early life, the school he went to, the experience he had that changed his life."

"I should think he might. I'd dream something up too. You're a funny one to complain about people dreaming."

"I'm not complaining, Miss Ingalls. I'm just impressed by it. He did it so well he really took me in."

"They're a clever lot," she said. "His daddy was a self-taught wizard. He collected fossils. He knew all about sunspots. Mr. Rainey said he was one of the first to shoot off a rocket."

"Shoot off what?"

"Some sort of rocket. He was born before his time, according to Mr. Rainey."

At the bottom of the photograph someone had printed, in pencil,

A New Home on the Prairie
Settler takes Pride in his Possessions

Miss Ingalls took the photograph from my hands, but a ceremonial image remained on my mind's eye. Was it the organ or the child that was being sacrificed? "I simply don't understand how the women endured it," said Miss Ingalls. "Some of them didn't. They simply went crazy."

"And the men?"

"Oh, they could *do* things. They could shoot at each other. They could shoot off rockets." She gave me the smile of an accomplice, then added, "And some of them would grow up and write fiction."

Back at the desk I said, "Do you suppose you might have anything on a family named Lorbeer? A Harry Lorbeer?"

"I'll look into it, Mr. Kelcey," she said, "if I can just find the time."

5

HAVE YOU NOTICED THAT SMALL, NEATLY
turned young women are often attracted to gangly, uncouth, foot-
in-the-mouth-type men? As well as the other way around? This
morning he brought the paper up the drive with him, and just
happened to meet Alice putting out the trash. My neighbor's wife
would say they made a cute pair. He took a moment to point
out a small local item to her, although nothing interests Alice
less than the local news. She has always had a peculiar distaste
for reports of the sort that she has just brought into the house,
clipped out, and read to me.

**500 BIRDS
DROP DEAD**

Liggett
Blair County

Birds were dropping dead from the telephone wires in Blair
County. Tim Conroy stopped his car to pick a few of them
up. He said they looked normal enough, except they were dead.
Conroy is one of Blair County's bird watchers. He identified
the birds, of the blackbird family, as being strange to the area.
They had blown off their course, lost their way, gone crazy,
or something. He took several of the bird bodies to the State
Fish and Game people in Liggett for analysis.

Two weeks ago she would have said, "That's your stink-
ing, awful bomb!" Now she said nothing.
I said, "Must have been something they ate."
"You want to know what he said? He said if he was a bird,
out in that dismal county, he would have dropped dead long ago.
There's not a tree in it. What is a poor bird to do? Nothing but
these awful wires for them to roost on. Imagine seeing it all as
clearly as they do!"

"They're *birds*," I said, "they're free to take off. We've got trees right here if they're looking for trees. Who told them to go out there and sit on the wires?"

"That's what he wants to know. He's sure they know something we don't."

She left me to think that over. A moment later she was back to retrieve the clipping.

"Alice," I said, "it's not all that unusual. They could have eaten some poisoned grain or something."

"Is that so usual?" she replied, and I've been sitting here reflecting on it. I know the country around Liggett. If you could put what is left out there on a truck and take it anywhere else it would be an antique. Before motels came in they used to have tourist cabins about the size of tool sheds. You parked your car in the space between them. On the windy days dust puffed up, like smoke, through the cracks in the floor. Around Liggett, when the dust was blowing, you might see cars with windshields like pieces of frosted glass, the paint sandblasted off the windward side. One thing I would like to tell Alice is that not only birds drop dead out there. I remember an old woman, out in the yard, her skirts blowing and flapping like wash on a line. A common turn of speech, if you can get one of them to talk, is the phrase "in all of my born days," followed by "I never saw anything like it." Birds dropping off wires would not receive much comment. Birds that *stayed* on wires would be cause for wonder. What I would like to tell Alice is that the craziest happenings are best described in the plainest language. If you see birds dropping dead, you say so. If you see someone walking on water, you just say so. If you see a hole in the sky, you say so. But if you see a flying object, unidentified, floating in over the tree-tops like a Frisbee, my advice would be to keep it to yourself.

Dahlberg stopped painting at four o'clock to work on a trellis for Alice's tomatoes. He thinks better of me now that he knows my saw is sharp. What is he thinking? I see only the back of his knobby head. I would have said his mind was a restful blank, like a farmer at the end of a plowed furrow, but knowing him as the author of *A Hole in Space* I see his brain pan twinkling like a constellation. Where is he off to? He envies me Alice. I envy the private world of his hands. One dangles like the claw of a machine, the thumb delicately tapping the second finger (a hangover of the days he dusted his cigarette); the other he has placed at the small of his back with the palm turned outward, the fingers paint-smeared. I can see that hand is anxious to get back to work. Whatever *he* is thinking *it* is eager to grip, heft, or touch something. If it knew what was on his mind it would make a swipe at the back of his head, as if rubbing a crystal ball. Dahlberg drinks from the hose, holding it upright, taking little slurps from the side. He is at once ungainly and fastidious. When he face is wet his eyelashes tangle and he looks very boyish.

I offered Dahlberg a beer, while he waited for Harry, and we sat on the part of the deck that had dried. I angled for an opening to bring up Fork River, but with me he gets defensive. Wouldn't it be more convenient, I asked him, if they lived closer to the city? He didn't think so. If I hinted I had found and read one of his books, I would never see him again. If the chance offered, I thought it might be possible to discuss Fork River with Harry Lorbeer who would not take it so personally. After all, he had put his name on a project that seemed to relate to the town's curious history. I considered it characteristic that Dahlberg's name had not been on it.

Harry Lorbeer was late, coming all the way from Crete, and honked at the end of the driveway for Dahlberg. "If you can find the time," I asked him, "we'd also like you to paint the garage door." The deck and the garage are both a gunmetal color, and use the same paint. I hope he appreciated that I did not ask if he'd be back in the morning.

"How did you two get along today?" I asked Alice. She'd picked up a little sunburn working in the garden. I knew they had got along very well, but she was weighing the intent of my question. It's a great challenge to feel that familiar motives have become complex. She had never had to guess at what I was thinking. Now she did.

"He's traveled. He's been to Italy." I said nothing. "And he was in the war."

"What war? That's hard to believe."

"Why is it hard?"

"I mean about the war. I don't see Dahlberg in a war."

"I don't see you in one either, and you were. He liked Italy but not the Italians."

"What did you say to that?" Alice makes a point of liking Italians, to justify her dislike of the Germans and the French. The Italians are more "human." They go through your bags while you're asleep.

"He thinks life is a joke," Alice said.

"He thinks *what*?" We were out on the deck. It seemed particularly foolish to hear that on the deck. We could see across the plain almost to Kansas.

"No, I think he said *hoax*. Life on this planet is a hoax."

"Oh my God," I said. "The thinking man's house painter."

"The thinking *woman's* house painter," she corrected.

"He said, life on this planet?"

"I did think that was silly."

"I take it he's had encouraging word from one of the others, right?"

"He wasn't just griping. He's really thought about it. I know it isn't so stupid as I've made it sound."

"I'll schedule a conference," I said, "I'm not too clear about these innovations. Imagine getting all this for three bucks an hour."

My sarcasm reassured her, showing her how much I cared.

"So how was *your* day?"

"No new planets," I said, "but talk of an old twister. They say this one followed along the Fork River to where it sucked up twenty or thirty people. They just disappeared."

"They scare me to death," she replied, and I knew that. The one thing she had insisted about the house was a basement.

"Not only people," I continued, "but real estate, including a new Victory garden. It left a hole like a mini-crater." I had the clear impression she had stopped listening. People who live in California shudder to hear about twisters: people familiar with twisters tremble to hear about quakes. Alice couldn't bear to hear about either of them. "I took a run out to look at it," I went on. "They call it Fork River. Except for the hole there's no sign that anything hit it. It's like a ghost town. The people just packed up and took off."

"I should think they would," said Alice.

"A self-respecting twister doesn't just drill a hole like that, then stop. It looks like it might have been made by an auger. It's not plausible."

"The poor people must have found it plausible. Why don't you ask Mr. Dahlberg?"

"I thought *you* might ask him. That you'd heard about this twister in Fork River. See what he says. If I ask him he'll clam up."

"Why shouldn't he tell you, if it's such a special twister?"

"There's just the two of them," I said, "in this ghost town. Flocks of cawing crows, a sort of lost world feeling. My feeling is they would like to keep it special."

"You're not thinking of doing a piece on it?"

"When something drops right in my lap," I replied, "I can't help but think about it. I don't know what I'm thinking. It's a subject that has some interesting angles. People are more open to unusual happenings than they used to be."

She knew I was covering something, but she wanted me to feel that she didn't know it.

"Is a twister so unusual?"

"The people in Fork River seemed to think so. After this incident, which is what they call it, they packed up and cleared out as if the place was cursed. They did not come back."

"If he brings it up, we'll discuss it. I am not going to pry into his background."

"Fine," I said. Knowing Alice I knew that she would, if I could keep Dahlberg around long enough. If he was talking about his travels already, he would get to Fork River sooner or later.

"While we've got him around," I said, "I've asked him to do the garage door. He's a good painter. You have anything you'd like Harry to look at?"

"Harry who?"

55

"Mr. Lorbeer. People refer to him as Harry."

"I'd like another bathroom," she said, "but I don't know where to put it."

"Contractors have these portable outbillies," I said. "We could rent one and put it at the foot of the garden."

Alice left me with the paper, and as I checked the weather it occurred to me that the Fork River twister—if that was what it was—should have been reported in the local journal. If Dahlberg came to work, interrupting my concentration, I might check back on the Heber County weather, during the war.

Dahlberg did not appear for work. I found that more of a distraction than if he had, since it magnified his rudeness. He knew to what extent this affected my work. Allowing for the fact that that might amuse him, he was equally rude to Alice. How little trouble it would have been for him to call and explain. At twenty minutes to eleven I phoned Fork River with a few good lines for their answering service. Dahlberg answered. On the phone he had a high pipsqueak voice. "Is it any of our business," I said, "why you have decided not to appear?"

"No," he replied. That found me at a disadvantage. I was certain he would give one excuse or another.

"Alice is anxious about her tomatoes. She's been waiting weeks for that trellis."

"I'll try to make it tomorrow."

"Is Harry there?" I asked.

"He's busy."

Having been there, having looked the place over and found it as dead as a cemetery, I appreciated his comment. "If he can find the time, I'd like him to call me. There's something I'd like to ask him."

"I'll tell him." Just by the voice and manner I would have thought I was talking to a child, about six years old. I hung up before he could hang up on me.

"For unmitigated rudeness and insolence . . . You heard me tell him you were waiting for your trellis."

"I am not *waiting,* and he knows that. The vines aren't long enough for a trellis."

"All he had to do was give you a call. I've already told him to reverse the charges."

About noon, having had no call, I drove in to the college campus. We have this great institution of learning which trains and exhibits a football team. You will have heard of the team. If a big cornfed local boy has heard of the team, just try and keep him down on the farm. In the fall one of my neighbors, a successful dentist, hangs a banner across the front of his house, screening off the picture window, which reads GO BIG RED. He loves it. His kids love it. He tells me that his wife loves it. On home-game weekends they wear red hats, ties, and jackets, and walk around like Irish children at their first communion. When we speak of an agricultural state, we mean one that grows big cornfed beef, on the foot and on the hoof. The local weather forecasts are as important as the oracles at Delphi. I had met the chief weatherman, socially, and found him agreeably full of his subject: a man who loves his work. Fred Rainey was also about my own age, and would remember—if there had been one—the incident at Fork River. He knew of me as the author of a piece looking hopefully forward to the next ice age. He loves ice ages. If there's a drop in the global temperature I hear from him.

"Sure," he said to his secretary, "send him in."

Another secretary, an elderly woman, sits at the back of his office wearing earphones, taking dictation from a tape deck. She didn't seem to be aware that I had entered the room. Dr. Rainey is a big, hulking man who belongs outdoors, but finds himself trapped indoors. He gets out just enough to keep a light tan on his face and hands. I felt almost indecently casual when I saw him, since I was wearing summer slacks, with a short-sleeved shirt, and open-weave, flat-soled sandals; he was buttoned into a dark brown suit that was too small for him. Including the vest. It's not often you see the coat and the vest. Rainey had just never had the excuse to depart from the customs he was raised in, such as cupping the elbow of your wife when you lead her down the walk to your car, or up the aisle of a movie house. As I came in I saw him tap out a lozenge from the packet in the drawer of his desk, pop it into his mouth.

"How are you, Kelcey?" he boomed, and pushed his chair back from the desk, so he could tilt back in it. His office is now air-conditioned, and I could feel a cool draft blowing on me from somewhere. Soon I would sneeze. I said I was fine, and what I wanted to ask him, if he had the time, was a little bit about twisters. Everybody in this state is interested in the weather, and if they stay long enough they get an interest in twisters. There is nothing in nature equal to them. The hurricane is more powerful, especially at sea, but you know well in advance if one is coming, and what to expect. The earthquake is as sudden, and more unnerving, but it's the aftereffects you remember. I've been in quakes, and watched the chandeliers swing in a theatre full of people. A quake is not much without the panic, and the crumbling walls. With a little luck out here in twister country, you can see the funnel shape up on the horizon, dipping and swaying, or a pillar-like column that is almost transparent, like a rain falling, but not frayed off like rain at the edges, and long before you hear it like a downgrade freight train you feel it in what my father called the *withers*. The terror you feel is primeval. It centers in the guts and radiates along the nerve wires. The hairs prickle at their roots. The fingers tingle. In the split of a second you're an animal in panic, either paralyzed or running for its life. In my boyhood most of the houses that didn't have basements had a storm cave, a mound of dirt in the yard with a cave beneath it. It didn't freeze in the winter and it was cool in the summer. People used it to store potatoes, fruits and jellies, churned butter. I remember my mother, crouched on a sack of onions, hugging me to her breasts so I could feel her heart throb. Nothing happened. I was carried back upstairs and was soon asleep.

"Anything in particular?" he asked me. His hands were clasped behind his head, rumpling his hair. Rainey married a local girl, who blessed him with four daughters, then returned to her position as a high school science teacher. Alice and I sometimes see them at the shopping plaza, or driving home from church. He will say, "Give my regards to Mrs. Kelcey," when I leave.

I'll thank him and say, "Give our best to Mrs. Rainey." I have heard him say that when people cease to do that, the game is up.

"You happen to recall the Fork River twister?"

He had been tilted back, savoring his lozenge. He tilted forward and looked at me over the rim of his glasses. "Where did you run into that?"

"It just so happens," I said, "we've got a fellow painting the deck from Fork River. I'd never heard of it and couldn't find it on the highway road maps, but Miss Ingalls, at the library, found it for me just below the Kansas state line." I could see that he was waiting for me to go on. "The story seems to be that it was a thriving town, mostly Swedes, until the incident of the twister. It frightened people so bad they packed up and took off."

Rainey tilted forward to open his desk drawer, find a paper clip, unbend it so he could use it to clean his nails. I thought of Harry, and his wire coat hangers.

"That's all hearsay," I said. "Is that how you recall it?"

He removed his glasses and polished the lenses with his tie. "During the war," he said, "I was in Washington. I didn't get back here till it was over." That's what you call a cardiac bypass.

"It's all history now," I said, "the place is like a ghost town. This house painter and his friend have it all to themselves. It must have been one of the nicest places in the state until the twister struck and the people panicked. The story is that quite a number of the natives were at work in the community Victory garden, just behind the school. The school looks fine. Just behind it, up the canyon, is this hole like a small crater. Almost perfectly round. The sides so smooth that if you fell in you might have a time getting out. No dirt anywhere. What sort of twister drills a hole like that?"

I tried to look suitably wonderstruck about it, anxious to know the exact name of this marvel. He wheeled his chair around so that he faced the louvers at the window. He's up about four floors, and has a good view of the plain, if he wants it.

"Twisters don't drill holes," he said, "—as a rule."

"That was my own impression. You'd have to get the twister

to stop right there, like the nozzle was stuck, and suck up the soil like a soft drink through a straw."

"That's a nice metaphor, Kelcey."

"I don't want to use it if it's not accurate."

"It's a vacuum," said Rainey, "on the human scale. The twister is a vacuum on the planetary scale. If you got one just a little bit bigger I suppose you could suck up anything that wasn't nailed down."

"Would you say that was highly unlikely?"

In the pause I could hear the clack-clack of his secretary's typewriter. The earphones gave her the aspect of a preoccupied spaceship pilot. Where was she off to? The reels wheeled on the tape deck.

"Would you say it was highly unlikely, Kelcey, to have a dinosaur put his head through the window?"

"I guess I would." I nodded.

"You get your time systems out of phase, and it would be more or less normal. You get your physical systems out of phase and you might get one hell of a vacuum, right out of the blue."

"Right out of the blue?"

"Why not? It's a smear of air around this planet, Kelcey, no thicker than the skin of your teeth. You prick it with something and you've got a vacuum."

"Rainey," I said, "what have you been reading?"

"It relaxes me," he replied, "more than the weather."

"Did you ever happen to read one titled *A Hole in Space?*"

Rainey's solemn, fleshy face is often like that of a Buddha. Meditative, without a clue to what he was thinking. "Is it a good one? I like the title."

"My current house and deck painter wrote it. His name is O. P. Dahlberg."

When you are testing melons for ripeness you want the one that rings hollow. I had hit it. Rainey picked at the lint on the sleeve of his coat. "You happen to know a P. O. Bergdahl?" I asked him.

Rainey said, "What were you reading?"

"Miss Ingalls mentioned him to me."

"A sort of wunderkind, Kelcey. Grassroots whizzkid. One of the first to relate sunspots and tree rings. Collected meteorites. Wrote a paper suggesting they might be flying objects. Designed and shot off a rocket."

"What became of him?"

"Working on a new rocket propellant he made a miscalculation."

We were silent. His secretary, clamped between her headphones, ticked away in her familiar orbit. At some point in every discussion you know you have come full circle. Just a few remarks back we were both headed outward: here we were back with the flying objects. At the door I turned and said, "Doesn't that damned typing get on your nerves?"

"Cuts down on the idle speculation," he replied.

"I just thought of something," I said. "What became of the rocket?"

Rainey peeled back the foil on a pack of fruit drops, pried one loose. "There's two points of view, Kelcey. You can settle for a theory that tells you what can't happen—or you can see what happens and forget the theory."

"That reminds me of the Fork River Space Project," I said.

"Fork River *what*?"

"Space Project. They meet on Sundays. I understand they listen to music and go into orbit." Rainey had tilted back to look at the reflections cast by the venetian blinds on the ceiling. "I sometimes get the feeling the old ball game is over. You ever feel like that?"

He wheeled his chair to face the glare at the windows. The prevailing wind had tilted the trees so that a gale appeared to be blowing.

"How do we start a new game, chum?" he asked me. Chum is the word he uses in a friendly putdown.

"The man to see is Dahlberg," I said, "if you catch him in time."

6

T**HERE'S NOT MUCH TO BE DONE WITH A**
hole but look at it. The cooling of the globe, the creation of the
seas, the coming and going of the ice, the dinosaurs, and the
Progressive Party were all reasonable acts compared to the mini-
crater on the Fork River.

What did Harry Lorbeer mean by a *space project*? Instead
of acting on the sly, to appease Dahlberg, which so far had got
me nowhere, I should persuade Alice to go along with me and
drive out to Fork River on Sunday. The Project was open from
2 to 5. There were questions I would like to put to Harry, knowing I would get nothing out of Dahlberg. If we appeared on Sunday with the others, there would be nothing underhand about
it. I would let Alice break the news to Dahlberg if she would rather
that we didn't surprise him. I'd actually like to hike up the river
myself, but it wouldn't suit Alice. "You hike, darling, then tell
me what it was like."

On Friday we had Dahlberg from 10:00 to 2:30, at which
time he had completed the deck. I walked out to admire what
he had done, which was not hard, since he is a good painter.
He made no objection to being admired, but neither did he appreciate the effort it cost me. He's a clever fellow. He knew very
well that Alice had put me up to it. He had only bought paint
enough for the deck, so he would have to wait till Monday to
start on the trim. He has mannerisms, when I am talking to him,
that make it hard for me to be civil. One thing he does is screw
his little finger into his ear right up to the second knuckle, grimacing as if it pained him. It could be a trick. He does it in a way
that implies he finds it hard to hear me. I've already mentioned
how he stands, looking away. Until I caught on to that one I
would move to see what it was he was observing. He implied

this was none of my business. The truth is that Dahlberg finds it hard to conceal his infatuation for Alice, his jealousy of me. This gives me a certain edge, a leverage, so to speak, I didn't have at the start. It led me to say, "I've been reading about Fork River. It's got quite a history. I'm thinking of driving Alice over to see it. Would Sunday be a good day?"

"How would I know that?" he replied. Sensing I had the advantage I felt different about his rudeness. "Well, if it happens to be, maybe we'll drive over. How long does it take?"

"You ought to know," he said, "since you've driven it."

I was willing to be caught in that lie to determine if the old man had reported my visit.

"I found the road pretty bad," I said calmly. "Is there a better way to get in and out?"

"Some walk," he replied. "They walk up from Bixby, about seven miles."

"That's fourteen miles. I don't think Alice would like it."

He gave me a sidelong glance, from the feet upward, implying that a person with longer legs would set a good example for Alice to follow. Dahlberg has the mannerisms, when he feels imposed on, of an aging rock singer bored with bobby-soxers. I'm puzzled why Alice finds this sort of thing appealing, since her taste has always been for mature-type men. My feeling is that what she enjoys is playing Dahlberg off against me. After all, he is only her second man.

While waiting for Harry to arrive with the van we sat on the deck, listening to Italian conversation records. Alice speaks excellent French, but her Italian, as she said to Dahlberg, was "rusty." She "knew" Italian (having got an A in the course) but she feared to speak it and make a fool of herself. I did not know it, and rattled it off pretty well. It had taken the bloom off our month in Portofino. She had so wanted to be my interpreter and guide, but she clammed up.

If the two of them knew Italian as well as they knew English neither of them would have said much more than *prego*, but a smattering of some language seems to encourage duffers to speak it. Alice had more assurance than she had had in the past, and

Dahlberg was an eager, appreciative pupil. He had never before sat on a deck listening to a young woman speak at him in Italian. Did he plan to go to Italy? No, not at the moment. It had been Alice's idea. They had got to talking about Perugia, where they had both been, and Venice, where they hadn't, and places like Sardinia they were eager to go to, and all that crazy country in the heel of the boot that the tourists had not yet got to.

Had either of them read *Old Calabria?* I asked. They had not. Until that moment I had not remarked anything complicit in their glances. At that moment I did. It was a veiled glance that plainly said, "Oh, *him*!" I was more amused by that than irritated because as you grow older it gets to be so common. To have read a few good books dates you. Have you noticed that?

The FM playing in the room behind us suddenly switched from guitar to orchestral music. A glowing surge of sound, like dawn breaking. Berlioz, Wagner, or one of the Russians. I stepped inside for a moment to turn up the volume, then came back to the deck to listen. Perhaps I *am* a little obsessed on the subject. A thin, tremulous, reed-like tone seemed to penetrate my ears and stay there, as if trapped in my head.

"You hear that?" I said. "That's Borodin. Russian space music. 'On the Steppes of Central Asia,' wherever that is. As I understand it, the steppes are open country." I gestured to the south, the wide view we have of it. It was one of those days we can see into Kansas, or rather over it. It was Kansas that spread out below me, with the visible tracings of the pack ice. "Hear that?" I said.

Alice said, "Hear what?"

"That tone, that reed-like sound." I put my index fingers to the tips of my thumbs and drew a long thin line on the air before me. With half-lidded eyes I attempted to whistle. Nothing occurred.

Dahlberg said, "Do we see, or hear it?"

"Listen!" I said, but what I heard may have been in my ears. It thinned to a sliver that gleamed like a knife blade. Alice eyed me with some apprehension. "It's not *just* a sound—" I said.

"Then what is it?"

"Well—" I said, "for one thing, it's like a space signal."

Was I right in feeling they exchanged glances?

"You're expecting one?" asked Alice.

I went back inside to turn up the volume, but the reed-like tone had vanished. It's what you hear in the ascending lisp of a saw, just as it dies off. Thinking it might come again I waited. I once had, but lost, the power to move my ears. Signals were whooshing past me all the time that a sleeping cat would capture and analyze later. Through the window I watched Dahlberg pour himself some Campari, a sweet vermouth they advertise on café umbrellas. It was not lost on me that he was more assured.

A loud honking in the street proved to be Harry Lorbeer, who had come by to pick up Dahlberg. Alice wanted him to come to the deck and join us, but fortunately he was too tired. From the deck we watched Dahlberg walk down the drive, his elbows up from his side, as if his arms were wet, a space between his legs you could ride a bike through. Just as he climbed into the car I yelled, "See you on Sunday!" but I'm not sure he heard me. He could always hear you, if he thought it to his interest, or he could wonder to what you had reference. His expression is the one you see on the dog at the gramophone horn.

I stayed in the drive for a while, sweeping leaves, watching the Mafia-type jays dominate the bird feeder, giving Alice time to clear away the glasses and make her way back from Perugia. When I entered the house she gave me a detached Mona Lisa smile.

7

UNABLE TO CONCEAL HER SATISFACTION

Alice brought another clipping back to my study. She placed it on my desk without comment.

BIRDS KEEP DYING

Liggett
Blair County

More birds fell from their roosts in and near Liggett over the past few days. Some observers report finding birds in the open fields, where there was nothing to fall from but the sky.

"I think they probably picked up some kind of poison," said Wayne Dorrance, of the Fish and Game Dept. He said an infestation of one thing often led to another. He did not elaborate.

Why is this bad news for birds good news for Alice? She sees it as a triumph of the unlikely. Things were going well if they remained mysterious. Was she beginning to see, like me, what was on the lids of her eyes? Would it surprise me to hear from her in space? In all soberness I ask the question in the hope it will help me face it.

In the mail this morning I received an article from Miss Ingalls. "Time Warp," by P. O. Bergdahl. She found it in a magazine devoted to local history and train buffs. It was published in the spring of 1958, on high-quality, glossy-stock paper, selected to enhance the illustrations, provided by H. L. Lorbeer.

The writer tells how trappers and buffalo hunters used to spend their winters at the fork of the river before it had a name. In the ashes of their campsites, a century later, he had found the bones they had gnawed on. Lead bullets and arrowheads were easier to find than the location of the fork of the river. The first order of business was to get it on a map. To get it on the map was to make a beginning.

Everything in the state, once it became a state, or in the unmapped regions west of the Missouri, had a beginning as clearly defined as the heavens and the earth in scripture. One day it wasn't there at all: the next day it was "discovered." The writer asks in passing, "Was the discovery of America a mistake?" The systematic looting, polluting, exploiting, followed on the "discovery" as night follows day. That marked the beginning. The trapper and his traps, the wagon trains headed for the goldfields. Was it a beginning to be celebrated or an ending to be mourned? At that point in his article, as well as in time, the writer asked that question in hope of an answer. He wanted to know.

All animals leave traces (he goes on) but few can compare with the leavings of man. In a gravesite on the rim of the canyon, a fully clad body was found with the toes sticking out of his boots. He lay on his face, the toes of his shoes were worn away by the hole he had been digging to crawl into. Once you left the canyon for the open plain there was no place to hide.

Some time after the turn of the century a Colonel Lorbeer, on a surveying trip out of Bixby, Kansas, came up the river to spend an unforgettable night at the fork. That was how he described it to Olivia Bayliss, his prospective bride. The Colonel had camped in a grove of trees, under a canopy of stars. Through the night he heard the water purling. His bride-to-be had often mentioned her love of water and trees. An Eastern girl, she was spending that summer at the Dells in Wisconsin. She had never been west of Rockford, Illinois. She thought wherever he was sounded delightful, and asked him if it offered a view of the mountains. That letter, and that question, went unanswered. In others she wrote to the Colonel he gathered that the thought of the "open" treeless plains distressed her. What *was* there where it was open? Was there nothing but buffaloes and Indians? He reassured her that with the coming of the railroad, with the coming of progress, with the coming of a woman like herself all of that was history. He was a maker of history, being nothing if not a man of his time.

Fork River proved to be a town created for the bride of a railroad mogul. The man who builds, as the Colonel did, a nine-mile spur of railroad up a dead-end canyon for the convenience of his wife has what we call panache, and is not without interest. She liked trees and the sound of running water, and that was what she got. The article is illustrated with a map, some drawings, old photographs, and a snapshot of the author. It's him, all right. He sits on the boardwalk in front of the stores with his bare feet dangling in the flooding water, a Fork River Huck Finn.

The writer gives the impression that he knew Olivia Bayliss, the Colonel's wife. There's a picture of her, a flattering soft-focus portrait in the turn-of-the-century manner. Soulful eyes, billowly light brown hair gathered in a loose and improvised manner. The well-brought-up children—three girls and one boy—often stood at the door while she fussed with her hair. The bone hairpins between her teeth made it hard to follow her instructions. A very up-to-date man, and an empire builder, the Colonel wanted, but did not get, an old-fashioned girl. She was several inches taller, musically gifted, a flighty creature who needed to be hooded, like a falcon. (The writer actually said that.) She wore (he tells us) long strands of beads that she worked like pulleys when the conversation was animated. If it was dull she might protrude her lip and twist strands of her hair to droop like a moustache. These are all things, of course, a child would remember. She kept a butterfly collection in glass cases, played mah-jong with her children, shot off the Colonel's pistols. But the long summers were a heat-tossed sleep. The Colonel let her spend some of them in England, from where she wrote him letters he found it hard to decipher. Did he cycle? she asked him. Wouldn't a little exercise do him good? The letter clearly suggested she expected it of him. The word *expected* was so appropriate to Olivia that the Colonel felt obliged to fulfill her expectations. They cycled in France. There is a snapshot of the Colonel wearing plus fours and a cyclist's cap. Shortly after they returned to Fork River, however, Olivia is afflicted with a "nervous ailment." It took the form of laryngitis. She could not speak in a manner they could understand. The children and her husband were obliged to read her lips. Years later it led her son, Harry, to interesting speculations about sign language on the plains. What led it to arise? The problems of space. The human voice simply didn't carry. At the distance it was safe for strangers to meet shouting was pointless: so signs developed. The antelope, indigenous to the plains, exposed the white underparts of his tail to signal a warning. The writer does not elaborate on what it was Olivia Lorbeer was trying to signal. Harry remembers her often saying to her husband, "Please don't shout!" The girls were sent to school in the East, when they were old enough to travel, but Harry stayed at home with his mother. Did she need him? Was he a loner? He remembers sitting with her at the table under a cone of light that concealed all of his father but his hands. The effect on the boy was like that of a seance, mysterious, disembodied movements. A servant, named Jackson, a former dining car porter, cooked the food and served it wearing a white porter's jacket. The boy saw the jacket moving about the table, but not the hands.

It all makes good reading, with the illustrations. It shows to advantage the writer's early talent in blending fact and fiction. I recognize both, having been partially there myself. Just a few hours away, in Omaha, I was caught up in the adventures of Douglas Fairbanks and Tom Mix. Those were palmy days! My father was into real estate, the Orpheum Circuit, and chick incubators in Shenandoah, Iowa. What about Harry Lorbeer? Had he come too late for crystal sets and winding his own coils around Quaker Oats boxes? The last of the Colonel's four children, he was schooled by the Depression. The Wild West was receding, like a view down the tracks, and he had his first taste of lip reading. From both sides of his background he inherited a talent for fiction. How would he apply it? The one thing he saw the most of was the sky. But these are my speculations, not the author's, and his subject is the rise and fall of Fork River.

The men who turned the century built railroads the way we

now build freeways. A well-traveled man, the Colonel wanted a house that combined the best of the East and the West. The wide, runaround porches, with the gazebo-like bulges of the country homes that would soon become resorts, with the sprawling comfort of western haciendas. He kept it low to stay in the shelter of the canyon. Bay windows as wide as those of a Pullman diner, red tiles on the roof. I know how he felt. I once dated a girl who lived in such a home in Waukegan. The deep porch surrounded it with a moat of darkness. In the evening I could see her at the piano, her mother seated under a lamp with a beaded shade, sewing. In the dark of the porch a creaking hammock. What a time her evil-minded little brothers gave me. No matter where we were I could hear them giggling like fiends. I loved the house. It was the house I missed when we broke up. Just using the elegant, spacious bathrooms, with towels as large and fleecy as rugs, gave me my first taste of perishable grandeur. Was it the same with Harry? In a summer storm, in the thirties, the Colonel's house was struck by lightning and burned to the ground. That explains the empty space behind the meeting house, fenced off from everything else like a helicopter landing.

There is a picture of the Colonel, the empire builder, standing on the rear platform of the first train to enter Fork River. Lesser dignitaries are ranked behind him. The rear platform of a club car was the best pulpit for a substantial public figure. The Colonel was substantial. His open stance, fingers hooked in his vest, was loosely defined as "presence." He had it. William Jennings Bryan had it. An uncle on my mother's side had it, but missed the train. Very little of Fork River is visible behind him, but enough to appreciate the changes. The present meeting house, or church, was not there. In the space that is open behind it sat the house he had built for his wife. Among the cottonwoods and poplars along the south bank it is possible to see the first "company" houses, as they were called. Either the railroad or the Colonel provided the money to encourage people to settle at the Fork. All the houses were white frame buildings with two or three bedrooms, lightning rods, and no basements. Thanks to the railroad they didn't need cars. The block of business structures, set up on stilts, was dictated by the seasonal rise of the river. Shortly after the fire the Colonel moved his family to Colorado Springs. It was a fashionable spa at the time, and Mrs. Lorbeer had had enough of Fork River. The children adored it but she found the winters long.

Until the market crash the town flourished, but that put the skids to the railroad empire. I can imagine they began to close down on the mortgages. As the Depression deepened everything cut back, and most of the people of Fork River were laid off. Some hung on, of course, assuming that they would soon go back to work. Even the weather changed. There were crop failures and dust bowls. I remember days, traveling from east to west, that it was as dark at high noon as at dusk. Many of the younger people, understandably, took off. During the Second World War Fork River was bypassed. The train no longer ran in and out. Mr. Lindner continued to live there, and for part of the time, at least, Harry Lorbeer. I learned from Jake, at the gas station in Millard, that after the twister Harry used to drive in and out in a jeep. I've no idea as yet when Dahlberg joined him, but I would guess the late fifties. I'd like to have seen that occasion. Two oddballs that manage to roll into the same pocket. It does happen. Oddball people should know that and take heart.

I don't find it hard to see Harry, a typical sort of loner, learning to make do in Fork River. It's the boy who sits alone, in the hollow of a rock, or staring at the ashes in a dying fire, who sees unheard of things when he lifts his eyes and looks around him. Where does he look? In the Fork River canyon he looked at the sky. I recall dimly, for just a flickering moment, my own bafflement that it was so empty all day, and so crowded at night. That's a wondrous thought. A mind like P. O. Bergdahl's, or O. P. Dahlberg's, might have made something out of it. I suspect it was Dahlberg who gave Harry the clue to changing the world. You just renovate it, reassemble the parts to heart's desire. What I'm afraid of is that Dahlberg's faculty for fiction is going to make my own problem harder. He imagines what he pleases. He has no respect at all for the facts. How am I, or how is Alice for that matter, ever to know when he is speaking the truth? It seems reasonably certain Bergdahl was his father, but how be sure?

72

Among his father's many remarkable talents was a gift for fabrication. I use the word advisedly. Fictions were his stock-in-trade. This somewhat circumstantial tie is the strongest link between father and son. Congenital liars? It's hard to draw a clear line on the blue of the sky, or the green of the sea. They lived together, briefly, in Omaha, where P. O. Bergdahl is identified as a graduate of the Technical High School. Ten years later he surfaces as O. P. Dahlberg, author of *The Taste of Blood*. There isn't the faintest evidence he ever lived in Provo, Utah, had Mormon parents, or went to school in Walla Walla. There may be a fact in his reading *The Grapes of Wrath* and getting a hangup over the turtle. The rest of it is pure, or impure, fiction, indicating a very assured talent.

In a book I just returned to the library I found a marker that illustrates my problem. It's in Alice's hand.

Things not to do

> Tame the wilds
> Break the plains
> Subdue the rivers
> Alter the weather
> Crack the barrier
> Split the atom
> Run, walk, swim, leap
> Faster and higher
> Hit, kick, smash, gouge
> Harder and harder
> Get impatient
> Or expect too much of Kelcey

I must say I find that touching. But without setting myself up as a judge it does seem to me their expectations are unusual. Just this afternoon, making a bank deposit at the drive-up window, my eye was caught by Dahlberg, wearing his helmet, emerging from the lower floor of the shopping plaza on the escalator. It gave me a start. What might they think of next? He crossed the mall at an angle, in his creaky, spread-legged manner, entering the Small World Travel Bureau. This agency features a globe on the roof that revolves. I could see him in the office, leaning on the counter, talking with one of the clerks. Was he planning a space trip or an earth trip? What was I to do? Isn't this expecting too much of Kelcey? With the car behind me honking I had to move. Somehow it put me in mind of how I felt the first time I entered Taubler's apartment. I have yet to tell you about Taubler and Tuchman. On the wall before me he had painted this window, with its view of the sea. A real beach chair was drawn up to face it, the floor around it strewn with the hulls of hand-painted imaginary peanuts.

"He's got his own system," Tuchman said to me, "and you'd better believe it."

Let's say that I've come to believe it. What that still leaves undecided is what I'm to think.

8

A<small>LICE WAS BORN THE SUMMER</small> I <small>LEFT</small>
college to be a cub reporter for a St. Louis newspaper. Reporters
were romantic figures in those days. They went to Russia, to
Spain, to Africa, to the dogs. Many prominent writers began as
reporters, but most of them proved to have a talent only for begin-
nings. It's this talent that draws Alice to Dahlberg. I'm not sure
what drew her to me, but it's the generation gap that binds us.
Puzzlement over my baffling behavior keeps her occupied.

But I shouldn't say binds. Alice is not bound. Actually, there
is very little mucilage in our natures. In the days of our court-
ship she liked to read to me from the works of Rilke, a very cagey
lover. Binding ties were not his strong points. He spoke of two
solitudes that touch, greet, and protect one another. I highly admired the way he put it. Where else but in poetry will lovers find
two solitudes appealing? Alice reads very well, with a purr of
contentment. Sooner or later Dahlberg will have to face it. One
of our neighbor's cats is very fond of me until I scoop her up
and try to hold her. Then she goes wild. "Why do you pick her
up?" Alice asks me, as she puts iodine on my scratches. I've given
it some thought. I persist in feeling (as I did with Alice) that having for long respected her feelings, she might relax and give in
to mine. I doubt that she will, but it makes for a lively relationship.

"Where?" she queries, as if puzzled, when I suggested we
have a look at Fork River. "Why not, if you'd like to."

We didn't have a perfect day, as I had hoped, the light diffused to a glare by the high overcast, but I wanted to get this
visit in while we still had Dahlberg on the payroll. Few things
bore Alice more than "going for a ride," but she thought it might
do me good to get out of the house and into the open. I was almost
sallow. Had I noticed how tanned and healthy Dahlberg looked?

75

Distracted by his sulky manner, and pockmarked features, there were many things I had failed to notice. Had she noticed, I rejoined, that I was a writer, not a house painter? Actually, Alice had something of a tan herself from the time she was now spending in the garden. She wore a wide, floppy-brimmed hat to keep the sun off her face. In the past she had thought it too showy for the natives, but it might be just the thing for Fork River. I loved the gesture, so natural to her, of wiping back the brim with the back of her hand. At the last moment she had decided not to wear the arch-supporting space shoes she had bought just for such an occasion, if one turned up. She wore a sort of ballet slipper that enhanced the slenderness of her feet.

The Big Red had won the game the previous day, so we passed signs of local celebrations, and small fry sporting their red hats and ties. I cannot account for the distaste I feel for small boys dressed up like little men. I had once been one. As I recall I thought very well of myself. I took part in a play where I was henpecked by a wife at least a foot taller, but the funniest lines were mine. The strutting little dictator latent in the male comes out like the first cracked crow of a rooster. Toward little "wives and mothers" I am less venomous, but reserved.

"Are you supposed to be using this road?" Alice said. The high weeds were sweeping the underside of the car.

"It's what Harry and Dahlberg use," I replied, "and it keeps the place private." I wanted to surprise her. My first impression of Fork River had been so special I somewhat feared another. Explorers who came on abandoned cities, or Indian cliff dwellings, must have felt as I did, just for a moment. The time-stopped sensation. The miraculous and unforced overlapping of the past and the present. That it should be right here in the heart of the cornbelt was part of it. The curving road into the canyon seemed worse than I remembered because Alice seemed so apprehensive. It kept her eyes on the road, so that when we made the turn opening out over the river she was not prepared for it.

"Oh my," she said.

"The light's not good at all. When the light is right it's like—" What was it like?

76

"Who are those people down there?"

On the east side of the river, partially screened by the island willows, we could see a straggly line of hikers, walking along single file. Most of them had green or red packs on their backs. They wore visors or caps.

"They're hikers," I said, "they've hiked in from Bixby. They have a sort of open house on Sundays." Alice had not been prepared for so many other people. She stared at them. "Look up ahead," I said. "Look over there in the clearing." The light was not as crystalline as I had first seen it, but the row of structures, up on piers over the bed of the river, was still hard to believe. Today, however, eight or ten people were seated on the boardwalk, their legs dangling. A few leaned against the buildings, sunning themselves. "What is it?" Alice asked, "a rock concert?"

I'll admit I was not prepared for the hikers. My impression of Fork River—the one I valued—had been of a place empty of people. Others were seated in the sparse shade near the meeting house, eating their packed-in lunches. One small child was running about, spinning like a top. Two cars, one a bright yellow pickup, were parked to get the shade north of the stores. I could see the heat rising off the hood of the pickup. So many people around spoiled it for me.

"Oh, I like it!" Alice said.

I'll admit that surprised me. "I'd like it better without the hippies," I replied. "There wasn't a soul here but the crows and the pigeons."

"I'm not so different," Alice said. "I'm as expectant as they are." She glanced around at them, almost shyly. A few more years made the difference or I would have lost her.

"Harry will like that," I said, and as we moved along the main street I could hear a bell tolling, or rather clanging. A flock of pigeons swooped up from the bell tower and swept low over the treetops, their wings whirring. At the opening of the canyon they careened to the left, spilling their shadows on the hikers, and came back toward the square.

"There's Dahlberg!" Alice cried, and there was Dahlberg opening the doors to the schoolhouse. He was wearing perma-pressed khaki pants and infantry-type boots, with a high polish. He may have seen us approaching, but he moved around with that stiff-joined solemn caretaker manner he has, his eyes on the ground. His short-sleeved denim shirt was worn with the tails out of the pants. Alice complains if she catches me that way around the house.

"Must be two o'clock," I said, and looked for a shady place to park. I let Alice out, then crossed the wide empty square to a narrow slot of shade at the north end of the buildings. It would get wider as the day lengthened. I left the windows down, and stood there a moment watching the younger people cross toward the schoolhouse. It might have been a scene in a TV movie, stressing ecology and back to the soil. I have admitted to Alice that I regret having missed the tribal reenactment of the sixties. A boy's-life fantasy brought to life, the airways, the freeways, and the sexways open. It boggles the mind. Schoolboys with their knapsacks on the Spanish Steps, at the door to Keats's house. To be a boy for life! Isn't that the American dream? Old enough to shave, to have sex, to vote, but not committed to these options. I think it privately riles Alice that she just missed the early liberated woman pow-wows. She is very assured. They would have loved her. She has the class without the dark glasses. But she is long accustomed to the creature comforts of being a man's wife. Dahlberg had found her. He leaned on the still-polished rail where the departed citizens had once tied up their horses and buggies. His gangly leanness was attractive. He had never smiled for me, but from where I stood, two hundred yards away, I could see the ivory gleam of his teeth. "Ah, well," my Uncle Kermit used to say, and tap the plug from his pipe.

The visitors left their backpacks on the porch to the schoolhouse, creating a very pretty picture. Leder-hosened German wandervogels used to leave their blanket rolls on the steps of the Italian churches with one of their number left to guard them. So it was not new. Same roles, new faces. As I crossed the square a sudden surging swell of music poured through the doors, like the horn of a speaker. Was it a concert after all? The volume seemed too great for the structure. The pigeons strutting the roof had lifted into the air, as if on the wind of the sound. I had last heard the music in Kansas City, where we had gone to see the movie *2001*. The volume had been about the same, but the circumstances were more auspicious. I seemed to experience the first dawn on the planet. A small group of terrified primates huddled in the shelter of a shallow cave. I saw their terror-stricken eyes. I came very close to feeling as they felt. Not since my childhood had I felt a shudder of awe. Eerie. That awe-filled moment was still in my mind when I cowered in bed, hours later.

I stood with Alice and Dahlberg, facing the open doors, waiting for the volume of sound to diminish. As the crest passed I said to Dahlberg, "Does it need to be so loud?"

He shrugged. "That's how Harry likes it."

Inside the building I could see that the visitors were taking seats against the walls on cushions. There were no chairs. The light appeared to come through panels in the roof and had a curious subterranean dimness, as if filtered through water. From where I stood the walls appeared to be hung with a series of abstract paintings. Reddish browns, tans, pale greens, electric blues, appeared to be the dominant colors.

"Where's Harry?" I asked.

"Running the show," replied Dahlberg.

"Well, I'm going to catch some of it," I said, and stepped inside. Toward the front of the room, wearing a black cleric's gown, Harry Lorbeer stood with his back to the door, manually operating a slide projector. The screen was centered on the back wall, ten feet above eye level, so that it appeared to be part of the window that opened on the sky. What I had thought to be the moon, seen above the earth's horizon, proved to be the earth just above the moon's horizon. The upper half only was illuminated, so that it resembled the cranium of a human skull. The sensation of space travel was not new, but the experience of unearthly, celestial transport is a matter of imagination. If the astronauts had it, they did not report it.

At two A.M. in the morning, the earth turned from the sun's glare, a simulated TV version of space travel may achieve the appropriate illusions seldom present in a moon landing. I stood gazing at planet earth, floating in space. To grasp it, I must compare it. Is it a blurred cosmic eye, screened by cataracts? Is it a blue and white marble that I once referred to, accurately, as a snotty? But neither cosmic eyes nor marbles bring tremors to the mind's foundations. Off there we are, off there I am, even as I stand on the moon, gazing. My soul is moved in a way that my tongue is unable to record. The hashish eater and the mystic would make the same claim. The view into space is unending, and a measure of man's creative cunning, but the view *from* space compels the awe that will enlarge man's finite nature. It's a brief sensation. The shadow of a bird's flight, and it's gone.

The panels around the walls, taken from satellites in orbit, resembled abstract paintings. I would say it gave the painters some good ideas. The sea was usually jade green, or deep grotto blue. Deserts were sable tan or reddish-brown, the mountains like the crinkled backs of lizards. Clouds were wide paint smears, or brush splatters, or the pop of aircraft guns. Only the shadows indicated they were not flat on the planet's surface. That thin band of unearthly blue, like a gas flame, was the Valspar skin of air that bathes the globe. There were clouds over Texas and the Gulf, long streaming veils of cirrus, frayed off at the edges. A weather front could be seen to the west, near the Rocky Mountains, a dark crinkle of surface like crumbling blacktop. I could puzzle out the plains thanks to the Missouri, more brown than blue, edging Kansas and Nebraska, with a barely perceptible line showing the Platte River valley. One man-made thing seemed visible. The tiny pimple craters, if you knew where to look, might prove to be football stadiums, where on certain days a mystifying change in the crater's color might be noticed. Of Fork River there was nothing, nor of its mini-crater, nor of Harry Lorbeer's thriving space project, attracting four cars and as many as thirty hikers to share a new experience. The music filled the room like a vapor, in which we were all suspended. After the surfing crest of the opening section there was nowhere for Strauss to go but down. After their long walk some of the guests had dozed off. Harry showed about eight or ten views of the earth from space, climaxed with a full earth view from the moon. Then he switched off the projector but left on the music. His manner was that of a portly, preoccupied priest. The heat of the projector had warmed him up, and he walked through the rear door into the open. I followed him out. We stood together on a porch just high enough to see over the fenced yard, and feel the down-canyon breeze.

"I liked it," I said, "I liked it very much."

He bowed his head slightly, pleased but unsmiling.

"What you're doing here," I said, "is very original. I'd like more people to see it."

He pursed his lips, clasped his hands at the small of his back. In his cleric's gown his bald head and rather long wispy hair seemed part of his costume.

"It's not a matter of numbers, Mr. Kelcey."

"Not to you, but I know many would enjoy it They are eager to experience this sensation. I could give you the names of people at the National Science Foundation. Dr. Rainey, at the college, should see it."

"There is no time," Harry said flatly. "We go from day to day."

I had almost forgotten he had that obsession. How could a person of such imagination have such childish doubts about the future? What did he fear? The Fork River was just a few miles to the west of the geographic center of the United States, with no visible resources that would lead an enemy to bomb it. We were facing north, up the river ravine, to the mini-crater concealed from our view by the high fence around the play yard, or whatever it was. It had been raked smooth as sandpaper, strewn with a few dead leaves. I thought I would work up to the crater, by degrees.

"I like this," I said, gesturing over the fence, "whatever it is, it seems to promise something." He made no comment. "Is it for something?"

"For something? It's for *them*."

"Them who?" A mistake the moment I said it. Harry's solemn, widely spaced eyes looked over my face piecemeal, seeking a clue to my ignorance.

"Them, *them*!" he said, waving both hands at the sky. "It's for them, whoever they are."

"A place to land?" I said.

"A place to land." That pleased him. He felt somewhat reassured about me.

"You can't believe that," I said.

"What do you mean, I can't believe it? I *can* believe it. It's you that *can't* believe it."

Men of Harry Lorbeer's type are not humorists. I will go farther and say that a sense of humor shows a deficiency of faith in oneself, as well as others. If I were a true believer, I wouldn't smile. Through Harry Lorbeer I have come to question many things I took for granted. When you hear somebody say, "That's only human," be on your guard. If I had faith the size of a mustard seed I would arrange my affairs, close up the house, send Alice home to her mother, and stand here on the porch of Harry Lorbeer's chapel with my eyes on the sky. But I am deficient in faith. The glittering saucer-shaped object will prove to be on the ball of my eye.

"You're right, Harry," I said. "I don't believe it. I've got some kind of block when it comes to believing. I can accept anything after it happens, but less and less, so to speak, on credit. Why is that? I don't like what it implies."

"You better believe it," said Harry, "or it's not going to happen."

He did not say what, but it struck me as true. The fact that I'd better believe it. Why is it that people totally lacking in humor arouse in us feelings of compassion? *They* had all the fun. What was there to pity them for? I put my hand, briefly, on Harry's shoulder in puzzled, troubled good-fellowship. He did not seem to mind. I felt that what we both missed in life was a younger or older person to lean on. In the room at our back Strauss and Zarathustra were building to another climax. If anything was going to happen the time was ripe.

"They come in from the west," Harry said, "you know, with the airflow, with the planet's rotation." He put his finger out and made a stirring motion, glanced at me to see if I was with him.

I was, all the way. On the veined lids of my eyes I saw the swirling globe gather into its vortex assorted, nameless flying objects, some unidentified. "But not to take off," he continued, "takeoffs are counter clockwise."

"Of course," I said. We both saw them, through a giddy swirl of air, and soft humming top music, take off against the planet's rotation.

"It's *unconventional,* Kelcey, but it's not unusual." In his eyes I saw the expectancy of my father, holding the string on which the gyroscope twirled, like a dancer. "God dammit, boy," he said, "never mind *why,* the point is it works."

Alice and Dahlberg, Alice holding some tall weeds and seed pods for a dried arrangement, came down the path from the minicrater, but it did not seem to have impressed her. Quite the contrary. She looked as she did when coming into the house from her own garden, her arms full of flowers. I noticed again that Dahlberg—young as he was—seemed to find the manners of his elders congenial, his hands at the small of his back, the left wrist gripped firmly by the right hand. Did I detect in him the tendency to combine the mature and the youthful?

"There's Alice," I said, "she probably wants to get back. We've had a wonderful time. Can we come again?" Harry bowed slightly, a solemn guru. If I *was* a believer in the shots from space, better not to admit it, and keep him waiting. His belief would be larger. It would make my belief a childish thing.

"Harry," I said, "what if I come out on a weekday? I'd like to just sit here. We could skip the music. It might do something for my character." Such a remark was lost on Harry: or maybe it was *not* lost on him. I saw that he believed it. His head nodded.

"See Mr. Lindner," he said, "he will let you in."

I thanked him and went to look for Alice. The steps at the front were now in the shade, and Alice was seated on the low one, toying with her dried arrangements. Dahlberg leaned on the hitchbar. The music pouring out of the open doors made it hard to talk.

"Did you see the hole?" I asked. "Isn't that something?"

As I suspected, it did not have much impact on Alice. Both

Dahlberg's boots and her yellow slippers were coated with a film of dust. Alice's forehead showed the first touches of the prickly heat that enhances her complexion. The lobes of her ears were translucent.

"I think we better get back," I said, and she seemed willing. Dahlberg sauntered along with us, in his gangly way, to where the car was parked in the shade of the buildings. Another car was there, with an out-of-state license. If this kept up they would have a winner. How would they handle that?

"We'll be back," I said. With Alice there he didn't make his usual comment. Neither did I slip up and say, "See you tomorrow." He seemed even less inclined to talk than usual, and we drove off without the usual banter. A few new arrivals were straggling in from the south, some of them wading in the shallow water. Even the willows on the islands looked hot and dusty. "I'm glad we don't have to face that walk back," I said.

Alice seemed preoccupied. A woman seated, absently holding flowers, especially a dried arrangement, has something sadly wistful about her. The flowers suggest losses, illusions. There were many things I meant to tell her but I hesitated to intrude on her mood. She was in a "study," a word her mother often used. Out on the highway, I said, "A penny for your thoughts," usually good for a smile.

"When I asked him what he wanted to do, you know what he said?"

I did not.

"He said, *I want to restore awe.* Just like that. I just can't explain why it moved me. He has a deep religious streak in his nature."

"I know," I replied, "not everybody feels that life is a hoax." Again a mistake. I should have suppressed it, but she hardly seemed to have heard me.

"He said that without awe we diminish, we trivialize, everything we touch."

Something childlike in her acceptance was touching. I had the good sense to keep my mouth shut. I had meant to tell her about my talk with Harry, and his landing site for the UFOs.

"You'd *better* believe it," I was going to tell her, and laugh, but I knew she wouldn't believe it. She would merely think that I was silly enough to try to discredit Dahlberg. If there had been less rudeness in his nature I would have liked him better. Trivialize is one of my favorite verbs.

9

I AWOKE TO SEE THE LIGHT ON THE shrubs and trees near the deck. Alice had smoothed back the covers, but her side of the bed was cold. She likes to read cookbooks if she can't sleep, topping the night off with a pre-dawn gourmet breakfast. She'll get back to bed at about the time our neighbors are getting up. The Fitches are good neighbors, as they remind us at Christmas, with a UNICEF card signed by their five children, all but the last child, a slip-up, sensibly staggered at two-year intervals. The last child, Rodney, came six years after his sister, Charlotte. With the appearance of Rodney the first four children became aware of what they had in common. They were the in-group. Rodney was the out. I catch him spying on me through the slats of their porch, where he likes to sit with one of his pet chickens. The Fitches are aware of Rodney's problem, and he has things of his own, like chickens. The Fitch dog, Elmo, belongs to them all, but he spends most of his time in the station wagon, doing chores and errands with Mrs. Fitch. Mr. Fitch is a GO BIG RED man who likes to power-mow his lawn early Sunday morning and play with a snow scooter in the winter. Since the third Fitch child, Clarence, they leave the house for school in the morning passing just below our bedroom window. Mrs. Fitch comes to the door to see them off. "Bye now," she says. "Bye now," they reply. "Bye now," she repeats. The older children now take off on bikes, but Rodney maintains this tradition. I've noticed that Alice hasn't managed to feel for him as she should.

If I wake up at night I have trouble accepting the world. Darkness conceals it, as it once concealed the face of the deep. What I know to be real seems so unreal I put my hands to my face, covering my eyes. A strange gesture. I do it to see more, as well as less. What I seem to see best is mirrored on the balls of my eyes. In the last few weeks, few nights, it's been the earth in space. There it floats, vapors swirl about it, or I see it like a skull on the moon's horizon. They tell me that the wall of China is the only man-made thing that is visible. Those chaps looking at it from Mars would think it a canal. Knowing what it is, we grasp what we dimly see. If I then zoom in on points of interest to me, the patchy continent of Europe, or parts of North America, I experience a pleasurable quandary. I see *where* it is—France, the oceans, and the plains—but I do not see *when* it is. That's my own talent, or my own weakness. In my boyhood my father took me to the Rockies, where he had a cabin in Estes Park. Of all that I recall little or nothing. My memory is blocked by a single vibrant image, of the great plains spreading eastward from the mountains. I saw it from a train window. In a way, it was my first view from space. The plains fell away eastward in a manner that left me dizzy, as if the earth were spinning. My father pointed out to me that the wisp of smoke, far away and below us, was a train approaching. I strained to see it, but I saw nothing moving. How could he speak of it as approaching? "It's not moving," I said, or something like that, and he explained that was due to the distance. If one was far enough from what was moving, the movement seemed to stop. Sometime later we passed this train thundering past us in the opposite direction. What could my father have meant? How did distance bring a rushing train to a stop?

If we are a few hundred miles in space, nothing visibly moves on the surface of the planet. Like shadows, we see that they move when we turn away. If one carried this impression to its conclusion, apparent movement would cease, apparent time would stop, at some point in space. From some point in space, that is, given the view, I might zoom in and see a huge leaf-eating monster, foraging in the swampy ravine of the Fork River. From another point I would zoom in and find it all covered with ice. In the full light of day, of course, I doubt that, I make a clear distinction between fact and fiction, but in the full bloom of night I zoom down to watch the Druids dragging their slabs of rock to

Stonehenge. They wear pelts, but otherwise they look like a typical crowd at a football rally. Dahlberg is there. Harry Lorbeer is there. And I am there at the fringe of the circle, gawking. Alice cowers with other womenfolk around the fire. If we get over this idea of looking backwards, we will note fewer backward characteristics. These people were shorter, but otherwise the same as those assembled at Fork River on Sunday. They loved mystery. They looked with wonder at the sky. Among them was a man, a true believer, whose mind buzzed with nameless unidentified flying objects, requiring only the right incantation to bring down what was up, and lift up what was down. He wore a blackish pelt, a solemn air, and he was free of the frailty of humor.

I suppose it's the bleakness of this scene I like, perpetually bathed in a lunar twilight. I know the sun shines on Stonehenge, but not in my mind. Far off the sun either sets or it rises, and they are of two minds about it. What a sensation! Hooded with night, on whose authority could they assume the sun would rise? That's what moves me. Waiting for dawn after such doubt. It's this surging, miraculous dawn that I hear in Strauss's music, and the terror and mystery of it that I saw in the cowering primates. Somewhere on the planet, according to my theory, they are huddled in a cave's mouth as dawn approaches. Light is a physical presence that overpowers darkness. The terror they feel makes them a single creature. They cling to each other as to their mother. If I zoom in on them, however, my compassion gives way to pity. The poor dumb brutes! Thank God they do not know what lies ahead. This pity, in turn, is diminished by the knowledge of my own ignorance. I know as little of what lies ahead as the apes. I turn away from this scene to another where a fire burns at a cave's entrance. How this fire attracts me, clearing a small space in the dark! I feel its warmth, by the flicker of its flames I see the figures huddled about it. They are past merely cowering. The terror they feel lifts the hair on their limbs, as it widens their eyes. I recognize Harry Lorbeer, wearing a deerskin and a fur cap that makes him look very Russian, with his widely spaced eyes. He is not so frightened as puzzled at what he sees before him. He has a stick with a rattle on its tip that he rattles. More practical, the woman seated on his left throws wood on the fire. The flames light up the cave interior and on the wall at the back, along with his shadow, I see the gangly gawky figure of Dahlberg, daubing at the wall with a rounded stick. He is tracing the outline of a creature, one of many that charge across the wall's face. I see they are bisons. The flickering of the light enhances the impression of their movement. Suddenly the figure turns, feeling my gaze, and gives me a wild, hostile stare. His hair stands up around his head. The fire burns on his eyes. This fellow is possessed. He holds his paint-daubed stick like a club. At his side, crouching, in a fawn-colored pelt that goes very well with her eyes and complexion, I recognize Alice. She is stirring up a mixture of fresh colors. She prefers this more creative-type work to cutting up the fresh kill, or tending the fire. Glancing up, as if she heard me speak, I see that she feels a certain pity for me, a man too old to hunt.

In spite of the fur pelts they wear, and the dark, smoke-filled cave, reeking of the odors of burned flesh and dung heaps, I recognize these people as my friends playing their roles. There is a child howling somewhere in the exact tones of Rodney Fitch. There has to be a dog, but he is probably back in the shadows, asleep. As strange and as familiar as I find this scene, what I like is the sense of something dawning. They have the faith, and you'd better believe it! It will of course take some doing, but they are working at it. That woman stirring the pot has things on her mind. Sunset is surely a worrisome time for people who have no reason to believe there will always be a sunrise—and that's where belief came in. They needed that assurance, and they got it. Here's the way it all works, one of them said, and that was how it was.

Now if we zoom in on a point we refer to as later, just west of the Missouri River, some time following the Ice Age, we will find Harry Lorbeer a keeper of the faith in his off hours as a handyman and plumber. He's got a flock, of sorts, he's got a high priest, and he's got a dawn-plan for the future, the eternal reenactment of flying objects, unidentified. Lying there in the dark, I'm obliged to tell you, my heart belongs to Harry. It's a game of dawnings. We're all Stonehenge hunters at heart. To feel we are

90

in on the dawn of something is a pitiful, shameful, humiliating illusion, which you can see in the eyes of most of the respectable people you know. The things that they believe! My God, it would break the heart. But what we see in the eyes of the nonbelievers is even more disconcerting. It has been described. It is what we call the status quo. Thinking of it I felt a surge of warm fellow feeling for Dahlberg. He was no fool. He couldn't look me in the eye and tell me that he was a licensed flying saucer pilot. For that he needed Alice's eyes. I thought about him with sympathy, in this context, and regretted that I had been so peevish. I got up to see what time it was, and perhaps say something reassuring to Alice. They were young. What could they do with their feelings but have them?

By the clock in the hall it was five past four, not so late as I had thought. Alice was seated with her feet curled up beneath her, on the couch, but she was not reading. She had a pad in her lap, but the reading lamp was turned to shine through the window on the deck and the bushes. I could see she was doodling with a red felt-tip pen. Alice's doodles are small button-size creatures with shell-like whorls that go round and round. They looked to me like mini-traps. She was so preoccupied I couldn't tell if I was being ignored, or she hadn't heard me. "The Birkins leave a light on in their kitchen," I said, "have you noticed that?"

In her minor depressions Alice will doodle to avoid a tantrum or my conversation. I could see that she was doodling with the felt-tip pen she had given me for Christmas. "Why are things as they are?" she said.

You know, that surprised me. Simple-minded questions are often unnerving. For too many years I had seldom thought of H. Taubler. Now I thought of him. I said, "Are *what?*" Then I said, "We're all Chicken Littles. We can't kick the habit. Suppose you got up in the morning and found the furniture attached to the ceiling?"

"What a ridiculous idea."

"It has its appeal," I said, "it breaks the habit. By now I would say Taubler would have tried it. He was wild. He stood things on their heads. He painted himself into, then out of Paris. You keep at something like that long enough and one day things are no longer what they were."

"Who was Taubler?"

I shrugged. "I don't think he knew. He was still working at it." I could see that she was thinking of Dahlberg. "One thing I can tell you, Alice," I said, "don't look at anything too closely." She looked at me very closely. "Take the UFOs. You know when the jig is up? The jig is up as soon as one is identified."

I could see that didn't help much. I stooped to scratch at a spot on the rug. Was it fresh paint?

Foolishly I asked her, "What have you been reading?"

"Intellectuals are like a can of worms without dirt," she replied.

If there is something to be said for the young, is it picturesque speech? I used to fork up worms and store them in fruit jars, just for the hell of it. If I went fishing I put them in a can I carried by the lid. Not knowing the head of the worm from the tail I found it hard to slip them onto the hook.

I walked into the kitchen and switched off the night light, opening the drapes. The dawn was colorless as water. I felt the chill of those primates eternally huddled at the cave's mouth. Above the trees the sky was streaked with traveling light. All I need to see is something like that to know that dawn's chariot is approaching, hitched up to white horses with flowing manes. Growing up and growing old have not diminished that impression. The same flood of light washed me into space where I weightlessly tumbled in orbit. I saw the surface of the earth curve out of darkness into daylight, and then out of daylight into darkness. At the point where the light and the dark commingled, over Fork River, Kansas, I saw myself. The immense pathos of my situation was part of the cosmic perspective, as if I shared with the cosmos the vast indifference of the prime mover. In this way, momentarily, I had learned to live with things as they are.

"I'm going to scramble us some eggs," I said, and stood for a moment in the draft from the refrigerator, the chill, impersonal winds of space blowing into my face.

92

10

IN THE LAST FEW WEEKS, PASSING THE
new shopping plaza, I speculate on how it must look from space.
More than five hundred acres of blacktop parking. In the early
morning hardly a car in sight, just the blackboard surface with
the cross-hatched white lines in a bold hound's-tooth pattern.
As the day progresses the cross-hatching disappears and you
would see gleaming, metallic, checkered colors, with dazzling
jewel-like reflections. What would an orbiting spaceman make
out of it? A spacewoman might see a garden, blossoming in the
sunlight. A spacespy would see a changing, coded message. Alice
would see that she needed new glasses.

Directly across from the plaza is Burke's Salvage Emporium,
an eyesore collection of war surplus quonset huts. In with the
battered pickups and shiny hotrods I saw the VW van with the
metal ladders on the top. I didn't think it would be Harry's van,
but it was, both sides daubed with faded green and yellow flowers.
Had Dahlberg run out of paint? It seemed early in the day for
him to have stopped. Along with paint, Burke's sold at a discount everything any of us will need when it's too late. Flying
suits, sleeping bags, rubber blankets, inflatable rafts, rope ham-
mocks, plastic canoes, wind gauges, path finders, height
estimators, fallout helmets and goggles, shovels, guns and am-
munition, pocket warmers, food cookers, tents, balloons, pith
helmets, hunting knives, canned water, dehydrated food, snake
bite and survival kits, vitamins and water purifiers. I browse in
Burke's while Alice does the shopping. I could see how it might
appeal to Dahlberg. A few years back I bought a war surplus
field scope, but without the directions as to how to use it, or what
it was for. I thought it might be a good time to ask Dahlberg
about it.

I parked in the gravel at the back and went in under a ceiling of inflated rubber rafts, between racks of second-hand flyers' uniforms. It was easy to pick out the flyers that were not so lucky. Why did the uniforms look so familiar? It was the outfit Dahlberg wore to paint in. I saw him soon enough, his copper hair glistening under one of the domed ceiling skylights. He had one eye closed; through the other he squinted through the eyepiece of an instrument used by navigators to determine their position at sea. He looked great. One of those dauntless Swedes who are born and bred to explore something. The instrument he was sighting through, or trying to, was an astrolabe. High racks of second-hand clothes, jackets, and flight suits concealed the shorter person who stood beside him. I assumed it was Harry. A gleaming orange helmet sat on his head. People of the sort of Dahlberg and Harry, as well as certain types of men in general, have a weakness for war salvage, especially if it's of a mechanical nature. I have a telescope myself, along with its tripod, which proves to be so heavy I seldom use it, but once I saw it I couldn't do without it. The whole setup came in a heavy wooden case that we now use for storage in the basement. It cost the government $700. It cost me $39.95, plug freightage. So I was not so surprised at what I saw as curious. What the hell did he expect to do with an astrolabe? Ignorance as to how to use one, or what it was for, had always prevented me taking the leap. We have plenty of stars in Nebraska, but no pressing need for instrument navigation.

Now and then the person concealed by the clothes racks thrust an arm into the air and wriggled it through the sleeve of a heavy quilted jacket, electric blue in color, puffed up with insulation like a flight suit. Farmers out here wear them in the winter. People are no longer so fussy about how they look. I could see the way Dahlberg wagged his head he needed time to make up his mind. He's like a kid. He shifts from foot to foot, rubs his hand over his head. Alice likes that. It's the child in him she likes. Astrolabes are not cheap, however, and a house painter has little need of one. He helped Harry out of the jacket he had managed to get on, then lifted off the helmet, fluffing out the hair that stood around his head like a halo. Understandably it reminded me of Alice. It was her hair. She tipped back her head to look up at Dahlberg, and the exertion had heightened her color. She looked excited and pleased. I would almost say she looked as thrilled as a kid. Of course she had a look through the astrolabe, where she saw nothing but her lashes. What was it for? He patiently explained, gazing into the darker regions of the ceiling. To be perfectly frank, the pair of them belonged on the recruiting posters you see in post office lobbies. They were in orbit. They were where everybody wanted to be. The astrolabe also came with a leather case that he explained was worth the price by itself. Did he want it? Then he must have it. Her head dropped from sight as she scrounged in her purse. Dahlberg held off for several agonizing moments, dipping and wagging his head as if in pain, then he gave in. He carried the helmet and the astrolabe toward the cashier at the front end. I couldn't see much of Alice, but I think she went along carrying the quilted jacket. What were they up to? I didn't have time to think. I went out through the rear door I had come in, and moved the car to the back of the parking lot. We drive a Plymouth. Alice often forgets what it looks like when she goes shopping. I have to taxi over and look for it in the parking lot. They got into Dahlberg's van, where they had a discussion (I could see his big head wagging), then they drove out on the highway and headed east. You won't believe this, but I just sat there in the car. I didn't think about much. It did cross my mind that some predicaments lie out of the range of urgent decisions, such as the purchase and use of an astrolabe. Was I in shock? I could watch the hands move on the clock in the Fairview Shopping Center. When it was time for me to go home, that was where I went. Dahlberg's van was parked in the street, and one of his shorter ladders leaned on the house wall, his paint-smeared shoes at its foot. When I pulled into the driveway I saw them on the deck. Alice waved.

"Dahlberg took me shopping!" she called. "Wasn't that nice?" She stood up to look at me through her new cheap war surplus bird glasses. Not liking what she saw, she tried looking at me through the wrong end. "You look far away!" she cried, waving.

Was I wrong in thinking that she liked that better? Slouched in one of the deck chairs Dahlberg held up his glass, rocking the ice cubes.

11

IT'S A NEW AGE. I'VE WRITTEN ABOUT IT
myself. People—women especially—are free to lead their own
lives, and I'm all for it. Alice has often heard me say so. As I
would not be a slave, I told her, neither would I be a master.
She appreciates the lessons of the past applied to the present. My
own opinion hasn't changed, but my interest has grown in the
life she might be leading. I said, "I'm going to run over and see
Miss Ingalls—"

"You can take that last book back," she replied. She was
out in the garden, with her new bird glasses. Dahlberg was up
on the ladder, working under the eaves. He is careless about the
paint that he drips on the driveway, but a non-drip painter is
a slow worker. The book to go back to the library was a collection of Arthur C. Clarke's science fiction. Just a few weeks back
Alice would have burned it rather than admit she had read it.
But as I keep telling myself, it's her own life. She had left a card
in the book as a marker, with a few words scribbled on it. "The
moon is our first bridgehead into space." If I had said that in
my sleep she would have been on the phone to her doctor. Who
is *our*? I leaned out of the car to call to her that I might not make
it back for lunch. I'm a talented fibber, but it's not easy for me
to tell a lie. I had said I was going to the library to see Miss Ingalls,
so that was where I went. I saw her, checking books at the desk,
dropped off the one I had brought, then left. It seemed reasonable
to me that Alice, to save Dahlberg the money, would give him
his lunch. If I did not come back for lunch, they would both take
off. I parked near the intersection of the east-west highway with
our own street, Sunset Terrace, in the shade of a billboard advertising the State Fair. I've always made it a point to take Alice
to the Fair. To smell real manure, hear chickens cackle, and put

your hand for a furtive, incredible moment on the moist snout of a calf, or the rump of a hog, is a very earthy experience. Alice had been a forest creature, not a farmer, but she liked to put in a day at the Fair. We had been so preoccupied with Harry and Dahlberg we had both forgotten about it. The billboard assured me that it still had three days to go. The thing for me to do—I didn't have to think about it, it occurred to me as a package— was ask them both if they wouldn't like to take a little time off. That would surprise them. I could appreciate the effort it would cost Alice not to exchange glances with Dahlberg. In little surprises I hoped to maintain the initiative.

As peculiar as I personally found Dahlberg, with his facial tics and mannerisms, it was possible for me to understand that a girl like Alice might be drawn to him. I don't confuse that with the usual attractions. *Drawn* is what water does to divining rods. Grown-up boys will sometimes have a greater *draw* than male grown-ups. At ten minutes to one, sooner than I expected, I saw the van approaching me from the south, the driver wearing a sunflower yellow crash helmet. Glare off the windshield concealed his companion. Trailing them with several cars between us, I realized how many movies and TV thrillers relied on vans to get the dirty work done. You can't see into a van. Nothing looks so ordinary from the outside. Just as an example, they could have in it, for a quick getaway, one of those two-seater motorbikes. In the big vans they store cars. I've seen it in the movies. While they are cruising along, with an escort of cops, they paint the whole shebang and change the motor serial number. With a little imagination there are a lot of uses for a van.

To avoid the downtown traffic they turned north, then west again near the Aggie campus. Between the scattered houses and leafless trees I could see the bright arc of a ferris wheel, with its rocking gondolas. We have a great State Fair, acres and acres of cows, pigs, chickens, and horses. Alice is scared of hogs, but she likes them. Nothing else so big is so graceful on such small pins. Has your attention ever been called to the eyes of a sow? Her lashes are long. She favors the languorous, lidded gaze. A sow with a litter of piglets at her teats, snorting little snorts of pleasure, may well change your mind about pork chops. I owe all of that to Alice, but last year, unfortunately, she found that some creatures who won the prizes were marched or dragged off to the slaughter. Had it been Dahlberg's idea to take her to the Fair? That's where we were headed, and it was too late for me to turn back. Up ahead of me thousands of cars were parked in fields of corn stubble, looking like they lacked wheels. I lost track of the van while I was parking, then I spotted the pair of them, their helmets gleaming, walking along hand-in-hand like a pair of knighted hippies. Until that moment I had failed to grasp their strategy. Who would ever recognize them in such outfits? Her helmet was white, with a sea-green visor, the electric blue quilted jacket puffed her out like a kewpie. Naturally they were headed for the livestock exhibits, but it seemed to me that Dahlberg kept her moving. Alice liked to put her hand on the moist snout of a calf, and smell her milky breath. In a pen freshly spread with straw I saw this gangly farm kid, lean as a puppet, sprawled as if he had been tossed there in his sleep. Seated on a bale of hay, his straw hat tipped back, a cowhand with short, rope-polished fingers peeled off a cigarette paper, shaped it to a trough, then tapped the tobacco from a pouch of Bull Durham. A farmboy watched him, his jaw slack, a green wad of blowgum locking his teeth. Neither gave me a glance. A cream-colored calf gazed in my direction but gave no indication that he saw me, an object in space he felt no need to identify.

Had I lost them? The racket of the music and hawkers was deafening, but on a weekday afternoon there were few people. Most of the rides sat idle. One in operation was like a huge auger stretched out on its side, boring a hole in space. The cars followed the circling curve of the bit, doing the loop-the-loop. A ride like that scares me to death. Adjoining the loop-the-loop, and not a ride at all, as far as I could determine, two steel columns supported an object resembling a motorcycle sidecar. From another angle it might be taken as a car hoist, or a cement mixer. The sidecar had a snapdown lid with a strip of green plastic as a cover. In a prison camp or a war movie it might be taken as a device of torture. A steep flight of stairs connected the car with the ground. At the foot of the stairs, on a low platform, a chap wearing a cap with a duckbill visor sat smoking a cigar and reading a newspaper. The operator—if that was what he was—was like a businessman on a coffee break. People in his line of work interested me. What is it like, day after day, to sell a life of thrills and gaiety? He looked like a car mechanic. Did he swap joy rides with his colleagues? Somewhere—my guess would be Oklahoma or Texas—he had a wife at home watching TV and several hoodlum-type kids resisting the powers of education. Chances are they had never found the time, nor the money, to enjoy the thrills sold by daddy. When they were asked what their daddy did, what did they say? On the platform at his side was a megaphone wired to an amplifier. Shouting was pointless. He had to broadcast to be heard. How people in his line of work must hate the slow-witted, tight-fisted yokel who would not part with his money just to have a good time. The ride was short and sweet, but life was long. Mechanical constructions designed for pleasure have a special melancholy when they are idle. Especially merry-go-rounds. It occurred to me that these new monstrous rides were like objects fallen from space and wrecked. I wondered if Harry had thought of that. Or was Dahlberg the one who liked to speculate? The loop-the-looping cars, called the SCREW-DRIVER, had pulled in and stopped but the two passengers just sat there. They wore helmets, and looked like Mamma and Papa bugs. Were they stunned, or merely dazed? The operator had to lean over and shout at Dahlberg. That seemed to revive him, he squirmed in the seat, then wriggled to where he could squeeze a hand into his pocket. What did he want? He wanted the fare for another ride. It was not a long one, maybe seven or eight loops, but I could see that two rides were enough. They needed a little help getting out of the cab, and recovering what we call our balance. I had observed this in returning astronauts. They left the SCREWDRIVER, stood for a moment feeling the good solid earth beneath them, then proceeded directly to the object I have described. The operator explained that only one person could ride at a time. There was a brief discussion between Alice and Dahlberg, with Dahlberg conceding that ladies went first. She went up the ladder to the cockpit, and the operator went up to buckle her in, check her out. Dahlberg stepped back from the apparatus to watch her take off. What it proved to be was one of these flight simulators that puts you through the full works of flying: over and over, tilts and dips, with a few of the drops you get in elevators. Not long. Although it seemed long to me, the lady being my wife. He let her sit there for a moment to recover or scream, then he went up and opened the hatch. They had a brief discussion, but she seemed to be all right. The operator helped her down, then he was thoughtful enough to let her sit in his chair while Dahlberg went into orbit. My visceral feelings were that the shorter person had the better chance. A tall gangly test tube, like Dahlberg, had too great a gap between his head and his feet. What if the fluids of the inner ear slipped out of place? Alice had opened her visor to get a breath of fresh air, but I could not see her face. While Dahlberg was dipping and tilting in orbit I took off.

I hurried back through the stock barns (the boy in the hog pen still drugged with sleep, sprawled on the straw) then across the fields to my car, the windshield waxed by a Halloween prankster. I drove to a diner near the airport where I sipped coffee and watched the planes glide in and roar out. It's not what you know that proves to be the problem, but what you admit. A farmboy could have seen what I had seen and drawn the sensible, obvious conclusion. Some people are determined to get into orbit. Was it so unusual that one of them was my wife?

On my way home I stopped at the market for a six-pack of High Life, Dahlberg's beer, and a bottle of Wolfschmidt's vodka. Alice liked gin for standing-up drinking, vodka for sitting down.

"You just missed him," Alice said, putting ice in the glasses. "He put in a long day—how was yours?"

How slender she looked! I would say the flight training had done wonders for her circulation. A glow to her cheeks, but a palpable tremor to her drinking hand.

"There's a fair on," I said, "would you like to go?"

She pretended not to hear me.

"You're going to miss him," I said, "aren't you?"

"You're shouting," she replied, "why are you shouting?"

I suppose I was compensating, as we say, trying to get through. Weightless in space, do we have communication problems?

"Cheers!" I said, hoisting my glass, and glanced up to see a reflection in the deck window that surprised me. It proved to be myself.

12

WHEN I CAME OUT OF MY STUDY THE
door to the bathroom stood ajar, the mirror reflecting a corner
of the living room and the deck. They were out on the deck, standing at the rail. Dahlberg had placed both hands on Alice's
shoulders and held her off at arm's length, like a framed painting. There was something so solemn, so ceremonial, about it,
I was neither startled nor offended. Her face tilted upward, as
I had often seen it, radiant with expectations. If one view of
Dahlberg is better than another, it's the one from below. If he
had sprinkled her with water it would not have surprised me.
She wore a caftan that hung to her ankles, and looked like a child
home from communion. Rather than spy on such a moment I
backed off.

A moment later I heard them talking in their usual carefree manner and joined them. Slouched in one of the deck
chairs, Dahlberg way saying that the way to change the world
was to change one's perspective. No one should see it up close:
even the man who made it. It should look like what it was,
not what it had become. One should see it in space, round and
luminous as a lantern, with swirling clouds that both concealed
and revealed it. Inside its film of air it would float like a cosmic
eye. When the time came to launch the first landing party, they
should collect only soil, beer, and peanut butter. No people. People were the contaminators. There should be a new way of
breeding people, like in eggs. He personally felt that the egg was
the perfect solution since nobody could determine which came
first.

It was quite a little sermon he delivered, and not the first
time Alice had heard it. She amused herself fishing for a cube
of ice. In a casual, passing-the-time sort of manner I asked him

where he planned to go on his trip. I may have said *drip,* an understandable slip. We once had a guest drop into one of our sling chairs the moment after the neighbor's cat had left a puddle. He wore the same expression as Dahlberg. Just a few expressions have to serve for countless circumstances. Alice sat with a cube of ice clamped in her mouth.

"I just happened to be passing Small World," I said. "You know, the agency. Saw you through the window."

Alice spit up her ice cube, said, "Oh, that was for me. He was asking for me."

"*You're* taking a trip?"

More toying with the ice cube. "I was thinking maybe *we* might, after New Year's. You're always complaining about the long winters."

"I complain," I said, "but I don't plan to move. It's cold here, but nobody's shooting at us. What place you have in mind?"

Dahlberg said, "The Bahamas, Guatemala, Honolulu—" He sounded like an airport plane caller.

"All he was doing was *asking,*" said Alice. "If there was something special we were going to surprise you."

"Oh, boy!" I chortled. I simply couldn't help it. A single glance passed between us like a pool shot. How avoid implicating remarks? "Alice knows I don't fly," I said, making it worse, and leaned forward to stuff my mouth with Fritos. I felt terrible. The salt on the Fritos burned my lips. "God knows, Alice—" I said, "you're free to take a trip anywhere you'd like to. Guatemala, Honolulu, the moon, or wherever—" There's no stopping something like that once you start it. I suddenly popped up, said "I feel like some music. Any requests?" There were no requests. I hustled inside, dusting the salt from my hands, and made a to-do of looking through the record albums. They sat like the lovers in a Bergman movie. I picked Benny Goodman's *Sing, Sing, Sing,* turned up the volume on Krupa's drumming. Alice went to the bathroom for a few minutes, leaving Dahlberg on the deck, rocking his beer can. People are crazy. If we admit to that, we can do pretty well. Alice and I danced a bit to the "5 o'Clock Stomp," then we both stepped

104

out on the deck to cool off. She looked radiant. How I look is well known.

"You were great," said Dahlberg. I think he meant it.

"We used to cut a bit of rug in the old days," I said.

"Oh they were not so old," said Alice.

"You know what," I said, "I'm going to take the Fifth Amendment." That broke it up. We all shared a common fit of laughter, and when it passed the music had stopped. I went to the kitchen for some more cold beer. When I came back Alice was studying Dahlberg through the wrong end of her new bird glasses. Was that the new perspective that he had recommended? she asked. It made him look far away. It pleased me to detect in Dahlberg's quick glance that the feminine mystique was a shared problem. Woman would be the same, no matter from where we saw her. In spite of Dahlberg's high-pitched, almost squeaky, voice, he had an appealing, mocking way of humoring himself. Now and then he wagged his head as if to free it from cobwebs. In a small, private fit of wheezing laughter he sucked air through his teeth, making a noise like a siphon. In the dappled shade of our open deck he looked mature and melancholy, having lost a little weight. I felt a twinge of concern about his health. Was he getting enough sleep? I don't think he would have minded if I had asked him, directly, if he anticipated certain navigation problems, but in the perspective I had at the moment it seemed a matter of little interest. We were all navigators. We did what we could with whatever we had.

Without warning Alice said, "Read him your poem, read him your poem!" A sure sign of her excitement was the way she failed to show it. Dahlberg looked stunned. God knows, I knew how he felt. This was something strictly between them. Why in heaven's name did she want me to hear it?

"If you won't, I *will*," she said, pushing up out of her chair, and stomped off the deck. Dahlberg sat with his head tilted back, as if gazing, dumbstruck, into space. His jaw was slack. He couldn't seem to believe what it was he saw. Alice was back in an instant with a piece of cream-colored deckle-edged paper. It appeared to be written in some sort of script, with flourishes. "You won't read it?" she asked.

He was speechless.

"Then I will," she said, and read it. The one clear impression I had was that it was not for the first time.

Some creatures are fierce, others are gentle, still others have remarkably peculiar customs, including birds of the air, fish of the sea, and animals that read newspapers.

When I read that Africa is rich in diamonds, Arabia is rich in oil, the seas are rich in minerals and America is rich in gold, I know that people are crazy.

On a recent night, sleeping fitfully, I heard the earth crack along one of its seams like an apple . . . Soon I will hear it again. The sound goes on and on, like the ringing of an axe in the forest.

Creatures are various, some of them foolish, and the earth floats like a skull above the moon's horizon, almost within our reach.

"Hey, that's good," I said. "That's really good."

"I forgot to read the title," said Alice. "It's *Coda*."

"It sounds great," I went on, "but I suspect it *reads* better. You've got a lot of meat in it. I'd like to read it."

"Somebody's *got* to publish it," said Alice. She gave me the first direct look I had had in weeks. An appealing look. I mean a look full of appeal.

"Of course," I said. "If you'd like me to I can mention it to this fellow at *Harper's*. We've had some correspondence. He likes me to keep him in mind."

One of the big jays that daily raids our feedbox swooped in like a falcon, scattering birdseed. Dahlberg leaped up to flail his arms in a surprisingly aggressive manner. Was this the man of peace, including birds of the air, or a mere reader of newspapers? The people we are comfortable with are fictions: if the real person speaks up we're shocked.

"I don't know about you two," Alice said, "but I feel like a *real* drink," and left us to make one.

106

Leaning on the deck rail, gazing across the plains to the south, Dahlberg said, "You know, Kelcey, I'm going to miss it."

I'm not going to say more than tell you quite simply what it was he said.

13

WE HAD DAHLBERG FOR TWO DAYS,
working on the trim, one day with his ladder right here at my
window, his spattered desert boots on my eye level. I caught
him giving me a glance through the trailing vines of ivy. Was
he on the ESP channel to Alice? At her invitation he had his lunch
with us on the deck. For my benefit, I think, he expressed the
opinion that the planet was in for a new weather cycle. Nothing
spectacular. Just drought and famine. The rising of the seas would
come later. London, New York, Los Angeles, Tokyo, and Venice
would experience a cleansing burial. How would those bells sound
under water? He yawns after eating, tapping on his tummy like
a gourd. He has a boyish uncouthness of manner, slouching down
to sit on his spine, knees forward and spread, knobby head lolling, an elegant, somewhat simian manner of lifting his beer can
by the top brim, sloshing the contents. Alice wears her dark
glasses, avoiding the burn of his glance. It might have been a good
time to bring up *A Hole in Space* but I had no idea what he might
say. Almost anything he said, it seemed to me, would be in
character.

Wednesday morning, just before nine, Dahlberg called. That
caught me so unprepared I was almost eagerly friendly toward
him. Harry had to drive to Plattsville, he said, which was more
than forty miles due east, and made it impossible for Dahlberg
to be traveling in the opposite direction. He was sorry. In my
confusion I think I said we would miss him. When he hung up
I found I rather regretted his departure from custom. Harry would
not have done it. He would not have departed from principle.
In Harry's view everything depended on the non-dependable state
of affairs. I feared that it meant Dahlberg was feeling the pull
of new contradictory attachments.

"I never expected him to call," I said to Alice.

She replied, "He's bringing me some real cider."

People have such exchanges all the time. We both appeared to be pleased. I waited till lunch to tell Alice I had some work at the library, so it was after two o'clock before I left the highway for Fork River. It was not a good day. A high, gauzy cirrus diffused the light and increased the glare. We have days when no apparent wind to speak of will lean on the car. You get little response when you depress the gas pedal, as if you were climbing a grade. Some weeks back I read in the paper of these cars that proved to be *coasting* uphill. Somewhere in the Near East, I think. They were descending a grade, but when they let the cars coast they came to a stop, and then coasted upgrade. We all know the answer. An optical illusion. It looked upgrade because of the slopes and angles. It's amazing how irrational people are if you say, "Oh, that's an optical illusion." They feel better right away, although what you have told them is that they can't trust their eyes. When I have a similar disquieting experience I cast around for some rule of thumb to reassure me. The experience is unnerving, but the *rule* is reassuring. Things do not roll uphill. Any fool knows that. So when you see a car coasting uphill you're not at all disturbed, since you know it's downhill. Going up the slight incline toward Fork River I could see by the ditch weeds I had a strong tailwind, but the motor had a carbon ping, and was sluggish. Was there a problem? I reassured myself I had a tank of bad gas.

On the rim of the ravine, where the road suddenly dropped, did I imagine I heard a windborne surge of music, like that of a drifting radio signal? It blew away as the road lowered, as if it was part of an upper layer of air. It seemed to me there were fewer leaves on the cottonwoods but otherwise it looked the same as when I had last seen it. The willows looked less green in the diffuse light, and the shadows hardly cool enough to seek out.

I parked near the schoolhouse, the car crackling as it cooled. The customary pigeons were not clustered around the bell tower, or pacing up and down the ridge of the roof. There were no cawing crows or barking dogs. A village without people has a troubling stillness. Where was Mr. Lindner? I had assumed he had

110

spotted my arrival, and would come out of the woodwork to discuss the weather. In which house did he live? Did *they* live? As I came in I had passed, on my left, a post with what was left of a box-like sign, about chest high. Looking back I could see the word ROOMS on a cracked piece of painted glass. If a lantern was put in the box at night, the sign would light up. I had all but forgotten that pre-motel period when local people took in tourists. The house that went with this sign, with a covered porch at the front, was boarded up on the first floor but had two dormer windows above the porch. One window stood open. Spread out to dry on the shingled roof of the porch were several undershirts, pairs of socks, and two pairs of Levi's, still so wet they looked black. I left the car, letting the door hang open, and walked around to the rear of the schoolhouse. The back door was ajar, propped open with a brick. Mounted on the inside of the door pane, like an ice card, was a sign that read

To Whom It May Concern
WELCOME
Back before dark.

I assumed the door had been left ajar to let out the heat. The building had a roof of sheet metal and glass, and would soon heat up. I opened the door to see Dahlberg, at the room's center, seated in the prescribed lotus position, his hands placed forward on his crossed legs, the palms up. He wore nothing at all, that I could see, but a film of perspiration. He looked like a heathen idol. On seeing me he closed his eyes.

"I'm sorry," I mumbled, thumped the door backing out, and heard him cry, "Kelcey, come back here!" I was not sure that I cared to. "Come back here!" he yelled. I let a moment pass, then I stepped in. He had several beer cans on the floor at his side: he patted the spot on the floor where I should sit. "Sit down," he said. I sat down. "You're not intruding, Kelcey. This is *your* project as much as it is *my* project. You like a beer?" I did not want a beer. We sat facing, high in the north gable, the glass

111

panel showing the planet earth rising above the moon's horizon. Spellbinding! Prodigious! Stupefying! and ordinary. It would soon be on T-shirts with Brahms and Beethoven.

"Do you grasp it, Kelcey?" I liked the way he called me Kelcey. I felt it helped me to grasp it.

"It's the perspective," I said, prepared to go on. I knew quite a bit about perspective.

"No, no, no!" he groaned. That wasn't it at all. His head lolled forward on his chest as if suddenly heavy. It saddened me to have failed him. He had thought me smarter. Perhaps he had thought me smart enough to be included in. My heart pounded. I was ripe for the word, but it escaped me.

"Then what?" I asked, my mouth dry, but he had withdrawn into meditation. His eyes were closed. Here and there, like constellations, I detected buzzing clusters of insects. It's hard to get away from the world's fictions. Why couldn't I see what was there instead of what I'd read about? High in the gable wasps droned at the mindless business of creation.

"Kelcey—"

"Yes?"

"You remember what He said?"

"Harry?"

Once more I had failed him. But he was quicker to recover.

"He said, It is finished. And it *was* finished. In two thousand years this is the first new beginning. It is the *earth* that is resurrected." I admired the way he had put it all together, nodding my head. "Love, hate, grand illusions, small illusions, you name it—"

I said, "Name what?"

"It's all been tried. Nothing works. If this doesn't work we'll have to write it off."

"The planet?" I asked.

"The planet."

"I think it might work," I said, "if what it takes is awe. It's the most awesome thing I've ever set eyes on—and failed to grasp."

"Kelcey, I've seen it on restaurant menus. The world in space. An old planet of the apes."

"What about yourself? You're a pretty reluctant prophet."

I regretted having said that. He looked chagrined, shame-faced. He moved his hands from his lap and saw, just as I did, that he was naked. "Harry's the true believer," I said. "He's got what it takes. And one thing it takes is no sense of humor. You're a very funny man."

He glanced at me, appreciatively. I just wish that Alice could have seen him.

"He's the believer," I went on, "you're just his first disciple. You really make a first-rate space John the Baptist. I can go right along with you on that hole in space."

"You're kidding."

I shook my head. I was about to ask him if it *really* happened. What held me back? "It's sure beautiful from here," I gestured at the earth, floating in space, "but what do you propose to do when you get back?"

I could see that question alarmed him. Was I going too fast? "I've been giving some thought to it," I said, "and I wouldn't rule it out that I might be helpful. Besides the believers, you need the ones who just stay and wait."

My feeling was he was right on the edge of including me in. His head bowed, the vertebrae in his spine were prominent. Alice had remarked how scrubbed his scalp looked through the short pelt of hair. You get the same effect around the eyes of a short-haired cat. Dahlberg liked the heat, the oozing perspiration that relieved the soul's pollutions. I knew his manias. As a boy he had signed his name in blood.

"Look, Dahlberg, if anything should happen, somebody should be here to report on it. Who would know it? What will it be but another hole in the ground? I'm so close to the edge I no longer see the sunrise. It's the earth that turns. I see it curve out of the darkness into the sun's rays, like the globe on the Pathé news reels. You remember that? I've been a space bug ever since. That one whirled too fast for the better effects. Day and night are everlasting. It's the spinning globe that gives the wrong impression. Nor is it a mystery to me that we feel as we do at three o'clock in the morning. Look where we are! At the back rim of the night. What if the globe should stop spinning?

113

I've given it some thought. Can you imagine what would happen when the word got around? No more sunrises? No sunsets. Just the light burning like a crack in a curtain at the rim of the world. But that's science fiction. Have you been to the mountains? You know how small things look on the plain? If you're up high enough, trains stop crawling. Higher yet, jets stop moving. Now if you just carry that to its conclusion, at some point in space time has stopped. It's all in suspension. My game is to zoom in from space on the Mesozoic period. Late research points out that the dinosaur was not just a big slug, but had strong family feelings, with what you might call stereo vision. He had to have something. Look how long he lasted. Another period I like is the dawn of man. Was it me Tarzan, you Jane, or less basic? I suppose the novelty was lost on them. Have you followed the latest rumor that he was a friendly, bow-and-arrow-type hunter? She was a hefty homebody and bone reader. They had a good life— while it lasted. Imagine looking out from that smoke-filled cave over ice fields in the winter, in the summer wooly mammoths wallowing in the swampy hollows. The moon anything you wanted to make of it. The caves appeal to me more than the grassy plains. For one thing, no place to hide. Why do the primates have this up ahead vision, with nothing behind? After all, there's more to be seen looking backward. You give up? Well, I'll tell you. It's less what they see than what they imagine. One thing leads to another, then another, and they all lead to where we are. Who sees what is there? From here how empty it looks! A new beginning, right? Time for a landing party. If you had your pick, where would you choose? High in the Himalayas, or low in a primeval jungle? In the pure white Arctic, hunting for puppy seals, or right here in Fork River, no smog and no crowding. Good dentists, heart transplants, and air-cooled movies. Whatever you find on Mars you'll have to take it with you. In strictly practical terms this is the site for a landing. So why take off?"

I didn't want a casual, offhand answer. I could see he needed time to think it over. Who could explain to a creative landing party, zooming in on what appeared to be a crisp mini-crater, that the armored thugs, battling like gladiators, were schoolboys at play on Saturday afternoon? A peace-type game, played during periods of cold war. How explain it to a spaceperson? "Well, I hope you know what you're doing," I said, "you *are* going to need a good navigator."

I didn't wait for his reply. It seemed cool outside, thanks to the film of perspiration inside my clothes. More leaves had fallen on the surface of the playground, and I was tempted to sweep them off. It seemed obvious, as Harry had pointed out, that the landing approach would be from up the river, gliding in as I had seen it done in movies. On the top of the saucer a revolving blinker: the entrance through a trapdoor in the bottom. I found the space machinery convincing, but the prospect of the spacepersons disturbing. Why these comic-strip Martians, with their repulsive hooded heads, fishy eyes, and dangling antennae? Why not invisible, the ultimate triumph! Just the stir of air, the irresistible attraction. I could see myself tempted. "Yes," I would say, "it came in like a top, with a purring vowel sound and an odor like crushed blossoms. Indescribably alluring, but not at all corny. I felt drawn myself. After all, what was there to lose but my clichés?"

Someone had closed the door to my car. On the windshield I found a penciled note on the back of a discount coffee coupon.

> **Not responsible for cars parked**
> **near schoolhouse.**
> **E. B. Lindner**

Mr. Lindner was nowhere in sight. The clothes were still drying on the roof of the porch, and I noticed a small throng of birds, flocking. The winter in Fork River would be something to deal with. More of a sense of resignation, of abdication, but what a crystalline sky at the north chapel window, the earth swimming in the vibrant ether. Surely it would take less faith in the winter, but more body heat.

On the highway I was so absentminded I drove past my turn-off, into Millard. They had strung a banner across the street advertising the days of the covered wagon. The men were growing beards. There would be a big parade on Halloween. Suddenly I felt the discomfort of a wireless set jammed with interference. What did these antics have to do with the view from space? What had led me to confuse the history of the planet with the history of man? Compared with his fellow creatures he was frivolous and fragmentary. He lacked history. Nothing human was alien to him, but who could say what was human? Until he had more history he was the missing link himself. I sat at the counter in what had once been a pool hall, but was currently a restaurant, dunking a cinnamon roll into coffee under the observant eyes of the waitress. In her disapproving gaze I saw the look of the first visitor from space.

14

WIND WE HAVE ALL THE TIME. IT'S THE
absence of wind, or a slack in the wind we notice. One of my
vivid memories, as a boy, is that of a windless day. I remember
the puzzled, concerned glances people gave the sky. On the plains
the sky is where you look for what seems to be missing, or when
something goes wrong. I looked up at it too, and saw one sky
going by overhead like paper blowing, and through the gaps in
it I saw another sky, with a rippled surface, pink as if the sun
was rising or setting, and still above that, strips of cloud thin
as gauze blowing to pieces right before my eyes. The wind that
seemed to be missing, on earth, was up there in the heavens, blowing the sky around. I was old enough to grasp that this was highly
irregular. Later that evening we learned that three twisters had
struck in Heber County, the town of Alston all but wiped off
the map. That phrase strongly impressed me—a town wiped off
the map. It makes sense in this country to speak like that, since
the surface of the plain is map-like, the roads run straight east
and west, or north and south, with sharp right angles at the in-
tersections: from a few miles up it actually looks like a map, and
the wonder is not that something blows away, but that it stays
in place.

Last night, right out of the black, I woke up as if I'd heard
a clap of thunder. The silence of the windless night made my
ears ring. As if stirred by a bat's wing the curtain stirred at the
window: a creak went through the house as if a weight pressed
on it. Above the trees a diffuse phosphorescent glow made
everything flat, with one dimension. Flat, rippling cirrus clouds
drifted eastward. I had this wild fear that the air was departing.
I took a breath and held it, as if it might be my last. And right
at that instant a suck of air, as if in the wake of an invisible object,

clawed up fistfuls of leaves and dust as if a helicopter was landing. Above the clouds screening the stars I seemed to hear a cosmic
wind. Nights speak to us profoundly of what once happened,
of what might happen in the presence of darkness. I gripped the
sill but I felt no terror until I came back to bed and missed Alice.
I chilled all over, as if I had been dipped in a deep freeze. My
sensations were so primal I lacked a word for them. A plant might
feel as much, or as little, as I did. There was not a shred of consciousness in it. I was in the world like a stalk of celery. Alice
found me sitting up staring, as in a nightmare. She had been to
the refrigerator: her breath smelled of low-fat milk. She says that
I resisted her efforts to wake me although I was not asleep. I didn't
want to give up, I didn't want to come back, from where I had
been. In the morning I would say I had the damnedest dream—
and it would be lost. I would not recover the sensation that must
be common to everything but people. A purely sensuous being
in the world. I lay back on the pillow and had this dream—is
there a better word? In the yard below me two or three dozen
little girls, in their birthday suits, stood in a circle like kewpies,
while the sprinkler wet them. At its center stood Alice, wreathed
in veil-like clouds, poised like the Venus in Botticelli's *Primavera,*
her head tilted so that the sprinkler water pelted her face. The
children danced clockwise around her, shrilly piping some nursery
rhyme. I gathered it must be a celebration, since they all looked
so blithely happy. Water streamed down Alice's face, and clung
to her skin like drops on a window. The scene was moonlit, or
rather earth-lit, the glowing, cloud-wreathed planet filled the sky,
and was growing larger. Were we coming in for a landing? I
remarked the absence of polar caps. Had they melted? The great
globe of the earth was like a painted balloon. How beautiful it
was! Out of a vast jade green sea only one peak jutted. The
cleansing flood had come! I looked for Noah and his ark. I saw
it all as clearly as the details on the globe in the Pathé news reels.
We were coming in! As it all swept below me I realized there was
no place to land. It was all one sea, the peaks had vanished, I
saw fish leaping and birds flying, but in all of that vast sea no

sign of man. I cried out something because Alice woke me, and switched on her light to have a close look at me. Seeing her troubled, puzzled expression I said, "Don't be surprised if people act crazy," as sober as a judge. It seemed to calm me, and in a moment I was asleep. I next remember waking to see Dahlberg and Alice at the foot of my bed, whispering to each other. His hands were green with paint, as if he had walked in from the woods.

Alice said, "Are you awake?"

I said that I was. I could be wrong, but I felt that Dahlberg almost looked at me with concern. God knows he's gangly, he's awkward, he has lumps on his neck, but there's something undeniably appealing about him. Something vulnerable, something expectant.

"You've been talking in your sleep something awful," said Alice. "Who is Towper?"

"It might be Topler," said Dahlberg.

It pleased me to see them so anxious. With his green hands they made an interesting couple. "I know no Topler," I said, "but I once knew a Taubler."

"Who was he?"

"He was a genius," I replied. "He was crazy."

"You're running a fever," said Alice, and put her cool hand on my forehead, taking my pulse in a professional, nurse-like manner. "You've got to rest," she said, "you're overexcited."

I accepted that fact as obvious. Alice tilted the blinds to keep the light off my face, casting luminous reflections on the ceiling. Taubler would have loved it. He preferred the illusion to reality. On the wall of his studio he had painted French doors that opened out on a view of the Mediterranean. At night the sky sparkled with stars he put on with the paint they used on watch dials. The moon was there, a green-cheese color, and the upper half of the planet earth. If we studied it through his telescope it proved to be the upper half of a human skull. Art Tuchman thought he was a genius. It was all new to me. I didn't know what to think.

15

HAVE I SUPPRESSED IT? WAS TAUBLER
the space trip of my life? In the summer of 1939 I was a student
in England, soaking up culture. All the talk about war led me
to go to Paris for a two-week vacation while it was still there,
and inhabited by Frenchmen. I arrived about daylight, in the Gare
St. Lazare, and found it easier to walk than lose myself in the
Metro. I saw that the secret of Paris was that the people who
lived there lived everywhere: the air in the street smelled of all
the rooms, kitchens, and closets being aired at once. I had been
told about gay Paree: I didn't know what to make of its resigned
sadness. Some people brushed against me, some made way for
me, but none gave any sign of having seen me. I towered above
most of them. Little they seemed to care. A girl with teeth so
black I thought they must be missing turned to give me directions, but not look at me. I had never experienced such indifference. I was amazed that a great teeming city could be so profoundly melancholy. No one had troubled to tell me. I had made
this discovery all by myself.

Toward mid-morning I sat on a bench in the Luxembourg
gardens, composing a postcard to my mother. I had seen Paris.
I had not been too impressed by what I had seen. I found the
gravel paths, the old women, the shrill-voiced children, more
depressing than the small fry where I had come from. On the
bench across the path, an older man—not elderly, but with his
best years, as we say, behind him—sat slouched, his legs astrad-
dle, his arms stretched along the back of the bench as if crucified.
I thought him a handsome man, really, in a scholarly way, but
down on his luck. The bottoms of his pants were not merely
frayed, but so chewed at the back the cuff was missing. His right
foot, turned on its side, showed the hole in both the shoe and

121

the sock. His hands and the balding top of his head were tanned. This dozing old man symbolized for me what I had come to feel about Paris. A sadness bordering on dejection: a past with no prospect for the future, with another war rumbling on the horizon. I was touched and depressed by the impression that such a state of soul had become a way of life. I was about to leave when I noticed that he was not napping, but observing me through half-closed eyes. Was he thinking of asking me for money? Before he did I stood up to leave, but he signaled for me to remain seated. From his pocket he took a piece of white chalk and pretended to draw, on the air around me, the details of an invisible room. He put in the windows, the door, and hung pictures. On the bench at my side he added a figure. The large hat, with fruit or flowers, indicated that it must be a woman. Then he stooped and on the gravel path at my feet he signed the picture

H. TAUBLER

Unmistakable. Then he stepped back to look at what he had done. That habit of squinting through half-closed eyes seemed to be his custom. Did he like what he saw? He seemed to be of two minds. From the inside pocket of his coat, where it was fastened with a clip, he removed a sheet of paper, handed it to me. The page was ornamented with printer's devices, hands with pointing fingers, cat's eyes, capital letters, a clock without hands and the word OUI! OUI! OUI! in a row across the top and bottom. At the center of the page, in small type, I read

> Don't be surprised if people act crazy.
> Be surprised if they act human.

I looked up to see his hand extended toward me, palm up, so I gave him two French coins, and he thanked me. He was perfectly sober, he stood for some time with his fingers hooked in his vest pockets, then he strolled away on the frayed cuffs of his pants.

A day or two later, it might have been three, my time sense

being affected, I was going along the wall of a cemetery when I saw the name H. TAUBLER. Was he a man who wrote his name on walls? A large piece of this wall had been peeled of its plaster, exposing the red bricks beneath. Along with the plaster part of a poster advertising an apértif had disappeared. Was that his picture? He might think so, if he was crazy enough. Later that same day, on the Boulevard San Michel, I saw him scrounging in one of the big litter baskets for candy and cigarette wrappers. For the first time I noticed how, when he strolled along, he looked about the same from the front and the back. I didn't really know in which direction he was going until I moved in close.

I went to the Louvre, and on two occasions I went to a movie just to watch the newsreels, but most of the time I just wandered around, thinking I might stumble on Taubler. The light in Paris has a glow about it, as if full of blowing snow or sparkling dust. I found myself squinting most of the time, through half-closed eyes. I found the name H. TAUBLER on two of the pissoirs, signed to strips of torn posters, and early one evening, near the Gare Montparnasse, I was approached by a dirty book peddler. He had them under his arm. The one he showed me was a volume of Jules Verne, *Voyage to the Moon,* with tipped-in pornographic illustrations. The peddler was a hulking black-haired young man, wearing green-tinted motorcycle goggles. He looked more German than French. In French I said, "Not now. Perhaps another time," to indicate I was not the usual sort of tourist. It brought on a fit of wheezing laughter. He pushed up his glasses to wipe at his eyes. "Oh, Christ," he said in English, "that's a new one." He had a Brooklyn accent, a cheerful, blue-jowled smiling face. "You're American?" I asked him.

"Me?" he wheezed at me, "I'm Tuchman. Wait till he hears that one."

"He who?"

"You got to meet him. He won't believe it."

He took my arm and we walked up the street to the Metro stop on the Avenue du Maine. Three old men, seated on folding stools, were playing haunting, melancholy music. One of them was Taubler. He sat with a clarinet across his knees while the accordion player did an encore. When the music stopped I was introduced to him.

"What's your name?" Tuchman asked me. I told him. "Kelcey," he said, "this is Taubler. Taubler doesn't believe Americans are real. He thinks they're a hoax made up by the movies."

I could see that the idea pleased Taubler. He gripped the lapels of his coat in the manner of a public speaker, but he said nothing.

"Don't let me intrude," I said.

"He don't play," said Tuchman. "He's hard of hearing. But if he sits here with them people give them more money."

"Is he crazy?" I asked Tuchman.

Eight or ten people gathered around us to watch Tuchman laugh.

So this is what Paris is like, I said to myself. It was all new to me, and I liked having someone crazy to talk to. We stopped and had a *café noir* at a sidewalk café where Tuchman sold one of his books to a tourist. We all shook hands. At no time was I possessed by the feeling that I had come to Paris to be flabbergasted. It all seemed normal enough. It had simply never occurred to me that grown-up people, of their own free will, might actually choose to be peculiar, or that opinions might differ on what being peculiar was. Now that it had occurred to me it was not yet something I was prepared to admit.

That afternoon we went to see the newsreels together, where we saw the world preparing to go up in flames. Everybody was marching. We sat in the dark watching them march. Then we went to a Chinese restaurant on the Boule Mich which was up one flight, with tables at the windows. Right there below us an organ grinder was having an argument with his monkey. The monkey would throw his own hat on the ground, then stamp on it. Then they would change positions and each one would stamp on the other's hat. A large cluster of people formed a circle to watch them, blocking the walk. Taubler had the seat at the open window, framing the view. Using one of the bits of crayon he carried in his pocket—he needed different colors on different occasions—he printed H. TAUBLER on the sill of the window. It was new to me, but I did not let on that I found it unusual. When we got to the fortune cookies I had one that said I would make new friends and begin a new life.

In the days that followed I saw the name of Taubler all over Paris. Wall posters that were torn or defaced in some manner were his specialty. He did not modify or improve these exhibits: he appropriated them. He filled his pockets with select samples of litter he found in the gutters, or the trash bins. Anything that had served its own purpose was ready to serve his. He did not buy newspapers, but he would take the time to read everything posted at the news kiosks. He stood back, being farsighted, his hands firmly gripping the lapels of his jacket. I had the clear impression that an invisible person was holding him up. On the Friday of my last weekend I saw this blind man in front of the Gare Montparnasse with a telescope pointed at the clear blue sky. It was Taubler. He had put on a beret and a pair of blind man's black glasses. He looked scholarly. A sign fastened to the tripod said

---

EARTH VIEW
1 Franc

I dropped a coin into the cup that hung from Taubler's neck. In the eyepiece I saw my own lashes, but not much else. Then I made out the half shell of a walnut pasted to a piece of blue litmus paper. The seas were dry. It made a very convincing image of the shrinking globe. "How was it?" Taubler asked me.

"Shrinking!" I cried. I was beginning to get the hang of it. He folded up his telescope, took off his glasses, and we walked together up the Rue de la Gaieté. Along the way he bought a loaf of bread, a yard long, which he carried under his arm like an umbrella. We met Tuchman in the hall of the building we entered and walked up the stairs. I held the bread while Taubler went down the hall to use the water closet, then came back to unlock a door that was padlocked. It opened on an oblong room without windows, under a grime-dimmed skylight. On the back

125

wall I could see a huge Paris Metro map, showing all the stops. At each stop the heads and arms of dozens of people sprouted like flowers, with the faces of red-cheeked, happy children. Faces also stuck up through cracks in the map, but not so happy. They clenched their teeth, or appeared to be howling. Here and there an arm thrust up, or a hand stretched out to grip something, hanging on for dear life. Tuchman beckoned me to come closer. At the Metro stop on the Boulevard Montparnasse one of the heads sticking up was mine. He caught my likeness. I had a brush cut hairdo and fuzzy cheeks. Until I stood in the room I didn't see the French doors in the south wall. They were framed by bright lemon yellow drapes, the green shutters thrown open on a view of the sea. The drapes were real, but the wine dark sea was a wall painting, with Taubler's name on it. The color was so brilliant I squinted at it, half closing my eyes. Drawn up to face the view was a real canvas beach chair, the floor around it strewn with the hulls of painted peanuts. They were so real birds would have pecked them. To the left of the doors, flush to the wall, was a planter's seed box, the bottom covered with gravel. Out of this box grew a plant, or rather a beanstalk, the huge green leaves painted on the wall to where they grew through a hole in the ceiling. Two long strands of real rusted wire supported this plant against the wind, and held it upright. The light off the sea cast the pale leaf shadows along the wall. Turning back to the view I saw a lopsided moon low in the sky. Peering closer I recognized planet earth and noted its resemblance to a human skull. There were cracks in it, or rather fissures, and on the bone-dry surface he had painted jewel-like cemeteries, the stones shining like gems. America appeared to have sunken, like a dead sea. A tiny white polar cap sat at the pole site, like a bandage. I turned aside to look at Tuchman, seated on a stool that had a high chair back painted on the wall. He leaned against it. "He's got his own system, Kelcey, and you'd better believe it."

I could believe it. Hadn't he already painted me into it?

"You can either work on the Metro or you can paste candy wrappers into dirty novels. We've got a new system going, but it still takes work."

126

"What would you say's the idea?" I asked him.

"You've got to make your own world, then live in it," said Tuchman. He was one of those big shaggy-dog types of people with the touch of something sweet and hopeless about him. I felt drawn to him. He had a pelt of black hair on his chest that made it hard for him to button his collar, gray eyes, and a big, soft Jewish mug. With Tuchman in it, Taubler's crazy system might work.

A week or so later, I've no idea, since we were living in our own time zone, Hitler and his pack invaded Poland and I was on a boat headed for the States. I said I would write. Tuchman said he would write. Taubler, of course, said nothing. That was more than thirty years ago. All I've got to show for it is a copy of Zola's *Nana* illustrated with hand-torn candy wrappers, signed by H. Taubler. Wherever he is, I'm prepared to believe that his system works.

16

ALICE'S DR. FRIEDMAN WILL SAY MY
state of mind arises out of rather special circumstances. A fevered
mind: a pattern of leisure: nights of lying awake rather than sleeping, and so forth. If an explanation is what you want, it is what
you will get. On Monday I felt well enough to go with Alice over
to her clinic. Nothing specific. A routine blood test. The elderly
lady who took my blood seemed to see better if she removed her
glasses. You know the routine. You extend the bare arm, the
palm up, a remarkably vulnerable position. The rubber tourni-
quet is applied, the invisible vein is supposed to appear. Mine
did not. She probed about for it. If I were picked up on the street
I would be taken for a drug addict. She doubted aloud that I had
veins, and an intern was called into finish me off. He found my
blood pressure high, and suggested rest. Might this be described
as a special circumstance? On the way home we stopped for gas
at Spivak's station, which gives Alice Blue Stamps, and I sat in
the car while she did a little shopping. Spivak's boy, Ernie, had
raised the hood to check the water and the oil. Through the gap
between the hood and the cowl I could see his disembodied hands,
working, the soiled fingers and bruised knuckles caked with
grime, like belt pulleys, the nails blackened, the fingertips blunted,
the back side of one finger glistening with nose drool, like a snail's
track, the acid mantle of skin (I had been reading some offbeat
medical papers) chapped along the seams, filmed over with oil
impervious to water, groping with assurance for the dipstick, then,
as if blind, for the battery water, a new kind of creature born
out of the need millions of cars have to be serviced, a selective
speeded-up evolutionary process, but when I blinked my eyes
what I saw on the lids was beautiful beyond the telling of it, the
planet earth, veined like marble, its torments stilled, its seas like

glass, on which at that moment I sat in a trance observing myself observe. Is that so peculiar? Taubler would have signed it. Earth rising above the hood of a '72 Plymouth.

"You all right?" Alice asked me.

I could see that Alice thought I looked a little strange. On reflection, it is my opinion that I should have spoken up. I frequently detected in Alice's gaze a willingness to share what I was thinking—even more than what I was thinking—but we both had our vested interests. Mine you know. The interests that weighed on me were hers.

Dahlberg had finished painting the trim and we had our last lunch together out on the deck. There was nothing more to paint. The front door was a possibility but Alice could not make up her mind about the color. Dahlberg smelled of the turpentine he had used to clean his hands and his brushes. He had that slightly peevish, boyish look that I knew Alice found so attractive. Alice loves to fuss with olives, celery stalks, radishes, bowls of nuts, and a variety of cheese dips, but she does not like to cook or open cans. This being the last day I also felt that his hostility had diminished. He was almost relaxed. He sat without cracking his knuckles or twisting his neck. We sipped vodka martinis, in chilled glasses, and nibbled at olives, celery stalks, bowls of nuts, a variety of cheese dips and stone ground wheat crackers. Dahlberg was very observant, but I wondered if he had noticed that Alice likes to fuss with food, rather than cook it. It often takes years to observe the obvious. In my own case, how long had it been that I had failed to notice Dahlberg's quick, lidded glances. Was it my pallor? I felt his concern. Alice seemed distant. Since she knows I dislike an open show of feelings, that is her way of admitting that she has them. For the first time I felt that I was part of the solution, rather than the problem. Was it my health? I felt a little queasy, but well enough. Would it surprise them if I said that it did not strike me as peculiar that two men shared the same woman? There was much to be said for it. My reluctance to say it stemmed from the fact that I didn't feel it with sufficient assurance. People in a moral dilemma who have lost their morals might feel very much as I did. I saw the

130

dilemma clearly. I simply didn't feel the need to choose. If Alice or Dahlberg felt more strongly I would be the first to acknowledge their feelings. My queasy feeling stemmed from the fact that I often felt in abeyance. The man telling a story who interrupts it to say, "Where was I?"—that's very close to my problem. Somewhere between where was I, and where am I, is where I am. In a physical context I felt buoyant. Platforms that are built out over the water always give me a pleasurable apprehension. A loss of bearings. A giddy exhilaration. Some get that sensation with their second cocktail, but I could get it just by closing my eyes. In the blackness of space, under a lacquer of air, cloud-wreathed and condemned the planet floated, approaching the heart of the football season. Did Dahlberg grasp that? Was this the time to bring it up?

"We're going to pick up some plants at the nursery," said Alice. "The big ones in the cans. Dahlberg is going to help me."

The mention of the cans had reference to the time I cut my hand badly removing a plant. It required several stitches. That particular plant cost us about $90.00.

That was all right with me, and I sat on the deck enjoying the full bloom of my feelings. I wanted to keep the vibrations of that particular luncheon, and the concern for me that they were feeling. That I felt a shade of disquiet was part of it. In my opinion the truest measure we have of contentment is on a scale that registers discomfort, like these indoor-outdoor thermometers. On one you read how it is on the outside, the other on the in. I enjoyed the shifting pattern of leaf shadows on the lids of my eyes. I could hear the band playing at the neighborhood high school, the horns windblown in advance of the drums. What clever primate, pounding on a log, or blowing on his fingers, started what nothing would put an end to? Marching bands. Each member blowing his own horn, beating his own drum. In tune, in step, in a heaven of clatter. The pied piper a baton-twirling, high-stepping Venus. Everyone a performer! No one a copout! Or was I seeing things too clearly? Who can gaze without blinking at perfect human felicity? That is something you have to learn to live with in space, but I wondered about Alice. I meant to tell

Dahlberg. In some respects I felt he was inexperienced with women. If you fall out of the habit of living with people their behavior can seem mighty peculiar. From space you can't take things one at a time. The stampede at the soccer match, the Miss America Pageant, and the oil slick off Santa Barbara are simultaneous events. You can't switch channels. It's all live, right around the clock. I dozed off, then I woke up with a start as a twisting gust of wind sucked the leaves upward. A top-lit moon, like a cone of lime ice, seemed to be tilted to dripping over Heber County. The night had the creamy pallor of snow falling in big butterfly flakes. What was it I heard? Dr. Friedman would tell me it was all in my ears. The cavemen had a gift for anticipation that was more than worrisome apprehension. Rainey identifies with early man, and seems to know. How those chaps would have guffawed, slapping their pelts, hearing us talk. Compared with those fellows our minds are loaded with shot, like a jumping frog's belly. Space traffic is quiet, comparatively speaking, but it seemed I could hear a few orbits creaking. Tedium with entropy? Had that troubled my sleep? How was I to explain to Miss Ingalls that all perception was extrasensory? It seemed obvious. The more extra the sensory, the more obvious. In the meantime, however, I lacked the gravity to consider what seriously concerned me. Where was my wife? Weightless in space her breasts would be bobbing. These are things that she may not have given much thought to.

I got up to use the bathroom and found a note from Alice tipped in a corner of the mirror, the one place, everything considered, I'm inclined to look.

> Kelcey darling,
>   Dahlberg says we can't be sure what this is, if it's not good-bye. In case Harry forgets, please have the light and power people turn off the lights. Also the phone. Who's going to need a phone? We're just not sure you really believe it. I've just got to. If he thought I didn't he'd do something reckless.
>
> > Love,
> >   Alice

I could appreciate her choice of words, since she did not want to leave a message that might start a rumor. No matter how much a woman looks to the future she doesn't cut all of her ties with the past. The water and lights would have been on her mind, spoiling her trip.

17

ARE YOU SURPRISED TO LEARN THAT THE
light and power people had no customers in Fork River? The last
account, a Mrs. Overholtzer, had been closed in 1943. That's
what the clerk told me but we had a very poor connection. I had
the impression that other voices were trying to get through to me.

"I received and placed calls with a Mr. Harry Lorbeer," I said.

"Not over these lines," was her reply.

It seemed to me I heard a hum like space static. Could it
have been Alice? When she hung up I heard no dial tone.

Over the weekend we had some gusty winds and heavy rains
which made a shambles of Alice's new tomatoes, and kept me
around the house. I find it hard to explain why I didn't miss her.
Friends and lovers who make solemn pacts to meet in the beyond
perhaps felt as I did. Less a loss than a period of waiting. It proved
to be more disconcerting to do without Dahlberg, and the smell
of the paint. Time and again I thought I heard the rattle of the
ladders on Harry's van.

On Tuesday I drove over to Millard, and found the Fork
River road gutted with a washout. The highway people had put
up a roadblock, with blinkers. I left the car off the road and
crossed the fields to the river, the west fork freshly clogged up with
sludge and debris. Broken bottles and glass glittered in the shallows like strips of clear ice. I found two clapboards, one side
smooth as if sanded, with pieces of yellow straw sticking through
them like arrows. New to me, personally, but not unusual. At the
heart of a twister many strange things happen. At a bend in the
river, where silt had accumulated, I found a half-buried doorknob,
like the egg of a seabird. Because the flooding had washed away a
stretch of bank, I crossed over to follow the bed of the railroad.
Weeds grew knee high between the rotting ties. The rails were

crusty with rust, like corroding paint. I walked along with my head down to ignore a flock of hovering blackbirds, with yellow hatpin eyes. If I paused for a moment, they shrieked and dived at me. Nothing gives me the feeling of being in the wrong place, at the wrong time, like aggressive birds. They are in their element: I am out of mine. They lead me to wonder what my element is. Fish have the water, birds the air, but man wanders with his head down, and with good reason. I used up a little time throwing gravel at the birds. They swooped in on me from the rear, their wings stirring my hair, my head down between my hunched shoulders. The creature buried in my nature strained to surface: the skin tingled on my neck, cords pulled at my ears. A smarter animal than I have become would have turned back. Why is it that some places accommodate so easily to bizarre perspectives? Huge creatures once grazed here, tiny, dog-sized horses; saber-toothed tigers crouched on the rim rock. Red men speared their fish, white men set their traps, horse thieves, scoundrels, buffalo hunters looked up this ravine, screened by the willows, to the sanctuary of their imaginations. When I rounded the curve of the tracks up ahead, what would I find? The sun-cured, time-preserved, and suspended village, waiting for the return of the departed, or a ruined, shriveled ghost town given over to birds and vandals? Would I stand there, as we say, getting my bearings, wheeling slowly to look around me. Where was I? That is to say, in what element? Dahlberg would say that I had lost my nerve, but Alice knows my reluctance to see things too clearly. My talent's for waiting. I don't believe in rushing what is bound to happen. It wouldn't surprise me at all to feel the earth tremble, or note, on the sky over the canyon, the turbulence of air like ripples on water. The sense of buoyancy, of unearthly lightness, I had already felt and welcomed. The saucer-like object, gliding like a squid, tilted slightly as it zoomed in for a landing, would have lights around its rim like an electric eel, and give off a whirring sound like a musical top. On the veined lids of my eyes the whirling globe gathers into its vortex assorted flying objects, some identified. But I don't let it unnerve me like some people. You see, I don't believe in rushing what is bound to happen. Seeing planet earth, as I did this morning, rising on the chaste moon's horizon, I was seized with affection and longing for how things were in Fork River. I mean *really* were. Assuming, of course, there was such a place.

FIRE SERMON

B O O K   O N E

1

WHAT THE BOY SEES WHERE THE CHILDREN
are crossing makes his eyes squint. It is a long city block to the
grade school exit where the old man gleams in the sun like a stop
sign, and that is how he looks. He wears a yellow plastic helmet
and an orange jacket with the word STOP stenciled on the back
of it. The flaming color makes the word shimmer and hard to
read. He might even be a dummy—the word GO is stenciled on
the front of the helmet—but anyone who knows anything at all
knows it's the boy's great-uncle Floyd. He's actually pretty much
alive but those who don't know it cry out shrilly, "Are you a
dummy, Mr. Warner?" When it's a boy who asks he better move
fast, but if it's a girl the old man gives her a pat on the bottom
with his Stop sign, just to hear her squeal.

One reason the boy likes to stand a long block away is that
he doesn't want to be part of this horseplay. The squealing girls
clap their hands, jump up and down, and shout some of the things
they've heard the boys say. They don't mean it, not really, but
the boy would just as soon not hear it, since he is known to all
of them as the *old man's boy*. Actually, he is not the old man's
boy, but it's hard to explain. Strictly speaking, he's an orphan,
and the old man is just his next of kin. But the fact that he lives
with him, and in a trailer, is more important than such an explanation. A further complication is that his name is Kermit
Oelsligle. No one can explain how he happened to have such a
strange name. When they ask him what his name is and he says
Kermit, they say Kermit *what*? He no longer says *Oil-sleekle* at
all, since it makes them laugh. My name's *Kurrr*-mit, he says,
and only now, after more than a year, has the name stuck. His
friend Manuel Gonzales says, "Hi, Kermit," and that's who he

141

is. Everybody else, including his Uncle Floyd, calls him *boy.*

It's a five-minute walk, the way he loafs and dawdles, from where he stands on the corner to the schoolyard exit. Children are crossing. Some of the girls hold hands and skip. It is painful for a growing boy to watch a girl skip. Seen against the light of an October afternoon their dresses are transparent and their legs skinny. For weeks now two of them have cried

> *See you la-ter*
> *Al-li-ga-tor*

to the Uncle. They are sisters, and chant the same thing when they leave the house in the morning. He finds it no excuse that at five and six they are but half his age.

The other thing he can't stand is the teakettle warble the Uncle makes blowing on his whistle. The whistle has a "pea" in it, to give it the warble, but only when blown with a strong blast. The Uncle no longer has a strong blast, so the sound he makes is a wet gurgling. The saliva in the whistle drips on his front when it hangs by the thong from his neck. He also wears it at meals. It drags in his egg when he lowers his head to eat. The two eggs the Uncle eats every morning account for his old age, his health, and his "perk." He is eighty-two and has a lot of "perk" for a man his age. If he eats only one egg in the morning he feels a loss of "perk" before lunch. The two hard fried eggs, the slice of fried mush, the crumbs and butter from his toast floating on his coffee, are things the boy knows the way a bird knows its nest. All that he knows often makes it impossible for him to eat. He likes his egg not quite cooked so hard, but the old man doesn't like him to eat a "live" chicken. That spot on the yolk is the eye of the chick, looking out. The Uncle no longer tells him to eat, insists that he eat, or even threatens him to eat, but merely slides the uneaten egg from the boy's plate to his own. Not being cooked as hard as it should be, it calls for more salt.

Neither of them like oatmeal, or eat it often, but it frequently comes up in their conversation. "A little oatmeal would stick to your ribs, boy," he says, since the boy always seems to be hungry. In spite of all he eats, he does almost next to nothing. At the

142

boy's age (which is almost twelve) the Uncle got up at dawn, harnessed the horses, plowed forty acres of corn and alfalfa, fed and watered the team, then milked five cows and separated the cream before he sat down to supper. Thanks to a big bowl of oatmeal he was able to do that, although he preferred eggs.

Aside from food, the boy's big problem is waiting for the old man to finish his work. He is paid to stand at the crossing till the kiddie schoolyard is empty. Sometimes he has to go in and shoo the little ones out, like chickens. If one proves to be missing, he has a key to go and look in the schoolrooms. They hide in closets, or might be found sitting under desks. If the boy is around while this is going on someone will surely ask him what his name is, or why his name is so different from the old man's. If he is *not* around, where the Uncle can see him, the old man will shout to anybody he sees, wanting to know if they have seen that boy of *his*. It's just his way of talking, but talk like that has caused the boy a lot of trouble. He is related to the Uncle on his mother's side, and not especially close. Just a year ago, with his father, his mother, two four-month-old Hereford calves, and his dog Schroeder, the boy was riding from their ranch, near Palmdale, to the State Fair in Sacramento. He never knew what happened. He and the dog had been sleeping in the back, and when he woke up it was all over. His mother, his father, his dog, and the two Herefords were dead. The boy wore a brace that kept his head from moving, and the nurse, Mrs. Seilers, had to feed him. She also read him the letters from his Aunt Viola, and replied that he would write to her when he could. His right arm itched day and night in a plaster cast.

If the boy had made a good adjustment to the fact that he was now an orphan, it was surely thanks to his Aunt Viola. She had carefully explained where his mother now was, waiting for him, and that she never for one moment stopped thinking of him. Here below, she had asked Aunt Viola to take her place. She sent the boy fudge, postcards of kittens and puppies, and a jigsaw puzzle that proved to be the face of the Saviour, a young man with a sad face and a pointed beard.

The boy's next of kin, and the person to take him, was of

course his Aunt Viola, but she had been an invalid much of her life and needed a friendly neighbor to take care of her. Next in kin was his great-uncle, Floyd Warner, who also happened to be a lot nearer. He lived alone in a trailer, right beside a school the boy could go to. The Uncle came over to the hospital in a bus, because his own car was up on blocks in the trailer court, and it was not advisable to pump up the tires for such a short trip. The boy was brought down to the lobby by a nurse, where he saw this old man who looked like a cowhand. His coat was just the regular one to a suit, but the pants were tucked into the tops of his half boots. He wore a two-gallon hat. Kermit had seen old geezers like him on the TV serials, but considered him too old to be his next of kin. "God-a-mighty, boy," he said, "don't you know who I am?" The boy didn't, but he said, "You're Uncle Floyd?" "Seems I am, boy," he replied. "Where your duds?"

The boy had very few duds he hadn't managed, just lying in bed, to grow out of. What he hadn't grown out of, he had on. His mother's things had been sent in a trunk to Aunt Viola, and what the boy could still wear he had in a duffel. The old man used it as a pillow to rest his head on during the bus ride back. He was not much of a talker. When they got to where they stopped he said, "Here's where we get off." The boy didn't *dis*like the Uncle, understand, he simply didn't want it known he was his *next* of kin. Especially when he wore the hard hat that made him look like some sort of bug.

From the backside, which is how the boy usually sees him, he looks even sillier than from the front, since a face has been painted on the hard hat to fool people into thinking he is looking toward them. The face wears goggles and a big friendly smile. If his back is turned, the people in cars might not hear his toot on the whistle. There is no longer much difference between his long blast and his short. He lacks the wind. The boy has tried it himself, and the fault may be that the pea in the whistle, which is made of wood, is so wet and heavy with saliva, blowing on it doesn't do much. The warble is like that of bird ornaments on Christmas trees.

At the schoolyard gate the boy steps inside and slurps water

144

at the fountain, forcing a thin stream of it through the slit between his front teeth. That is something new: he owes it to the accident. "Just don't you forget," his mother liked to tell him, "every dark cloud has a silver lining."

A small boy with a bandaged eye stands at the curb waiting to cross. He has already crossed the street four or five times. He thinks it's a game. The Uncle says, "Run along home, kid," and gives him a strong nudge with his Stop sign. He does not like kids. He thinks they are all a pain in the ass. The fact that he has never had kids of his own he thinks the greatest blessing of his life. They grow up to be hippies, criminals, drug addicts, sex maniacs, or basketball players. The boy should be grateful he is too short to be a basketball player.

The Uncle notes he is there, and goes along the fence to a large wooden box at one end of the schoolhouse. The box contains playground equipment for the kiddies, and the sloping lid is padlocked. The Uncle's keys are on a chain attached to his belt. One key is for the padlock, one key is for the school (if a child is missing, that is the first place to look), one key is for the car, now up on blocks, one key is for the trailer, and four or five keys no longer serve any purpose. One is to the car he traded in on the trailer, and one is to a garage he rented in Ojai, where he kept the trailer while he had his prostate operation, which he paid for in cash. The other keys must have once fit something, and there is always a chance they might fit something again. No one with the sense they were born with ever throws away a key. He raises the lid of the box and puts in the Stop sign, his yellow hard hat, and then the orange jacket, folding the jacket so it won't crack along one of the seams. From the box he takes a cap, tan in color, with the earflaps up, tied in a bow at the crown, and a folded shopping bag in which he will carry the laundry. He puts the cap on his head, and when he turns to face the boy he looks like Bugs Bunny. Other old men the boy knows either go without hats, or wear something that hides what they should be ashamed of, but his Uncle Floyd looks like either a bug or something worse. This couldn't always have been so, since his Aunt Viola, who would rather die than say something

145

untruthful, often took a full page in one of her letters to say how the girls had carried on about him. "Dear Boy"—she would write (these were really Kermit's letters)—"there were broken hearts all over Humboldt County when he married Muriel." The boy had to accept that on faith, and he did, since Viola had faith enough to save half the people in hell. That was the sober opinion of a man with no faith whatsoever, Floyd Warner. Now he walked toward the boy pulling on the sweater his sister Viola had sent him for Christmas, the sleeves so long he had to roll the cuffs up. The cook in the Acme diner said he looked like Popeye the sailor. The boy could believe it, although he had no idea how Popeye looked. Sometimes the boy lagged behind, to give the impression they were just walking along, but not together, or he might walk a step or two ahead as if he needed more room to play with his yo-yo, which he often did. The Uncle said, "Think you'll ever learn to work it?"

After fourteen months the boy understood this was just his way of talking. He did not talk just to hear himself talk, or spoil you with praise. "You hatching that egg?" he would say, when the boy fried one, or "You waiting for hell to freeze over?" He was full of expressions that made no sense whatsoever. How did hell freeze over? It was something *he* might have heard as a boy. Kermit had never seen anything frozen over larger than a milk can or a feed trough, although he understood everything froze up back on the plains. His Uncle and his mother both came from there, and his great-aunt Viola still lived back there. His father was from Texas, which he often said was cold as a witch's tit.

Most of the people in Rubio knew the Uncle as the crossing guard to the grade school corner. They said "Hi there!" to him, when they saw him on the street, and the children cried "Hello, Mr. Warner!" There was nothing to gain in being unfriendly with a crossing guard.

The boy lagging, they go along Alameda, the sidewalk steaming with the city sprinklers. In the Uncle's opinion, the hippies in Rubio would never wash their feet if it wasn't for the sprinklers. They walk in the wet grass in the street divider, leaving the tracks of their feet as far north as Tracy. At Tracy and Alameda there

146

is a movie, a drugstore, and shops for people who carry their groceries. If they shop every day but Sunday there is a very little for the boy to carry. They eat a lot of potatoes. Neither of them understand where all the margarine seems to go. In the hot weather, as it is in October, in order to help keep the trailer cool, they cook less and eat a lot of frozen meat pies. They come in four flavors: beef, chicken, turkey, and tuna, which they heat up in a small electric oven. Another thing the Uncle can't account for is where all the milk goes. The boy can. He drinks two glasses for lunch, then he has two more after lunch while the Uncle is busy at the traffic corner. He likes his own milk straight from the carton just before he goes to bed to settle his stomach, the night air in the trailer cooled by the draft from the refrigerator door. The boy would like to have ice cubes made from grape Kool-Aid, but the ice compartment is used to store frozen berries and meat pies. The boy likes the berries while they are half frozen, and may have already ruined his stomach. The Uncle likes them on his cereal, or in a tall glass covered with canned milk.

The boy's yo-yo casts a shadow on the wall of the school like a ball he was trying to throw away and couldn't. In this part of the walk he lags far behind, stopping in one place so he can watch the shadow. His own shadow is six feet tall, or almost. Not much can be said about how he looks except for the flap of hair on his forehead. It is always there, like a tilted awning, and explains the birdlike cock of his head. If he had real long hair, like the Beatles, he would wipe it back and it would stay there, but the sides and back of his head are clipped. "Goddam it to hell, you want to look like a hippie?" He didn't know. It would take some pondering. He couldn't bear the shame of somebody taking him for a girl. Nor did he want his mother turning in her grave (as the old man said she certainly would), since Aunt Viola had written how she was buried with her father, her mother, and her mother's mother, in a plot so small there had not been room for *his* father, or a marker of her own. In a way he hadn't noticed while she was alive he was now aware of his mother's presence. "Dear Boy," Aunt Viola wrote him, "your mother's loving eyes are always upon you—" Even allowing for her having other interests that could be a lot. He thought of her as younger than he remembered because she had been "a little girl" to Viola, who had last seen her three years before she was married.

The Uncle is not concerned that the boy lags behind, or is held up by the light at Alameda and Shoreline. He didn't especially like kids, and in his eighty-first year this ten-year-old boy had moved into his trailer. It was not the boy's fault he had no nearer relations, nor that Floyd Warner didn't care much for his mother. It was her child, one year behind in his schooling, thanks to the way they moved around when they cared to, that he now saw stringing beads when he opened his eyes in the morning. Did people send a boy to school to learn to string beads? If the Uncle had five more years of life, which was two more than his own father, this boy would still be a kid in the Rubio high school playing with his yo-yo and stringing beads. The trailer would be full of his hippie friends, all smoking pot.

The Uncle's anger was divided, and weakened, by his worry about what might happen to the boy, and his rage against the pack of mongrels that would soon take over his trailer. It had been his home for twenty-seven years. No trailer in the camp was as neat and clean. No teen-age boy could be expected to learn how to use the stove, how to change the gas, how to save the lights, and how to get rid of ants. An old fool and his wife (the Uncle will *not* stop thinking in such terms) who live in an apartment facing the trailer court have been waiting eight years for Warner to die, and to buy his trailer. He has heard from Mrs. Leidy, the court owner, that the woman is making curtains for it. Just to think about them renews the Uncle's lease on life. But renewal or no, he will not live forever and one day they (both still in their sixties) will make the boy an offer and move in with their three cats.

If the boy is underfoot, the Uncle is seldom easy of mind. If he lags behind, or is held up at a light, he might lose him for five or ten minutes, there being one drugstore and two markets he will have to check. The old man has a deal with Mr. Brundage, of Self-Serv, that if he spends as much as five dollars he can take the cart along and let the boy bring it back, Mr. Brundage knowing that Floyd Warner is as good as his word. With that in mind he will pick up their laundry, fluffed and folded (you can't do laundry for a boy in a trailer), and a ten-pound sack of charcoal briquets, on sale at Varney's outlet. The Rubio Laundrolette is full of new washers, a new gas fluff and drier, a playpen for babies, and a machine that will give the old man four quarters for a dollar. He has used it three times, and it makes no mistakes. The Laundrolette attendant is a girl in her second year at the Rubio high school. She has five lower teeth, no upper teeth, and a child fifteen months old. These simple facts are on display six days a week, but the old man can't believe them. He accepts them: believe them he cannot. At eighty-two he has all but two of his own teeth (impacted molars pulled in Kansas City) and to actually see this toothless girl, with her child, is no help at all in helping him to believe. He thought her one of these Okie women who came out in the thirties and forties. Her color is sallow, free of makeup, and her public expression is that of a seamstress with a row of straight pins between her lips. This habit was formed when her teeth hurt her, and without her teeth she still has it. It was not something she learned to conceal the few she still has. They are bunched all at the front, like the teeth of prairie dogs poisoned by grain, or hit by something, lying sprawled on their backs with their feet in the air, their mouths open. The old man had seen thousands of them in his day, and he knows how they look. Under the sacklike dress of an oatmeal color her breasts hang loose and get in her way when she is folding clothes. Out of a lifetime of habit Floyd Warner asks a person his or her name, the first time he meets him, but he cannot bring himself to speak to this girl. Would he rather she *didn't* have a name? Yes, he would rather that. She has displayed no interest in his and lets him find his own bundle, when he calls for it, while she goes on folding clothes, or nursing her baby. That too is something the old man has seen when he let a sow litter in the warmth of the kitchen, sitting up all night to keep her from rolling on her own brood. She goes to school: he has seen her seated on one of the idle teeter-totters, in the playground, and as much as he detests the idle gossip of women he is curious about the child's father. What possessed him? His puzzlement is greater than his disgust. The girl's infant (they all looked alike to Floyd Warner) often occupied the hamper that sat on the scales for weighing clothes. It did not disturb the mother if a nearsighted customer dumped her bundle of laundry over him, her, or whatever it was.

Shoreline Avenue in Rubio is lined with palms and parking meters. The palms are now so high that only people traveling south on the freeway see their tops, said to be the hideout of a new breed of tree-climbing rats. This rumor persists because the fire department has no extension ladder that will reach to their tops. The west end of Shoreline is Rubio Beach, once a sedate, almost exclusive promenade and bathing center, now the site of a swarming hippie love-in during the spring of the year. They come straggling along the streets, singly and in clusters, thousands of them, some love-ining as they go, like the strayed and lost remnants of some deranged but irresistible Pied Piper. Colonel Gertler, who served on the Western Front, compares it to the flow of refugees from the east. Many of them were children. They too wore the stoned vacant expressions, but carried no flowers. During this invasion the older residents attempt to confine the younger ones to their playrooms. Beach fires light the sky. There is frequently a rumbling noise that compares to that from the freeway. The old man and the boy watch it all from the safety of the trailer court, where the gate is locked, seated on two armless camp chairs at the door of the trailer. This 4 x 5 spot, a mini-verandah, is filled in with green gravel, to give a grassy effect, and is sheltered above by a metal awning with alternate bands of yellow and white. There is room to one side for the barbecue grill, on which they do most of their summer cooking, charburgers being the old man's speciality.

FRESH HORSE MEAT DAILY is still visible on the window of Augie's Pet Emporium, but it was not sold only as pet food when Floyd Warner settled in Rubio. He had tried it himself. Few things disturb him so much as his squeamishness in this matter. He liked horses no better than cows. He thought them as dumb. But along

150

about his third juicy bite of mustang filet, the best cut, he had to push his plate away and settle for a strong cup of black coffee. It was one of many things he had not mentioned to the boy. With several other kids he was inside the pet store trying to get the myna bird to say f—— Nixon. Floyd Warner doubted he ever really said it, but that was the story, and it made good business. The old man did not use such words himself, but he had always been free with most of the others. The name of the Lord or his earthly son figured prominently in these outbursts, since the old man considered religion—all religions—the scandal of the century. The long and fluent relief of cursing was still one of his respected talents. Bigger and tougher men had stood slack-jawed to listen to him. This strain of rage in him revealed itself in various abuses: the beating of horses, the breaking of tools, the frightening of children, and fancy cursing. His sister Viola had written to the boy, "No one curses so elegantly as dear Floyd," which both pleased and distressed him, since he had not known he had cursed before *her*. But more than likely he had, their father being the first great hate of his life.

"Come along, boy," he said, and they go along together to where dogs blocked the entrance of the Self-Serv market. Five dogs, two of them the size of yearling calves. The way things were going he would not be surprised if they one day turned and just gobbled him up, but they probably wouldn't because they had it softer the way it was. Like people, they were now too smart for their own good.

The boy tried three carts before he found one without a flat wheel. Another thing he didn't like were front wheels that wobbled, or one wheel that stuck when he made a turn. Cart wheels were damaged by old men, or old ladies, who sneaked off with them without asking permission, and bounced them off curbs, or ran them over bricks, or kept them at home for children to play with. (There were two market carts right at this instant being used as playpens in camp trailers.) Today the old man buys a sack of white potatoes, a sack of red potatoes, two bunches of carrots, two cucumbers, two half gallons of milk, two dozen brown eggs (white eggs had yolks so pale he could hardly see them), two pounds of margarine, one jar of peanut butter, one jar of strawberry jam, three loaves of sourdough bread, five one-pound packages of ground chuck, three pounds of chicken wings, one pound of legs, and the leg and thigh of a tom turkey, big as a dog's. At the checkout counter they buy two packages of gum, and one plastic bag of Hershey kisses. They both watch each item as the cashier, Miss Tomlin, rings it up. The young man who puts it in the brown bags is Skip Fletcher, a basketball star at Rubio High School. The boy is afraid to look for his face in the big muff of hair. The old man says, "Put all of that in three bags, will you, boy?" Kermit has been waiting for him to say that, and now that it is said he takes a grip on the cart. The old man holds up the line to open the sack of Hershey kisses, fish one out, and fumble with the foil wrapper. He pops it into his mouth and moves toward the door. In no way whatsoever does he show the faintest inkling that he has just escaped with his life. Skip Fletcher doesn't show it either, stuffing his hand into a bag, but everybody else in the market knows it, and just waits for Floyd Warner to drop dead. The boy is so sure that one day he will—if first Skip Fletcher doesn't kill him—that he has a little speech he plans to give when they ask him what in the world happened. This speech will explain, as most Rubio people know, that the old man calls people "boy" if they are younger than he is, which includes all but four or five people in the county. He says "boy" like other people say "Hi." He doesn't mean one thing or another by it, he likes white boys just as little as black boys, and possibly even less than people in general. If this speech will not make him popular it will nevertheless explain that although he might be peculiar, he is not what you would call a racist, or anything like that.

Nothing happens, however, and they go through the doors that open with a swish, and keep the dogs out. They stop next door for the bag of briquets stacked in the wheelbarrow in front of the hardware. Mr. Muzzey, who owns it, looks as old as Uncle Floyd but he says "Hi there, you kids," and makes change from his own pocket. The old man does not like this "kid" stuff, but he considered Mr. Muzzey so old and senile he has to be excused. It is people like Muzzey he refers to when he speaks of "old farts," which is quite often, as distinct from "oldsters," in which group he considers himself.

Now the boy takes the cart, and they go east toward the barren embankment of the freeway, the guard rail at the top level with the blur of passing cars. At this hour of the day it is picking up. Traffic from San Jose is streaming north, and traffic from as far as San Francisco—where the boy has not been—is roaring to the south. This sound is now so consistent they don't actually hear it. It is a wind-noise, or a sea-sound, to which he has grown accustomed. In the morning, early, he is aware of its diminished roar and thinks of that as morning—just as now, and on through the twilight, he will think of this noise as evening. There is seldom no sound, even late at night. In moments of silence his Uncle Floyd will jerk in his bunk, and pop his head up. Sometimes he will say aloud, "What the hell was that?" When he was inexperienced, early in the winter, the boy would say, "Nothing, Uncle Floyd," but in time he learned this was worse than if he pretended to sleep and said nothing. How could it be *nothing*? It had to be *something* that woke him up. He would lean on his elbow, listening, until he caught the whine of an approaching car, and by the time it had come up and passed he might be back asleep.

The main entrance to the trailer court is two blocks east, at the exit to the freeway, but in three years it has been seldom used because most of the guests are on a permanent basis. It is now a camp, more than a court, and the sign on the freeway had been changed to say so, but people who were new or just plain dumb sometimes pulled off and were disappointed. They were often people traveling late at night, having come up from L.A., or come down from Portland, and the lights of their cars, stopped at the entrance, always made the boy think of accidents and police cars. They shone directly on the Warner trailer and lit up the inside like a bolt of lightning. His Uncle would have to get up, pull on his pants, and go out in his bare feet to speak to the people, then try and help them get turned around so they could

153

get back on the freeway. These were the times his Uncle might curse from the time he got up till he came back to the trailer. The boy did not understand what his Aunt Viola meant by elegant. He was not shocked by cursing since he had been raised among cowhands, who like to curse at horses and cattle, but none of them went on and on half so long, or cursed as if they really meant it. His Uncle Floyd, with his head in the lights as if a police car spotlight had caught him, would talk a stream without any letup, his head pumping like a dog barking, his face so red it made his hair look white. He used a few words the boy had never heard, but he never used the words the boy heard the most. These were the "dirty" words kids wrote on buildings and on the walls and doors of lavatories. He couldn't help but know those words, but he was never so furious he used one. No, not once. Twenty yards down the street, where they could see it and turn, hung a NO VACANCY sign with the NO on a blinker, but either they thought it was out of order, or didn't see it, or were just ornery, since they would drive right by it and then honk at the chain. This chain was taken down and a high fence put up after what was known as the "incident." "We don't want an incident like that again," Mrs. Leidy had said, and the fence had stopped them. Anyone could walk around it, or either side, but no one with any sense would try and drive through it.

The boy recalled the incident very well. It had rained all day and Uncle Floyd had gone to bed even earlier than usual, leaving his boots and his lantern-sized flashlight where he could reach them if something flooded. If a wind came up and blew down a lot of leaves the three drains in the camp would clog up in a jiffy, and there was nothing to do but straddle one and rake off the leaves by the handful. The boy held the lamp, wearing a poncho-type raincape that dragged on the ground.

He slept right through the noise they must have made coming in. That was unusual in itself, since Volkswagen motors, especially the old ones, make quite a racket. Someone had got out and let down the chain, then they had pulled right over it into the camp, parking under an oak. When the boy did wake up the old man was pulling on his boots, and cursing. It wasn't raining so hard, just a light drizzle, but a film of water glistened over the bricks in the drive. Out there in the dark, where he couldn't see a thing, there were yelps and shrieks like you hear in a dog pound, some of them worse. The boy couldn't see a thing until the old man had clapped on his rain hat and stepped outside, switching on his light. About twenty yards away, directly in the beam, what the boy saw looked like a jungle movie. They had a broadside view of the Volkswagen bus and it was painted every color of the rainbow, but most of it green, red, and yellow, like flowering plants. The windows were curtained, and like something he saw through a screen of foliage. No lights. Just the crazy yelping and hooting. The Uncle kept his light trained on the cab and when he got up beside it he banged on the door. Nobody answered. There was too much racket for them to hear. The Uncle set the lantern on the ground and using both hands he tried to get the door open, and gave it several kicks. The noises eased up and the old man yelled, "What in the God-a-mighty hell are you up to?"

"We're havin' an orgy!" came the reply. "What the hell you think?"

The boy head that as plainly as if he had said it himself. The old man was so flabbergasted he just stood there, holding the light. The yelping started again, and the boy would swear he saw the bus rock. The old man went back and tried the rear door, then he picked up a brick that marked the edge of the drive, gripped it with both hands, and slammed it against the side of the bus. The noise of it made the boy wince, and close his eyes. He did that maybe four, five, fix times, each time a little harder than the previous, when the rear door of the car swung wide, with a bang, and a long-haired girl leaped into the drive. She was absolutely naked except for her streaming hair. Another girl followed her, then a boy (he could see well enough to tell the boys, all right), then a girl swinging what might have been a dress, then two boys in shirts but without their pants, their stiff peckers looking like horns as they ran into the dark. Another boy followed, dragging a girl along with him, then he let go of her hand and took off by himself, leaving her to wheel around, like she was dizzy, then stumble off in the same direction. The last one leaped out with an armful of blankets, tripped on a trailing corner, and sprawled on his face. The boy would not soon forget his naked straddle-legged stance as he scooped things up. How many were there? It would be hard to be sure. The boy felt they would keep coming, like the next fireball out of a Roman candle. But it stopped, and behind the soft drizzle he could hear sounds like deer scrambling through brush, or a pack of hounds. None of them ever came back. They left the car to sit right where it was so everyone in camp looked it over in the morning. There was not much in it but piles of old bedding, several pairs of blue jeans, and maybe two dozen girls' panties, some of them left over—in the Sheriff's opinion—from orgies somewhere else. There was also marijuana in the dashboard ashtray and two gallon-sized jugs of Mountain Red wine, one about half full, but nothing at all to indicate whose car it was, or who *they* were. The Oregon license had been swiped from another car. Until this incident occurred nobody had known that where the camp now stood was once known as the "jungle," and was used by high school boys and girls who parked there to neck. These looked like young hippies, they couldn't have been that old, but they must have smelled it out or heard about it somewhere, since they all ran off and disappeared as if they knew their way around. When he spoke about it to Mrs. Leidy, Uncle Floyd referred to them as "young heathens," and a striking example of what the world was coming to.

Floyd Warner's arrangement with Mrs. Leidy—he did not consider himself in her "employ"—paid him sixty dollars a month plus free trailer parking. For his part he raked the gravel walks, watered the plants, and kept an eye on the place. Some years back Mrs. Leidy had felt that Floyd Warner might have filled in well for Major Leidy, but when he turned up with a boy who had no other close kin her manner had grown cooler. Since Major Leidy's death she ate mostly nuts she cracked herself, and no meat. "The energy you use digesting meat," she told the boy, "you could convert to a higher consciousness." The boy replied that he ate it because he was hungry and liked the taste. In the old days Floyd

Warner often set up her grill, knowing how to get the most out of the charcoal, and if he didn't stay for supper, having food of his own, he would drop around later to watch "Gunsmoke" with her on the TV. Her trailer had a living room almost twenty feet wide and watching TV in it did not give the Uncle headaches. All of that had stopped, and perhaps just as well, or the boy might have become one of those TV addicts, with nothing but "TV snow" on his mind.

2

THERE ARE TWENTY-SIX TRAILERS IN
Live Oak Camp, plus eleven dogs, nine cats, and four children,
not counting Kermit Oelsligle. Dogs are not allowed to roam,
and when walked on a leash have to make their mess off the gravel
paths. Live Oak Camp is modest, by most standards, having no
swimming pool, public showers, view of the sea, or cable TV,
but it does offer shade, reasonable rates, and walking distance
to schools and shopping. Nineteen of the twenty-six trailers have
been here for at least ten years. That also pretty well dates them—
and the people you will find in them. When they settled for a
trailer good rentals were scarce, and they considered the move
temporary, something to live in while they took time to look
around. In less than half the time most of them took land prices
doubled, and the dollar dwindled—which happens to be why,
they tell the boy, they are where they are. A boy his age could
hardly care less, but he is new to the camp, old enough to talk
to, and brought up to say "Yes, ma'am," when asked to do
something. He has also been nowhere, knows very little, and
therefore should find the stories of old men of interest. Most of
these stories begin, "You wouldn't believe it, my boy—" and most
of the time they are right.

The trailers sit in three rows, in a herringbone pattern, each
row divided by a narrow strip of blacktop. The boy considers
blacktop the best surface of all for roller skates and food carts.
The noise is reduced, but not so much the dogs don't start barking when they pass by. Mrs. Leidy's Welsh corgi does not like
the boy, and claws at the metal screen door to her trailer, although
all the boy did was catch him peeing on one of their own trailer
wheels, and gave a bang on the wall. The corgi had kicked gravel
all over the place as he took off.

"You go along, boy," the old man tells him, and turns off at the entrance to Mrs. Leidy's. She has a flagstone walk leading to her door, with a picket fence around her rock garden. The day's incoming mail will be in the birdbox sheltered by her patio awning. One of the Uncle's chores is to deliver the mail. On the average it takes him half an hour or more if he gets into a discussion. The older trailer residents (fifteen years or more) feel the younger residents are noisy and irresponsible. They don't talk to each other. There have been two unverified cases of dog poisoning. The younger residents don't speak to anybody, but the older ones talk to Floyd Warner with the idea that he will speak to Mrs. Leidy. Her point of view is, if anybody doesn't like it, they can move. Floyd Warner has made few complaints himself, but he has made so many for others Mrs. Leidy may feel he identifies with them, and when she says *if anybody doesn't like it, they can move,* it's very clear that she means *anybody.* Move where? She knows very well he hasn't so much as had air in his tires for years.

Because he gets his rent free, the old man's trailer is separate from the rest, under the oak at the entrance. It takes up less room. The boy likes the trailer sitting where it is, since it is more like they were off somewhere, camping. The Uncle's car is under an olive green tarpaulin. Both the car and the trailer are up on blocks (with boxes of ivy cuttings under the trailer), but you would never believe the trailer dated from the thirties if it wasn't for the Model A wheels. The man who built it, then living in Arizona, must have gone on to make his fortune somewhere, since this trailer looked ahead to the bullet-type aluminum numbers in the fifties. All the joints in the shell were hand welded, and the only leaks, in all those years, were at the windows. He had even thought of screens, on the inside, and a water system you could attach to a garden hose. It suited the Uncle fine, but it proved to be small for a man and a boy. Only one person could move around at a time, so one had to stay in bed, or go for a walk somewhere. The boy's bunk was an upper, put in by his Uncle, but it was twelve inches shorter and eight inches narrower than the bunk bed below it. A crib mattress was just the right length, but not

160

so thick he couldn't feel the ropes that held it. When an acorn from the oak fell on the metal roof he jumped a foot. All winter long it pinged like a helmet when it rained. His only serious complaint was that the old man, all winter long, got up before daylight to cook breakfast, which they would eat by the hissing glow of his camp lantern. It seemed hours would pass before the boy went to school. In the empty playground he would swing on the swings, balance the teeter-totters, play with his yo-yo, and be so hungry he was almost starved by the time the bell rang. He was able to stay alive by eating the Fig Newtons his Uncle believed kept them both healthy and regular. If your bowels don't move, he said, you just help yourself. The boy did just that, scooting back to the trailer for a handful of them at recess, and gulping down milk if the Uncle was off somewhere. Floyd Warner was accustomed to a big dinner, having been up for six or seven hours, after which he took off his shoes and took a nap. If he was still asleep at the afternoon recess the boy would make himself a peanut butter sandwich, gulp some more milk, and grab a few Fig Newtons on his way out. It sometimes seemed that the more he ate, the hungrier he got. Coming back with the groceries, he had to be careful not to go hog wild and make himself sick, or eat so much he lost his appetite for supper. If he couldn't eat, the old man knew he was sick. His cure for sickness was not to eat anything at all, and starve into submission whatever it was that was troubling you, or take three tablespoons of castor oil and wash it out. The boy had learned to leave nothing but grease streaks on his plate.

On a day like this one they would barbecue chuckburgers on the new grill. Floyd Warner did not believe in Blue Chip stamps, nor would he patronize a store that promoted such hooey, but a woman whose child used the school crossing had one day just given him all these stamps. It had been the boy's chore to lick them and put them in the books. Rather than risk losing them all in the mail, the Uncle rode the bus with them to San Jose, where he went to the store, exchanged them for the grill, and returned home. A metal hood protected food from the wind, and there was a crank to turn roasting chickens. The boy took charge of the grill, and prepared the fire. He had reduced to eight the number of briquets necessary to charbroil four chuckburgers, leaving heat enough to percolate the coffee. With the hamburgers they ate strips of fresh cucumber, sprinkled with garlic salt.

A privet hedge a block long and almost eight feet high screens the trailer camp from the school. Floyd Warner had planted that hedge himself and saw to it that it was clipped and watered. He did this after supper, when the boy could help him, since it required moving the hoses from nozzle to nozzle. The stooping and pulling was something the boy was young and strong enough to do. By the time they had reached the end of the hedge, on Shoreline, it was time to start all over again. Some trailer residents complained that the flowering privet gave them hay fever and sinus headaches, but Mrs. Leidy believed that all such disturbances were in the mind. She liked the sweet smell of the privet herself, and if people didn't like it they didn't have to breathe it. Floyd Warner liked it. It reminded him of a lilac bush that bloomed on one side of the porch when he was a boy, filling a house he otherwise hated with its almost sickening fragrance. He had a very good nose. Viola used to say he could see through his nose. The boy did not understand why anyone should hate a house, or even find the smell of flowers so sweet they were sickening, but he listened to this story with his eyes wide since it was the first that the old man had told him. He had thought, when he arrived, that his great-uncle Floyd would be like his father's uncle, Harvey Stambaugh, who began to talk once he had swallowed his food, and went on talking till he had once more filled up his mouth. He had some remarkable stories to tell, but the boy had already forgotten most of them. His Uncle Floyd said next to nothing, day in and day out. He usually talked only when he gave orders, which he had been accustomed to do as a farmer with as many as fifteen hired hands during threshing time. The boy would have liked to have heard more of that, but there he stopped. The only time he did more than give orders was when he read to the boy from his books or read him Aunt Viola's weekly letter. These letters were addressed to Kermit Oelsligle, not to Floyd Warner, and the boy could read them very well for himself, but either his Uncle didn't believe he *could* read, or he liked to get and read letters. Aunt Viola seemed to know this, as she would say, "and now, Floyd, you old rascal—" and say something that was meant personally for him. Floyd was five years younger than Viola, and she had always been his favorite sister. How his sister could have lived for eighty-seven long years and still believe the foolish nonsense their father had taught them was something that Floyd Warner could not understand. He would put the letter face down in his lap, and put a hand to his eyes. The boy did not understand what this "nonsense" was except that it had to do with religion, living forever in heaven, where she would rejoin all those who had died. It did seem a little farfetched, but the boy didn't know much about it. There was a God, of course, but he was vague on the details. His Uncle Floyd had given his life to this study, and expressed himself very strongly. "You can tell her she'll have to do without me!" he shouted. "I'd rather burn in hell than be with that old bastard!" That old bastard was *their* father, so the boy knew better than to ever write and tell her. But the Uncle had also told her that, time after time, when he wrote in the past. "Don't let that old scalawag tell you his stories," she wrote Kermit. "There's so much the Good Lord has to forgive him already!" But she wasn't really worried. The boy knew she felt it would all turn out all right. The Lord knew everything, and one thing He knew was that Floyd Warner was a true and a good man, one who belonged in heaven, in spite of the foolish things he said. The boy agreed with that. If good and true men were in heaven, that was where he would be.

Two or three times a month he might read to the boy from Colonel Ingersoll's *Forty-Four Complete Lectures,* a volume with a faded red binding and Colonel Ingersoll's picture on the cover. The type was in two columns, and most of it so small Uncle Floyd took his glasses from his nose and used one lens like a magnifier, reading with his head tipped to one side.

There never has been a man or woman of genius from the southern hemisphere [What was that? the boy wondered] because the Lord didn't allow the right climate to fall upon the land. It falls upon the water. There never was much civilization except where there has been snow, and an ordinarily decent winter. [Uncle Floyd had it in his youth, so he no longer needs it.] You can't have civilization without it. Where man needs no bedclothes but clouds, revolution is the normal condition of such a people. It is the winter that gives us a home; it is the winter that gives us a fireside, and the family relation, and all the beautiful flowers of love that adorn that relation. Civilization, liberty, justice, charity and intellectual advancement are all flowers that bloom in the drifted snow.

The boy had never set his eyes upon drifted snow except on the TV or in the movies. He planned to buy a snowmobile one of these days and test the theory out. A favorite passage he had heard many times had to do with the making of Adam and Eve.

After the sleep had fallen on this man the Supreme Being took a rib, or, as the French would call it, a cutlet, out of him, and from that he made a woman; and I am willing to swear, taking into account the amount and quality of the raw material used, this was the most magnificent job ever accomplished in the world. (Uproarious laughter from his listeners.) Well, after he got the woman done she was brought to the man, not to see how she liked him but to see how he liked her. He liked her, and they started housekeeping—

Uncle Floyd found all of this so funny he would have to stop reading and sit muttering curses. "Jumping Jehoshaphat!" he would say, "O Jesus save me!" along with remarks the boy censored. He might just sit with his head in his hands and forget where it was he had broken off reading. "Where was I, boy?" he would ask, his eyes shiny with laugh tears, and the boy often wondered. He did understand that Colonel Ingersoll had him doing the two things he liked to do most, laugh and curse. Next came dominoes, which was something he could do with the boy. The boy liked to play games, especially checkers, but not with someone who took the game so seriously. The Uncle kept his finger on the piece till he had figured all the moves and made himself almost dizzy trying to peer around it. If he overlooked something it made him so furious he would curse, and blame it

164

on his eyes. "Goddam it to hell, boy, I must be color-blind!" The Uncle liked to win, but he wouldn't cheat. The boy liked to cheat. "Is that a cockroach, Uncle Floyd?" he would ask, and stare into the corner behind him. When the old man turned to look he would give himself a checker, or take one off. Thinking about cockroaches also took his mind off the game. The boy paid for all of this when his Uncle read to him from *When a Man's a Man,* by Harold Bell Wright. The book had been given to him by Aunt Viola, with her name at the front.

> There is a land where a man, to live, must be a man. . . .
> In this land every man is—by divine right—his own king; he
> is his own jury, his own counsel, his own judge, and—if it must
> be—his own executioner.

Hearing that the boy felt what he knew must be guilt, and knew himself to be a lesser man than the Uncle. On the other hand, with his Aunt Viola's help, he might improve himself. In the same breath the Uncle described her as a silly child and a saintly woman, a portrait the boy accepted as true to her remarkable nature. Until she wrote to him he had never received a letter, or known that all letters were once hand-written. She still wrote a "fine Spencerian hand," but recently it had become a little shaky. The boy felt he had come to know her pretty well—the big house she lived in, the two cats she lived with, and the presence of the Lord in all of her thoughts. Aunt Viola's picture of Uncle Floyd was perhaps even stranger than his picture of her. Her letters always ended with the question "How is that wicked old scalawag you live with?" Uncle Floyd *wicked*? What in the world was a scalawag? When he read that Uncle Floyd would take off his glasses and rub at his eyes with his knuckles. The boy was dying to know, but feared to ask him what a scalawag was. He would also just as soon read his own letters— they all began, *My dearest boy*—but he considered the old man a better reader of her Spencerian hand. First he would hold the letter to the lamp, to see which end was the best one to open, in case it had clippings inside. He never failed, after he took out the letter, to shake the envelope to make sure it was empty.

Aunt Viola's weekly letters were often read several times because the first time might get the Uncle so aggravated he found it hard to go on. Not all of Viola's letters were in that vein, but at her age her old friends were dying, and she felt the need to reassure Floyd that he would see them all again, and they would see him. "Only if they all burn in hell!" he had shouted, and thrown that letter on the floor as if he meant to stomp on it. He didn't, of course. He put it with the others in his locked metal file. They were the *boy's* letters, addressed to him, personally, but all he wanted to do was make sure he wouldn't lose them, and have them to read when he got a little older and had some sense.

Aunt Viola wrote the letters to "her" boy on Sunday, and unless something went wrong they were received on Tuesday, and nothing had gone wrong. His Uncle Floyd placed the letter right in front of the clock face, to make sure he wouldn't forget to read it. When they finished with the watering he would turn up the lamp and wait for the boy to climb to his bunk. From up there the old man looked different, especially without his hat. He had most of his hair, but it lay flat on his skull and had the same color. At the back of his head the red lining of his cap had stained it orange. With his glasses on the boy thought his appearance very dignified.

"That Aunt of yours thinks I'm lost to the Devil!" he would say, as if he was pleased to hear it. His Aunt really thought no such thing; was that what she meant by scalawag? The boy gathered it was a person with an ornery streak, who pretty much did as he pleased.

"You attending, boy?" he would say. The boy had learned to be attending.

My dearest boy, your Auntie's batteries are not so low she can't say her own prayers and write her own letters, which certain people who shall go nameless find it increasingly difficult to do. My girl has left me alone [she called her neighbor, Mrs. Gertheimer, her "girl"] and I'm lonesome for my loved ones. No, I do not send Xmas cards. If God had wanted the world to celebrate Christ's birth date he would have said so, and we'd

166

know what day it is [Aunt Viola believed there was some doubt in this matter] and it would not be the horrible event that your darling Uncle assures me it is. And you must not send me chocolates. This old tabernacle won't take it anymore—the Lord knows how I'm tempted—but make it dates if you must send me something.

Your Auntie loves *small* animals better than big ones, and she hopes the Lord will forgive her. A puppy came into the yard—I was lying in the hammock—and when I spoke to him he came cautiously forward, making funny little puppy overtures and whimperings, to sort of feel out my attitude about puppies—and when he realized I was friendly [Floyd Warner said, "She means *it* was friendly, to agree with attitude"], you never in your life saw such a happy creature! He pranced and made such happy little yelps I guessed he must be hungry ["She always thinks *any* animal is hungry!" the Uncle said] and gave him some food. He just wanted to gulp it up, pan and all. It takes so little to make God's creatures happy ["That excludes you and me, boy! and don't you forget it!"], one just knows the power that Satan has in the souls of men. I'm enclosing a little booklet for you, dear boy, and I want you to read it with your eyes and heart open. The Lord will take care of you, wherever you are, if you'll just let him. The trouble is our stubborn wills get in the way so often, and the stubbornest will I ever set my eyes on is our old scalawag! If he would just not be so willful he could look forward to a life eternal ["God help me!" cried Uncle Floyd] but I have not lost faith that he will stop being so stubborn and let himself grow up.

You've a cousin in Viet Nam—did you know that? Orien Moody, Ethel's boy. It wouldn't hurt for you to pray for him, as I do. He writes as if there was nothing so commonplace as a war. I love you dearly, boy, and know that your mother has her eyes on you right at this moment.

"Just that's enough," said the old man with a sigh, "to give a person the creeps." He returned the letter to the envelope, then turned a few pages of the little booklet, "The Man You Must Know." He tossed it up to where the boy was lying. "You better read it, while you've still got the brains you were born with."

It was not lost on the boy that this was in the nature of his first compliment.

167

3

IT IS SEVEN LONG BLOCKS, OR ABOUT A
twenty-minute walk, from the Live Oak Trailer Camp to the main
post office. On a hot day it seems more like a mile, and on a
cold day an offshore breeze is blowing, and there is usually some
fog. Nevertheless, hot or cold, the old man and the boy take this
walk once a week to post the letter to Aunt Viola. ("I can't tell
you what it means to me, dearest boy, to find your letter in the
box Monday morning.") Whether she can tell him or not, that's
where the letter is going to be, or should be, if the U.S. Postal
Service was not in the hands of dropouts, copouts, hippies, and
politicians. Considering that it is, it's amazing it works as well
as it does. The mail service is the one general topic Floyd Warner
will discuss with anybody, which includes such extremes as Mr.
Yawkey, in the service, and a potential employee, Kermit
Oelsligle. The pay was bad, but in uncertain times the government managed to stay in business. Men walked farther daily, and
received nothing for it, playing golf. Uncle Floyd's scorn was
shared equally with the mysteries and abuses of the mail service,
and the new Leisure World of fun and games. Rubio has a park
with a shuffleboard alley, and a strip of green lawn where the
oldsters play "bowls," and though Uncle doesn't play himself he
sometimes pauses to watch the others. His head wags. He looks
all around for someone who finds it as funny as he does. If he's
so smart, and he is, why doesn't he see that *he's* the one that's
funny? The boy stays clear of him at such times, not wanting
to be mistaken for his next of kin. What is so funny about old
men playing bowls? "God-a-mighty, boy," Uncle Floyd says. "If
you don't know that how can I explain it?" In any case, he doesn't.
There is no better exercise than a good walk, although there may
be better walks than the one they take. The palms are so high

they cast no shade, and if the old man isn't careful he will step in some dog crap. He does not mince his words about dogs. The town has no law about unleashed dogs, there having been so few of them in the past, but the present population numbers in the thousands. They are free to wander, obstruct traffic, block open doorways, copulate in public, and endanger life and limb with their droppings, some of them pie size. What kind of dogs are they to turn their backs on the earth and prefer cement sidewalks? The food they eat out of cans makes the smell of it worse. Floyd Warner dislikes all of this so much he complains to the Sheriff, if he can find him (he might be in his car, listening to the ball game), but as a rule he has to settle for Mr. Yawkey in the post office. Yawkey is old enough to have known better times, and smarter dogs. He is not important enough, however, to have any influence in the matter, and Uncle Floyd believes he is fearful of speaking his mind, if he has one. He has a job. He has no jurisdiction over unleashed dogs. The important thing about Mr. Yawkey's job is that he is paid to stand at the open stamp window, where Floyd Warner, or anybody else, can engage him in a discussion that may or may not have to do with the mails.

It comes to more than that. Mr. Yawkey is the one man in Rubio, available on call at the stamp window, who is actually part of the mindless forces that are taking over the country. Neither insult nor discussion will draw him out. On the other hand, neither does he walk off and start sorting letters at the back of the room. He stands there, his pale face green in the shadow of his visor, the shirtsleeves turned back on his hairless arms. As many as eight or ten pens—ballpoints, felt points, etc.—fit into a plastic holder that protects his shirt pocket, although the only pen the boy has seen him use lies on the metal counter with several rubber stamps. Now and then he takes a puff of the cigarette he balances on the rim of the scales, right over one of the pouches, and there is no way to explain why the place hasn't burnt down.

Not to obstruct public service Floyd Warner will stand to the left of the window, near the mail slots, sharing the remarks he directs to Mr. Yawkey with whomever he is doing business.

Not many seem to mind. Many agree with his comments on the state of the Union. It was at this window that Floyd Warner had his first confrontation with the postal service. Mr. Yawkey (looking very much the same, but not so thick around the middle) refused to insure the package wrapped in the manner he had received it. (Insufficient twine, he said, or something foolish like that.) Floyd Warner, naturally, had threatened to complain to the Postmaster General, whose picture hung on the wall. It was at this point that Mr. Yawkey said something crucial.

"Mr. Varner," he said (misreading the name Warner on the package), "all I do is work here." A simple fact, of course, but a mistake for him to have said so. He has had to live with it for sixteen years. "I know all you do is work here, Mr. Yawkey—" he has heard Floyd Warner say at least once a week, and all things considered his temperament is still good, even sunny. If Floyd Warner actually *misses* a Friday, Mr. Yawkey is the first one to know it. When the mailman on the route comes back to the P.O. he asks him, "How's the old man, o-kay?"

If the seven-block walk is not constitutional, why does the old man take it? There is a large red and blue mailbox on the corner where he stands, daily, directing crossing traffic. It is tilted slightly, leaning forward, as if waiting for the light to change. The mail is picked up daily, rain or shine, at five o'clock. This metal box has legs equipped with bolt holes, so that it can be bolted to the curb or sidewalk, but it actually occupies the corner with no more assurance than its own weight, which is not much. Boys have accidentally moved it, playing tag, and purposely transported it on Halloween to one of many corners without one, a federal offense. Into this "litter" can (it has been used for that, too, and on at least on occasion half filled with water to which goldfish were added) Floyd Warner is expected to drop the weekly letter to his sister Viola? It beggars belief, one of the many expressions he owes to her. Nothing has been done to improve this situation (as if painting it red and blue would improve it!) in all the years Floyd Warner has lived here, which is why he will walk, come hell or high water, to the post office itself to mail a letter. It's an outing for the boy, who walks ahead eating a Dixie Cup fudge sundae.

Rubio's business district is a block from the beach, with an area of benches and trees that cars are not allowed to enter. This had all been done before the hippie invasion and there was no legal way to keep them out of it. They took naps on the benches. They gathered in a cluster under the trees. In order to get them out of the Mall, the merchants let them have the empty Penny Arcade building. It had neither a wall nor windows at the front, and the boy could look in and see real hippies seated at the tables, talking, smoking, and eating. Food cooked by hippies was spread out on a counter, under a menu painted on the wall, like a mural. A meatloaf sandwich could be bought for twenty-five cents. The boy understood that if he ate such food he would get hepatitis and turn yellow. He didn't want to turn yellow, or worse than yellow, bleached out to white like a fish's belly. Not that it mattered too much, since he seldom had the twenty-five cents. What he liked to do was just stand there and look. If he stood in the ninth grade section of the schoolyard some smart aleck would tell him to go back where he came from, but no hippie would ask him to do anything as foolish as that. While Uncle Floyd went to speak to Mr. Yawkey, which might occupy him for twenty or thirty minutes, the boy would stand at the front of the Open Grave as if he was waiting for somebody. He saw plenty. He could fill a book with what he saw. He didn't hear much because the rock music made it impossible to hear anything else. If someone said, "Hi, man," to him, and it was not a girl, he would say, "Hi, man," back to him. Clear at the back of the room was a lavatory he had gone into and found a girl there, combing her hair. "Hi," she had said to him in the mirror. "Hi," he had said, washed his hands, and left. They smoked *grass* back there, and the one coming out would give the joint to the one coming in. He could fill a book with what he saw if he could be sure his Aunt Viola wouldn't find it and read it. She read a good deal, there being little else for her to do in bed.

If the weather was bad the hippies sometimes hung sheets at the front of the store to keep the wind and rain out. They kept

172

the boy out, too, and he would either go down to the Thrifty Drugstore and read the comic books on the magazine rack, or go back to the side hall in the P.O. building and look at the pictures of the men Most Wanted by the FBI. Hardly any of these men had beards or long hair. The boy was shy about looking at *Wanted* people (wouldn't he shy off if they were looking for *him*?) until he found that not one of these people, as hard as he looked, ever looked back at him. They faced him. But at no time did he catch a look. These men were always alias one thing or another, which he could easily understand from the pictures, the same person looking one way from the front, another from the side. He would not himself have believed it was the same person, and wondered if the photographer might have got them mixed. These pictures of Wanted men were across the hall from the Army and Navy recruitment office, where an Army man, with his coat off, usually sat doing crossword puzzles. The office had a pair of scales against one wall, and a chart with large and small letters for checking the boys' eyes. He could read it all, easy, even from where he stood in the hallway. The one thing uncertain was how much the Army would want him to weigh. On the scale in the drugstore he weighed ninety-seven, which was up nine pounds from what he weighed in March. In the Army if he grew out of his clothes he would be able to get more free.

All of the stamp windows, those with metal grilles and the big one with the scales, operated by Mr. Yawkey, were just inside the lobby doors on the front. The boy took special pains to get in and out of the doors without being seen by Mr. Yawkey. Why was that? Mr. Yawkey never failed to flick him a friendly, conspiratorial wink. The boy agreed, almost without reservation, that Mr. Yawkey had lost what little brains he had been born with, but in one way or another he could not explain he still had more than Uncle Floyd. He could wink. He could share with the boy a joke about the old man. It embarrassed the boy to share this sort of knowledge with a person as dumb as Mr. Yawkey, who naturally assumed he was smarter than Uncle Floyd. His Uncle would be there, just off to one side if Mr. Yawkey was doing business, or leaning in the window to make remarks about how to improve the mail service. Mr. Yawkey no longer took this personally. At one time he did, and would slam down his window when he saw Floyd Warner come through the door, but that had got him nowhere since the Uncle would stay right there till the window was opened. The Uncle's point had been that he refused to pay taxes for the delivery of mail well known to be junk, and Mr. Yawkey's point had been that the U.S. mail service could not make an exception for Floyd Warner. This meant that Floyd Warner turned back all mail addressed to OCCUPANT, which was nearly all of it, and the local mailman, Mr. Dexter, often carried away more mail than he delivered. If he wouldn't take it away, Uncle Floyd would dump it in the "litter" box on the corner, where it would have to be sorted out in the post office. That was how it had begun. Over the years, however, Uncle Floyd had got tired of writing *Return to Sender* on so many junk letters (if he didn't, he got them back two days later) and just let them collect in a cereal carton and threw it out when it was full, about once a month. His argument with Mr. Yawkey was more of a discussion growing out of different views of the Postal Service, one from the inside, which was pretty complicated, and the other from the outside, which was getting worse. One of Uncle Floyd's beefs was the female hippie who delivered early Special Deliveries in her nightshirt, a point that Mr. Yawkey considered well taken, and saw that it was stopped. What the boy waited to hear (out of sight but not earshot) was the slap of the old man's hand on the counter, which signals that he is preparing to leave.

"I don't want the Postmaster General, Mr. Yawkey, to think you've got nothing to do but entertain the public!"

The boy tried to sneak out while Mr. Yawkey turned to wink at one of the mail sorters, or stood tossing packages into the mail pouches at his back. That had once been a sore point with Uncle Floyd, but he no longer mentioned it.

On their way back to the camp Uncle Floyd might buy a pint of French vanilla, to eat on sliced peaches, since the long walk gave them both a bigger appetite. He also felt more like eating if he got a few real gripes off his chest.

174

4

FLOYD WARNER KEPT A CALENDAR ON
which he jotted what sort of day it was, every day of the year.
Windy, overcast, drizzly, rain, clear and cool. clear and warm,
and all though October he put simply, *Dandy.* Practically every
day was dandy, and that had been true over the years. They might
get a few gale winds up from the south, and maybe patches of
morning fog along the coast, but day after day it was weather
to suit the creator. The boy thought that an odd way for the old
man to put it, with his feelings on the subject what they were,
but he spelled creator with a small *c,* and meant no nonsense.
Something had to have started the whole shooting match, and
that was what he called the creator. It stirred in him reverence
and awe, but mostly awe. He could experience this by looking
at the sky, and the veil-like scarf of the Milky Way, and he could
also experience it closer at hand by lowering his eyes and gazing
at the ground. Years ago he had done that, while herding sheep,
having very little else to do. He had sat down on a rock, and
let his eyes rest on the small hole of some earth creature. Not
so big as a prairie dog hole, or a mouse hole, but somewhat larger
than most ant holes. Heaped around it, as in most cases, were
the sand and pebbles kicked up out of the hole. A tiny volcano:
that was how it would look in a photograph. He was struck by
the color of one of the pebbles, and took a closer look. Separated
from the others, in the palm of his hand, it looked very much
like the stub of a pencil, only not so large. One end of it was
sharpened to a very fine point, and it had six smooth polished
sides. The other end was just a crude stump of dirt and sand,
as if left unfinished.

At that point along the valley of the Pecos River Floyd Warner
was twenty miles from the road, and about a mile from the shack

he lived in. No one had passed that way before, so far as he knew. In the distant past there had surely been Indians: had one of them fashioned it for an arrowhead, or some sort of tool? It was a very great puzzle to Floyd Warner, but not, to his mind, a mystery. Someone had made it as it was, and for a reason. One day he would know. In the next few weeks, his eyes searching for ground holes, he found more than a dozen of these strange objects. A few were perfectly finished off at both ends. Some were tiny as beads, others thick as pencils. All colors, but he thought it one kind of stone. He soon had a small coin purse full of these gems, and when he brought his herd back from their grazing he showed them to an old-timer in Carlsbad. He had seen them many times. "Pecos Diamonds" were what they were called. They weren't really diamonds, of course, and not worth anything on the market, but they were found all along the Pecos and always had that particular shape. Who had made them? Aunt Viola and people like her were quick to say they were made by the Lord. They showed His hand. But they didn't show at all what His hand was about. The proper question was *what* made them?—and in time Uncle Floyd has his answer. He showed them to a mining engineer in Roswell and this man immediately described them as "crystals," said that *nobody* had made them, but in the nature of things they just made themselves. He used the word "snowflakes." Rain needed to turn colder for snow, but rocks needed great heat to become crystals. It was a matter of temperature, not the mysterious hand of God. Understandably, the Uncle had shown the boy a pouchful of these objects, and had been pleased to see the boy's eyes widen, his jaw hang slack. That was awe, much to be preferred to reverence. The boy was privately certain Indians had made them, but he was not so foolish as to say so. "Goddam it to hell, boy, didn't I just tell you *what* they were?" He thought they were great, whoever made them, and for keeping his mouth shut he had one of his own, not quite so fine as the others, but every bit as hard to explain. He had shown this example to the four or five people he thought bright enough to appreciate it, two of them girls. One of the girls, Eileen, wanted him to drill a hole in it, put a string through it, and let her wear it, if he wouldn't himself. She was certain anything made by Indians would bring you luck. The boy liked beads, even strung beads, but he surely knew better than to wear beads, or let *any*body drill a hole in his rock. He kept it in the watch pocket of his jeans, and it had already been twice through the laundry. One day he would have it polished, put it in a ring, and send it to Aunt Viola. He would say he had found it. It was all right with him if she believed it was made by the hands of the Lord.

The boy's best friend was Manuel Gonzales, whose father was janitor of the grade school. Manuel came early to school, then stayed late in order to ride his mini-bike in the empty playground. He could ride in a circle with the handlebars spinning, or jerk the front wheel up and ride around on the rear wheel, like an acrobat. The only person he allowed to ride his bike was the boy. All he did was ride around the playground while Manuel sat on the exercise bars and watched him. "You ride good," he said to Kermit, who had shared with him a close look at the "diamond." His only observation had been that it looked like a "doll's tit," but had no taste. Manuel dipped popsicle sticks in ketchup and sucked on them as he rode around on his bike. He envied Kermit living in a trailer and showed no interest at all in his being an orphan, or why his Uncle Floyd, his next of kin, happened to be so old. Mrs. Todd, his teacher, considered Kermit a nice clean boy, with good manners, but less carefree than most boys of his age. "Are you happy?" she asked him, hoping he would say yes, but his eyes filled with tears and he couldn't speak. Not that he was *un*happy, but he did seem to miss the rides in the pickup, with his father, the dog Schroeder sitting between them so that he looked like a hippie girl from the rear. Every evening they rode out to look at the steers, white-faced and clean in the green feed lots, the air sweet with the smell of the sprinklers and bundled hay. It was understood between them that the father talked to his son through Schroeder, eliminating the sort of confrontation they both had with the mother. Not wanting Schroeder's fleas, she had stopped riding with them in the cab.

He was not unhappy—one of the trailer ladies paid him one dollar a week to walk her Doberman pinscher where he wouldn't

see other dogs or frighten people. The dog had had an operation on his ears, and looked to other dogs like a giant rabbit.
The boy spent this money on cream soda and potato chips. On
Saturday nights the hippies had a rock concert at Adelphi Hall,
four blocks west on Shoreline, which the boy could listen to like
the carnival music he had heard in Palmdale, the lights on the
Ferris wheel visible from where he lay in bed. He understood from
what Mrs. Leidy said, and others, that his Uncle Floyd had been
quite a "cutup" when they held the square dances in Santa Cruz,
until his knee got tricky, and he had to give it up. What people
did now he did not consider dancing, or anything else. The boy
was privately of two minds about hippies, not wanting, at any
cost, to be mistaken for a girl, but very much attracted to beads,
bare feet, and far-out hats. He liked their talk. He looked forward to hearing someone call him *man*.

The boy was back from school, in the kitchen of the trailer,
concealed behind the refrigerator door he had opened, when he
saw the mailman approach and slip a letter under the screen. His
mouth was full of Fig Newtons, he made no sound. The mailman
went away without knocking, and he saw the letter was a
telegram, the name Floyd Warner behind the glassine window
of the envelope. He wondered what had happened. He
understood that telegrams were always bad news. He put it on
the table, where his Uncle would see it, then decided he should
go and tell him about it. At this hour of the day, he was the crossing guard at the playground exit. The boy did not mosey toward
him, playing with his yo-yo, but walked right down and stood
at the corner. His Uncle was surprised to see him, but let him
wait. Having a message to deliver distracted the boy from what
the Uncle was doing, and how silly he looked. He was also a
person of some importance to receive a telegram. When he didn't
cross over, but just stood there, the old man said, "Well, boy,
what is it?"

"You got a telegram."

"I got what?"

"You got a telegram. The mailman brought it."

"Why didn't you bring it?"

The boy had no idea. It simply hadn't crossed his mind to bring it. "Should I go get it?"

No, he didn't want it. He had only a few more minutes to go, and then they could both go back and read it. "A telegram?" he repeated. "Who sent it?"

How would the boy know that? He began to feel the urgency, however, and the five-minute wait seemed a long time. "Skeedaddle!" said the old man to the last child, and gave her a thump in the rear with his Stop sign. Without going to the storage box to change his jacket, he led the boy back to the trailer, the Stop sign still in his hand when he stepped inside. He held the envelope to the light at the window, turning it one way then another, straining to read it.

"Why don't you *open* it?" asked the boy.

"I think I know," said the old man. Did he think that was an answer? "It's your Aunt," he said. "Something to do with your Aunt."

The boy had guessed it was from Aunt Viola. Who else? His Uncle put the telegram on the table, then sat down. Between his legs he held the Stop sign, gripping the metal rim with both hands.

"Aren't you going to read it?"

"You read it," the old man replied.

That was how the boy was the first to really know that his Aunt Viola had passed away in her sleep. Arrangements were pending, and they wanted instructions wired. The boy wondered what sort of instructions, and where they would have to go to wire them, but her brother, Floyd Warner, said nothing whatsoever, his face concealed by the hard hat. The boy felt embarrassed to see his Uncle's stubborn will bend like a branch under Aunt Viola's faith, who was already up where she said she would be, watching them both.

Later that evening the boy and his Uncle walked the seven blocks to the Western Union office, where the Uncle wired that Viola Warner should be buried in the plot with the rest of the family, if there was room. If there was not room, as near to it as she could get. This still left twenty-three words in a night letter

179

so he said he would be coming to settle her affairs as soon as he could make the proper arrangements. At nine-thirty, the usual time, they were both in bed. The boy tried not to think of Aunt Viola, up in heaven, because he knew that his Uncle would not be there. He would be in the other place, wherever that was, wearing his yellow hard hat, his orange jacket, and holding up his Stop sign to people like the boy who might want to get in.

Mrs. Leidy advised him that he could fly there and back in less than twelve hours. She had flown to Oklahoma, attended a funeral, and visited friends in Fort Mills, Arkansas, then returned to Rubio in less than three days.

Or:

Traveling by bus, he could leave Monday morning, be there on Thursday, and then back by Monday, seeing much of America in the comfort of an air-conditioned coach.

Or:

The City of San Francisco left Oakland at ten in the morning, then went through the Feather River Canyon and across Nevada, Utah, through the heart of the Rockies along the Colorado River to arrive in Lincoln just before midnight, if it was on time. In the morning a bus would then take him back to Chapman in about two hours.

At least it was one thing or the other, Mrs. Leidy said, since no man of his age should try to drive it. Drive it? Uncle Floyd might have forgotten that he could drive it if Mrs. Leidy hadn't brought it up, it had been so long since the Maxwell had been off the blocks.

Floyd Warner liked to sleep on major decisions, but he lay awake most of the night on this one. The boy could hear him scratching himself, and smacking his lips. In the morning his mind was made up, however, and he woke the boy to tell him. "Get up, boy," he said, giving him a shake. "We got to get packed."

It had taken him all night to sort things out and understand what had happened back in Chapman. Aunt Viola could be buried, in one plot or another, and rise as she knew she would to heaven, but there remained the house in which she had lived all but a few years of her life. As the family died off they had left things with her, and now there was no one left but Floyd Warner. Himself and the boy. Soon there would be only the boy. If Kermit Oelsligle had the brains he was born with on his mother's side of the family, he would see that something had to be done, and know what it was. But he didn't seem to.

"Goddam it to hell!" he old man shouted. "Don't you know who you are?"

"I'm Aunt Viola's boy," he replied.

That surprised Floyd Warner. The boy stared at him through a blur of tears. If he blinked they would run down his face, so he stared without blinking.

"Blow your nose!" the old man said, handing him the dish towel. "We've got a lot to do."

What they had to do first was take the tarpaulin off the car and get the battery charged. The Maxwell coupe still had its original paint, a dark-green color, but it had crackled to look like imitation leather. On the right side running board were three cans, in a rack, painted red, white, and blue, for gas, water, and oil. Experience had taught the Uncle to put water in them all. The smartest thing he had ever done was install an electric starter when he had the motor overhauled in the forties, since he was now too old, and the boy was still too young, to crank it. Without the trailer in tow, the car had last made a run up the California coast to Seal Beach, near Portland, where Floyd Warner had once been tempted by a bit of land speculation. He had decided against it when an earthquake gave the whole area a shake. The Maxwell even had a heater in the cab, but it was not very effective until the water was hot. If the water got hot they would have bigger problems than cold feet. While the battery was charging, the boy pumped up the tires. The two on the rear of the coupe were new when Uncle Floyd had driven to Seal Beach, but the other four, counting two on the trailer, were smooth as bicycle tires. Two of them they could use as spares, but what they needed were four new tires for such a long trip. The boy reasoned that if they were going to buy tires, why didn't they let the tire people put in the air—which was just the kind of reasoning his Uncle expected from a boy who had never done

181

a day's work in his life. These tires were on rims, and it was something of a problem to get the tire off the rim, even with tire irons, and nobody in the tire business today would go around the corner to replace a tire, or do that kind of work. The boy saw that if the rims were slipped off the wheels he could *roll* the rim and tire the mile to the tire shop, but since he *did* have the brains he was born with he did not make the suggestion. He pumped ten pounds of air into each of the tires, and let it go at that. Packing the trailer was no problem—after all, it was already packed—but getting it and the car down off the blocks proved to be a headache. In the entire trailer camp there were only two jacks of the sort you could stick under an axle. The new style jack wouldn't fit on the Maxwell, or raised the cab in the air and left the wheels on the blocks. They were all set to go but they couldn't get the wheels down on the ground. The Uncle would fool around beneath it with the jack, thumping his head, then he would get up and stand off to one side, where he could see the whole rig, and soberly curse it. Some of the men had heard such language, but the ladies in the camp said they had never heard it. He didn't raise his voice much: he just folded his arms and went on and on. The problem was solved by five of the men using one of the railroad ties as a lever, lifting the Maxwell just enough to slide out the blocks. The trailer could just be pulled off, once they got the Maxwell motor started. Mr. Gonzales, the janitor, who worked part time at a gas station in the summer, went home for his supper, then came back and stayed until after dark, when he got it started. He advised putting in five gallons of gas and letting it run. The Maxwell motor had a good even sound when it idled, but it wouldn't idle without backfiring. First it would cough two or three times, then go off like a bomb. Someone in the camp called the Highway Patrol, who pointed out that the car had a four-year-old license, and lucky for him it was not out on the road. Lucky for him also, Floyd Warner proved to have his car ownership papers in his green metal file with Aunt Viola's letters, but unlucky for him his driver's license was four years out of date. Taking care of all of that took three days, since he flunked his first two driver's tests, but it allowed time for

Mr. Gonzales to get the motor in tune and reduce the backfire. It also gave the boy time to study the map and figure out that it was 1,948 miles from where they were to where they were going, following the route the man in the gas station laid out. At a cruising speed of thirty miles an hour they would hope to do two hundred miles a day, most of it early in the morning, before the desert sun got hot. Long trips by car were not new to Uncle Floyd, who had once been all the way to Guadalajara, but he had given up traveling when the freeways made it all one big racetrack. Did he think it had changed? No, he did not, but this was a trip that couldn't be helped. He was through with traveling. He and the boy were going home. Thanks to the awful freeways, once they were north of San Francisco they could go all the way without big city traffic, free to pull off the road and sleep where they chose. They would leave at dawn, going north along the coast, and before the morning traffic was jamming up the city they would be crossing the bridge, over the Golden Gate, considered by the Uncle to be one of the seven wonders of the world. Those situated in far-off, superstitious places he considered out of date.

B O O K　　T W O

1

EVEN THE BEST-LAID PLANS MAY FAIL TO
take into account the early-morning traffic in San Francisco, where
Uncle Floyd, confused by two bridges, ended up taking the wrong
one to Oakland, three miles long with no place he could turn
off. A Highway Patrol car with the blinker revolving followed
them across.

"Pop," he said, "you're under the limit."

Uncle Floyd was certain he had heard it wrong. They had
been going twenty-five, maybe less, in a thirty-five-mile-limit zone.

"You got to go *over* it, Pop," said the cop.

"Boy," said Uncle Floyd, "it won't *go* over thirty-five!"

He proved to be a nice, friendly cop, however, and gave them
directions instead of a ticket. What they should do was get off
the freeway until the traffic let up. The cop went ahead of them
to a freeway exit where they could drive under thirty and not
get arrested. To help pass the time until the traffic let up, they
had their second breakfast in a Richmond diner, where they could
also park on one meter at the curb. The cook in the diner, who
lived in Vallejo, explained how to drive under thirty on the
freeway. They should stay over to the right as if they were preparing to get off. If a cop stopped them for slowing up the traffic,
they would simply tell him they were pulling off. If they had
to pull off, they would get back on and do the same thing. Once
they got to Sacramento the road got wider and there were lanes
for slow traffic on the grades. To be on the safe side, in case they
had to pull off where there was no place to park, and nothing
to eat, they let the cook make them up a bag of sandwiches.
Highway travel had changed since Uncle Floyd had come west
in 1941.

They were back in the car, looking for the freeway entrance, when the boy noticed the paper under the windshield wiper. A ticket? He decided to ignore it. If they were leaving the state the cops would never find them. But when they pulled into a station to ask directions the attendant found it and had a look at it.

"Hey, look at this!" he said. "You got a cash offer."

"I got what?" said Uncle Floyd, but he couldn't read it, and passed it on to the boy. Someone had written

For CASH OFFER call
Wilner 386-9886

on the back of a canned tuna fish wrapper.

"Cash for what?" Uncle Floyd asked.

"Your car, Pop. People collect old cars."

Uncle Floyd didn't believe such nonsense for a moment.

"They might give you even more than you paid for it," said the attendant, "in case it's paid for." He gave the boy a wink.

"God-a-mighty, boy," he said, "now why would I sell it? I'd only have to go and buy me another."

"I've one I'll sell you for three seventy-five," said the attendant. "All it needs is tires."

"Young man," said Uncle Floyd, "you may take me for a fool, but I'm not see-nile!"

"If I were you I'd keep the offer," he replied, "just in case."

"If you were me, boy," Uncle Floyd said, "you wouldn't." But since they were there he let him put in five gallons of gas.

The traffic on the freeway was still pretty bad, but they fell in behind a truck pulling a wide house trailer, with flags out on the side. The truck's speed averaged about twenty-five, and cut down on the wind. They tagged right along behind him through Sacramento, where a new, wider freeway led into the mountains, and the old man called the boy's attention to the color of the leaves. Born and raised in California, as he had been, he had little or no idea of the change of the seasons, the whiteness of the winter, or what it was like to look forward to spring. It led him to ask the boy what, if anything, he looked forward to. Just as he feared, the boy didn't know. He looked forward, that's all.

186

If it was evening, he looked forward to morning. If it was Monday, he looked forward to Saturday, and that sort of thing. He just looked forward. Where else was there to look?

Uncle Floyd said he was thankful to hear what he said, since it surely confirmed what he feared the worst. California was a place to grow old and die in, but not to grow up. He, Floyd Warner, was of the opinion, having lived for some years in both places, that no man on whom the snow did not fall was worth a hill of beans. While there was still time the boy had damn well better get himself under it. The boy had heard this before, but not so well put, and in this context it left a stronger impression. If people were divided between those on whom it snowed, and those on whom it didn't, it would prove to be a help in sorting them out. Snow had fallen on his mother (no way to tell about his father), on his Aunt Viola, on his Uncle Floyd, and once it had all but buried his grandfather, who had been found with a pack of ice in his hair. It may have frozen his wits, but it didn't kill him, and he had gone on to preach his religious nonsense, the snow, unfortunately, not being a cure for some human ills. The boy would do well to keep all of this in mind when the time came for him to choose a wife between some female with her brains sunbaked, her hair the color of baled hay, or some woman with skin like snow, and the sun in her heart. The boy slept on it, his head lolling from side to side, as the cab tilted, but his eyes were open when they rounded a curve and there, up ahead of them, were two people. Snow might have once fallen on the young man with the beard, but the girl had hair like a bale of hay, and almost as long. The young man carried a pack on his back, and had thin, hairy legs.

"They hitchhikers?" His Uncle did not reply, his gaze far up the road as if he didn't see them. The girl wore stockings of a purple color and a skirt so short she didn't seem to have one. Her long hair hung below it. About her shoulders she wore a green shawl. The boy had never seen a girl with a bigger, friendlier smile.

The old man said, "No hitchhikers. About half of them just as soon shoot you."

As the car came up and went by them the boy thought the

187

young man looked familiar. His expression was sad. His black beard came to a point on his chin. The girl put up her arm and waved to the boy; he waved back.

"Besides," Uncle Floyd said, "we've got no room. It's against the law to ride in a trailer." In the side mirror the boy saw the young man put a thumb to his nose and wiggle his fingers at them, then the curve of the road cut the two of them from view.

Just before dark Uncle Floyd discovered that the lights didn't work. He cursed elegantly for about five minutes and walked around the car giving the lights a hard thump. But none of that helped. Uncle Floyd was knowledgeable about the magneto, the distributor, and the carburetor, but anything to do with electric wiring he preferred to leave to other people. But not Mr. Gonzales. He had always found that people full of good will seldom proved to know their ass from a hole in the ground. In fixing one thing they managed to ruin something else. Fortunately, the lamp in the trailer used gas, and the boy walked back down the road and held it. A young man in a Chevy pickup stopped by to help them, but he was not familiar with a car so old.

"You should be lucky it runs," he said. "What do you want, everything?" He meant that as a joke, of course, but his Uncle didn't laugh. What he *could* do for them was fall in behind and flash his high beams far up the freeway. That way Uncle Floyd could see where he was going, and they drove along on the tail of their shadow. About ten miles ahead they reached a camp for trailers, where they could stop for the night.

The camp had no lights of its own, but it was all lit up by Mr. Cowles' mobile home. He and Mrs. Cowles were traveling west to visit Disneyland and see their grandchildren. Mrs. Cowles had retired the moment they arrived because winding mountain roads always left her queasy. She sat in their living room watching the news on the TV. Mr. Cowles was not much help with their lights either, but he was very much impressed with Uncle Floyd's Maxwell. Not himself, but his father had owned a Dodge touring that he couldn't seem to wear out and became very fond of, driving it around during all those years when new cars were scarce. Mr. Cowles would never forget the characteristic ping the old Dodge motor made. He would say to his wife, "Here he comes, Laura," two or three minutes before he pulled in the yard. In 1949 he turned it in on a Plymouth, which he drove till his death. Even his father, however, would never have dreamed of driving that car across the mountains, and pulling a trailer with it. What he proposed to do was take some Polaroid snapshots of Uncle Floyd, and the Maxwell, in the morning, which he would send back to have printed in the *Motor Trails News,* in Racine, Wisconsin. They ran a special section on antique cars every month. He personally believed this was the first antique he had ever actually seen pulling a trailer, but there might be others in out-of-the-way places, and parts of the South. In the morning, when the light was better, he would take some shots. He and Mrs. Cowles had started their trip with their dog, but somewhere in Wyoming he had taken off and left them, all of which proved, in Mrs. Cowles' opinion, that he had more sense than they did. She didn't care much for campers. If she ever took a trip like this again, she said, it would be in a box.

During the night Uncle Floyd decided he didn't want pictures of either himself or the Maxwell, so they were up before it was light and left the camp without eating breakfast. A few miles down the road they pulled off the freeway rather than go through the tunnel up ahead without lights. A rancher going west, with two crates of leghorn pullets, stopped to see if they were having trouble. His own car was a '37 Ford V-8 so he knew what to expect when he lifted the hood. "You've blown a fuse," he said, fiddling around, and used the one they had blown, wrapped in a piece of tinfoil from his cigarette package, to make one that would work. The way the Maxwell worked, they had really good lights when they raced the motor, and not so good when they didn't. But there was always light enough so the people coming toward them could see them.

Although the road was new, and the boy had the impression they were cruising along on the level, the radiator boiled every ten or twelve miles and made the windshield a solid rust color. It might take the boy a quarter of an hour to get a bucket of water from the shallow river. Ten miles farther it would all go up in steam and spray. One thing it did was clean out all the rust, so the spray on the windshield also helped to clean it. But they took almost all day getting over the pass. On the far side of the mountains they could coast, and almost get back the gas they had wasted, but the old man was so tired he couldn't stay awake. He thought it best to stop and take a little nap, which proved to be until morning, and the sun woke him up. He swore to the boy he had never in his life slept so long as that. They both woke up hungry, and the boy was collecting firewood when he heard someone yelling at him from the freeway. The girl with the long hair, all of it wildly blowing, sat at the rear of a truck with her legs dangling, giving him her big, friendly smile and waving her arm. The boy waved back. The young man was seated out of the wind with his knees drawn up, his head resting on his arms.

"Who was that, boy?"

"That was them," he replied, but the old man didn't ask him for an explanation. The truck had been used for hauling hay or straw because bits of chaff blew in the windstream behind it, one of the girl's brown legs swinging in front of the taillight so it seemed to blink.

2

IN THE MORNING THE BOY WAS UP TO SEE
the sunrise behind what he thought must be the Rocky Mountains, they looked so far away. The old man had planned for
them to leave about daylight, but he hadn't slept well with the
soreness in his legs, and the noise in his ears. He didn't notice
this crackling, like bacon frying, till he put his head on the pillow.
Then it went on all night. The boy had heard his own ears go
pop, but he would rather they did that than do nothing at all.
It was part of traveling, like the nosebleed he had in the men's
room. He was doing nothing more than just looking at himself,
when his nose began to bleed. He was ashamed to face his Uncle
with his nose bleeding, so he sat in one of the booths, his head
tipped way back, swallowing all the blood he would otherwise
be losing, till it finally stopped. But something like that was what
you had to expect when you were traveling around.

Another thing about traveling: if you would like to save
money, what you do is always order some sort of breakfast. His
Uncle Floyd might eat eggs three times a day, boiled in the morning, hard-boiled for lunch, and fried hard in the evening but
since *he* didn't like eggs he ate hotcakes in the morning, cold cereal
for lunch, and maybe hotcakes for supper with a piece of ham.
They had planned to eat in the trailer, which they could do on
about half the money, but after riding all day they both liked
to get out and walk around the town, then eat in a diner. If he
couldn't walk somewhere to eat, his Uncle Floyd would rather
not eat at all. Only walking took the kink out of his legs that
seemed to be there every time he stood up, and made him so stiff
and sore in the morning he could hardly move. The foot he used
on the gas pedal would go to sleep for so long he couldn't feel
the pedal. If he took off his boots his feet would swell so he could

hardly get them on in the morning. Was he feeling his years? He asked himself that when he thought the boy was out of earshot. It was also better to stop every hour or so than drive for three or four hours, then take a nap for six. Once he really fell asleep right after lunch he couldn't seem to wake up. Some of that might be caused by the elevation, as Mr. Cowles had mentioned back in the mountains, but most of it, in Uncle Floyd's opinion, came from sitting too much "at the goddam wheel." Just gripping the wheel made his fingers so swollen he could hardly butter his toast in the morning, or pick up a spoon. Added to that, the noise and rattle of the cab went on all night, as if trapped in his ears. It was too goddam bad, the old man said, that the boy wasn't just a year or two older, which was not exactly old enough to drive but surely big enough to sit at the wheel out here in the open where he hardly had to do anything else. The boy replied that he *had* sat at the wheel, and even more than that he had once shifted the gears in his father's pickup. It had been his father's custom to let him sit at the wheel and move the car if time ran out on the parking meter. He was older and bigger now than he was then by more than a year. The old man said if he could just sit, and not drive, he wouldn't have the kink problems in his legs, and it would not be necessary for them to lose five hours while he took a nap. At the rate they were going, ninety miles a day, it might even be snowing before they reached Nebraska, where a blizzard in November was every bit as common as roses in May. So what happened was, about three miles out of Lovelock, the old man stopped the car and slid over in the seat, while the boy got out and walked around to climb in behind the wheel. His legs were almost as long. His brown hands looked good on the wheel. He put in the clutch, he pulled back the shift, and he let it out so slow they both thought it was slipping, then it caught, and without even a lurch they were off.

"Can you stop it, boy?"

Yes, he could stop it. Unfortunately, he also killed the motor. But that was because he was inexperienced, and the old man watching him made him nervous. There was nothing to it. He felt he would like to drive both day and night. "If the town's big

192

enough to have lights, we stop, and I take over. You understand that, boy?"

The next town with lights had so many the boy could see them from miles away. An airplane beacon swept the cooling sky. The old man had been dozing, his head on a pillow, and when the car stopped moving the quiet woke him up. It took him a moment to remember where they were. "That Lordsburg?" he said, sitting up.

The boy had never heard of Lordsburg. The town ahead, according to the map, should be a place called Winnemucca. Winnuh—who? It was right there on the map. In Winnemucca there were gas stations with showers, and they both took one and felt a lot better. The trailer camp provided ice water, and the boy had never before seen a slot machine. They walked through the door into a darkened room like a movie lobby, full of these machines, cranked by men and women. They had entered the building under a sign that said BREAKFAST AT ALL HOURS, but the boy was a minor, and minors were not allowed. Floyd Warner took exception to that, and said he and the boy would eat where they pleased to, which proved to be a smaller place farther down the street. The sky was lit up all night long by the blinking signs. That and the ice machine made it hard to sleep and they were not up at daylight as they had planned. The old man refused to wear dark glasses, and ruin a pair of eyes that had never caused him trouble, but the boy, now that he was driving, felt it important for him to see clearly. At eight in the morning he had the sun hot in his face. According to their new plan the old man would drive to the edge of town, out beyond the traffic, where he would stop and the boy would take over. He was ready. He wore the new glasses that made the brown desert almost look green. Thanks to them, surely, he was able to see the hitchhiker far down the road. She was no longer wearing the purple stockings, and appeared to have on nothing but her long hair. The boy thought she was out there in the desert, all alone, and he would surely have stopped if he had been driving, but when they were closer he saw the young man lying on his back in the ditch grass, his head resting on his pack. In order to get a good suntan he had taken off his shirt.

"That's them!" he cried, and he would have stopped, or at least slowed down, or something. For maybe four or five seconds, it might have been longer, the old man let his foot ease up on the pedal—then he saw who they were and pushed it flat to the floor. The girl waved both her arms and threw the boy a kiss when they went by. It didn't seem to bother her at all that they didn't stop. They were going up an incline, with the road so straight he could see them in the rear-view mirror for miles, the sun gleaming on her yellow hair. How did the pair of them always end up ahead, although the old man and the boy always passed them? Where were they going? Was it some sort of game? Floyd Warner didn't say one word or another, or even let on to the boy that he had seen them, but he drove the car for another hour just to make sure he had put them behind him. With the wind at their backs, they cruised along at almost forty miles an hour.

His Uncle took the wheel again, out of Elko, then the boy drove for more than four hours, once coming within an inch of falling asleep with the right wheel off in the gravel. It scared him awake, so that after that he was all right. They had to have a conference in the city of Wells as to how they planned to cross the Great Salt Lake desert, and on the advice of the gas station attendant they bought a water bag and let it ride on the fender. By sundown they had come almost three hundred miles. Floyd Warner had hardly driven any of it, but just riding all day had worn him out. He wasn't hungry either, and went to bed while the boy drank pop and ate two hamburgers. The clerk in the store looked like Carlos Gonzales but the boy guessed him to be an Indian. He read comic books and made change from money in an ashtray. They were in Utah, but the difference was not too noticeable. The boy was able to see, from a rise he walked to, almost all the way back to Nevada, where the girl with the big warm smile was probably smiling at somebody. She continued to do that even when people didn't stop. This impressed him as unusual behavior that required some sort of explanation, but he understood he was not going to get it from the old man. He would like to meet this girl in a filling station and ask where it was they were going. That was not uncommon. They had already been asked four or five times. If she continued to smile he would then ask her how they always happened to be up ahead, right after the boy and his Uncle had passed them. This would all be easier if he was sitting at the wheel when they came into the station for a drink or something, and he could say to her, "Be seeing you!" knowing that he would.

They were still in Nevada when he saw, far up ahead, this roiling, mud-colored river obstructing the road. It proved to be sheep, thousands of them, and when he stopped the car they flowed around behind it and they could move neither forward nor backward. Mixed in with the flock were hundreds of invisible bleating lambs. Such a moiling sea of creatures gave the boy a fright, but Uncle Floyd got out of the car and waded in among them, clutching the wool on their backs. He could hear him shouting elegant curses, as if he knew some of them personally. The movement of the flock carried him along with them, as if he rode on their backs. If sheep were the dumbest things alive, as the boy had been told, why did the old man seem so fond of them? It was no accident, he said, that the Lord Jesus spoke of his followers as sheep. The huge flock was kept in order by several dogs that ran along beside the pack, as if stalking, their heads and tails kept low. The sheepherder himself, with a blanket roll on his back, was so far away the boy could hardly see him. In his excitement, clutching the sheep for support, the old man was carried off with them. Did he know what he was doing? Off maybe one hundred yards he wheeled around and cupped his hands to his face, as if shouting something. The boy heard nothing but the bleating lambs. The old man did not move—a single buffeted figure, a snag in the river that flowed wide and fast—but tried to hold his footing against the current. The boy leaned out the window, as from a bridge railing, shouting, "Uncle Floyd!" as if that would help. The old man held his place by reaching forward to clutch at the wool streaming toward him. The boy continued to holler. The lambs continued to bleat. In spite of his age the boy had never questioned that his Uncle Floyd could stand up to anything—even God, if necessary. Mr. Yawkey, Mrs.

Leidy, the U.S. Postal Service, or a bus full of heathens could not budge him. Aunt Viola called this strength his stubborn will. Had it proved equal to everything but a flock of dumb sheep? The boy's fury was in part his dim awareness that he, too, was helpless. Against a force as mindless as this he could only rage. And then it was gone: he watched the tail end of the flock recede, leaving the old man high and dry in the desert, his back humped from the posture he had held while standing his ground. When the boy ran toward him, he waved him off. He needed no help from a pre-teen boy to get himself out of what he had got into. That was his point. He took his own good time coming back to the car, stooping here and there to pick up a few pebbles, but it was not lost on the boy that his hands were still trembling when he got to the car, his shirt tail stuck to his back. Some miles down the road the boy caught him sniffing the fingers of both hands, oily and smelly with the sheep wool. Did he like it? He made no complaint. The sheep stench had also rubbed off on his pants, so it was like having one in the cab with them. As strong as the smell the boy had the impression that his Uncle would have liked someone older to talk to, it not being every day that he was carried away by a flock of sheep. When they stopped for the night the hard-boiled egg his Uncle first peeled, then handed to him, had the taste of all that wool he had clutched. "You wear it off, boy," he said, catching his eye, "you don't wash it off."

3

THEY TOOK OFF BEFORE SUNRISE, WITH-
out breakfast; was that why, in a long, long day, he didn't see
them? Not even once. He did manage to see the Great Salt Lake,
and sent a small bag of it to Manuel Gonzales, care of his father,
the janitor at the school. In the afternoon heat, there being no
shade, they both took naps lying under the trailer. What it led
him to discover was that one tire had a wobbly spot that had
worn through the rubber. A new tire, but the wobble had worn
it out. The tire man at the station explained that the wobble was
not due to the wheel, but to the wag of the trailer, and that it
might not be an easy thing to correct. At fifteen miles an hour
it might not wag, but they would be a long time getting where
they were going. The other thing they could do would be to buy
a new tire every thousand miles.

While they were waiting for the tire to come out from Salt
Lake City the boy sat in the station observing the travelers. Most
of them took him for one of the natives, which he thought was
fine. He was seated on the fender, beside the water cans, when
Mr. Simpson, of Long Beach, spoke to him. He drove a Chrysler
sedan with windows so dark it was difficult for the boy to see
Mrs. Simpson, if that was who she was. She kept the windows
up because the air-conditioner was on. Mr. Simpson had stopped
to have his oil changed, which he liked to do regular as clockwork.

"What's that you got there, son?" he said to the boy, meaning the car.

"It's an antique," he replied, showing he was not born
yesterday.

"I can see that for myself," Mr. Simpson said. "You think
it ought to be pulling that trailer?"

"It's all right except for the wobble," the boy advised him.

Uncle Floyd had been resting inside the trailer, but hearing them talk he put his head out. "I'm Arthur Simpson, of Long Beach," Mr. Simpson said, "and I've been having a chat with your boy."

"He never talks with me," the old man replied. "What did he say?"

"He was saying you had a little trailer wobble. You know, that's hard on the tires."

"We're acquainted with that," the old man replied.

It was hard on the car, too, said Mr. Simpson, and he would like to make him an offer. He liked old cars. He liked to save them from the hazards of the open road. This fine old car, which still seemed to run, should be taken off the road before it was ruined. He would give Floyd Warner $1,500 for the car, just as it was, and pay the trucking costs to get it back to his home in Long Beach. He wanted to know what Floyd Warner thought of an offer like that? Uncle Floyd said he thought it a reasonable offer for a car that burned oil, and was now burning rubber, but over thirty-six years he'd got accustomed to it and saw no reason why he should give it up.

"Make it two grand," Mr. Simpson said, "which will buy you something a little bigger. How about a Buick? How about a late model Olds?"

If he could believe what he'd heard, Uncle Floyd said, all the late model cars weren't built to give service. The Maxwell had given him no trouble to speak of, outside of a little oil.

"Make it an outright sale of three thousand dollars!" said Mr. Simpson. If he didn't want another car he needn't buy it. He and the boy could take a train, or the plane.

"I was offered six thousand dollars," Uncle Floyd lied, "even back before I put the new rubber on it. With the new rubber on it I feel obligated to wear it out."

"My offer stands on the car alone," said Mr. Simpson. "I've no need of the antique that comes along with it."

Uncle Floyd said, "Mr. Simpson, what would you say is the yearly fall of snow in Long Beach?"

Mr. Simpson could see he was crazy. "If it snowed in Long

Beach, Mr. Warner, you think Mrs. Simpson and I would live there?"

"That I don't," said Uncle Floyd, and took the boy for a walk to take the kink out of their legs.

They were three days crossing Utah, part of it because the boy took the wrong turn on the freeway and they were forty miles north, almost to Ogden, before he realized what had happened. Floyd Warner did not realize it at all, because he was riding in the trailer, sleeping. There was a law against that, but if anything happened the boy would say the old man had been taken sick— and that was how he looked. The boy thought he might have caught something from the sheep, or overexerted himself. If he didn't feel too well, and he didn't, he would go without eating until he felt better. That was how he got the "poisons" out of his system. If everybody would do that, in his opinion, eighty percent of the doctors would go out of business, and the remaining twenty percent would take care of women's backaches. Every woman in the world, including Aunt Viola, had an ache in her back.

In the mountains east of Salt Lake it got cold at night, and the wind rocked the trailer. The only food the old man would touch was hot water, with canned milk in it. It's a shame to say so, but riding up front, alone, the boy was afraid. He stared up the road hoping he would see the smiling face of the girl, waving to him. There was room in the cab for two more people, now that he was alone. When he stopped to see how the old man was doing, he looked dead. He didn't snore. He just lay out on his back, with his mouth open. But he always had strength enough to shout at him to close the door. The cold mountain weather seemed to suit him, however, and he was up the next morning for an early breakfast. According to the map he spread out on the counter they now had less than seven hundred miles to go. But they were only going about two hundred miles a day. The town of Chapman, where Viola was buried, appeared to be near the middle of the Platte River, but the old man assured him that was a mistake on the map. The town set to the north. The river itself was a mile away. You could tell it by the willows that grew along it and the quicksand that would swallow up horses and wagons. Floyd Warner had sunk in it to his waist when he had been a boy.

Being anxious to get there, and feeling better, his Uncle Floyd took the wheel. They had a strong tailwind that wagged the trailer, but it pushed the car right along with it, saving gas. In country so empty everything looked small, the mile-long freight trains were like toys, and people along the highway crouched on their bags to get out of the wind. A fine powdery dust settled on the boy's lips, and mixed with his gum. He was just sitting there, not driving, when he saw the girl with her long hair blowing, looking half frozen, but with the big warm smile on her face.

"That's them!" he cried. The young man was crouched off the road, out of the wind. It might have been because the girl had hardly any clothes on, her arms clasped tight to keep her shawl from blowing, or it might have been just seeing her so often, always smiling, as if she knew them, but whatever it was the old man stopped the car. The girl didn't seem to believe it. Maybe it was hard to tell, they went by so slow, that they had actually stopped. She just stood there, watching, while the young man came running toward them, swinging his pack. He came up on the boy's side of the car, and put his head in the window he had run down for him. Was it the blackness of his beard that made his lips so red? Seeing him so close like that, and so clearly, the boy knew why he looked so familiar. He was the Lord Jesus of the jigsaw puzzle sent to him by Aunt Viola, with the eyes that were said to follow you wherever you went. But they didn't have to follow anybody who was trapped right there in the car.

"Far out, Dad," he said, looking them up and down. "Where you people headed?"

The Dad bit caught the old man off guard. "Up a ways," he came back. "Where you headed, boy?"

"Ohio," he replied. "Have a job in Ohio."

"Wouldn't it pay you to take a bus and get there?"

That caught the young man off *his* guard. "It's not much of a paying job," he said, "just a job."

"We've got no room in the cab, boy," His Uncle peered around as if he might find some. So did the young man.

"Far out!" he said. "Really far out."

"How's that, boy?"

"Far out, Dad," he replied, "a real gasser."

Did he mean the car, the old man at the wheel, or the whole kit and kaboodle? The boy did not speak this language but he understood it was complimentary. Before the old man replied the young one withdrew his head to make room for the girl, with her wide, white smile. Tangled strands of her hair crisscrossed her face. "Hi!" she said.

"Hi!" the boy echoed.

"We've been expecting you," she said. "*Honest!*"

The boy said, "We had to stop. We had to stop and buy tires. We wear tires out fast because of the trailer."

The old man said, "Shut up a bit, will you? That's more than he's talked since we left California."

"We're from California, too," she said.

"I was just telling your friend"—the old man did not look at him—"we've got no room here in the cab. For one maybe, not two."

The young man said, "We could ride in the trailer."

The boy sat silent, his eyes down the road. Was the old man going to say there was a law against it, after he had ridden in it himself?

"There's a law, you know," he said—the girl seemed to know that, her head wagged—"but I can't leave you out here, with night coming on. I suppose we can take you where you can find shelter."

"Find shelter?" said the young man. "That's a gas!"

"Boy," said the old man, "what are you saying?"

"He means that's just wonderful! He really does, don't you?"

The young man had walked back to get in the trailer. Uncle Floyd yelled at him, "Hey, hold on there!" and shut the motor off to go back and check on him. The door to the trailer had to be locked to make sure it wouldn't fly open. His Uncle unlocked it, then stepped inside to see what was lying around that somebody might swipe. There was quite a bit.

The young man said, "Why don't you let me drive, Dad, and you ride back here."

"God-a-mighty, boy, you got a nerve!"

"We can't run away with you in it, Dad," he said, "and the kid up front." When he said *kid,* the girl tilted her head to catch the glance of the boy: he lowered his eyes.

"Stanley's honest," said the girl, "I mean, he really is."

"His name's Stanley?" asked the old man. "What's yours?"

"Joy," she said. Her hair just naturally hung in strands over her face, and she had to keep parting it with her fingers. Her lips were so chapped the boy knew it must hurt her to smile.

"What I'm going to do," the old man said, "is let the boy ride back here with you. If that's all right with you."

"Is it all right with *you?*" the girl asked the boy.

"Oh, sure," he said.

"I know he'd welcome the chance," Uncle Floyd said, "to talk to somebody besides me." He stepped out of the trailer and let Stanley step in; he looked all around it, then sat down on the chair. The girl said, "Oh my, isn't it groovy?" and sat down on the bunk. The boy stood off to one side, in the kitchen. "Sit down, boy!" Uncle Floyd said, "or you'll fall down when she starts to wag." The boy sat down at the other end of the bunk from the girl.

"Now make sure you latch the door when I close it, you hear?" The boy knew how to do this, and got up to latch it. He sat himself down again, then waited forever for the car to start.

"Your old man a good driver?" Stanley asked.

"He's not my old man," the boy answered. "He's my next of kin."

Suddenly the dishes began to rattle, and the girl took a grip on the bunk post. "Fasten your seat belts," Stanley said, but she did not laugh. The boy had never ridden in the trailer when it was moving, and he didn't like it. He felt trapped. Stanley didn't seem to mind and took an orange from his pack and slowly peeled it, sniffing his fingers. He put the strips of peel in his jacket pocket,

202

and divided the orange in three equal sections, offering one to the boy, who shook his head.

Stanley said, "Take it, kid," so he took it. It was better to sit and eat than do nothing. The wagging of the trailer was not so bad, but the rattle of the dishes and pans was deafening. How had the old man been able to sleep in it? He had been sick. The cars coming toward them now had their lights on but it was not dark in the trailer. The windows tilted upward and the sky behind them was bright. After a while the girl used paper towels to try and stop the dishes from rattling, and before she had finished Stanley pulled her down on his lap. "No," she said, but he held her. He put his right hand up under her dress into the top of the purple stocking she was wearing, his other hand took a grip on her hair at the back of her neck. In order not to see what they were doing the boy rolled over on his side, facing the wall, his head thumping on the side when the trailer jerked. The smell of the exhaust was strong on the grades when the motor pounded, and they were hardly moving, but on the down side it would blow out and the boy could smell the peel of the orange. But he was not feeling so good by the time they stopped. The lights of the gas station flooded the trailer and the girl stood up to look at her face in the mirror, using a paper towel to wipe around her mouth. When Stanley opened the door the old man was right there, peering in.

"You people all right?"

"We're gassed," said Stanley. "You ever been high on pollution?"

He stepped out to stretch his legs, followed by the girl, then the boy. Some real Indians were standing by a Coke machine looking at them. A freight train was passing through, the crossing bell clanging, and the racket was so bad the boy could not hear a word the old man said to Stanley, or what Stanley said to him, although he could see their lips moving. The girl followed Stanley out to the highway, where she turned and waved to the boy, then the two of them walked along the edge of the road into the town. The main street was all lit up, an arrow flashing downward above a diner, where five or six double trailer trucks were parked at the front. Most of the noise had left town with the caboose, the lights blinking up the grade to the west, but the old man didn't ask him, then or later, how he liked riding in the trailer, nor did he have much to say about it himself. On the menu in the diner he read that they were in Rawlins, a Great Place to Live.

4

ALL NIGHT LONG TRAINS RATTLED THE
dishes as if the trailer itself was moving, and the boy often had
that impression when he peered through the window. The letters on the boxcars drifted one way, then another, but who was
moving? Puffs of wind rocked the trailer as if they were tilting
on a curve. How could Rawlins be a great place to live if nobody
slept?

The old man did not get up till the trailer was warm inside
from the sun. He asked the boy about the smell of the orange,
and the boy explained. Apropos of nothing special the old man
said that he'd been studying the map on the wall of the gas station, and there was a route, going south out of Rawlins, that
went like an arrow right down to the Rockies, which he thought
the boy, instead of just passing by, might like to see. Did he think
the boy was so dumb he didn't see through something like *that*?
Did he think they were going to duck them *that* way? On the
other hand he did want to see the Rockies, and he also didn't
want to seem ungrateful. With his own eyes, however, from the
window of the diner he could see what must be snow on the
Rockies, but his Uncle said he probably couldn't tell snow from
clouds. He did take the trouble to ask in the station and the attendant said, "Mister, you kidding?" There *was* snow in the
mountains, but he was mostly concerned with the rap he could
hear in the motor. It was louder when the engine idled than when
it pulled on a grade. He said a bearing like that might run for
weeks, or it might wear a hole in the motor by evening. He recommended four quarts of his heaviest oil, and no higher cruising
speed than twenty miles an hour. With one thing or another they
didn't leave Rawlins until almost noon, taking it very easy, so
they were going little more than twenty miles an hour when they

approached the turnoff east of town. Both Joy and Stanley were seated on the guardrail so you couldn't be sure they were hitch-hiking or not. The girl waved to the boy, who could see that Stanley was hunched over playing his harmonica. About fifty yards down the road the old man stopped. The girl was the first to reach the cab window, and put her big, friendly smile right into the boy's face. Just sitting there in the sun had made her smile whiter, and her nose red.

"Isn't it a groovy day!" she cried.

The boy said it sure was.

"You want to let them in the trailer?" the old man asked him, but he did not tell him to get in with them. They had to wait for the girl to go back and get Stanley since he hadn't even troubled to get up off the guardrail. He went on playing his mouth organ as if the boy wasn't there, holding the trailer door open, and the girl said, "You can lock it if you want to. We don't care." He didn't lock it, he just banged it shut and came back and got in the cab with his Uncle. After a while the old man said, "I don't like that smart-alecky boy." That was all. It was a groovy day just like the girl had said. They had a tail wind from the southwest so that they cruised along with no more pedal than if they were idling. In the midafternoon the old man got sleepy and they pulled over to the side to let the boy take the wheel. They both got out of the cab to stretch their legs. Even better than in Rawlins the boy could see the Rockies, like a row of white teeth on the horizon, with high thunderheads of cloud piling up to the east. On the flat bottom side of the clouds a veil of rain was falling, the purple color almost the same as the girl's hip-length stock-ings. He thought the view was something she shouldn't miss.

"Hey, you people," the old man said, and slapped his hand on the door of the trailer. Nothing happened. Had they fallen out or something worse? The old man slapped the door again, then pulled it open as if he thought they would step right out. The boy was the first to see the hairy ass of Stanley lying on the bunk, his pants wadded on the floor, and he first thought he was just sprawled there, taking a nap. Then he saw, behind, the white leg of the girl thrust straight up so that it touched the upper bunk, but the rest of her body, except for one brown arm, was sunken into the bunk that Stanley lay on top of, his face twisted toward them with a wide, grimacing smile. His Uncle Floyd had to put his head in to see clearly, and then it took him longer to figure it out. Didn't he believe it? The boy saw it all very clearly right off. Shrilly, the old man shouted, "What in the name of Jesuschrist are you doing?"

"Fucking," he replied, and went on with it.

The crash of the door broke the pane in the window, and most of it fell inside, like breaking glasses. The old man went around and got behind the wheel, forgetting that they had stopped to let the boy drive, then he had to lean over and run down the window to ask the boy if he meant to just stand there, or get back in the car. He got back in the car, and not far down the road that veil of purple rain he had seen near the mountains mostly proved to be hail that bounced like popcorn on the engine hood.

The boy got behind the wheel a little after midnight, and drove all night. When he stopped for gas he thought Joy and Stanley would get out and sneak off somewhere, the way *he* would, rather than wait for daylight and have to look the old man in the face. But they didn't eat, use the toilets, or anything else. The old man slept in the cab, and the boy saw him only when the car lights flashed through the windshield, his arms around the pillow that was tucked up under his chin. The strange thoughts he was having were largely due to the people riding in the trailer. He hadn't thought of it, as he did now, as a trailer with something in it. A cattle trailer. His father had one for horses and steers. They had been pulling such a trailer, with the boy's Hereford calves, the night of the accident near Palmdale, and he awakened to see the leaves burning in the pepper tree over the smoking wreck.

Just before sunrise he could see North Platte but he thought he would starve before they reached it. He parked the car across from an all-night diner, the long counter full of truck drivers. The boy sat in a booth, near the jukebox, while his Uncle went back to the men's room. The window reflected the counter, and the fluorescent lights, but if he put his face to it he could see out. The door to the trailer hung open, and the girl stood there, combing her hair. Stanley sat on the running board of the car, lacing his shoes. The boy was glad for them that it was still dark and they could sneak away without the old man seeing them. He watched them closely to see if Stanley tried to swipe something from the trailer. The girl closed the door, wrapping her shawl tight around her, but instead of walking off in the other direction they came across the parking lot toward the diner. Were they so hungry? How could they think about eating after something like that? They came in together, and knowing the boy was there somewhere the girl looked all around until she saw him, then she smiled and waved. Stanley gave her his pack, some change from his pocket, and she came toward the booth while he headed for the men's room.

"Whoever slammed the door broke the mirror," she said. "Now we've got no mirror." She sat across from him, smiling. "Your eyes are red. Didn't you sleep?"

"I drove almost all night."

"You should smile more," she said, and smiled at him. "It's being together that matters. Don't you know that?"

By being together did she mean what he thought she meant? Smiling, she tipped her head to one side, like a bird, and sang

"Come to-gethhhhhh-ur"

clapping her hands softly. Did it lead him to smile?

"That's better," she said, "don't be such a sourpuss."

Stanley came from the men's room and sat down beside her, his beard speckled with paper towel lint.

"Where's the old man?" Stanley asked him. "Throwing up?"

"He's not sick," he replied. "He's just pooped."

"He's sick, too, kid," said Stanley. "All the non-fuckers are sick. Maybe you're sick, too."

"He's not sick," said the girl. "He's just been driving all night."

The boy was not stupid, but he was still less than twelve and this sort of discussion made his eyes smart and water. He

208

could hardly see the old man coming down the aisle toward them, rubbing at his glasses with a piece of paper towel. Without his glasses he didn't see, until too late, who the boy was sitting there in the booth with. He did not sit down. There was towel lint on his glasses when he put them to his eyes.

"Breakfast is on us," said the girl, looking at Stanley. "It really is, isn't it?"

"Far out, Pop," he said. "All you can eat."

Uncle Floyd just stood there in the aisle, winding his watch.

"Sit down, Dad," said Stanley, but the boy knew he would not sit down, and dimly understood why. It was not because of Stanley, or because of the girl, or even whatever it was they had been doing, but that the three of them were now seated together in the booth. They were all young, and he was old. They were on the one side, and he was on the other. The boy knew that on the instant. He knew it better than anything else.

The old man said, "What do you people do? Besides, that is."

"Very funny," said Stanley. "A real gasser."

"He's a Weatherman," said Joy, "aren't you, darling?"

"You're a what?" said the old man. "Where'd you learn it?"

"I picked it up the hard way, Pop."

"I suppose they teach that in the schools now, don't they?"

"They teach everything in the schools now," said Stanley. Joy smiled.

"This what you plan to do in Ohio?" asked the old man.

"I've a big job waiting for me," said Stanley. "A real big job."

"I'm starved!" said Joy. "Isn't everybody starved?" She turned to look at the menu on the wall behind the counter. "I want a dozen eggs, a pound of bacon, a bowl of oatmeal, and prunes, and three orders of toast."

Uncle Floyd checked his watch against the clock on the wall, then he said, "You got fifteen minutes till the bus leaves," and walked off.

"Uncle Floyd," the boy cried, "you didn't eat!"

At the door he stopped as if to think that over. "I lost my appetite, boy," he said, and walked out the door.

"He don't like to watch us eat. He don't like to watch us—"

The girl placed her hand over Stanley's mouth, then yelped when he bit her finger. All the men at the counter turned to stare at them, the girl sucking her finger, the boy with his face pressed to the window where the reflection revealed it was just the three of them against all the rest.

BOOK THREE

1

IN NORTH PLATTE, NEBRASKA, AT SIX-
thirty in the morning, in a diner with people who urged him to
do it, the boy had the first hot cup of coffee in his life. He liked
it better with two extra spoonfuls of sugar, and more cream.
When they came out to the car they found the old man asleep
in the trailer, in the boy's upper bunk. He lay facing the wall,
and didn't move when the girl covered him with a blanket.

"Why don't I drive?" said Stanley, so he drove and the
boy sat on the seat near the window, the girl in the middle.
A hazy overcast sky kept the morning sun out of their eyes. The
girl sang songs the boy had never heard, clapping her hands. People who tried to sing without a piano or something embarrassed
him. You couldn't see it on the road, but all across Nebraska
the road was downgrade, and easy on the motor. Except for her
singing, he liked riding along with them in the cab. "I knew he
wasn't your old man," said Stanley. "You know how I knew?"
The boy didn't. "If he was your old man, and worth a shit, he
wouldn't have asked you to get back in the trailer with us. We
could have dumped you. We could have dumped the two of you.
He was more interested in what he thought we might swipe than
he was in you."

The girl said, "Oh, Stanley!"

"It's time he figured out who his real friends are," Stanley
said. "It's not some old fart."

"You like your Uncle?" the girl asked.

The boy pumped his head up and down. He pressed his lips
together to keep them from trembling.

"You're still a kid," said Stanley, "and that's kid stuff. When
you grow up you'll see it different.

The girl sang

> "You never give me your money
> You only give me your fun-ny pa-per
> And in the middle of negotiations
> You break down"

which made no sense at all. He wondered what they would all do when they reached Chapman, and how long it would be before someone picked them up. Would he miss them? Would he never see them again? On a sign in Grand Island he saw the name CHAPMAN and yelled, "That's it!" and pointed at it.

"Half an hour," said Stanley. "Just in time for lunch."

"Your people live there?" asked the girl.

"She died," said the boy.

"You don't know it," said Stanley, "but you're lucky. I had to fight 'em. All *you* got to do is let them die off."

A few miles out, the boy could see the elevator, with a grove of barren trees to the left of the tracks; along the highway there was nothing but a gas pump in front of a false-front store.

"Oh, look!" cried the girl. Off where she pointed, in the direction of the river, gravestones shimmered in the high noon light. Rows and rows of them. Did that explain the emptiness of the town?

"They're all buried there," the boy said firmly.

"Oh, it's lovely!" cried the girl. "I want to see it!"

A smooth dirt road led off the highway toward it, and far down at the road's end they could see the willows. "That's the river," he said with assurance, just as if he knew. A quarter mile or so south they turned to the left, then to the right at the cemetery entrance. Trees grew high around it on three sides, and the grass on the graves had recently been cut. An old hand pump with an enameled dipper attached to the nozzle stood near the gate.

Stanley said, "I'm thirsty, but not *that* thirsty."

"Can *anybody* be buried here?" she asked.

"You got to be dead first," said Stanley.

"Don't be stupid," she said, and left the car to run to the gate, where she kicked off her sandals, then she ran between the rows of stones flapping her arms like wings, her shawl trailing out behind her like the tail of a kite.

"Somebody see you they'll put you in the nut house!" yelled Stanley. He stopped at the pump and worked the handle. Nothing happened.

"First you've got to prime it," said the boy, who knew about pumps.

"What you mean, prime it?"

"You put water in at the top, then pump it."

"If you've got water, why bother?" said Stanley. He bothered, however, taking the canvas water bag from where it was squeezed between the hood and the fender. There was still water in it, and the boy poured it in at the top while Stanley pumped. The rising sound of the water was like that of an animal being sick. Stanley raised the dipper, took a taste of the water, and spit it out. The boy did it the way he had learned from his father, by cupping his hand over the nozzle then pumping the handle until the water had backed up in the pump. Bending over he drank what didn't splash in his face. The girl had stopped running up and down between the stones, and stood leaning on one, her foot turned up so she could look at its bottom.

"Ohhhhhhhhhh—" she cried.

"You have to put on an act!" Stanley yelled at her.

She did not reply. She let herself sag down on the mound of a grave so she could pull up her foot and look at it closely. Her long hair was the color of the grass that grew tall as hay at the edge of the clearing, or in yellow tufts close to the stones, out of reach of the mower. When she did not reply Stanley picked up her sandals and walked between the stones toward her, reading off the names. "Hofer, Seidel, Manson, Klinger, Cook—"

"What Seidel is that, boy?"

Stanley turned from the stones to see the old man, hatless, with his hands cupped to the pump nozzle. The boy was pumping. He thought it made a lot of noise for a cemetery pump.

"Lyle C.," replied Stanley, reading it off the stone.

"And which one of the Cooks?"

"Esther."

Both Stanley and the boy waited for him to say something. Uncle Floyd cupped the cold water to his face, then shook his head like a dog, his skin shining like leather. In the flat noon light he seemed to have no hair at all.

"Sewell, Wells, Horde, Youngblood—" Stanley chanted, then he stopped and shouted, "Where are the Jews, Dad? Don't they bury the Jews?"

"One of the Hordes married a Jew," he replied. "Forget his name." He thought a moment, added, "They went to live in Grand Island." He stooped for the hat he had dropped in the grass, then walked to stand in the road behind the trailer. The boy hadn't thought of him being bandy-legged, but he was. With a wet brown hand he shaded his eyes and looked across a field of corn stubble toward Chapman. With all of them here in the cemetery, what was there left to see? One grain elevator, two or three houses, a barn with a MAIL POUCH sign on the roof, all of it in what might have been a grove in the summer but the trees were now either dead or leafless. The old man in the road would see what he remembered, but the boy's squinting eyes saw only what was there. He didn't think it much.

"You hear that?" Stanley yelled to the girl. "One ran off with a Jew. Pretty lucky, right?"

The girl didn't seem to hear him. She crouched almost bent double, with one leg pulled up and the foot twisted around so she could look at its bottom.

"That's it, boy!" said the old man, and wagged his finger at a two-story house with a run-around porch. At the upper-floor windows the green shades were drawn. A lightning rod topped the roof. The grass had not been cut, as in the cemetery, and it grew hay-high along the sides of the house, giving the impression that the porch was sinking into the ground. The barn with the MAIL POUCH sign set so far behind it the boy wasn't sure that it went with the house. Uncle Floyd put his hat on his head, said, "She sat there for fifty years looking over here, and now she can lie here forever and look over there. If you feel a pair of eyes on you, boy, that's sure to be her grave."

This cemetery had looked small to the boy from the road,

but it contained a lot of stones. Some were too old and weathered for either of them to read, others were so new they looked like samples. The boy found Aunt Viola, not because he felt her eyes, but her stone was so new it looked plastic. There had not been room for her with the others, but Uncle Floyd pointed out she would have cooler summers with more shade. It embarrassed the boy to see the stone was so small. Viola Warner had lived twelve years less than a century and he felt that her stone should look like it. His impression was that she must be small and almost brand new. The sod cut to dig her grave had been put back on it like strips of carpet. The crumpled tinfoil had peeled away from the coffee can with its withered flowers. His Uncle Floyd stooped to take the flowers from the can, toss them aside, then sprinkle what was left of the water on the grave. It disappeared without a trace, and the boy was certain he could hear it dripping on the lid of the casket. Every time it rained it would drip and ping, drip and ping. . . .

"Your mother's here somewhere," the old man said, and wheeled slowly as if he might see her. The boy didn't want to. For *his* mother to be here was all a mistake. What was right for Aunt Viola, with her great faith, was not right at all for his cheerful, foolish mother, with her Bible on the shelf with the cookbooks, a file for the candy recipes she had collected. If his mother's eyes were actually on him they were checking his ears and neck. Uncle Floyd was not strong in that department, and for a week now the boy had drunk a lot of water, but not washed with it.

Cries like the shrieks of birds led him to turn and look toward the bearded Stanley, seated on a grave. The girl was sprawled face down across his lap. He had her skirt pulled up and her panties pulled down as if he intended to give her a spanking. Before she got it, sensibly, she shrieked. Her dirty bare feet wagged in the air, and when the boy got closer, and saw better, he noted the prickly red spots on her creamy white bottom. Stanley was using the point of his hunting knife to fish for the burrs. They were all over the soles of her feet as well, but first he had to get them out of her bottom. Several clusters of the sandburs were stuck like ornaments to her mini-skirt. The boy knew from experience that when you pulled a burr off, nine times out of ten you didn't get the prickly thorn. It had to be found before it was sat on, or it might disappear. Another thing he knew from personal experience was that you could *feel* them better than you could see them, but he was not in a position to be of much help.

Coming up behind him the old man shouted, "What in the God-a-mighty hell are you up to now?" Couldn't he see?

"She's got her ass full of burrs," replied Stanley. "What do you think?"

The girl made little yelps when he jabbed her, and her toes curled inward like fingers. The boy thought he might lend a hand with her feet, his eyes being very good for small splinters.

"Kid," said Stanley, without looking up. "You people got some mercurochrome or something?"

Yes, they did have something. The boy went off on the double, collecting burrs on his pants, to the tin of Band-Aids in the cabinet drawer. Stuck in with the Band-Aids was a bottle with skull and crossbones on the label. That meant it would sting, and anything that stung would do you good. He galloped back, passing the old man, who had stopped to pump his hat full of water, his face dipped into it for a drink.

"She can do her own goddam feet," said Stanley, making big red spots out of the small ones, "but first I've got to get them out of her ass." The boy hated to agree, but he could see the logic of it. Nor had the sting gone out of the treatment, from the way she yelled.

When Stanley had done what he could—he planned to do more later—he had to carry her piggyback to the trailer since she couldn't walk. The prickly itching was so bad she just sprawled out on her face and bawled.

"You're like a bunch of goddam kids!" Uncle Floyd yelled. "When the hell you expect to grow up?"

"Up where?" replied Stanley. He would have peered at the sky but the old man slammed the door in his face. They drove back into town on the road they had come out on, then along the highway to the Texaco pump in front of BELLE'S CAFÉ.

216

Three or four old cars and two pickup trucks were parked at the side. A short gray-haired man, not so old as Uncle Floyd, came to the screen. Before he could speak he had to swallow the food in his mouth. Turning away, he said, "Emma, look at this!"

A gray-haired woman in a blue polka dot apron, her hair in curlers under a hairnet, came to the screen. She held a wad of apron squeezed in one hand, but what she saw didn't impress her. The boy was sorry she couldn't see the California plate on the rear.

"You people want gas?" said the old man.

Inside the café a voice said, "What'd he want gas for? That burn gas?" Then he guffawed.

"I'm Floyd Warner," Uncle Floyd said. "Would you be the one to have the key to the house?"

"We got one key, Mr. Warner," she said. "There's a lawyer in Grand Island with the other."

"Guess one key is enough, if it works," said Uncle Floyd.

Inside the café the same man guffawed. "He bring that wreck back for the auction, too?"

Everyone in the café had stopped eating to listen. The boy could hear them laugh.

"You'll find it pretty much the way she left it, Mr. Warner. Anybody will tell you that's how she liked it. Is that your boy?"

"We're related."

The woman gathered up a wad of the apron and squeezed it. "You plan to have an auction soon?" she asked.

"Let him get settled first, will you, Emma?"

"She's got a regular store of things, Mr. Warner. If the kids didn't want it, they left it to Viola. There's a lot they didn't want."

"There's always people to buy what you don't need," said the man.

"I wouldn't have thought that," said Uncle Floyd. "Where are they?"

"They're not all dead, if that's what you're thinking. We get two, three hundred people for a good auction."

From the broken window in the door of the trailer comes a sound like somebody gagging.

217

"Kids," said the old man.

The woman nodded her head. "You're going to need more room." To the man she said, "Key is in the cash drawer," and he left the screen to get it. The boy could hear the bell ring when the door banged open, again when it shut. He came back with a long, lead-colored door key on a paper clip, with a tab attached. The woman took it, said, "It's to the rear door. I suppose you know that. Nobody's used the front door since Mr. Warner."

"Him and God," said the old man.

The woman wasn't sure she had heard that right. Before she replied there was a racket in the trailer that sounded like scuffling. The voice yelled, "Stanley *don't!* Stan-ley DON'T!" The old man ran down the window on the driver's side and slapped his hand like a board on the car door.

"Quiet, goddam it!" he hollered. "You kids hear me?"

It was quiet, inside and out.

The woman said, "How many you got?"

"Three in all."

"You're going to need more room than you'll find," said the woman, and gave the boy the key.

"We'll look around, ma'am," Uncle Floyd replied, but when he let out the clutch it was so loose they just sat there, giving off smoke. Then it caught, and they swung around to head west, the old man waving at the faces crowding the screen door. The trailer rocked so bad crossing the tracks the boy could hear the dishes in the cabinet rattle. "That hasn't changed much either," the old man said, but mostly to himself.

2

ON THE NORTH SIDE OF THE TRACKS BASE-
ments had been excavated for two stores that hadn't gone up.
One was full of cans and the bodies of wrecked cars. In the weeds
back from the road a cement sidewalk ran from one vacant corner to the next vacant corner, spears of grass shooting up between the slabs. Over one corner a street lamp, the once milk-
white globe marked with overlapping rings of mudballs that had
stuck for a while, then dropped off. Far to the back of a grove
of trees the boy could see a chain swing and two teeter-totters,
indicating it had once been a park. Aunt Viola's place, the house
with two floors and the green blinds drawn at the upper windows, sat in a clearing of knee-high grass with a windbreak of
evergreens at the back. Even above the ping of the motor he could
hear cawing crows. A driveway went between hedges back toward
the barn, but they had not been clipped for so long the room
between them was narrow as a cow path, the branches dragging
on the car and sweeping the trailer. Between the barn and the
house there was no visible path. The one people still used came
in from the side and led to a small white house across the street
where chickens scratched in the side yard. A lawn swing tilted
on its side in the front.

Uncle Floyd slapped his hand on the trailer. "We're stopping here. You people better move on."

"On what?" came the reply. "She can't sit or walk."

They could hear Joy moaning.

Uncle Floyd did not open the door to check. "Come along,
boy," he said, and they waded through the high yellow weeds
toward the house. The rear porch was screened in, but except
where it was patched, with new pieces of screen, the boy could
not see through it. The screen door had a thread spool for a knob,

219

a hole kicked in the screen at the bottom. Chickens had wandered in and out, leaving their feathers stuck to the wire. "How she ever managed without a man," the old man said, "I'll never know." He opened the screen and they stepped in on the porch. Along the house wall, blocking the window, were four or five golden oak iceboxes, of assorted sizes, topped off with milk pails, enamel water pails, and a high pile of straw hats. Back in the corner, their tops hooded with flour sacks, were machines that the boy had never seen. They appealed to him, however, because they had cranks, and were good for something.

Aloud the old man asked, "Now who'd want a cream separator?"

There were also bushel baskets of pots and pans, and a brass boiler, with its lid. The boy still had the brains he was born with and said, "If they're antiques, Uncle Floyd, they're worth money."

"Quiet, boy," he replied, and unlocked the house door. They were in the kitchen, a room flooded with light from the window without curtains or a blind. Along one wall sat the stove, a kitchen range with the wire handle thrust up from one of the stove plates. Otherwise the top was clear of everything but burned matches. Someone had used the stove to scratch matches on it, and nothing else. The scratches made a crisscross hatching on the plates that turned from soot color to sulphur. All of the matches had burned down and died before the end. Before he said a word the old man's head began to pump, priming up his curses.

"Jesus H. Christ God-a-mighty!" he swore, and used the plate lifter to bang on the stove. The boy listened to him curse and saw what else there was to see. A round coal oil stove, with a wire handle, was topped by a large enamel teakettle, with oil-smoked sides. On the table that sat against the wall in the corner dishes and glasses were stacked to the boy's shoulders. He had never seen so many, even in a store, or glasses of so many colors. At the back, in a pile, were lampshades, and on the top of the shades a woman's hat with feathers. When the old man was quiet the boy could hear mice running in the walls. Besides that there were chairs, stacked with their legs up, and two kitchen cabinets, back to back, so you could use either one or the other, two or three ironing boards, and a carton full of iron handles, irons, and iron wax.

The door out of the kitchen was on a swinging hinge. The old man gave it a push and said, "That's new. When did she do that?" He pushed it inward to where it caught on a rug. The light through this door seemed to be all there was in the room behind it. The shade drawn at the window reflected the light back onto the bed, one end of it stacked with pillows. An afghan spread was turned back on wrinkled sheets. Aloud, as if he expected an answer, the old man asked, "Does it have to be so goddam dark?"

The boy said, "Aren't there any lights?" and looked for the switch on the wall. There was no switch, but on the table at the beside stood a lamp, with a green shade, a wick curled in the bowl of clear oil. Uncle Floyd kicked the door, opening it wider, then stomped in to throw up the blind at the window opening out on the porch. That did little good because it was blocked by the iceboxes. The room smelled of burned lamp wick, coal oil, and the odor the boy associated with his mother's clothes closet, at once sweet and sour. On the floor was a saucer of soured milk, the edges nibbled by mice. A shoebox full of postcard pictures of cats, kittens, and puppies, along with postcards and letters, sat on the shelf below the lamp. The boy recognized the last letter, with the Smokey the Bear stamp, as his own. On the table at the foot of the bed, where they could be reached through the iron frame, soiled towels and dishcloths were piled in a washbowl, held down by a plate dirty with food smears. At the side a comb was stuck into the bristles of a brush with a silver back, and a small oval picture in a frame stamped with colored flowers. The picture showed a bearded man, seated erect on a chair, with a child on his knee holding a bird cage. The boy moved closer to see if the cage held a bird, but it is empty and the door is open. A woman stands behind him, one white hand resting on his shoulder, her hair parted and gathered in a bun at the neck. The white lace at her front is like the wings of a butterfly. The man's face is clear, his gaze directly forward, but the woman's eyes are so pale they look filmed. The boy thinks she looks frail and very young.

"Hand me that, boy," Uncle Floyd said, and turned so that the light fell on the picture. "That's him. That's the old bastard."

"Did the cage have a bird?" the boy asked.

"If it did, it's the only thing that ever got away!" Then he added, "That's either Viola or me, I don't know which."

The boy's gaze has moved to a case on the bureau behind him. It has a faded velvet lining, the color of dust, and in the clip of the lid there is the ivory frame of a mirror without glass. When he touches the lid the frame rattles. In the bottom of the case, in the velvet pockets where there had once been other objects, he sees three large bullets with dull brass casings and the ivory handle of a shaving brush. All but a whisk of the bristles are worn away.

This had once been the dining room, and the round oak table is now backed into the corner behind the door. The top of it is littered with pillboxes, medicine bottles (some of them with the skull and crossbones on the label), a lamp with a broken chimney, the wick in an empty bowl, glass salt and pepper shakers, cases for glasses, a cigar box without a lid, full of pins and bone hairpins, a cigar box with the lid made into a pin cushion, stuck full of threaded needles, hatpins, and a lady's cameo. There is a ball of tinfoil, a pocket watch with a chain, a flashlight, a pocket knife with a broken bone handle, two bed casters, a shaving strop, and a shoebox lid full of black and red checkers. There is more, but it would take all day to sort it out. What would an old lady want with a man's long-handled razor, a box of shotgun shells? He turns away to see the old man trying to pry open the folding doors. One is stuck. He curses it, kicking at it with his boot heel. One of the doors slides back so they can squeeze through into the parlor. A big coke burner with smoked glassine windows sits on a fireboard with the floral pattern worn away at the front and two sides. The fender of the stove shines like a bumper where somebody recently has sat on it. The nickel-plated ornament on the top has been pushed to one side to expose the fire lid, which is covered with half-burned matches like the kitchen range.

"Who in the goddam hell did that!" Uncle Floyd cried. He swept the burned matches off the top with his hand, then looked at the smear of soot and dust on the heel. "Who the hell do they take me for!" he cried, and the boy wonders what he means by that. There is a space around the stove, as if it might get hot, then the room is jammed with bureaus, chairs, and sideboards. The boy sees his reflection in a half a dozen mirrors. At the large front window there are glass curtains that he sees like webs on the drawn yellow blind. In a corner near the door, where light falls on it, a three-legged table is covered with framed pictures. Maybe a dozen of them, with the larger ones at the back. Above it, as if through a window, a wild-eyed white horse with a flowing mane has been frightened by two yellow bolts of lightning, and rushes forward as if to leap into the room. The door itself has a center of beveled glass, the oval rim frosted to show off the engraving, and there are three panes of red, blue, and yellow church glass at the top. Perhaps they explain the curious color of the light in the room. Most of that color can be seen on the stairs where the red glows as if the carpet were burning, and the boy can see motes of dust sparkling in each beam of light.

"Wait here, boy," the old man said, and as he walked up the stairs the dust rose in a cloud at his feet. The boy hears his feet stomp the ceiling above him, then go from room to room, the doors creaking. In one room he stands: the silence of the house is like a tomb. The boy would leave, but his limbs will not move. He is able to gaze, with parted lips, at the two yellowed pages of sheet music on the rack of the black upright piano. A hymn book. The title of the hymn is "Crossing the Bar." One thing the boy has never learned is how to read music, and he wonders how this hymn sounds. His Aunt Viola loved music. He understood that she played as long as she could. A cushion had been placed on the piano bench, the lid of which would not quite close on the music. There were also pictures on top of the piano, but all he could see were the reflections of the window, where a fly buzzed behind the yellow blind. When the fly stopped buzzing he cried, "Uncle Floyd!"

No answer.

Fearing to look behind him, he went forward yelling, "Uncle Floyd! Uncle Floyd!" as he went up the stairs. At the top of the stairs the door ahead of him stood open, jammed with boxes and barrels like an attic. He could see little more than their outline against the dim light. The closed door he ignored, and came back to the front where the corner room looked empty. No rug on the floor, no clutter of objects, just a rocker facing the open window where the blind was half raised. Floyd Warner sat there, or rather he sagged there, his hands hanging limply between his knees, his head tilted as if to catch small sounds from the yard. Below the window the knee-high grass was like a field of grain. Beyond it the road they had just come down, leading across the tracks to the highway, and farther beyond, framed in the trees, the gleaming stones of the cemetery, the air smoking with the sprinklers that someone had turned on. The boy saw it plainly enough, but he doubted that the old man could see it. Had he fallen asleep? He was accustomed to an afternoon nap.

"Uncle Floyd," the boy said, but remained standing in the door. The green blind softened the light, and with nothing in the room to block it or absorb it the boy felt its presence. Within it, captive, he saw the figure seated on the narrow-backed armless rocker, both the seat and the back covered with pads made of patchwork quilting. Two dozen patches on the back side alone, in all shapes, colors, and materials. Everything left over had been put into it, as into this house. The old man who sat there did not impress the boy as his own great-uncle, Floyd Warner, but another object preserved from the past. Perhaps this corner room had been reserved for objects of that sort. Surely Aunt Viola had had something in mind when she cleared this room of all but the rocker, and came here, when she was able, to sit by herself. The boy really knew nothing about such matters and perhaps that proved to his advantage. He brought so little to what he saw, he saw what was there. This old man before him was not sleeping, since he sat in too strange a manner, his head up like a bird, rather than lolling on his front. "Uncle Floyd," he repeated, then he strained to control his terror as his legs ran on the stairs. He banged into things, he fell once, but he had only three doors to pass through and three rooms to cross. Out on the screened-in porch he shrieked, "Stanley! Stanley!" and saw that he was seated

224

at the door to the trailer, examining the feet of the girl who lay on its floor. "Stanley!" he yelled, waving to him, and the young man stood up, taking the time to put the tail of his shirt into his pants, before he came at an easy lope toward the house.

"Uncle Floyd!" the boy cried. "He don't answer!"

"Maybe he's in the can."

"He's *not* in the can. There isn't any can. He's in a room upstairs. He doesn't answer."

"Cool it, kid. Maybe he just wants to be alone."

"He's sick, too.'

"How you know he's sick?"

"He looks sick."

He let Stanley go ahead of him, one room then another, waiting while Stanley peered around, his head shaking, pronouncing the words "Far out, man," as they went up the stairs. The old man no longer sat there, perched like a bird, but had slouched to one side with the curled fingers of his right hand touching the floor. Stanley removed his hat to look at his face. "Hey, Pop," he said, "how you feel?"

What a question to ask a man who had died, the boy thought. Surely he could not be alive, and look as he did. Gray like putty, his jaw slack, but gleaming on his forehead was a film of moisture. Did the dead perspire like that? No, they did not. He was not dead, and when Stanley fanned his face with the hat his eyes opened. "Let's get you out in the air, Pop," Stanley said. "Air in here make anybody sick," then he started to lift him, but the old man shook him off.

"Boy," he said, "where you at?"

"Here, Uncle Floyd," he replied, and moved to where the old man could see him. He took a grip on the boy's arm, at the wrist—to take his hand would imply he was helpless—and pulled himself up. They stood there a moment while he got his bearings, his hand moving to the boy's shoulder.

"You going to stand here?" he said. The boy walked a half step ahead of him, slowly, down the stairs. He seemed to get a bit stronger crossing the kitchen, and as they stepped out on the porch he released the boy's shoulder, opened the screen himself.

225

"How you feel, Dad?" said Stanley. "You feel better?"

"I had a queasy spell," the old man said, breathing the fresh air, and went slowly ahead of them through the weeds toward the trailer. The girl was about to sit now, in the door of the trailer, with her right foot curled up so she could pick at its bottom. Her arch was so flat her foot was prickled all over, like a pin cushion.

"You poor darling," she said to Uncle Floyd. "Don't you feel good?"

"I feel as good as might be expected," he replied, "but I'm going to take a nap." She moved from the door to let him into the trailer, sprawl out on the bunk. His left leg hung down to the floor, and she leaned forward to slip the boot off. "Leave me alone!" he yelled.

"If the old fart wants to be left alone, leave him alone," said Stanley.

The boy said, "He'll be all right when he's rested."

"I'll either be all right or be dead."

"You mind we go sit on the porch?" Stanley asked the boy.

No, he didn't mind. Stanley crouched in the yard as if he meant to spring, and signaled to the girl to straddle his back, which she did. As they went off through the weeds she sang

> "I never give you my number
> I only give you my situation
> And in the middle of investigation
> I break down."

"What is she saying?" the old man asked.

"It's a song," said the boy. "She's singing."

When the boy glanced in to see if that answer satisfied him his eyes were closed, and he looked asleep. The mournful sound he heard was the keening of the doves somewhere in the barn.

226

3

IN THE LATE AFTERNOON THE BOY SAT
at the door of the barn's loft. Like the house, it was crammed
with all sorts of objects, some of it junk. A pile of horse collars,
horse and buggy harness hung along the walls like decorations,
corn shellers and grinders, a foot-treadle grindstone on which
he sharpened the knife in his pocket, kegs of nails, a barrel of
tar, tied-up bundles of asphalt shingles, cans of paint, brushes
glued to the bottom of cans where the turpentine had evaporated,
numberless shovels, hoes, and pitchforks, two unused rubber-
tired wheels of a buggy, fly nets for the horses, and numerous
machines supplied with cranks. They would all do something if
cranked, but few would crank. In a box of articles he considered
swiping the wires and loose parts mystified him, all related to
a project he could no longer grasp. An oatmeal carton, like the
one in the trailer, wound a third of its length with thin, covered
wire, to which other wires, and strange articles, were joined. In
the bottom of this carton he found rocks that he understood to
be crystals, gleaming like mica, but to what use had they been
put? This collection he considered to be so valueless it would never
be missed. He put it to one side, along with a doorbell that needed
only a battery or something to ring it, and sat himself in the loft
door, facing the south. He had the same view as the window at
the front of the house, but it was wider and he saw more. A train
that had passed left a veil of smoke over the town. He understood
that a person might actually live here, as well as die. All her long
life his Aunt Viola, troubled with her health but supported by
her faith, had lived on here while the others died and left to her
those things they valued. These things, many of them useless,
had survived. Into his pocket the boy had slipped a coin found
in the pocket of a coat, draped on a doornail, that had survived

227

all the people who had spent or saved it since 1879. The meaning of this escaped him in a manner he found satisfying. Already he was old enough to gaze in wonder at life.

While he sat there he watched the old man ease himself out of the trailer and stretch his limbs. His hindquarters were cramped like an old dog's. Still bent over, his gait uncertain in the soft loam of the yard, he moved away from the trailer toward the corral adjoining the barn. As he walked his fingers fumbled at the buttons of his fly. The gate stood ajar, tilting inward, with a bucket upside down on one of the posts, the bottom of which he gave a slap as he passed. Patches of corn and grain, planted by cowpies, sprouted in the corral like a garden, the ground sloping away from the barn to the marshy tangle that drained the farm. The outside rail of the fence was almost lost in the weeds. All this long walk he had never stopped fumbling at the buttons of his fly, and they were open to his satisfaction by the time he reached the partial shade of a tree branch. His knees flexed, he pee'd down a stalk of stunted corn. When Uncle Floyd had been no older than the boy who now watched him from the barn loft window, he had watched another man pee in this manner, or was it something he had thought of himself, after milking the cows in the evening, or on his way to the barn after breakfast? A good pee in the open: not in the barn or the smelly, breath-catching stench of the privy. Was this one of the few things in the present that connected him to the past? He stood there, as a man will, with his gaze fastened on something or nothing, enjoying the great relief and pleasure it had been to pee. But he had also seen something. Almost at his feet, a step or two to the left; he bent his back, not his legs, to peer at it closer. Something on the ground. From where he sat the boy could not make it out. Curious, he called, "What you see, Uncle Floyd?" which naturally gave the old man a start.

"Where the hell you at?" he answered, peering around.

"Up here," called the boy, and waved, but he had turned back to what he had found. The boy used the ladder to come down from the loft, and the stable door to get into the corral. When he came up and stood beside the old man he saw nothing on the ground of interest. That was how well it was all one piece of earth.

"A horseshoe?" he asked.

"An ox shoe, boy."

Whether or not it was an ox shoe (don't believe everything you hear, the old man had told him), this shoe was elevated above the level of the corral on a pedestal that was shoe shaped. The boy would have said the pedestal had been made for this particular shoe. It was an inch or so above the ground on the barn side, but at least two inches or more on the slope side. Two shoe nails firmly attached it to the pedestal.

"What pushed it up there?" the boy asked.

"Nothing pushed it up there," he replied. "It's the earth that washed away from it. It's just where it always was. It's the earth that fell away."

The boy reflected on that for a moment. "You going to leave it?"

"What would we do with an ox shoe, boy?"

The boy was thinking they might nail it to the trailer for luck. They could use some luck. The old man said, "You like them, eh?"

Like who? The boy guessed his meaning only because he had turned to look toward the house. Now that the light had dimmed the flaking paint above the screened-in porch appeared to glow. The blue ball on the lightning rod blazed like a cold planet in orbit. But what held his eye was the warm glow behind the yellow blind at the window.

"You hear me, boy?" the old man asked.

Did he *like* them? He hardly knew. What he wondered was, did it matter?

"I'm glad it's you, boy," he said, "and not me. It goes against my nature, more than it does yours."

That took the boy by surprise. He had assumed it was the same nature they had, somewhat young in himself, somewhat old in his Uncle. How was he to know what this other nature might be?

"They've lit a lamp," the boy said, pointing toward the house, and the idea pleased him. It was the dark that made the house so spooky.

"They've what?"

"Lit a lamp," he repeated, and the old man strained to see it, squinting his eyes. "Them f—king goddam kids!" he swore, and went off toward the house. The boy couldn't see what was so bad about lighting a lamp. He tagged along behind the old man's trail through the weeds and saw him bang the screen door as he entered, then come back to grab the mop handle sticking out of a pail. As he moved closer he could hear the girl laughing; that was what he heard. Then he heard them talking, more than shouting, and two or three whacks like slapping a pillow. He crossed the screened-in porch into the kitchen, where the door to the room with the bed was half closed. Uncle Floyd stood behind it, the handle of the mop thumped it as he talked. The open half of the door framed the bureau mirror at the foot of Aunt Viola's bed, reflecting the glass shade and the smoking chimney of her lamp. The wick was up too high, causing it to smoke, and the boy could smell it on the draft through the door, along with the sweet scent he knew to be grass. The lamp glow was so bright he didn't at first see Stanley and the girl in the shadows to the side. They were sitting up, propped by pillows, side by side, in Aunt Viola's bed. Both of them were naked, but Stanley didn't look it with all that hair. His arms were folded, and he held the cigarette so that the heat of the lamp sucked the smoke under the shade, then out at the top. Of the girl, he sees mostly the top of her head, as she is bent over to peer at the bottom of her foot, her long yellow hair hanging around her like a screen.

"We don't dig it dark, Pop," said Stanley. "We're scared shitless of the dark, aren't we, baby?"

Maybe she lifted her head to speak to Stanley, her fingers combing her hair from her lips, but in the mirror she faces she sees the boy. "Hi, darling!" she said, and gave him a big smile. From where he stood the boy could not see the old man, but he could hear his wheezy, labored breathing: he saw the shadow of the mop head rise on the wall, then come down with a loud

230

whack on the bed quilt. The girl began to laugh, and Stanley pulled up the quilt to cover them both. The boy could see they were hugging each other, laughing, when the head of the mop whacked them. All that it did was fill the air with a cloud of dust.

"You-you-you-you-YOU—" the old man yelled, building up with each *you* the boy's expectations, but all he ended up saying was "Blow out that lamp!" Whatever it was, he didn't want to see it. The two under the covers went on laughing. Did the old man do it? All of a sudden the room went dark. It went sooty black, with no more noise than the sound of clothes falling from a hanger. Muffled in the darkness the two of them went on giggling like kids.

"Uncle Floyd!" the boy yelled, but he was too scared to push the door wide open. The air smelled of what the two of them had been smoking, but on the draft he caught the whiff of something stronger burning. In the cave of darkness behind the bed, as if a match was struck, fire flickered. "Uncle Floyd!" he shrieked, "something's burrrr-ning!"

"I hope it's the two of them in hell. Serves 'em right!"

As if he had poured kerosene on it, the fire leaped up. The boy did not cry out: maybe the crackle of the flames recalled a terror better forgotten. He turned and ran, kicking a pail someone had half filled with water, then he was out on the porch, through the screen door with a thrust that almost unhinged it, and like a rabbit he cut through the weeds as if the fur on his back was burning. He passed the car and the trailer, then he entered the clearing of short grass approaching the barn, where he heard, like a timber splitting, the loud bang of the screen to the porch. That was the way the old man would slam the door to the trailer if the boy left it open. He did not look back, fearing he would see him, in his gleaming yellow hard hat, coming toward him. In the field on the left a startled cow lifted her head to watch him pass. On he went to where a wide ditch fenced the pasture, and he sank into it like feathers, the soft matted grass sweet smelling as hay. Insects droned above him, others crawled beneath him, and far behind him the confused sounds of commotion. Horns tooted. Near, then far, several dogs bayed. When he pushed himself up, eyes level with the ditch rim, the sky behind the barn was like one end of a rainbow. Black and white smoke billowed, and in the roiling cloud he saw tongues of flame like bolts of lightning. Stanley would like it. He would have liked a better view of it all himself. The tolling of a church bell made him think of Aunt Viola, and that her eyes would be on him right at this moment. What would she think? At least she would know he hadn't started the fire. The dying crackle of it now came to him faintly, and once he imagined he felt its heat. Anyone approaching would have seen the last of the glow in his eyes. Some of the trees along the driveway had taken fire and sent up showers of sparks, like fireworks. It was very much like Uncle Stambaugh's yarns about the Fourth of July. Then it all died away, like a sunset, and he was suddenly cold. A heaviness that was in neither his arms nor his legs, but like something he had swallowed, persuaded him to just lie there. Nobody came for him. Nobody hooted calling his name. He had once felt that he would surely die to be alone like that in the night and forgotten. But nothing happened. He felt nothing but the ants inside of his clothes. He might have lain there all night, just to show he could do it, if it hadn't been for the invisible cows, their movements like that of approaching monsters in a horror movie.

From the corner of the barn he could see the brick chimney tilted like a ladder toward the wall that was missing. A fire still smoldered in the kitchen range and smoke came out of one length of the stovepipe, like a truck exhaust. Just a yard or two away— that was how it looked—the coke burner in the parlor glowed like a piece of charcoal. He thought it all looked small, as if the great heat had caused it to shrink. All around what was left the weeds had burned away but still smoked and flickered at the outer edges. There was very little rubble. The cream separators, once on the porch, had toppled in a pile like so many milk cans, but the blackened iron frame of the bed, where the two of them had lain, looked ready for making. The strong odor he smelled was that of hot metal and smoldering weeds.

Until he walked toward the fire, and had to move around

the trailer, he hadn't noticed that the car was missing. The weeds that had swept the underside of the car were shiny with grease. Without the car to support it, the trailer tilted, and the coupling bolt was sunk into the yard as if someone had banged it with a hammer. The girl sat in the tilted trailer doorway, combing her hair. Behind her Stanley sprawled out on the lower bunk, smoking. Neither was surprised to see him.

"Where you been?" asked Stanley. "You missed a good fire."

He said, "Where's Uncle Floyd?" and peered around as if he might see him. Beyond the glow of the ashes, like dimmed car lights, were the faces of the people who had gathered to watch. They sat in their cars, or stood back under the trees, their eyes glowing like gems. The boy guessed that they had waited for the fire to cool in order to see what there was, if anything, behind it. None of them spoke or moved. They had probably expected to see more than they did.

Stanley said, "Too bad you missed it, man. It was a really good fire."

"Pay no attention to him," she said.

"You should ask *her* about fires," said Stanley. "She really digs fires."

"Where did he go?" the boy asked.

"Who knows?" replied Stanley. "Maybe up in smoke."

"Pay no attention to him," the girl repeated. Her hair, fanned out over her shoulders, appeared to have real lightning bugs trapped in it.

Stanley said, "He didn't care if we burned up or not. He took off without looking back. I watched him. You can see the way he took off in the way the trailer dropped."

She said, "It broke three cups and the percolator top."

"That was already broke."

"Not in *pieces*. There'll be no more *perk*-olator coffee."

Stanley asked, "Where you suppose he took off to?" The boy had no idea. Now that Aunt Viola had left them, what other place was there? "How about that place across the tracks?" said Stanley. "Maybe he wants to bury that car there."

"Pay no attention to him."

"What you plan to do?" said Stanley. "You can't stay here, man. What else is there to burn?"

"He's doing what we're doing," she said, "aren't you?"

Why didn't he ask what they were doing? Through the film forming on his eyes he seemed to see Stanley through rain-weighted branches.

"Don't look at me, kid. It's not my idea."

"Stop calling him *kid*," she said. "He's not a kid anymore, are you?"

Stanley got up from the bunk and spread his legs to step over the girl into the yard. At the edge of the smoking grass he unbuttoned his pants, pee'd on some of it. "What a tool!" he said. "First you start a fire with it, then you put it out." He turned back to the girl. "Which is sorer, your ass or your feet?"

"I'd rather sit," she replied.

"You two sit," he said, "while I walk over and get us some food." He walked around the smoking rubble where the house had been and they could see him outlined against the firelit faces. Far back on the highway a neon sign flashed the word EAT.

"He just took off?" the boy asked.

The girl put up her hands like a magician who had just dissolved something into the air. The idea pleased her. She seemed to see it drifting away, like smoke.

"Why'd he leave the trailer?"

"For us, silly. Besides, where he's going, maybe he won't need it."

She raised her eyes from him to look at the sky behind the barn. Part of it was still glowing with the sunset, and the boy could see the branches of the trees against it. Two of the trees were so full of birds they looked like leaves. The racket they made was like the grackles back in Rubio. Had they gathered like the people to watch the fire?

"You know about birds?" she asked.

"What about them?"

"You know what *old* birds do when their time has come?"

No, he didn't. Was there anything of interest he actually knew?

234

"Well, when they are old, and their time has come, they just go off alone in the woods and die. That's why you never see any old dead birds, you realize that? There's just millions of birds and they have to die, sometime, but you never see a one of them unless they're hurt."

It amazed the boy to realize the truth of that, and shamed him to think that he hadn't known it.

"It's nature's way," she said, "and people should live according to nature. Some people really do." She stood up, suddenly. "You hear that?"

All he heard was the cooling crackle of the fire, like a piece of crumpled paper unfolding. Her eyes remained on the orange glow behind the barn. "That's the really big fire. You hear it?"

He stands before her, listening. Raising her long arms skywards she moans, "OOOOOooooooo MMMMmmmmmmmmmm," then again, "OOOOOooooooo MMMMMMmmmmmmmm!" He thinks it must be an animal call of some kind, or at least for birds. "Fire transforms," she pronounced. "You hear it in the fire."

He stands feeling the warmth of the one they had had on his back. She has tilted her head back to gaze at the sky, where the light on a plane's wing blinks like a planet. It reminds him of his Aunt Viola, and her faith. Already she is up there, somewhere, peering down. Soon now his Uncle Floyd would be up there, too, in spite of his mocking, stubborn will. The boy is relieved to feel that his eyes will be closed, not fastened on *him*. A man like his Uncle Floyd would not have the time for something trifling like that.

"The stars are balls of fire, too," she said, but gazing upward for so long has made her dizzy. The hand she had raised to shade her eyes she lowers to grip the boy's shoulder, ease the weight on her feet. With the other she seems to point to the corral, where the gate stands ajar. The boy feels a pleasurable chill of terror that someone stands there, beckoning to him. Would it be the old man, personally, or his ghost? "Look here, boy," it says, real as life, and points to the ox shoe that the earth has moved away from. There it sits, firmly nailed to its pedestal. He is glad to be reminded of the ox shoe, and plans to go and look for it in the light of the morning. It is in light like that that things are most easily found. In spite of all the eyes on him, and all the faith for him, he's going to need all the luck he can get. *They* are, that is. His Uncle would have been the first to tell them that. He is distracted by the girl's tightening grip on his shoulder in order to steady herself, stand on one leg, and by the glow from the fire examine the sole of her blackened foot.

"Fire purifies," she said, and gave him her big, warm, friendly smile.

A LIFE

For Winona Osborn 1888–1973

1

FROM THE HIGHWAY TO THE EAST,
where his car is parked to the left of a mailbox propped in a milk
can, we can see him standing in the knee-high grass at the edge
of a field of grain stubble. He stoops, one hand at the small of
his back, in the manner of old men who find it painful. A grove
of cottonwood trees, blighted or drought-killed, rises about him
like masts with half-furled sails. The old man was born in this
country, and it might be misleading to say that he had left it.
If asked if he could use a pair of shoes, he would reply, I have
a pair of shoes. We see them on his feet. They are high-top shoes,
with box toes, the metal hooks and eyes hard on the laces. He
wears out more laces than anything else. Neither shoes nor laces
are what they used to be, and neither are his feet. The car we
see back on the highway is a Maxwell coupe, acquired in exchange for a Dodge touring in 1928. He could use a better car,
and will think about buying one when this one wears out. The
grass he stands in is green compared to the yellow grain stubble,
and might be classed as weeds by the men who farm the land.
It's not a grass they mow, or a grain they harvest, so it must be
weeds. This man is old enough to know better and remember
when it was grass from horizon to horizon. His father had taken
grass, as he did most things, religiously. Before the land had been
plowed, or some would say broken, he had distinguished a dozen
or more varieties of land cover, the nameless grasses that kept
the soil from washing and blowing away. One thing he showed
his son was how the shorter the grass, the longer the roots. Reluctant to heed or learn anything from his father, the boy had learned
that. He knew that the tall bluestem slashed his legs like sabers,
and made cuts between his toes that itched like crazy. He liked
the sour grass from the way it tasted and the blue grama from

239

the way it sounded, along with buffalo grass, big and little bluestem, and the tall, sweet-stemmed switch grass, as good as its name. Wheat, too, was grass, along with barley, oats, and rye, and on the same authority the tall corn was grass, but the pleasure of the grassland was diminished if everything growing on it proved to be grass, except for the trees. It pained the old man, as a boy, to watch the grazing cattle jerk their heads upward to tear loose a patch of cord grass, a stem of which he holds, the head wagging, between his teeth. In his mind, thanks to his father, the word of God is tangled in the names of grasses, and the mention of one evokes the other. Being as old as he is, he thinks of that and the paleness of the grass on the grave of his sister, green as winter wheat. Dead now three weeks, the last of the family, excepting himself. "How is my darling old scoffer?" she would ask him. For weeks now nobody has asked him. It occurs to him that from now on nobody ever will.

His name is Warner, but people refer to him as "the old man." "You mean the old man with the kid?" they would say, although the boy was only his kin by marriage. It occurs to him that from now on he would not hear that, either. The boy had taken off with a pair of hippies picked up on the road. Warner had been born and raised in this country, but as soon as he was raised he had left it. He had not liked it much then; he did not like it now. Even as a boy he had learned to stand with his back to the wind. Just ten days ago he had left California to come back here and settle the affairs of his sister, who had recently died. Now they were settled, his sister was buried, and what she couldn't take with her had gone up in smoke. As for the boy, Warner would check to see if there were people locally on the mother's side of his family—Holtorfer by name, once said to be from Archer. Warner would tell them what had happened, and where, if they wanted him, they might find him. Would the boy ever believe that Warner would be relieved to find them all dead?

On the south side of Archer, where he stopped to buy gas, he mentioned the name Holtorfer to the station attendant. He learned that one Holtorfer, a Miss Effie Mae, old now and a little dim-witted, lived with a Miss Amanda Plomer. To the gas

240

man's knowledge she had always lived with her, but how would he know since she was older than he was? Surely Warner had heard of Effie Mae's brother, Ivy, the last man in the county to be killed by Indians. Warner had not heard it, but now that he had heard it he thought it highly unlikely. As a boy, he had seen more gypsies than Indians, and they scared him worse. Effie Mae, a little girl at the time, had never got over what had happened. Now that she was old, nothing else seemed to occupy her mind. For years now Amanda Plomer, a religious-type lady who had never married, looked after her. The two ladies managed better living together, since they could pool their Social Security money and keep only one house.

The elm blight had ravaged the town south of the tracks, but left the north, and poorer side of town, in the shade. After so many years in California, Warner found the elm-lined street like a tunnel, almost a strain to his eyes. The first house on the block, recently repainted a white that seemed luminous in the darkness, sat flat on the ground, the baseboards trimmed with grass out of reach of the mower. On the track side of the house the shades were drawn as if to reduce the racket of a passing freight train. A woman came to the screen to watch Warner pass, as if the sound of the Maxwell was familiar to her. The Holtorfer place, a cottage-type dwelling, was more or less concealed by two huge lilac bushes at the front. The clapboards on the visible side of the house were so free of paint they were like boards in a walk, or a weather-beaten fence. So much time had passed since the lilacs were trimmed, the upper branches formed an arch at the entrance to the porch, like trees planted at the door to a tomb. The yard grass had grown so thick and matted it provided a billowy hay-colored carpet, spongy with the growth of grass that tried and failed to reach the light. At the front of the yard blocks of the sidewalk tilted to accommodate the elm roots, but it seemed clear that the tenants walked in and out of the driveway to the door at the back. In Warner's boyhood only hobos used the door at the back, so he thought it better to use the one at the front. A thread spool (it pleased Warner to see it) had replaced the handle to the screen, the holes kicked through it at the bottom patched with pieces of shoe-box cardboard. In the cool of the shade, the draft from the house was like that from an old icebox empty of ice. Just inside the door, sprawled so flat on the couch he thought it a dress put out for airing, a woman lifted her arms toward him as the porch boards creaked.

"It's Will!" she called. "Is that you, Will?"

Before Warner could reply, from a room at the back a figure came toward him he thought to be a crippled child. The walk was that of a creature accustomed to crutches, or trained to get along without mechanical braces. She, too, her arms extended, called out to him in a voice like a parrot. Warner stopped in his tracks, an arm's length from the door, unable to move forward or backward. He watched her toddle toward him, push open the screen, then grasp him about the hips like a child. Warner reached to his back to release her hands, but she held him tight. Sometimes the very old, reduced to skin and bones, give an impression of unusual strength. She held him fast, her frizzled hair tickling his face. The woman on the couch, seeing that he was not Will, had pushed herself up and come out on the porch to persuade the little one to release him. It was not easy, but the way she went about it, her voice calm, her manner assured yet gentle, suggested to Warner this sort of greeting was more commonplace than unusual.

"Effie Mae thinks you're her daddy," she said to Warner, "she thinks gentlemen callers are her daddy."

Effie Mae had stepped back to see clearly who he was: the look she gave Warner led him to wonder. Short frizzly bobbed hair stuck out from her temples, straight up from her scalp. The startled look this gave her seemed at odds with her pleasure in seeing him. She might have been Warner's age, or half again his age, suds dried on her arms as high as her elbows, the strings of the apron she wore dragged behind her like harness traces.

"You're him," she pronounced, "you're just older."

Amanda Plomer said, "She frightens people, she's so possessive. She's never got over losing Ivy."

The word "losing," otherwise so ordinary—everybody spoke of losing someone—tallied with Warner's impression, the day

242

before, that he had lost in the last few days a part of himself, measurable as weight. It seemed unlikely, however, that Effie Mae would ever lose what she fastened her grip on.

"At least the Indians didn't get you," she said to Warner, "did they?"

"No, ma'am," Warner said, and turned to smile at Amanda.

"Effie Mae's not forgetful," Amanda said, "of anything she chooses to remember." She returned his gaze, smiling serenely. Warner was thinking if people lived long enough, would they all look alike? He had not seen his sister in more than forty years, but he could guess how much she looked like Amanda Plomer, her straw-colored hair thin to baldness at the back of her skull. In her pale blue eyes, the mild radiance of her manner, he felt she approximated Viola in saintliness. "You're Mitchell, aren't you?" she said. "Desmond's uncle?"

Warner shook his head. No, he was not Desmond's uncle, so far as he knew. He was related, by marriage, to Hazel Holtorfer, who in turn had married a Vernon Oelsligle, and on their death in a car accident a year ago, their son Kermit, a boy of ten, had come to live with him. This boy he had brought with him from California in the hope of finding some of his own people. Both ladies were attentive. Warner assumed that Amanda's silence was that she found it so upsetting. On the ribs revealed by her dress she moved the tips of her fingers, as if stroking a washboard. Had he forgotten that women of Viola's faith found very little seriously upsetting? "He's met up with some younger people," Warner said, "more his own age. His next of kin should know he's off my hands."

"Holtorfer?" repeated Amanda.

Warner nodded.

Effie Mae cried, "You tell him about Ivy? You tell him they buried him where they killed him?"

"There's Ivy Holtorfer," Amanda said, "if he had lived. Otherwise there's just Effie Mae. . . ." Her eyes scanned the room as if she might have overlooked someone.

"Of the Warners," he replied, "there's just me. It's not natural for a boy to live in a trailer cooped up with a man as old as I am. Along the road we picked up these young people, and it was natural for him to fall in with them. Now he's off my hands." He rubbed the palms of his hands together.

Did Amanda Plomer find that of interest? The yellow fingers of one hand passed before her eyes as if searching for strands of loose hair, but found none.

"The boy needs raising. He needs an older woman." But once he had said it, it led him to wonder. The boy would deny it. The hippie girl was as old a woman as he would like. Young people had learned to make do with each other, to do without the old. "He's off my hands," Warner repeated. "I left him with his friends back in Chapman."

The gaze of Amanda Plomer, who stood facing the door, was fixed on a figure too large for the opening. To peer in, she stooped, pressing the bulge in the screen inward. At her side, a handbag dangling on its strap to her shoe tops, a creature with a spread-legged stance peered to the right and the left, in a birdlike manner. In her free hand she gripped a folded newspaper, which she used to fan the air.

"Mrs. Lindblatt! Miss Belle!" said Amanda. "Do come in."

"We didn't know you had company," replied the tall one. The screen open, she stepped to one side to let the smaller one precede her. Effie Mae moved to take a firm grip on Warner's arm.

"He's mine," she said. "You can't have him."

Rather than dwarf those who stood in the same room with her, Mrs. Lindblatt stood back, waiting to be encouraged to step forward. "He wouldn't be if he knew what it meant, would he?" Did this refer back to Effie Mae's statement? Mrs. Lindblatt's broad face lacked both features and expression. The lids of her eyes were swollen, as if stung by bees.

Miss Belle said, "I smell chocolate chip cookies."

"Not today," replied Amanda, "perhaps Wednesday or Friday."

As if a voice called her from the kitchen, Miss Belle started for it, her handbag swinging.

Mrs. Lindblatt said, "If she gets ahold of something, she

244

brings it bad luck. Look what happened to Cleo. Look what happened to Honey."

Amanda turned her gaze on Effie Mae, who strengthened her grip on Warner. "What did happen?" she asked.

"They died," said Mrs. Lindblatt, "didn't anybody tell you?"

"Things slip her mind," said Amanda.

"She handled them too much," said Mrs. Lindblatt. "You can't handle kittens the way you do some things. It gets their insides jumbled." She looked behind her, then around her. "Miss Belle, where you at?" Miss Belle had disappeared. Unhurried, touching objects as she passed, touching the plants that crowded the sunny window, where artificial birds were perched on sticks, Miss Amanda entered the kitchen. A moment later, with Miss Belle, she reappeared, Miss Belle clutching a sprouting potato. Was it her eyes sparkling, or the light on her glasses?

"She don't eat it," said Mrs. Lindblatt, "she hoards it. You ought to see her room. It's like a fruit cellar."

Amanda said, "Well, bless her heart. She can have it if she wants it."

Effie Mae cried, "She can't have him. He's mine!" and tightened her grip on Warner. Amanda stooped to help Miss Belle add the potato to the contents of her handbag.

"*White* bread?" Amanda asked, holding up a bread wrapper.

"For birds," replied Mrs. Lindblatt. "Some birds like it."

Warner said, "If you ladies will excuse me—" but his effort to move was checked by Effie Mae.

"Don't let her get a grip on you," said Mrs. Lindblatt. "It's bad luck." Amanda turned to Warner, lifting his arm to gently pry loose Effie Mae's gripping fingers. Effie Mae watched, as if unaware that the hand was her own. Her fingers had left their impression on Warner's wrist, white bands the blood was slow to return to. "If you ladies will excuse me—" he repeated, but Amanda gave no sign that she had heard him, and turned away to make a clear space in the center of the room. Chairs were moved back, and Warner thought for a moment she meant to recite to them, or sing. Mrs. Lindblatt and Miss Belle had played the game before, however, and stepped forward to offer their hands to Amanda. Warner's right hand was gripped by Miss Belle, and his left by Effie Mae, so that they formed a circle.

"God protect him from Indians!" cried Effie Mae.

"Not so fast, dear," replied Amanda. They stood holding hands, observing the silence, attentive to Miss Amanda's concentration. She had lowered her head, allowing it to tilt slightly to one side. In repose, Effie Mae's slack-jawed face seemed larger, the wide eyes like those in a mask, the hands dangling at her sides like clumps of roots. The tilt of Amanda's face exposed to Warner a profile like that of a dreaming child. Behind the lids the eyes were moving. Warner could not explain the tremor, like a chill, that began at his fingers and passed through his body, affecting him so powerfully that his knees trembled. He glanced upward to see, pinned to the rafters, postcards and pictures of a religious nature, the details somewhat blurred by the film on his eyes. For the second time in twenty-four hours what Warner knew to be commonplace seemed strange, and what he knew to be bizarre seemed commonplace. His hands held by these gentle elderly ladies, in a manner he knew to be childish, he felt a child's terror that if Effie Mae released his hand he would rise toward the ceiling. This would surprise no one. The giant Mrs. Lindblatt would put her hand up and pull him down. That this would surely happen led his limbs to tremble, so that Effie Mae took a firmer grip on him.

"I'm scared for him!" she cried, jarring Amanda out of her trance.

"You can let him go, dear," Amanda calmly replied. "There's nothing can happen that hasn't already happened," to which she added, "Amen."

"Amen," echoed Mrs. Lindblatt and Miss Belle. Something in what Amanda had said escaped Warner, but it seemed to reassure Effie Mae. She released Warner's hand, and watched it rise to rest, gently, on her frizzled hair. The impression that his life flowed into her was so manifest that he trembled. It would not have surprised him if he had fallen, or risen, effortlessly, toward the rafters. Effie Mae did not seize him when he turned and walked to the door. He let himself out, without glancing

246

back, and no sound came from the house to indicate they were watching. "He's buried where they killed him!" Effie Mae pronounced, as if in answer to a question put to her. Warner's first glance back was from the turn at the corner, where the spear pointing to heaven, on the lightning rod, appeared appropriate to all that had happened.

What had it been? Two or three miles south of town, the prayer ceremony had left his mind fuzzy, like a blow on the head. He let the car straddle the center of the road, like a horse that knew its way home better than he did. Through the cranked-down window a cooling breeze dried his damp face. Just before the house had burned down, and he was still in it, like a ghost in the upstairs bedroom, he had experienced a similar sensation. The weakness in his limbs had led him to sag to a chair, facing the cracked blind and yellow light at the window. His impression had been that his eyes, his *own* eyes, hovered above him like a presence, seeing the things of this world about him for the first time. The view from the window, framed like a painting, impressed him as timeless and unchanging, and the old man seated on the armless rocker was within the scene, not outside of it. For a fleeting, breathless moment he took himself for dead. This sensation was more agreeable than unpleasant, a moment of suspended animation, recalling to his mind the silence that followed the singing of a hymn. *I'm crossing the bar,* he thought, *crossing the bar.* This seizure lasted only a moment but it left him pleasurably addled. Did he hear a voice ask him, "Old man, how are you?" or did he put such a question to himself? His opinion was he was still as good as might be expected, had been for years. The query "Who's next?" put to him like a barber, might pop into his head at the least likely moment. The crux of the matter was all in whether he replied, "He is," or, "I am." It hardly seemed to matter. To the query, "Old man, are you crazy?" he has both a smile and a ready answer. He may well be crazy, but he's certainly no crazier than anybody else.

As a small boy, twirled in a swing until he felt queasy and

the world tilted, his return to normalcy had been accompanied by a sense of weightlessness, as in twirling he had lost something. He felt that way now. It had come over him, like a mild illness, so common to his sisters before they fainted, as he stood in the prayer circle, his hands held by the women. Was it common to people made dizzy by twirling, or by prayer, to inwardly smile? For a brief moment did they feel free of this world, like children tossed in a blanket? If prayer did this for people, it was something that his sister had never mentioned. He had never once said to her, as he might now, "I know how you feel." How she felt was free, disembodied, outside herself. Warner had felt it. That he continued to feel it led him to straddle the road and drive slowly. If he zigzagged on the highway would they think him drunk? Off to the left—would that be east? he had lost confidence in his bearings—a cluster of abandoned farm buildings sat in a grove of dying cottonwoods. A weedy, winding lane, like a dried-up creek bed, led back to the road where the turnoff was marked by a mailbox propped up in a milk can. The lid of the box gaped open, and he could see that it was still stuffed with circulars. He let the car drift by, then brought it to a halt to check the side of the box facing the direction of delivery. Worn away, but guessable, if you know what you are reading, like the weathered MAIL POUCH sign on a barn roof, was the name D. Ho torfe . No *l* at all, nor much *r* at the end, but if you know what to look for you could supply it, as Warner did. He left the car and walked back to check it, just to be sure. Curiously, it was easier to read at a distance, but Holtorfer it was. Warner did not of course believe what such a coincidence suggested, but he would have liked to have shared it with Viola. "You see," she would have said, "you old scoffer!" He loved to hear her say "scoffer." Such things were coincidences, they happened all the time, and his coming along this road was one of them.

The Holtorfer place was being farmed by a neighbor who had left some of his machinery in the yard. Warner stopped beside a wagon, the floor sprinkled with wheat grains the size and color of mice turds. The sheds and barns lay to the south, the barn dilapidated, the roof sunken so that it looked like an ailing

248

monster, bats hanging from the rafters where Warner could see them through the unhinged door. He did not like bats. The eerie whisper of their wings brushing his face had scared him silly when he was a boy and slept on an open porch. Bushes had grown at both ends of the porch and he knew bats were crossing by the movements of the leaves in the breath of their wings. The Holtorfer house depressed him, all the windows broken by hoodlums for the pleasure of hearing the glass crackle, and he walked wide around it as if it were haunted. The trees were dying, as he had seen from the road, their top branches sticking up into the sky like fingers, but the lower branches provided foliage to darken the grove and keep weeds from growing. Cows had had the run of the place for some time, the ground spongy with their crumbling droppings. Shady groves of cottonwoods had been rare on the plains in Warner's boyhood, and they would soon be rare again now that the groves were dying. The land they occupied could be plowed and seeded with wheat and corn. At the west end of the grove, where the sun got at them, there were clumps of weeds just out of reach of the plows. Warner was drawn by the light at the end of the grove, nothing more. As he approached, the view widened to include the green village of Archer, he tripped on a post in the knee-high weeds, paused a moment to curse. Back on his feet, but still tipped over, one hand at the small of his back to assist him, he saw that the post was a piece of stone about the size of a table leg. Such things were once used to determine claims, establish boundaries. This one, of moss-greened marble, had on its top the initials IH, plain as a cattle brand.

It was at this moment we first saw him from the road, where he had parked his car, his profile like that of a man relieving himself. The time he took, allowing for his age, was longer than that. It took time—his condition being somewhat light-headed— for the pieces to come together and register on him their proper effect. He had stumbled on the grave of Ivy Holtorfer, believed to be the last white man in the county to be killed by Indians, his age seventeen. The stone had no date, two sides marble smooth, two rough with a pelt of moss. Deeper in the grass he found a rusted can containing a piece of crumpled tin foil. Since the age of tin foil, that is to say, someone had come here with an offering of flowers. All of Warner's long life this youth had lain here dead to all that had happened, dead to all that would ever happen, dead to even the fact of birth and dying, since killed by Indians as he stood daydreaming, or stooped over a plow. Warner's feelings, if he had cared to admit them, were so bizarre as to be ghoulish. Ivy Holtorfer seemed as real to him as himself. Not only in his youth, that of a boy who had all of his life before him, but also in the predicament of his death. Had he looked up, or failed to look up, before the bullet or the arrow had found him? If Warner did not, one could only say that he lacked the strength. The presence of his own death was so real it awed more than it scared him. As if held by the hand, bemused by voices, inwardly smiling at the novelty of it, all the deaths of this world that had escaped him, mother and wife, five loving sisters, one so fresh in her grave little grass grew on it, he was able to grasp the irretrievable loss to Ivy Holtorfer of his own unlived life. It shamed him to think how little of life he had yet to lose.

Is he so old as that? He's eighty-two, but with Viola gone he has no proof. It astonished and pleased him that no living person could testify to his age, only the dead. If he so desired he could pick a new one. He might say he was up to ten years younger, as people often remarked. A man in Santa Cruz had made a new life for himself by declaring he recalled the sight of Lincoln, at the end of the Civil War. Any fool with eyes in his head knew he was lying. Warner recalled Buffalo Bill, on his white horse, leading the Hagenback and Wallace circus into Schuyler, the envy of kids who had never set eyes on a buffalo. When Warner told that story to his nephew Kermit, the boy had replied, "Who's Buffalo Bill?" It hadn't seemed a good question to Warner at the time, but now it did.

2

T<small>HE NAME OF</small> W<small>ARNER IS WELL KNOWN</small>
in Merrick County, Nebraska, where Myron Warner settled a
homestead on the bluffs south of the Platte, and the town of Chapman would have borne the Warner name, or that of Osborn, his
wife's name, if she had not feared to offend the Lord with such
a show of pride. Five of the Warners' surviving children, all of
them girls, learned to love God and fear Him, but the son and
firstborn refused to observe the Adventist sabbath or accept any
day as holy. Even as a boy he hated his father, and equally loved
and pitied his mother, seldom out of bed with unwanted children.
On the Adventist sabbath he often stayed in his room and read
the works of Colonel Ingersoll, the great agnostic. At fifteen, slight
of build but active (the Warners ran small, but never stopped
running), he hired himself out as a threshing hand and left his
father's house never to return. That same summer, a few weeks
later, he had the first of the loving, taunting letters from his sister,
and in return sent her the first of the numberless postcards ridicul-
ing everything and anything she believed, or he feared she might
happen to believe. These letters, filed in shoe boxes, salvaged
from the attic of the homestead, were among the items and
perishable objects that went up in smoke the previous evening,
traces of the smoke still visible in the morning, dimming the lights
of Grand Island off to the west, and the Pony Express stop nine
miles to the east. The Pony Express had ceased, of course, with
the railroad, the gleaming two-way track bed of the Union Pacific.
In these spare facts there is much of Warner's history. He saw
railroads come, he saw horses go, he once rode in a Franklin with
its air-cooled engine (this before his own home had indoor plumbing) and sixty years later he drives, when it will run, a 1927 Maxwell coupe. Now that it is no longer pulling the trailer it seems

to have a lot of pep, but the body rattles. Like a kite without a tail, the motor acts skittish when going downgrade, or caught in a tailwind. He has to keep a firmer grip on the wheel than he used to, his eyes on the road.

Has he aged overnight, or is that an idle question, already being too old to begin with? Is he so old that having aged overnight means nothing, except in his head?

Viola would ask him, "How is my old darling?"

How is he? He is old.

The day before, of all the days of his life, just a few hours in time and a few miles in space, had been the most eventful. He had seen the past, lock, stock, and barrel, go up in smoke. A column of hot air, rippling like water, had risen from the blackened yard where the house had stood, lofting ashes and pieces of debris to where the cooler breeze had set them blazing. The beams of car lights, parked back in the trees, had crisscrossed at that point where the house had vanished, like footlights playing on a stage. At the center of the stage, two small figures had cast huge shadows on the barn behind them. The very sight of them aroused Warner's fury. Everything that had happened, everything yet to happen, could be laid at the feet—at least two of them dirty—of that pair of kids. As he knew it would, and as it always had, one goddam thing always led to another, and this was the last in the series that dissolved his past into a column of air. And *that* event was now receding before he had managed to grasp it clearly, like something that caught his eye at the car window, displaced, a moment later, by something else. An event that was nearest to him in time now proved to be to its disadvantage. The wheel of his life having come full circle, the past was now coming toward him as the present mysteriously receded. What had happened last night fell away, slipped away, like the road visible in the rear-view mirror, but what had happened in the distant past flowed toward him like objects approaching on the highway.

Where was he now? With the sun on his right, he was driving south on route 183. Where that leads he'll know when he gets there. One thing he never told the boy, and would now never

252

have to, was that he once got up at dawn, in Liberal, Kansas, and drove eighty-five miles before the sun came up where he thought it should set. That added up to one hundred and seventy miles of wrong road, all of it pretty bad. Give or take a county line, the route he was now on he had first taken in a topless buggy to pick up his bride-to-be in Oberlin, Kansas. Then with her and her dog, a little half-breed spitz that took weeks to get used to Warner, they took sixteen days, not pushing the horse, to get to the homestead on the Pecos River, just east of Roswell, New Mexico. Then it took him almost half a day to find what little it was he had left there. Just forty years ago he had left more, but would it prove easier to find?

It was a comfort to Warner to be off the freeway and back on a road where the turns were at right angles. One reason he had put the car up on blocks in California was that the winding roads were confusing. In the space of ten miles the sun in his eyes would be around at his back. The lack of any right angles made it difficult for him to find his bearings. With the angles gone, what did a man have left but up and down? It now occurred to him that up or down pretty well covered his available options, up to heaven with Viola, or straight to hell with everybody else.

The car appeared to stand still as the road swept beneath it, spinning the wheels. Coming toward him, from shadow into sunlight, the "memory" of lumber for a house, brought out from Omaha on a flatcar, dumped in the knee-high weeds along the track bed. From there it will be floated across the spring-flooded river, then dragged up the bluffs by a team of lame oxen, exchanged for a wagon by people headed westward. What is the lumber for? To build a house on the bluffs. In his haste to complete this house for his wife, who is expecting, the builder forgets to put in the stairs between the first and second floor. A hole has to be sawed in the ceiling of the kitchen, a ladder inserted, as into a barn loft. That Warner should "remember" this is amazing, since he was the child the woman was carrying, and this was why he was born in the kitchen, and not upstairs. All of her children will be born in the kitchen, then carried up the ladder to grow up. The father is too busy running a farm, the mother is too busy rearing children, to take time out to restore the missing stairway. Besides, the children like it the way it is. Floyd Warner's first memories—as distinct from what he has heard—are of heads popping up through the hole in the floor, like a jack-in-the-box. In the kitchen he sees the ladder against a blaze of light, like a trellis, the rough steps fuzzy with the wool of their mittens and stockings. The draft that blows through this hole in the winter gives them all colds. Peering through it—is he a child or a boy?—he sees several women seated at a quilting frame, their heads bowed, the backs of their necks exposed. If he married Muriel Dosey—and not one of the Claytons, big soft girls who needed a man's help up and down from a buggy—it was because he had seen Muriel Dosey baptized in the Platte River, near Chapman, her slip clinging, her neck and shoulders exposed when she dipped and then popped out of the water, gasping for air. The copper glint of her skin was due (it was rumored) to the one-quarter Indian blood in her veins.

It occurs to him now, more than sixty years later, that he seldom again saw so much of her uncovered. She had been baptized. What other reason for exposing herself to men's eyes?

Warner is old, but he sees her as clearly as if he had left that riverbank this morning, and had the sand in his shoes. Others have been baptized, the men have waded to where they stand, knee deep, in the shallows, but the women, including his wife, prefer the concealment of the deeper water. The Clayton girl, Maude, covers with her hair the bust that floats her, as if inflated. Muriel Dosey is stooped, her hair dangling into the water, as if she were gazing at her own reflection, her hands placed across her breasts in what he feels to be an imploring gesture. Its meaning distracts him now as it distracted him then.

Another way to put it is that he is like a sock, turned inside out. What is nearest his skin, he feels the least, what is distant he knows the best. Veiled by the dust raised by the cantering horse he sees the hands of his sisters waving to him from the buggy. They are on their way to church, with their father. He sits on the rear stoop of the porch or at the upstairs window, having

254

refused to either ride to church or walk there. Soon enough, he refuses to ride, anywhere, with his God-fearing father. At seven years of age he walks three miles to school and three miles back. He is a child, but his stubborn will proves to be as inflexible as that of the father. This battle of wills will determine the course of his life. He will neither ask for help nor accept it when reluctantly offered. With the mother dead, he is like an unloved adopted child. As plainly as he saw the hands of his waving sisters—like ribbons blowing at the sides of the buggy—he sees that each of them, father and son, had effectively destroyed what they had loved. He sees that they each, if they had it to do over, would do it over again.

Would it be said that he was living, or merely seeing, parables? Leaving California, the morning sun in his eyes, he had sensed that he was traveling backward, but that the boy, in the seat at his side, at the same moment was hurrying forward, free as the wind. The same direction in space proved to be the opposite direction in time.

While the boy was there on the seat at his side, he could think of nothing that he wanted to tell him, although there were one or two things he might have told him, if he had been asked. All that he had not told, and not been asked, would end with himself. A film passed over his eyes as if a blast of cold air had chilled his face. He was relieved that the boy was not there to witness these involuntary shows of emotion, a sign, surely, of his weakened condition. He had long lived with the dread that one night he might wet his bed, or his pants. He understood from the complaints of others that something of this nature was not uncommon, although it was one of many things that exceeded his grasp. He had once watched the blood ooze from his arm, the result of a bullet he hadn't heard fired, his first experience with his body defying his inflexible will.

One thing he had meant to tell the boy was about the balls of fire. Seated on the padded board, across the arms of the barber chair (his head in a cloud of scented powder), he had heard the crash and the crackling like thunder, and blinked at the flash of light, like an explosion, opening wide his eyes to see the ball of fire that rolled like a hoop—he could see right through it—to where the road ended at the cattle loader, where it had popped, like a balloon bursting, the blades of straw, picked up as it rolled, driven like copper nails into the planks fencing the corral. "How come?" the boy would ask him. Electricity had done it. What it did, or might do, in those days was beyond belief.

Beyond the belief also (he now remembered) of some of those who had heard the story, and pointed out that if he had heard the explosion, which he did, it was after he saw the blinding flash, light traveling faster, even there in Chapman, than the noise it made. This obliged him to admit that what he had described was what he had *heard,* firsthand, from the barber, who had described it so well he had no need to see it himself. A boy's ears, his own especially, were often bigger than his eyes.

Was that why he had put off that story until he had been asked? Balls of fire, so common in the past, had grown so uncommon they might sound peculiar, or even downright stupid, to a boy who had watched a landing on the moon.

Had his sister Viola felt herself unraveling like a ball of yarn? Or was this caused by the car, the riding, the ceaseless glide of the road coming toward him, slipping beneath him, and then on the instant (in the rear-view mirror) spilling out behind him. His feeling was that this movement added nothing to him, but carried something away. Surely Viola had been spared this humiliation, alone in her bed, shrinking all by herself. It was the old man's impression that his shadow had narrowed, as if drying as he looked at it. It also looked paler to him, as if cast by something that lacked substance. Nor could he keep track of the numberless ways the car seemed to unreel him, loosen his parts, shake him down to something less than he had been. Curled up in the trailer bunk he felt himself dwindling; he awakened from sleep to feel he had shrunk. In the washroom he did not glance up at the mirror until he was alone. The boy's knobby head impressed him as being larger than his own: a balloon full of air, as compared with one from which it had leaked, the skin wrinkled.

Had he dozed off at the wheel? He put his head to the window, into the whistle of a lark's song, certain that he had heard someone singing a hymn. Nothing is there. The telephone wires, on their tilted poles, rise and fall as they approach him. Some moments pass before he realizes the singing, the humming, had been himself, the last words of the hymn dry in his open mouth.

Brighten the corner where you are!

Hadn't he hated hymn singers all of his life? Or didn't that include hymns? A few moments of his life he had sat in a pew, his feet extended before him, listening to the choir and the throb of the organ. Before hymn singers there had been hymns. After almost eighty years of silence he remembered their verses. The way the past was coming toward him seemed to free him from the present and the future. He was no longer bound, as he had been, to his own life. The uncanny impression the day before, then his weightlessness in the circle of women, was not a fleeting sensation but his knowledge of the loss or gain of something. What gain could come from a loss of life?

He let the car coast to lift his hands from the vibrating wheel, and consider them closely. Hawks and Effie Mae had such talons. The fingers curled to form a rake. An injury of boyhood—a house jack had fallen to crush the first joint of two fingers—showed like the stitching of a glove seam. A doctor in Grand Island, where he had appeared to be drafted, put it down on the form as an "identifying scar." That had aroused him to the knowledge of his body as a place inhabited he would one day abandon. He had made much of that in a letter to Viola, citing the injured fingers, and the nature of the scar, so that no impostor, as he put it, might be mistaken for him in heaven. Just his letters to her were more than enough to see him in hell.

In the bunk of the trailer, his knees hugged to his chest, he would clasp the soles of his feet in his hands, holding himself like a wrapped package. Night by night, week by week, the contents of the package seemed lighter to him. From the sack of skin and bones something had evaporated: was it life? What he hugged in his arms was like a pod of dried seeds. His concern proved to be what he could clutch and hold to him. Skin and bones, the saddle-smooth soles of his feet. If the bedclothes had been thrown off his body he would have looked like a just-hatched bird. If dead, would he have been found clasped in his own arms? The thought of this so shamed him he tried to sleep in his customary manner, his legs stretched to lie one on the other, but they were so fleshless, the knees so bony, this actually proved to be painful.

Old man, this voice would ask him, what is on your mind? Need he admit it? He felt that he owed it to his age, his weakened condition. So what was it? The womanly emotion of tenderness. This unmanly concern for his dwindling remains he felt with embarrassment and confusion. Had Viola been alive she would have been startled, and for once in her life unbelieving, that an emotion so frail, so womanly, had overcome his stubborn will.

IN HIS PERIODS OF REFLECTION THE CAR might drift to the center of the road, and straddle the white line, as if it meant to relax. He fought his inclination, if he was not daydreaming, but the Maxwell had a will of its own. It, too, was old. It felt better, it felt safer, straddling the line. In Humboldt County, Kansas, there was not so much traffic that it proved to be a problem, unless he crested a grade. The Maxwell's speed was reduced on the grade to hover between twenty and thirty, so he didn't come on other cars as fast as they came on him. On the grade the motor tightened up, and ran quiet (it also ran a little hot on a long one), but on the downgrade the hammer of the loose rod could be distinguished from the general motor racket. The ideal condition was a speed of about thirty-five, against a slight headwind. The wind took up the slack in the motor and made it almost quiet in the cab, where the jolt of the wheel edging off the road was all that kept him awake.

If no one sneaked up behind him and honked, the Maxwell would slow down to the point it started bucking, and wake him up. He prided himself the way he could doze off and wake up just in time to keep the wheel out of the ditch grass. He couldn't do that with anybody's car: it had to be his own. Both east and west of Roswell the blacktop road was crossed by cattle barriers, made out of pipes or old rail ties, just wide enough that when the wheels hit them at about thirty-five it was like an electric shock: the vibration in his arms, the tingle in his legs, would last for miles. In the past, the dog would bark all the way to Alamogordo. The dog disliked the barriers, but what he couldn't seem to stand was to be held up at a crossing by a freight train. Did he think it was alive? Warner would have to whip him to shut him up. He lacked experience, that dog, he couldn't stand gas stations or the cough of a John Deere tractor engine, dislikes he may have picked up from Warner. All that muttering he often did under his breath was not lost on the dog.

Was there anything that dog liked? He liked a car with a real quiet idle. Warner could leave him in the car, and no trouble, if the motor had a quiet idle. The finest idling motor he had driven had been a Dodge five-passenger touring. What year? He had never given it much thought. The motor had what he would almost call a *ping,* like a good coin dropped on the counter. He might have been driving it now if his wife had not complained about the side curtains. He had been astonished. To his knowledge, until he married her, she had never ridden a mile in anything but a buggy. A mistake to have come up so fast? So he had thought. He had wooed her in a buggy, one that he had rented from the livery stable in Aurora, an advantage of the buggy—he had been led to reflect on it later—being the easy way the spring seat could be removed and carried through the cattail rushes to the river. She had asked no questions. It seemed to be acceptable to her for him to park the horse where it could graze on the ditch grass, or low-hanging willow branches, and go off with the buggy seat toward the river, but, later, if he stopped the *car* he had to leave the motor running, and let it run hot. "Muriel," he said, "I don't understand you!" It had made no impression on her. Perhaps it was the way she always said so little that led him on. Her nature was reluctant: one way or another, one place or another, seemed a matter of indifference to her, but in the matter of side curtains on the Dodge she drew the line. He traded it, in Amarillo, for the Maxwell coupe, never liked by the dog.

The blast of a horn, wind-borne toward him from the rear, led him to pull off the road and let the truck whoosh past, the suck of the wind stream lurching the cab. Up and down the rear of the trailer were the battered license plates of numerous states, like a patchwork quilt. A black exhaust plumed from the pipe at the front, drifting eastward on the prevailing wind. That hadn't changed. A wind like that infuriated him first, then ended up mystifying him silly. Why did it blow? His wife replied, "To turn

260

the windmill, pump up water." The Indian in her found that perfectly sensible. Viola would have said, "God wills it," and both women would have exchanged glances, amused and baffled by the things that troubled men. When his wife took ill and lay awake at his side, resigned to illness, the wind and dying, the whir of the wind wheel, the clatter of the vanes as the wind veered or shifted, made him aware of a force in nature to match his own stubborn fury. This had led him (his wife dead, not there to turn her gaze on him) to let the wind simply batter the machine to pieces to be free of its ceaseless clatter. Was that accurate? He had believed it until this moment. Or had he, in this battle of wills, let the wind destroy a part of something bigger than he was? A visible reduction of the invisible forces he opposed?

From the bib of his overalls he slipped his watch, saw the face plainly, then put it away. For the *time* he cranked down the window and squinted at the overcast sky.

Why does that bring to mind the fire?

In the dusk of the yard he had watched the windows light up a moment, as if in a sunset, those on the first floor suddenly darkening as if with clouds. There was a pump right there at the door to the barn, with pails upside down on the corral fence posts, but it had never crossed his mind to put out the fire. Was there something inside he wanted burned up? Against the flames gusting out of one window he saw the hippie girl. He was struck by how much she looked like a stilt-legged boy. Feeling the heat of the fire (the sky was lit up with a shower of sparks), he turned to unhitch the car from the trailer, letting the hook-up drop in the yard with a thud. He got no help from anybody—the boy had tailed off somewhere like a frightened rabbit—but the bearded hippie, without a rag on his body, lit up on the front as if he was half-roasted, stood holding his blue jeans watching the house burn. Ringed with fire, he looked like the devil personified.

It had been the old man's intent, no more, to move the old car back from the fire, out of range of the sparks, but the sight of Stanley put him in such a fury he headed down the driveway and just kept going. The way he hit the track crossing shook him silly, but didn't slow him up. Thinking he had come for help, and expecting him to stop, people gathered at the door and outside the café watched him go by. A fire hose cart had once been parked in the weeds beside the livery stable, but he had no recollection of an actual fire. This was an actual fire, and cast a flickering glow in the tops of the willows along the river. One sensible thing he did was slow down approaching the bridge. It had been of planks, the loose ones clapping like thunder, with a turnout near the center allowing buggies to pass. This half-mile-wide river (he had described it to the boy as not particularly deep, but a mile wide) appeared to be no more than a sandbar with pools of water too shallow to wade in. (Where, he wondered, had they baptized the women?) At the south end of the bridge, standing on the rail, he could see the peaked roof of the privy at the edge of the bluff. Gone? Willows screened it off. His father, his eyes on the horizon, had staked out his homestead on the bluffs, for the view. To enjoy it privately he faced the privy to the valley. His son often caught him there, his britches down, with *nobody to spy on him but God,* warming his knees in the sun. The fact that he had said that, and never tired of saying it, had always spoiled the view for Warner, both the summer and the winter prospect tainted with his monstrous love of God, and God's love of him.

Nevertheless he had been right about the view, and would have enjoyed the fire. It had been rumored of him, but never proved, that he had set his own haystacks on fire to watch them burn, like sinners in hell. Viola's house burned much better than a haystack, going up with a whoosh, once the roof caught, some of its heat borne on the breeze that rose off the river. The lights of the cars, focused on the smoke haze, made him think of a lynching witnessed by his father, but never described. It had made him more God-fearing than ever and an orator on the question of slavery. It shamed Floyd Warner, this man's only son, to hate him after eighty years as he had as a boy. "You're too much alike," Viola had said, "you both want something all to yourself." She didn't say God. There were always things she thought that she didn't say.

Except for the privy—at the edge of the bluff where the

plowing left it undisturbed—nothing remained of the house and barns his father had built with his own hands. Back in the thirties, dust, blowing like smoke, had settled in drifts around the house like snow, burying tools and implements no longer of any use. A bulldozer had flattened the house and outbuildings to provide extra acres of rented pasture. What had not gone back to dust—including the nine in the cemetery—had now gone up in smoke. He found it strange the way his fury cooled with the fire, so he was able to gawk at it, like a neighbor. Car lights picked up the trailer, gleaming like a helmet, the enamel buckets on the posts fencing the corral, and nearer the fire, wavering like flames, the unmistakable figures of the boy and the hippie girl. Was it a trick of the light, the heat rising from the ashes forming streamers that flowed upward, that caused him to see her arms stretched over her head like a dancer? They lowered and raised, as if she stood there exercising. To his astonishment, he was able to see that she faced away from him, her back to the fire, observing the shadows her movements cast on the barn. He had forgotten her powers, the thralldom she cast over the boy. He had left the fire, he had driven to the bluff, and he had watched it all go up in smoke, not for one moment doubting that he would drive back when both he, and the fire, had cooled. Back to what? Had he reason to doubt all that he knew, as well as what he saw? Not only the house, not only the past, but the ties that had bound the boy to it, insofar as the boy was concerned, had gone up with the smoke. Nothing would be gained in going back, since there was, in truth, no place to go back to. He would not find in the ashes anything he valued, or what, until this moment, he had hoped to salvage, the boy being the one remnant of the past he had already lost.

Old man, so where are you?

He looks at the map. Kansas lies before him, a reassuring patchwork of straight lines and right angles. If he goes south, the west is on his right, the east on his left. Viola had written him of her concern when the center of the country, believed to be in Kearney, Nebraska (where she had attended the teachers college), was found to be instead near Osborne, Kansas, one hundred miles to the south. People living in Kearney, where everything was Mid-City, had to adjust themselves to the fact that they had never really been at the center of something, as they had thought they were. His answer to her had run to several pages—the vanity of man being one of his better subjects—with pointed asides as to what God would think of such fools made in His image. Actually, the news had put him in such a rage he had written to the postmaster general (the object and source of most of his complaints), asking who in the hell the government thought it was to make such a decision without consulting people, the center of anything being where they thought it was, until they were told or persuaded to think different. The center of a town was something people knew, and not something to be decided by a crew of surveyors, none of whom really knew their ass from a hole in the ground. He did not say that in so many words, but his intent was clear. Four or five weeks later he received a large packet of government bulletins, mailed without postage, on every subject except the one in question. As to where the center of the country was *now,* he couldn't care less.

One thing he would like to know—the car drifts to straddle the line in the road, as he thinks about it—is where the boy now is, where he will end up. It had seemed of small importance when it first crossed his mind—now he could not understand how it had happened. There had always been Viola to write and ask. There had always been a place. On the insurance card in his wallet he had written Floyd Warner, Chapman, Nebraska. There had always been a Warner in Chapman. The boy's name was Kermit Oelsligle. People wouldn't believe it even when they heard it. That he would never again hear it had not occurred to him. How was it possible to believe, to accept, something like that? Never hear it. Never really know where he was. All his long life the old man knew, and believed, that Viola's childish beliefs were impossible. Childish they were—but possible, graspable. Better the boy up in heaven, with Viola, than where he would never again set eyes on him, hear about him, or know where he was.

"For chrissakes, boy," he would say, "where you been?"

"Oh, around," he would answer.

"Around where?"

"Oh, just around."

The boy had a chipped tooth he swore he got biting himself. His claim was that he dived into the water then came up, too fast, under the diving board and thumped himself on it, biting himself so hard he had chipped his tooth. The old man never believed that for a moment, but he lacked experience in swimming pools. He had been careful to conceal the fact that he couldn't swim. It would not merely puzzle the boy to hear it, but discolor in a way that might disturb him the stories the old man had told him about the river. He would see it all different if all he saw him doing was *wading* in it.

He was startled by the appearance, right there at his window, of a freight locomotive pulling a caboose. It had come up behind him, without whistling, the track bed running along parallel with the road. The hulking monster put him in mind of some prehistoric creature, running for shelter. That was not so unheard of: creatures almost as large had roamed these plains before the ice age. Their bones had been found. They had lived so long ago his mind could not grasp it. The magnitude of such things had been pleasing to him in proportion to the torment they were to Viola, who found them contradictory to her faith. Without her to torment, or the boy to amaze, his pleasure in such vast prospects diminished. He cared less for monsters, more for the freshly painted Santa Fe caboose. It appeared to have been taken somewhere for a cleanup, the windows gleaming, the hardware blackened, the letters A.T.&S.F. bright as the raised lettering on a bank window. The dull sooty black of the freight locomotive made it look like new. In a caboose with three brakemen, two of them wearing the high-crowned denim hats, matching their overalls, Warner had ridden with his Uncle Verne from the junction at Columbus through the rolling sandhills to what his uncle's wife Mae described as a dirt farm. What other sort of farms were there? He had had the wisdom not to ask. Verne's wife—known as Great-Aunt Mae—had come from a non-dirt farm in Ohio, and took a superior attitude to farms deficient in cows and chickens. That in spite of the fact that half the chickens would blow off with the wind. A cow wouldn't, but there was little for a cow to eat. She kept cows, nevertheless, cranking the milk through a separator that might have been one of those on Viola's porch, the cream so thick it had to be spread on his oatmeal with a spoon. What had become of her? With Viola gone he no longer had anybody to ask. Warner had actually liked his Aunt Mae, but sensed that he should not, if he could help it, show it. Did she like him? "Let him stay another week," she said, "if he cares to." Why did she call her husband V.B. if his name was Verne? Years later he had grasped that calling him V.B. was a *sign* that she liked him. Likes and dislikes were largely a matter of signs. If Warner felt himself not actively *dis*liked, he understood that he was probably liked. Aunt Mae had no children of her own and frowned on the troubles one had with children, until they were able, as she put it, to help with the chores. Approaching the house with two full pails of water, the wire handles cutting into the palms of his hands, Warner had heard his Uncle Verne, looking up from the wash pan, his face glistening with water, say that one thing he could say was that the boy was not afraid of work.

"Is it something to be afraid of?" she had replied.

But he had sensed that it was. His uncle had implied it. His own nature at times rebelled against it. So the fact that he did it, without complaining, demonstrated that he was *not* afraid of it. Before he had left she would pour water for him into the pan his Uncle Verne had just emptied, and he was free to use, like a hired hand, the other half of the towel placed on the drainboard, watching the letters come clear on the flour sack as it soaked up the water. Sometimes it proved to be sugar, instead of flour. He was *not* free, however, as Verne was, to toss his water into the yard through the screen bulge, but no one objected if he stood there with the towel and watched the hens scratch around the wet spot, or gazed out across the yard, booby-trapped with wire wickets left over from the previous summer when two of her nieces, who *were* afraid of work, played croquet for a week and then just left them in the yard to rust. They were city girls from near Zanesville, Ohio, and thought of nothing but boys.

At the top of the rise, white and looming as a lighthouse, a school building sat fifty yards or so back from the road. One side of the yard had been fenced, to keep in cattle, and the mesh of the fence was clogged with tumbleweed and paper blown there by the wind. At the back corners of the yard, equal distance from the schoolhouse, were two white privies with a chest-high wooden fence to screen off the doors. Through the film of chalky whitewash the old man could see the words stenciled on the boards: BOYS and GIRLS. A man who didn't *know* that, of course, might not *see* it, but he was experienced in such matters. Even more than experienced, he was at ease in such surroundings. Schoolkids. The empty yard suddenly alive with hooting and scrapping little monsters. That the bike rack in the side yard stood vacant meant that this was a holiday, or a weekend. He didn't know which. In either case he did not feel, as other strangers might, that in using the privy (so long as it was the BOYS) he was intruding or had an evil mind, waiting till the coast was clear to draw his own dirty pictures on the back of the door, or carve something on the seat. At the front of the yard there was also a pump, a tin cup dangling from a wire looped to the nozzle. Not to arouse the suspicion of local people (one thing they always knew was who was driving what car), he parked near the road and carried the canteen along with him. On the south side of the building there were two teeter-totters with splintered planks and well-polished seats. The nearer side was used as a playground, the windows protected by heavy cable screens. He noted with interest how the paint on the clapboards had been worn away by bouncing balls. Even around the pump not a blade of grass had survived the daily stampede. There was a caked mudhole, but no sensible seed would take root in it. It was a comfort to him to see it all, however, and imagine how it came to life at recess. In a wind like this they would never hear a whistle: he would have to ring a bell. Even the wind-swept yard, hard as concrete, provided him with familiar, friendly footing, the playgrounds and trailer parks of California being covered with

267

acres of seamless blacktop. His dislike of kids, well known to everybody, did not extend to the school grounds in their absence. The vacant yard, the idle apparatus, pleased him with more than its unexpected silence. He had the impression of time arrested, of something lost, recovered. The swarm of faces, many new every year—he felt a weakness in his legs to contemplate it—dissolved away to this pattern he found reassuring. The faces changed. He clung to what resisted change in himself.

The wind blew on him in a way that made his feet seem light. He would first have a good pee, then he would have a long drink. Considering it was something he had never really liked (the wind puts a hand on his chest, to delay him, to give him time to reflect on it), how explain the way he had learned, for most of his life, to live with it? It might have been—once he stopped howling— the first sound recorded in his ears. It leaned on the house nine months of the year, leaving a disturbing hollow when it stopped. Even his mother said that if the house should fall it would be toward the wind, not with it, reeling over like a drunk whose support had shifted. He had grown accustomed, even as a child, to the siltlike talcum on the sills of the windows, where the tassels of the curtains, or the cord to the blinds, left tracks like small night creatures. One of the few things he had said to his father was that he was sick and tired of the goddam wind—the "goddam" thrown in to give it the predictable effect.

What had been the effect?

He delayed the pleasure of this reflection until he stood out of the wind in the privy. There were two holes; one for small bottoms, one for large ones. At the end of his life he was back where he had started, faced with the same choice. A strong eye-burning stench blew from the larger hole until he corked it with his bottom. It had the effect of increasing the quiet, as if a draft had been closed. The backside of the boards obstructing his view were scribbled over with verses, names, dirty drawings. At his eye level he read

Here I sit
Broken hearted

The next two and unforgettable lines (Warner knew them so well he needn't see them) had been boldly printed over with

NOBODY CARES

He was mystified why any snot-nosed farm kid, evil-minded by nature, would overlook the chance to repeat something dirty. Wasn't one reason for a privy to get off a kid's mind what he couldn't throw up? Did he mean to have a fourth line to rhyme with it, or just leave it like that? *Nobody cares.* It seemed a strange thing for a kid to write. It was more what an older, more experienced person might come to feel if he sat here for long, the door open, the plain empty and rolling as far as you can see it, the sky topless as far as you can feel it, the wind howling like a ghost in the uncovered hole at his side. Did Warner know about boys, having been one? Kermit Oelsligle would never believe it. With Warner's family of sisters, what boy had he known? Better than he cared to he knew Vance Fry, a boy so evil-minded he made a joke of it. Warner seldom saw him his beady little eyes were not squinted up tight, his lips smiling. He had the devil's cunning. His pockets were always stuffed with the Kewpie chalk he used to make dirty drawings. His father had been obliged to scrub off the sidewalks in front of the stores. How explain, in a boy of his age, what he could make of the words on the back of a tin of Prince Albert tobacco? With his knife—the mother-of-pearl handle in the shape of a woman's leg—he would scrape off words and letters so that what was left was slyly wicked. Try as Warner would, since he didn't believe in devils, he could only see it as a work of evil, not that of an eight-year-old boy. Vance had a small-size head, which didn't help matters, with his hair sticking up at the crown like a feather, his pants pockets weighted with marbles he had won playing keeps. He carried cinnamon oil in a perfume bottle, into which he dipped toothpicks, then sucked on them, which he said made the girls crazy to kiss him. What if it did?

Sheets of newspaper, cut into small squares, were spindled on a nail to the right of the door, but the type was too small for him to read. In his father's *out*house—he did not like the word "backhouse," and frowned on the word "privy"—the previous year's Monkey Ward catalogue sat to the right of the holes, with a flatiron on it to keep the draft from flapping the pages. There were no scribblings on the door of *that* privy until farm hands, hired to help with the threshing, left it cluttered with drawings that had to be painted over before the father would let the rest of them use it. The girls walked the quarter mile to the Applegate farm, too small to need any hired help on it. These men were rough and foul-mouthed out in the field, but polite and respectful once they got to the table, yes-and-no ma'aming every move his sisters made. One of the younger men divulged to Warner what he did with his hard-earned threshing money. He went straight to Kansas City, where he got himself a good whore. He and this whore would get out of bed just long enough to eat, and they would stay in the bed until he ran out of money. He said he'd be glad to take Warner along with him, and "show him the ropes." This top and bottom side of men—he was a perfectly normal, good-looking young man when he was wielding a pitchfork, or sat with his head bowed while his sisters said grace—flabbergasted more than it horrified Warner, since he did not at that time actually know what a whore was, good or bad. Sixty-five years later he still did not know. He had rebelled at his father's God and Viola's religion, but what was clean and unclean derived from their example, and nothing in his experience would make the flesh of such a woman desirable.

A gust of wind blew cool on his bottom, escaping with a howl through the hole at his side. The wind along the Pecos, where he had taken his bride, howled like a creature trapped under the house. In the summer, up from Mexico, it blew hotter. In the winter it blew down from the snow-capped Rockies, lifting the sheepskins from the boards on the floor. You had to see it to believe it. Muriel never got over, being part Indian, the way the stove would howl like a coyote, the draft sucking up the flame so fast it would sometimes put the fire out. He had written to Viola that heathen superstitions seemed to him better founded than those she followed, and if he took it in mind to rise to heaven it would be on the draft up a stovepipe. She had

270

not replied. It tickled him at the time, but shamed him now, that he had given his new dog the name of Jesus. "Why you suppose I call him that?" he had asked her. "The rabbit's good as dead till Jesus spots him, then he springs to life." When he had told that story to the boy he had just stood there, looking sheepish, which was one way he couldn't stand *anybody* to look. There was nothing dumber on this earth than a sheep, thousands of which he came to know personally, and he respected the good sense of Jesus Christ in referring to his followers in this manner.

So why raise sheep? He didn't like dirt farming. He couldn't stand being at the "mercy" of the weather. The farmer's stoical patience with the whims of nature, and his mutton-headed belief that "the Lord would provide," were equally repugnant to him. He didn't mind the sheep being dumb, if he himself was smart. He thought one man and a dog could handle a herd of sheep, and in the first winter blizzard he lost four hundred of them, packed like snow into a corner of the canyon. Even the dog lost track of them. Without moving a muscle, their heads all pointing into the corner, as if swimming, they had silently, mindlessly suffocated. Little more than three inches of snow had fallen, but it had been enough, with the wind blowing, to bury them alive. Cattle would do that, too, but at least it took more snow to cover them.

Not a wind sound, more of a hingelike creak rose from the hole at the moment he did, as if the seat had a squeak. Something shiny—anything and everything might be dropped into the hole of a privy—moved as if stirred by the wind. Again it squeaked. The match he struck, and held to the hole, the draft snuffed out. He made a wad of the newspaper, let it flare to a ball of fire, and dropped it. In the flood of light, eyes like bolt holes in a stove's hot belly returned his gaze. A rat? The eyes were too big. The body was multi-colored like a bread wrapper. All eyes and ears, what he had seen was a kitten, or what was left of a cat. It clung to the narrow two-by-four ledge that served as the privy foundation. If the boy had been there, the old man would have directed the operations. He would have held his legs, that is, while the boy stretched his arm into the hole. He was not there, however, and Warner stood a moment distracted by a fact to which he

271

was not accustomed. It would have been a relief just to tell the boy what he should do. "You going to let a little stink be the death of that kitten?" The boy knew he didn't care much for cats. Now he kneeled to the floor, turning on his side so that his shoulder corked the hole, then reached to where his fingers closed on the knobby, furry head. A normal kitten would have clawed him good. This one did not. He drew from the hole such an object his impulse was to throw it back. It had been dropped—*dropped*—into the filth, and somehow managed to crawl up the wall to the ledge. Now that its eyes burned with light, it hissed at him, like a snake. He could bear neither to drop it nor to hold it, a tiny furry bundle of filth.

Naturally enough—he had to do something—he left the privy and headed for the pump. It needed no priming: water spilled from the nozzle and he held the creature beneath it, like a dirty ball of yarn. The little fight left in it stiffened the body, but it was too feeble to claw him. The dousing gave it the look of a long-whiskered fish. He hustled to the car, wrapped the creature in a T-shirt—one with "Smokey the Bear" stamped on it—then placed it on the floor in the warm draft off the engine. Once the little mouth opened wide, like a feeding bird, but it made no sound. Did it mean to frighten him with just a look? The eyes lidded, the head nodded, as it tried to hold the fierce expression. "Sleep! Sleep," he said, matter-of-factly, and fluffed the material to keep the light out. Had he never before looked closely at a kitten? Foxlike ears. Inside one ants were crawling. The nose was pink, the faintest vapor at one nostril. What sex was it? He recalled that Viola preferred female cats. At the thought of her he experienced her outrage at what he knew had happened. Some goddam kid—the word "goddam" was invariably followed by "kid"—had brought a batch of kittens to school and another goddam kid had thought of dropping one down a privy hole. The vileness of man made his eyes film over, and aroused his fury against heaven. "Dear Viola," he would say, "I thought you should know what the good Lord is up to here in Kansas." He resented her dying, since he could no longer torment her with his letters. "You're such a stubborn old curmudgeon I just feel sure the Lord

272

will have mercy on you!" What if that should prove true? Never in his life had he taken such nonsense seriously. But what about his death? He sat for some time, the cab rocking like a cradle in the wind stream of a cattle trailer, bits of straw and manure falling from the sky to ping on his windshield. Before starting up the car he glanced at the map to see where he was—to see where *they* were.

Garden City? On that previous trip they had stopped in Garden City to shoe the horse.

Under the spring seat of the buggy he had his own Gladstone, loaned to him by Wayne Wagstaff, a Burlington brakeman, and a fiberboard case, with straps, that contained her things and her *trousseau*. Where had she heard the word? It referred to garments that should never be worn. In those days she had been a girl with flesh so firm it took a good pair of teeth to bite her. With her dress over her head he was often tempted. Different than most women, she never squealed. One day into Texas a rattler struck her—a young one, almost too young to rattle. She had given him her hand, he almost fainting to see the blood spurt, where he had cut her, then shamed and mortified to feel desire for her as he sucked the wound. What sort of man was he? Like most, in her opinion. In the sand behind the house, some of it mixed with cement, he had taken her in broad daylight, while she strained to keep the laundry she was holding out of the dirt. He was something she learned to live with, like the weather, liking some of it, finding some of it irksome, but no cause for complaint. Was it the Indian in her? He had liked her being darker than his sallow sisters. She had a sentimental streak. If anybody said, "Have a good day, Muriel," she would make an effort to have one. Her older brother, Ivan, spent most of his time throwing his knife at trees.

Across the plains to the west, the tapering shaft of a grain elevator flashed like a mirror. On Mrs. Leidy's TV, in the trailer court, he had seen a moon rocket on its pad, waiting, smoking. "That's like an elevator!" he had exclaimed. She had never seen a grain elevator. He could not believe it. A woman from

273

Pennsylvania, sixty-eight years of age. An elevator for her was one that went up and down, nothing more.

It didn't make her any younger, but she seemed as far removed from him as the boy.

At about the boy's age, maybe a year younger, he had been lifted from the street on the Fourth of July to ride the same horse as Buffalo Bill, straddling the same saddle, his small hands gripping the horn. For a week his pecker had been sore, as if he'd rubbed it on the frame of a man's bicycle. That was something he had never told anybody, but he might have told the boy. He was not going to tell him anything he didn't want to know. When he began, "Now when I was a boy . . ." he could see him turn off. Did he think his Uncle Floyd had been somebody's uncle all of his life? The fact that he would always and forever be an uncle to the boy, plain and obvious as it was, was new to him. To the young, the old were born old, they came that way like old cars and old buildings. In the boy's mind that was how it was, and where *else* was he if not in the boy's mind? An old man with a trailer, a Maxwell coupe, and a sister, now dead, by the name of Viola. The youth Stanley had asked the boy, "Is that old fart your relation?" As he stood waiting for the boy's answer, Warner's eyes had watered. Would he ever answer? "Yeah," he had finally said, an admission forced from him by the need to tell the truth.

The strangeness of the fact that what he hadn't told the boy, the boy would now never know, made his limbs heavy. His hands keep their grasp on the wheel, but his foot slips from the gas pedal. Once more the car drifts to straddle the wavering center line.

What had he told him? That the way to clean a slate was to spit on it. "What's a slate?" the boy had replied. He hung around hippies and hippie places the way Warner had hung around gypsies. He is startled by how much they appear alike. The difference being that gypsies were gypsies, hippies were punks. What stories he might have told him—if he had been asked! These gypsies camped along the tracks, like hobos, and let their horses graze in the railroad ditch grass. They were known to be horse thieves. When the horses got old they sold them to glue factories, in Missouri. A kid of ten at the time, Warner would see their camp in the shadow of the railroad ties, west of town, or the glow of their fires under the water stack to the east. He had heard it rumored that they kidnapped white children only, and sold them for ransom, so he revealed himself, approaching so close they could see he was white by their own firelight, but nothing ever happened. Nor did he ever see them dancing. A woman nursing a child, dark as an Indian, came to the side of the buggy where Viola was sitting, rubbed the cloth of her skirt between her fingers, like money, then scuttled away. Viola would have given her the skirt if asked, but she was not asked. In the midst of a hailstorm he had seen some of the children running and hooting like little Indians, stooping to grab up a fistful of the hail and stuff it into their mouths. The boy, not knowing about gypsies, might easily think they were hippies. Their clothes were bizarre. They roamed about free as the wind.

If he had told the boy about these gypsies, their carefree ways, their adventurous lives, would he have been able to grasp that his Uncle Floyd had once been young? About this he felt a deeper injustice than he did about the two hippies. That had been his choice. But would he never understand that the old man, too, had once made one? Was it beyond him to grasp that Floyd Warner had once watched the big boys take their girls into the weeds behind the Chautauqua, and when they had left he would sneak in to lie on the still-warm trampled grass? He would never be told that. He would grow up and grow old without ever knowing how much, as *boys,* they were alike.

4

LULLED BY THE IDLING MOTOR, THE
kitten appeared to be asleep. How long since it had eaten? It might
have been in that filth for several days. That led him to think
of the cats back at the farm and who would now feed them with
Viola gone. They lived in the barn. There might sometimes be
as many as two dozen cats, half of them wild. It was not unusual
for a person not to see them till the cows were milked, and they
lined up to be fed. Once they got a whiff of warm milk their tails
went up. Since he could remember Viola had insisted that fresh
Guernsey milk was not good for kittens, unless they got it second-
hand in the customary manner. It curdled in their stomachs, she
said, or something like that. The old man didn't believe that for
a moment, but he did feel that this kitten, after such an experience,
should have something solid on its stomach. Mrs. Leidy, in the
Rubio trailer court, fed her cat canned fish.

The tower of the grain elevator, now that he was getting
closer, proved to be higher than he had imagined. The grove of
trees at its base looked like bushes, the houses and freight cars
like a toy village. It delighted him to see that this grain elevator
had been recently painted, and the church hadn't. It stunned him
to realize he no longer had Viola to torment with such observa-
tions. "There's this town in Kansas," he would have written,
"where they got eleven churches and seven people. The folks are
all so religious they just repainted the grain elevator." In recent
letters he had kidded her more than usual to make sure she would
write them right back, the boy being of an age he needed a good
woman in his life.

The way the cab jolted crossing the tracks led him to stop
the car and take a look at the kitten. He could see the light through
one pink ear. A tiny spider moved about in the hairs, as if they

were grass. A jumbled but appealing image of life within life, as small as this spider and as big as this earth, awed and instantly escaped him. In the river of his blood life swam. He had heard or read that somewhere. A woman known to Mrs. Leidy had once sat on a needle that turned up, years later, in her forearm, where it wanted out. It had traveled here and there in her body. She swore to it. That his own life had passed without his knowing about the life within him pleasantly dazed him. Over the Grand Canyon—so he had read—two huge planes had collided, having approached from opposite sides of the country, like two flies, a commentator had said, colliding in space. This awesome reverie was interrupted by the hiss of steam pluming to the left of the radiator cap. The column of red in the heat indicator pressed the flag at the top to signal *Danger*. Another time he might have instantly killed the motor. Now he let it run. He lifted the kitten from the floor—it seemed to be sleeping—and placed the bundle in the sun's rays on the shelf behind the seat, and as he entered the town of Minden Warner looked for a school building, which might have a water pump at the front or the back.

He bought gas in Minden, but rejected the suggestion that his fan belt needed changing. He had bought it new in California. The previous belt had lasted for eleven years. He did accept from the attendant a map of the Southwest, showing the roads to Roswell and south along the Pecos. At this time of year he could go in along the river, it would be so dry. Getting a buggy in and out was no problem, unless it was in the flood season, but once they had a car, which was not this one, getting in and out was often up to the car, there being no way he knew to keep the battery charged. After some months of experience he parked it on the rise halfway to the road, where a push might start it, but if the motor didn't catch it would set in the hollow until he got a horse to tow him, or a ride to where he could charge the battery. That car had been such a headache that when he did get it to Roswell he sold it for junk.

Across from the gas station a gleaming metal hitch bar ran the length of the street, the sidewalk shaded by a wooden awning. A horse was tied up at the hitch bar, a sight so unusual the

278

old man considered it for a moment. A brown horse, nothing to speak of, with an army-type saddle over an Indian blanket. A young fellow of the type you only see in the movies, no shoes on his feet, a blue and white bandanna around his neck to keep his shirt clean, came toward the horse with a transistor radio held to his ear, like it hurt him. "You want to buy a horse?" he shouted at Warner. Why did he think he would want to buy a horse? He got himself on the back of the horse, with some effort, and let it walk off with him as if he were wounded, holding his head. The music seemed to come from inside the horse.

Back in the shade of the awning a voice called out, "California? It wouldn't be Frisco?"

Until he said that Warner had forgotten the California plate. One of the things he had done in Chapman was wipe it off.

"It wouldn't *have* to be Frisco," said the speaker. "Salinas, Modesto, Bakersfield—you name it." The old man saw him dimly, back in the shade, until he came forward dragging an olive-green duffle. Above his reddish beard his face was the color of raw meat. Beside a pale, sallow man he might have looked healthy, his teeth gleaming as he smiled. Warner didn't like a man of his type in city clothes. The hoist he took in his pants revealed dirty feet without socks. Much as the old man disliked the young, in general, he disliked a canny old bum even worse. He had no sympathy for a man who would sleep in his clothes. This one was maybe twenty-five years Warner's junior, and from the way he acted he knew that. He resented Warner's having lived so long—never mind how he looked. The old man could judge that for himself in the way he was reflected in the café window. It was as if he sat on a stool at the counter, and had turned to look out. Behind him the street glared, so that his outline seemed to shimmer with a blue flame. He had always prided himself on being wiry. He had never before seen himself shriveled. What he saw was not a wiry old coot, but a shriveled old man. Back in Rubio, on the asphalt of the playground a child had printed

Mr. Warner is a potato bug

and he saw plainly as the nose on his face that the child was right. Buglike and bandy-legged, the head wider than the shoulders (the ears still growing), the hands dangling from the sleeves like roots. One would say that whatever he had been, the bug would out. It had not occurred to Warner, until he saw the reflection, that old men were impostors: inside they were one thing, but outside they were man-size potato bugs. This old bum with his duffle, who stood sizing up Warner, had not yet reached the stage of transformation. He looked like a people. Rolls of fat concealed the bug in him slowly emerging. He spit out the toothpick he had been chewing, prepared to come on strong with this stranger, this feeble old fart. "R-L-N?" he said, reading the letters off the license. "Now what county's that?"

Before Warner actually sensed what the issue was, he knew that it hung in balance. If he didn't call it, right off the bat, it would be too late. He thought of saying that it meant *Runs Like New,* which had been the boy's contribution, but it was not the best retort for a city-type bum like this one. "Owner's initials," he said, matter-of-factly, which was what the boy had wanted but they hadn't got, there being an extra charge for such nonsense. He dipped his head to pass beneath the hitch bar, then walked in the shade to the door of the café. A fan above the door blew the smell of chili into his face. A fly-specked mirror reflected the cook, who stood with his back to the counter, frying bacon. He was the nervous type who couldn't let a strip of bacon lie there and cook. The old man was crazy about hash-brown potatoes but not the ones that came frozen and they served half raw. He also had to keep in mind that he should eat something he could share with the cat. At one end of the counter a young man squeezed catsup from a plastic container onto a plate of French fries, and at the other a squat, broad-shouldered fellow leaned on the counter as he ate an ice cream cone. In the mirror behind the counter Warner saw his dark face, the hair, black as a crow's, that hung to his shoulders. He did not lift his eyes until he sensed that someone at his back was looking at him. A real Indian. Warner stood there, staring at him.

The cook said, "You don't have to sit at the counter, mister.

There's tables if you don't care to sit at the counter." Did he think Warner was one of those people who wouldn't sit down to eat with an Indian? He seemed to. If Warner had been free to, he would have told the cook that the Indian's being there was no surprise to him. Quite the contrary. Seeing him there was almost reassuring. Of all the things in this world, or almost all of them, there was nothing that Warner disliked more than a day full of happenings like so many leaves blowing. Since morning, one thing had led to another, and they had all led to this seat at the counter. He returned the cook's stare. Behind the menu finger-painted on the mirror he could see the Indian licking the ice cream, his tongue smeared with the chocolate color.

"This fellow here," went on the cook—he had turned from the grill to point his flipper at the Indian—"has been over there and come back. If you want to know what it's like, you should ask him." He put that question to the young man on Warner's right, who sat back on the stool in such a manner it pulled his pants far down on his buttocks, exposing patches of hair. Warner saw him through the eyes of the Indian. Clippers had worked around his ears and up the back of his neck, but below his ears he was a hippie.

"Man, I know what it's like." He gripped the bun he was eating with both hands to keep the slice of ham in it from slipping away from him.

"You know shit," said the cook. "You ever kill anybody? You ever see a man killed you just loaned money?"

"I ain't, and I don't plan to," said the young man.

To Warner the cook said, "Pop, what'll it be?"

"Two eggs, with hash browns," replied Warner.

The cook was relieved to have somebody as old and prejudiced as Warner to talk to. "Nobody knows till they been there, ain't that right, Pop?"

"Depends," he replied, "you been dead long, you don't know much."

The young man on Warner's right guffawed hoarsely, then choked up with a fit of coughing. No sound of any kind from the Indian. His attention was focused on doing one thing at a time. Warner knew about Indians, having once hired a boy by the name of Kira to herd sheep for him. He would spend days by himself on the open range. Warner had found the boy a slow learner but he didn't hold that against him. In those days the men would sell you the rings off their fingers, the blanket off their backs, if they had one. This Indian on his left had the smooth copper color of the one on the penny. On the right sleeve of his jacket he wore an emblem that looked newer than the jacket.

"What outfit's that one?" said the cook, giving Warner a wink. "The Cleveland Indians?"

Warner knew that was some sort of wisecrack, but he didn't get it. Were there Indians as far east as Cleveland? "You hear me?" said the cook. "What outfit's that one?" He moved to point his grill scraper at the emblem on the sleeve.

The Indian shrugged. "Not my jacket." He had nibbled the cone down to where he had to hold it between the tips of two fingers, like a cigarette butt.

"Not your jacket?" The cook saw he had a point there, but he decided not to make it. "I guess you guys get the surplus before we do, eh?"

Did the Indian hear that? Warner was thinking how the Pueblo-type Indians were a different kettle of fish from the Sioux and the Blackfeet, who lived in tents, and would as soon, or even sooner, kill a white man as look at him. This Pueblo-type Indian, a Navajo or a Hopi, turned on the stool to lick his fingers clean, like a cat. It reminded Warner of the one in the cab, and that he hadn't ordered food a sick kitten might eat. Getting no answer from the Indian, the cook had turned back to flip the eggs. "I've heard it both ways," he went on, to keep the conversation going. "If they don't like the war, they do like the girls. Ain't that right?"

The Indian raised his eyes to look right at Warner without seeing him. On the right side of his jacket, just below the shoulder, there were three small holes, one beside the other. They were brown around the edges as if they might have been burned with a cigarette.

"Ain't that right?" the cook repeated.

The young fellow on Warner's right replied, "If a booby trap blows it off, what good's a girl?"

"Hell," said the cook, "they'll sew you on a new one. They get a lot of spare parts in these wars, as well as jackets. You'll just never know what you'll find in war surplus till you go and look!" He slapped his flipper on the grill, then added, "Never mind how you like it, buster, just be glad you're back!"

"Why be glad am back?" replied the Indian. The cook had not expected him to answer that one. The old man was thinking there was nothing you could say to which somebody wouldn't take exception.

"Hell, you're alive," said the cook. "You're not in a goddam box." Having said it, he seemed to wish that he hadn't, but the Indian let it pass. "Nothing's perfect," said the cook, "but the killing's over—"

"What killing over?" answered the Indian. He showed no emotion. He asked as if he was ignorant, and wanted to know. From the napkin dispenser he removed one of the napkins and carefully cleaned his sticky fingers. The calm way he did it led Warner to feel he missed the gist of the cook's statement.

The cook said, 'You know what that napkin cost me? You're free to use it, but you know what it cost me?"

"No," said the Indian. "What it cost you?"

The old man couldn't figure out if it was what he said, or something in his manner. The cook said, "Let's forget the napkin. Let's just you and me forget the goddam napkin, no matter what it cost. Let me just ask you what it costs me to provide you with a stool for your ass to sit on while you sit and eat a fifteen-cent order. You know what my time is supposed to be worth? Let me ask you that."

The Indian had been served a glass of water. They watched him take two little swallows of it. Someone like the cook might be led to think that he had merely spoiled it for anybody else. To cool things off Warner said to the Indian, "Young man, what is your name?"

"George Blackbird," he replied. "Old man, what is yours?"

Warner was too flabbergasted to be offended. Did he mean to be like that, or didn't he know better?

"Blackbird?" said the cook. "That's translated from the Indian?"

The slow movement of his head seemed to be an assent. It took time, the old man was thinking, to get accustomed to their impassive manner.

"My name's Warner," he said, since he had been asked. "Floyd Warner."

The cook said, "Why you Indians so strong on the bird idea? Blackbird, Thunderbird, Warbird, so forth?"

"What's wrong with that?" said the young man. He took a swallow of his Coke. "I like it better than Clay, which is the name of dirt."

"Your name is Clay?"

"Clay's my first name. Another thing is, they often think it's my last name."

"It wouldn't be Clay Ridge?" asked the cook. He winked at Warner, assuming the Indian wouldn't get it.

"No, it wouldn't," the young man replied. He didn't say what it would be.

"Old man," said George Blackbird, "what you want?"

In the pause that followed they could hear the bacon frying. Warner really wasn't sure he had heard it right, or if it was something he had sat there thinking, having heard it before.

"His name is Warner, like he said," the cook retorted. "He'd probably like a cup of coffee, for one thing. How about a piece of pie?" He moved to one side so Warner could see the pie in the case. It was all pie with the meringue piled on it to look like a cake. It hadn't crossed his mind that the Indian thought he wanted more to eat. "I see you're driving," said the cook. "Which way you headed?"

"West," he replied. "Just east of Roswell."

"What's there to do in that country?" asked the cook. "You in cattle?" The old man sensed he didn't care a damn, but did it just to keep the Indian from talking.

"Sheep," he replied. "I'm a sheep rancher."

284

"God bless and protect you!" said the cook. He shook his head in the manner of a man well known to sheep. "I've seen more people lose their shirts in sheep—"

"Well, I didn't lose mine." It made him conscious of the old one he had on; he hadn't change it in weeks.

"You were either smart, or you were lucky. The only sheep I like is a lamb chop."

Warner restrained his impulse to point out that lamb was not sheep. A man that dumb was not a man to discuss the sheep business with further.

"I wasn't so smart. I just did it by myself. Me and the dog."

"I'm interested to hear you say that," said the cook. "You must be about the last white man in the business. I understand they brought in these Basques, from Europe, when they couldn't get Americans to do it. They go off and live on the range with them, for weeks at a time."

"I lived with them"—he couldn't help but say it—"day in and day out for seventeen years." He saw that the cook didn't believe it. "Then I gave it up and moved to California."

"So why you go back?" said George Blackbird.

The cook said, "You previously asked this gentleman what it was he wanted. I'd say what he'd like is to be left alone to eat, to finish his meal in peace."

The old man might have left it there, but he thought it curious for the Indian to ask him what he was asking himself. "I was just visiting my people, along the Platte. On the way back I thought I'd look in on the homestead."

"Was what you had a homestead?"

"Yes, sir, that was what I had." It pleased Warner to speak to someone who could appreciate a homestead. So far as he knew it wasn't yet of much value, but one day anything fronting on the highway would be. The way people were coming, they would crowd into hell once they opened it up.

The cook said, "You rent it out or sell it?"

"I let it set," he replied, and that's how he saw it on his mind's eye. The cabin sitting on a rise, not a good place for it, down in the hollow would have been better, but it was what Muriel wanted and what she got. Up there she could see to the Rockies in the winter, or turn and look along the Pecos in the spring and summer, the water as green as the willows until muddied with the rains. A nice place except for the goddam everlasting wind. "It sets back—" he said, waving his hand to the left, "not much on it but the cabin."

"How's it for fish?" said the cook. "Maybe I'll rent it. God, do I love to fish!"

Truth to tell, the old man didn't really know, not caring for fish. There were fish in the Pecos when there was water, but right now there would be little water.

"You go there now?" George Blackbird asked. Even the cook thought the question more respectful. Blackbird leaned on the counter, folding the napkin he had used into an airplane. He held it up as if he meant to sail it, then changed his mind.

"I'm thinking of just looking in," Warner said.

George Blackbird nodded. "Me, too."

What did he mean by that? What he meant, it turned out, was that he was just looking in on his own people, who were near Winslow.

"That mean they're Hopis?" asked the cook.

That wasn't what he meant, but it was what they were.

"I was a cook for two winters at the Thunderbird Lodge up at the Canyon," said the cook. "I got to know a lot of Hopis." He extended toward the old man the ring finger on his right hand. An uneven piece of turquoise, darker at the edges, was set in silver framed by six silver drops. "That's a real one, Pop. One of the old ones. The drops stand for rain. The turquoise in their language stands for the sky."

They all waited for George Blackbird to comment. The ring was there for him to see, but he ignored it. "I happen to *know* this is an old ring," said the cook. "The Indian put it in hock. They gave him twenty bucks for it. They don't give you twenty bucks for anything that's not old."

A cool draft of fresh air blew George Blackbird's paper airplane from the counter to the floor, where he let it lie. The cook looked to the door and said, "You're welcome to step in or step out, mister." In the mirror behind the counter Warner could see the bum with his olive-green duffle, framed in the door. He couldn't seem to make up his mind to step in, or back out.

"I don't mind waitin'," he said, "if I know I got a ride. You plan to move along soon?"

"Don't rush a man when he's eatin'," said the cook. "For chrissakes, nobody likes to be rushed. Let the man have his coffee."

"No rush," said the bum, "I just need to know if I got a ride." He put a smile on his face that made him look like Happy Hooligan in the mirror. Warner didn't speak. He let the cook add hot coffee to his cup. George Blackbird rose from his stool as if he meant to leave, and the bum at the door stepped out to let him pass. Instead of stepping out, he closed the door in the bum's face. The cook couldn't believe it. The bum couldn't believe it. George Blackbird stood there, his hands in his jacket pockets, so that the coat hugged him at the hips. Near the middle of the back, like buttons, were four bullet-size holes. Warner was thinking that the way they did things today it might have been only yesterday he was at war, somewhere in Vietnam.

"Bygod, you do beat all," said the cook. "You learn that in the Army?"

George Blackbird remained facing the door, returning the gaze of the man he could see through it. The bum looked more dumbfounded than mad. He wouldn't know what to think until something else happened. "The nerve of that old bastard," said the cook. "I wouldn't give him the time, if I were you. I'd let him walk."

George Blackbird's head nodded. "He walk—I ride."

It was neither a question nor an assertion. In either case, it was not what Warner was accustomed to deal with.

"Wouldn't you say that was up to Mr. Warner?" asked the cook. George Blackbird didn't say who it was up to. The cook would have preferred, the old man would have preferred, and even the young man, Clay, would have liked it better if he had turned from the door and faced the mirror, instead of showing them his back. Seeing only his back in the mirror led them all to turn and look to the front. The bum had moved from the door to lean his duffle on the front fender of the Maxwell.

"Unless I need someone to spell me off," said the cook, "I personally like to travel by myself. People got their own habits. Most of them either talk or they smoke too much. I picked up a kid west of Topeka who played the mouth organ all the way to Garden City, where I let him off."

One thing about Indians, Warner was thinking, was that they didn't talk much. In his first year on the ranch he had a boy named Awa help him with the sheep. He was pretty good with the sheep, and almost cheap as a dog. He disliked coffee. He didn't like water on his hands or face. Muriel couldn't understand until she asked herself how he lived in that wind without his skin cracking. The dust on his skin was like a talcum, until he washed it off. It was hard for them both to get over feeling dirty and settle for one or two baths a winter, but that was the way to get through the winter without their hands and wrists cracking with the chap. That little Indian could live in the wind like a bird. The only trouble they had was that there was no way to tell a dumb Indian from a smart one, both Indians being short on talk. Warner had given the boy a board and set of checkers for Christmas but later found he had used them as wheels to make toys and skates. Was that dumb or smart? If he had to go somewhere in a car, however, and choose between a white bum and a dumb Indian . . . "Mr. Blackbird," he said, "where you headed?" The Indian sat there as if wondering. "I'm not going so far today," the old man said, "but I'll take you as far as I go."

Did Blackbird think that was reasonable? He still didn't say. He did turn to look at a rack of Hostess cupcakes and select a pack with chocolate icing. As he accepted his money the cook said, "I ought to charge you extra for the napkin, you know that?"

Clay said, "Which would you rather have, napkins or trees?"

"You ever wipe your ass with a tree?" asked the cook. The old man had, as a matter of fact, but he was not fool enough to admit it. To the Indian the cook said, "You travel light, I will say that."

Blackbird paid for the cupcakes with pennies, stacking them

288

in little piles of five on the counter. He helped himself to a toothpick as the cook rang up the sum.

Warner said, "You wouldn't have some scraps for a cat?"

"They won't eat scraps. That's why I don't have one. You got a cat that eats scraps you got something special." He wagged his grill scraper at the cans of tuna arranged in a pyramid behind the counter. "That's what they feed cats now," he said. "I've seen it on the TV."

George Blackbird said, "Cats eat fish. Like fish."

"How much a can of that worth?" the old man asked.

"Cost me thirty-eight cents wholesale. It's worth forty-five to me; what's it worth to you?"

The old man was thinking how he used to buy fish, maybe it wasn't tuna, for nine cents a can. That was fish for himself. "I'll take one can," he said, then he added, "I'll never get it open. You got an opener?"

"This is a diner," said the cook, "not a goddam dime store."

"I just mean to open it," Warner replied. The cook put the can on his cutting board, then used an old-fashioned opener to cut it open, leaving the crimped-edged lid still attached to the can.

"Don't cut yourself with you pry it up. There's nothing sharper than a goddam can lid."

"Blade of grass sharp, too," said Blackbird.

In another situation Warner might have said, "You're one smart Indian!" but in this one he didn't. What he did was stand a moment looking at him. Would anyone but an Indian know about the edge on a blade of grass? Holding the can by the rim, careful not to tip it—there's nothing that lasts so long on your fingers as fish oil—he walked out through the door the Indian held open to the cool shade of the awning, the fan blowing at his back. Then he let the Indian lead him to the car, as if he might need help getting the door open. The old bum had his duffle between the hood and the fender, as if that was his customary place to store it, but George Blackbird, as if he did it all the time, as easy as a postman handling a mail sack, picked it up by the drawstrings and gave it a swing over the hitch bar to where it plopped on the walk under the awning. He did it so easy anybody would have said it was Blackbird's car. He opened the door for Warner to climb in—first leaning in to put the can of tuna on the back shelf—then he walked around the car to let himself in the door on the other side. That was the door that might open anytime, and the old man kept it wired. "Hold on," Warner said, and leaned over to unhook the coat hanger from the handle. Blackbird let himself in, then wired it up as if it were something to which he was accustomed. A really smart Indian. Was it the war that made him so smart? Warner almost felt grateful toward him for getting him out of a sorry situation with the old bum. He had a chew in his mouth—Warner could see it, the way he stood staring with his mouth open—and would have spent his time cranking the window up and down so he could spit. A smart Indian like Blackbird might smoke a little, but he wouldn't talk. In choosing a red man over a white man—and he didn't really choose him, he had been chosen—Warner felt less guilt than he might have since most people impressed him as no damn good, especially whites. Another thing about Blackbird, the moment he got in the car he didn't peer around and make smart cracks about it, or ask if it was a wood or coal burner. To an Indian a car was a car. One thing Warner would have done, if alone, would have been to see where he was on the map, but he didn't want to give Blackbird the idea he had to look at a map to see where he was going. The Maxwell bucked a bit when he put it in reverse, so that the canteen dangling from the choke handle thumped Blackbird on the shin. Without asking if he might, the Indian shortened the strap so that it wouldn't swing, unscrewed the cap and took a swallow of the water, put the cap back on, then sat with it propped between his thighs. How long was it that Warner, a foolish smile on his face, just stood or sat and watched such things happen? It seemed to him, since morning, they were watched by something in him besides himself.

Since Muriel had died, and he had gone looking for another wife, Warner had not sat this close to an Indian. On his way to California he had stopped in Gallup, where the all-night diner had been full of them. When he came out of the diner, unaccustomed to the traffic, he had been hit by a pickup without any headlights, three ribs broken and his leg sprained. The nurse who looked after him had been a young lady from Pasadena, named Eileen Coyle. She had come from California to put in a year of practical training among the Indians. She did not like the soft life of Pasadena. She loved the life of Indians on the reservation. In less time than it took for his leg to heal he had asked her to marry him, and she had accepted. She did not like many white men in general, but she liked him. Warner was not experienced in judging young women, and she was inexperienced in judging older sheep ranchers, believing right up to the moment they left the highway, east of Roswell, that he was taking her back to one of those Rancho Grandes, with a big hacienda, she had seen in the movies. They came in after dark so she didn't see much, but it had been enough.

Sometime toward morning, while Warner slept, she hiked back to the highway and got a ride somewhere. She never wrote to him, nor returned for her three suitcases full of clothes. A lawyer in Santa Barbara later notified him that the marriage had been annulled. To think about it now, almost thirty-five years later, left him as speechless as it had then. A woman old enough to flirt with him, to marry him, to give up, as she said, her career for him, had refused to get out of the car when she saw the house in the flickering headlights. Her expression had been that of a woman too startled to scream. He couldn't budge her—she had been a girl on the hefty side, almost as tall as he was—so he had left a lamp burning so she could find her way when "she came to her senses." Whatever senses she had come to had led her to climb out and take off.

Thanks to this young woman—Warner no longer had, if he ever had, a clear picture of her features—his appreciation of the woman he had married came too late. Muriel Dosey's only complaints had been about the flapping side curtains of their first car. She would rather walk, she said, but she meant that as a simple statement of fact, not a threat.

As if he smelled something burning, Blackbird tilted his head back and sniffed the air. The sun on the cab had made it hot.

"It's the fish," Warner explained, since he could smell it

291

himself. But Blackbird knew the smell of canned fish, and that was not it. He bent over low to sniff the air under the dashboard, as if it might be something wrong with the motor. Warner let the car drift and the motor idle: a good nose might save them both a lot of trouble. But what Blackbird smelled was not under the hood but in the hot air of the cab: he turned to sniff behind him. On the shelf at his back his gaze fastened on the soiled Smokey the Bear T-shirt. At one end of it the kitten's ratlike tail was visible. Blackbird moved his head closer, then drew back as if he didn't like cats, his lips pressed together.

"It's asleep," said Warner. "I'm letting it sleep."

Did Blackbird doubt that? He turned in the seat once more to sniff the air, then gripped the tip of the tail, the T-shirt falling away as he held up the soiled lifeless body. Blackbird looked directly at all there was to see, then flicked it, like a match, through the lowered window.

"Dead cat," he pronounced, "more surplus."

Why didn't Warner speak up? He had gone to considerable trouble to salvage the creature, and how could he be sure that it was dead? Did Blackbird see things more clearly? Could he be sure of Blackbird, if not himself? The Indian's attention had been diverted from the cat to the opened can of tuna on the same shelf. He picked it up, careful not to spill the oil, using the nail of one finger to pry up the lid, placed it on the seat between them, then tilted to one side to search in his pockets for a knife. With the small blade of the knife he speared hunks of the tuna, carried them to his mouth. Was that, too, something he had learned in the Army? He ate about half the tin, then pressed the lid flat on what remained, cleaning the blade of the knife on the leather of his boot top. Naturally he was thirsty, after eating the fish, and had himself several swallows from the canteen, leaving a film of fish oil from his lips on the spout.

The sun shining through the windshield increased the heat in the cab, and the smell of the fish. Into Warner's head, out of nowhere, popped a notion so strange it made him smile. The moment coming up, the one that came toward him like the line on the highway, then receded behind him, was something he had no control over. He could watch it coming, he could see it receding, but he could do nothing to avoid it. The Indian, the cat, and the prayer ceremony had come out of nowhere to take him somewhere. He could see it happening. He could see that it was not an accident. He had come this way by his own free choosing, and having chosen as he pleased, he was right where he was. One thing led to another, to another, to another, like the count of the poles that passed his window.

"What you say?" asked Blackbird.

Had Warner said something, or did the fellow hear what he had been thinking? He was one smart Indian. Warner didn't like him, but he paid him his respects. Now that they were driving west the lowering sun made Blackbird squint as if he was smiling, but Warner knew it was more of a grimace, as if salt burned his eyes. Now long accustomed to it, neither of them noticed the smell of the fish.

5

SOMETIME LATER HE WOKE UP WITH
Blackbird wrestling him for the steering wheel. The left front
wheel of the car was sweeping the ditch grass on the wrong side
of the road. Fortunately Blackbird, who proved to be stronger,
forced the wheel in the other direction. "What the goddam hell!"
the old man shouted, too worked up and startled to keep his
mouth shut.

"You fall asleep," said Blackbird, "drive off the road."

Warner could not deny it. The truth was he was accustomed
to being spelled off, especially late in the day.

"Old man, I drive," Blackbird stated, and Warner could think
of nothing to say. Blackbird seemed in no hurry, taking time to
pee in the car's cool shade when Warner stopped it. He also
seemed familiar with the gear shift, but he was not so adept at
it as the boy. The car bucked and died. On starting up again,
he almost shifted into reverse. The changeover had loosened them
both up a little, and Blackbird helped himself to one of his cupcakes; the old man declined. By way of explanation, not to hurt
his feelings, he explained that he didn't like to eat without his
coffee, especially anything sweet. He would often as not go
without eating rather than eat then find he had no coffee.

Blackbird said, "You like me, you got no people."

Actually, Warner had said nothing much about people. The
Indian always seemed to infer more than Warner had said. "I've
got people," he said, "here and there, but no more in this part
of the country. That's what brought me back."

"No people is bad," said Blackbird.

In most respects the old man would deny that, having lived
most of his life without them, but he understood that Indians
were of a more sociable nature. It was enough for them to be

around each other. They didn't have to talk. "What became of yours?" Warner asked him. Blackbird shrugged. The old man was sure he meant to go on, if for no other reason than he had been asked. "Not only Indian people have a bad time," he continued, "it's a bad time for people in general. Families break up. They move around too much. They don't have their own place."

"Indians move around, too," said Blackbird, "move around to hunt, to fish, to kill."

The old man was made ill at ease by the word "kill." It was the Indian's nature to speak like that, but in the context of their talk the word was disturbing. Why couldn't he have said to hunt and to fish, and let the matter drop?

"I suppose that's true," Warner replied, "but you still don't move around as much as we do. Pueblo people stay put, most Hopis and Navajos stay put."

"No stay put," said Blackbird. "Keep put."

The old man had to respect a smart Indian. He tried to catch his eye in the rear-view mirror, but Blackbird kept his narrow gaze on the road. "I suppose that's true," Warner added.

"Keep put till killing," Blackbird said, "then draft him."

If he wanted to refer to the war as the killing, Warner was not prepared to argue with him. It did seem he used the word more than he had to. Did he use it because he liked it?

"The killing is bad," replied Warner, to put Blackbird at his ease. He wagged his head as if to free it from the thought of the pointless killing, the millions who were now dead.

Blackbird also shook his head, then said, "Killing not bad— always killing something."

Warner gave himself time to think over what he had heard. There were good wars and bad wars, as everybody knew, but he would not refer to wars as good or bad killings. An Indian might. In that respect, among others, he was different from a white man. It amused the old man to see an Indian like Blackbird in a white man's war, the issues simplified to killing or being killed. Warner knew Indians, he had hired them, he took it for granted they weren't like white men, so his feeling about Blackbird's withdrawal was not a personal matter: no better or

296

worse than that of a stranger asleep in a bus seat. This would not, however, explain Warner's feelings when Blackbird took the trouble to look at him. His small black eyes were without expression. He did not wink or blink or move his head to indicate he was being looked at. If he had been a dog, he would not have wagged his tail. When the cat had stopped hissing at Warner like a snake, he had looked at him in a similar manner. Impersonal. Nobody knew, for sure, what was on an Indian's mind, least of all, maybe, an Indian, but Warner had not previously felt how little it mattered. There sat Blackbird. Here sat Warner. The poles made a sound as they passed the car window.

"Always killing something," George Blackbird repeated. Then he added, "My father kill his younger brother."

Not to show shock—Blackbird showed none—the old man said, "A family quarrel? They had a fight over something?"

"No quarrel," said Blackbird. "According to tradition, older brother kill younger brother." The old man did not speak. He did not feel, as he should have felt, a rising flood of anger; he felt only tired. Blackbird was a presence, Blackbird was a force, outside of his experience. He was like the boy Stanley and the girl Joy: he was too much. "No traditions now," continued Blackbird, "less killing. Older brother in jail now for killing. For an accident."

"An accident?" Warner echoed. He was not sure he cared to hear about it.

"My brother, four braves, go on raiding party. They ride three days into enemy country, raid tent of enemy braves, make many blows on him. Then my brother make a blow, but by accident kill him. A good raid, with good blows, but he kills by accident. They find and put him in jail. For killing by accident they put him on trial."

It was a long speech for George Blackbird; now and then he raised both hands from the wheel, the palms forward. There was something to be said about the white man's justice, but the old man could not say it. His wits seemed dazed, as if the *words* had been blows. In a similar situation—that one, too, in the car— the young hippie Stanley had said something that had outraged

297

him. But he had said nothing. He had done nothing. He had not relieved himself with a stream of curses. He had been faced with something with which he could not *cope,* a word he had picked up from the hippies. He had failed to cope then, and he failed to cope now. In a Reno washroom, as he stood buttoning his pants, he had heard one of the men in the booths telling a story, he did not know to whom. The gist of the story was that a woman being raped, if she was smart, would relax and enjoy it. He couldn't cope with that either, but perhaps his resignation was of that order. Did a woman after rape feel as he felt?

Slouched in the seat, Warner alternately dozed and watched the blood-red horizon darken, indifferent to the fact that this meant tomorrow would be a good day. Now and then lights came toward them like puffballs shot from Roman candles, exploding as they struck the windshield. He had been asleep when they stopped at a red light, and a car heavily thumped the rear bumper. A pickup truck, crowded with young hoodlums, honked to attract Blackbird's attention. The old man was relieved it was the Indian at the wheel, not himself. They drew alongside, leaning out to leer at them, howling their obscene remarks at the Maxwell. Only days before, Warner would have cranked down the window and cursed them silent. The young were amazed to see such fury in an old man. Now he observed them with a curious detachment, as if their speech were alien to him. Blackbird parked the car at the side of a diner where the windows were lit up. Warner might have been a child, on a railroad platform, peering up at the lights of a diner, but now he looked without envy, without wonder, without appetite.

Did Blackbird assume he was asleep? As if he thought the old man might drive off and leave him, he took the keys from the ignition, then walked through the diner to the men's room at the back. Before he came back to a seat at the counter, Warner had dozed off.

During the night, the car moving, he awoke thinking he was riding in the trailer. That was not unusual, but he could not carry the thought through to its conclusion. Who was driving? Where

298

were they going? He went on musing without knowing. On a rise, somewhere, he opened his eyes to see what he thought was the farm burning, but it was only the lights of a town reflected on the clouds.

6

WHERE WERE THEY?

A film of rust-colored water splattered the windshield, the
light coming through the window at the back of the cab. The
glare was so direct the old man thought it might be the light of
an approaching locomotive. It was the sun, however, looking
like an explosion in space. With blinking eyes, he seemed to wait
for the report. Out here where distances were hard to judge he
had learned to estimate them the best he could, noting the length
of the gap between the flash of lightning and the peal of the
thunder. That storm's about forty miles away, he'd say to Muriel,
and often it was.

No one sat at the wheel; the cab door hung open to show
the hard, cracked surface of mud in the ditch. On the far side
of the ditch was a tilted pole with a single glass insulator on a
peg at the top. The sun had faded its bright bottle-green color
to that of smoked glass. It no longer bore a wire, so the pole
would not hum if a boy pressed his cheek, or an ear, to it. Even
in the old days he had had trouble with the men who used the
glass insulators for target practice, turning off the power that
pumped his water. In the spring, when the Pecos ran clear, he
often carried water to the house in milk cans. Every drop of rain
dripped into gutters that carried it to oil barrels for storage. When
the level of the water was low there might be tadpoles swimming
in the dipper. Muriel refused to drink it. She feared they might
swim forever in her insides, or turn into frogs. Had living out
here shortened her life? The doctor in Roswell had made no comment. "I wouldn't say her life was easy," Warner had said, thinking the doctor might contradict him. But he did not. "No, I suppose not," he had replied. No woman had an easy life on a
homestead, but they had never lacked for essentials. Nor had it

301

been for the lack of money they went without luxuries. To bring a privy into the house had always impressed her as foolish. If it had been there, she might have paid money to get it out. They had both thought, when they were older, to get a little farm in Oregon, with some trees on it, with a woods nearby where he could hunt and fish. "I don't feel right in my side, Floyd," she had said, and two weeks later she was dead.

Would the Indian have said something *killed* her? Through a hole between splatters Warner could see him pouring water into the radiator. A vapor of steam slowly appeared, but did not blow off. The way the Indian was darkened by the cab's shadow, the old man felt it might be evening. What time was it? The moment he asked he knew where he was. The sun came up like that to warm the east wall of the house till the boards creaked, like branches, warm to his hand while his breath smoked white in the darkened room. It did not seem remarkable the car had stopped where it did, but merely the last in a series of inevitable events. One thing led to another. No accidents.

"What happened?" he called to Blackbird.

"Motor run hot. No fan belt."

If I were you, the man in the station said to Warner, *I'd change this belt.* But the man was not him. He was a man called Tex by the boy at the pumps. Warner unhooked the coat hanger from the handle of the door and pushed it open so he could climb out. For a moment he stood beside the car, unable to straighten up. Blackbird moved to look at him. "Old man, you sick?"

He was old, not sick. He asked, "Where we at?"

One hand shading his eyes, the Indian stared down the road to the east, as if he saw something. A moment passed before Warner saw the girders of the bridge, as if slowly approaching. They were painted white. He could not recall a white-painted bridge.

"Pecos River," said Blackbird.

On the hills around him Warner saw the sparse growth that only a fool would have tried to graze sheep on. A man like himself. Not to question what river it was, he said, "I don't recall the white bridge."

302

"Painted white," said Blackbird, "so drunken Indian see it better at night."

"If that's the Pecos," said Warner, "we can let the car set. The road to my place turns off just beyond it. I can let it set till I get into Roswell, get a new belt."

George Blackbird had raised both sides of the hood so the motor could cool; he stood gazing at it. Warner recalled how the Indian boy Awa would marvel at the Dodge and feared to crank it. In his Indian mind that made it come alive, and dangerous. Blackbird knew about cars, but he was still an Indian and perhaps he also marveled at what made it run. Like an animal it needed water when it ran hot.

"One thing about the road through here, Mr. Blackbird, is that there's a lot of traffic on it. It's a main route. You'll have no trouble getting a ride." Warner felt he couldn't make it much plainer than that, that this was the end of the road, for them both. He leaned back into the cab for the ignition keys, the flashlight behind the seat, and the canteen. A half carton of Fig Newtons, left by the boy, was stored under the seat for an emergency such as this. Warner took them, but left the half can of tuna—although his by rights—for the Indian. Mrs. Leidy, back in Rubio, had trained him to be suspicious about anything left in a can. Out of the cab he said, "What you might do, when you get into Roswell, is ask the Texaco people to see I get a new fan belt. Some gas, water and a fan belt. Forget his name, man who used to own it, but I've always used Texaco products. Tell him the car is right here west of the bridge, a little less than twelve miles. If he'll toot his horn a bit I'll hear him—I'm just back off the road, on the rise."

Blackbird looked in the direction Warner pointed, seeing what Warner could no longer see. The wind wheel, if still there, might be visible. The cabin would not. Along through here Warner had kept his eyes on the water in the Pecos, like a crack in the earth. There was always something. There was always the dread that it might dry up. Even before he had left, the weather had turned the cabin the color of rusted iron; no color proved harder to see unless it snowed. The two windows in the house were around to the front, facing the west, where the sunsets were like the mountains on fire. A good thing about sheep was the way they soaked up the blazing noonday light. "I'm off about a quarter mile," he went on, "road leaves the highway just beyond the bridge. I don't plan to use it. While I'm here I'll walk in and out."

It was good that Warner knew Indians, or Blackbird's silence would have disturbed him. "I want to thank you for your company," Warner said, but with his hands full, as they happened to be, he didn't offer his hand to Blackbird as he otherwise might have. He noted the hint of stubble along Blackbird's jawbone. That surprised him. Did it mean his blood was mixed? The blast of the diesel horn, although two hundred yards away, led Warner to throw up his arms but seemed to paralyze his legs. Blackbird had to reach out and jerk him off the highway as the westbound van, throttling for the grade ahead, went by with a wind stream that rocked the Maxwell and sucked the breath out of Warner's mouth. The deafening roar of the throttle made it pointless to curse. A cloud of diesel exhaust veiled off the sky, through which they could dimly see the van lights twinkling. "Shhhheeeeeeee-it!" Blackbird hissed, and Warner took off. Walking head down, gripping the carton of Fig Newtons, the canteen swinging on its strap to sweep the ditch grass, he recalled the black man in the gas station back in Nevada who had banged his finger with one of the tire irons. "Shhhheeeeeeeeeeeee-it!" he had cried. Warner had thought it was air escaping from the tube. It was a new curse, not to be mistaken for the old one Warner tried to spare the ears of the boy. The black man had had it, the red man had it—was it a new way of cursing the white man? He avoided glancing back until he reached the bridge and had the partial concealment of the girders. He did not see Blackbird. The door of the car still swung open on the ditch side. Was he seated in the cab, spearing the smelly tuna with the blade of his knife? Something about George Blackbird appealed to Warner, but something about this appeal disturbed him. The fact was it relieved Warner to realize he had not, in the confusion, said good-bye to Blackbird, nor shaken his hand, implying that they had seen the last of each other. He regretted that he hadn't mentioned to Blackbird that fish left in tin cans might be tainted, but he was reassured to feel that that was something he could smell out for himself, like a dead cat.

7

THIS BRIDGE WARNER WAS CROSSING

proved to be a new one, without the planks he could peer through
at the glint of the water. They had also made it wider. People
who didn't know better might think it was a road. In the past
Warner would stop on the bridge for the view it gave him up
and down the Pecos. It was almost a canyon: over thousands of
years the stream had cut a deep crack into the earth and rock.
Viola refused to believe that. This river and canyon, in her opinion, had been made by God, like everything else. Warner had
once sent her postcards of Carlsbad Caverns showing stalagmites
higher than houses, made by the drip of water over millions and
millions of years. He couldn't grasp it. Over him she had always
had the advantage that she didn't *need* to grasp it. There it was.
The Lord had made it. That was that. What a strange thing it
was that his love for her now seemed to be the greater for it.
Downstream to the south—it took him time to see it, the canyon
being in shadow—the townspeople held picnics where the stream
was blocked by old car bodies, dumped off the bridge. They had
weathered and rusted to the color of rocks. On those days the
kids would climb around on them, and the men would sit there,
angling for trout. He recalled that Muriel, although part Indian,
never cared for fish because of the bones. She liked the canned
sort better, such as sardines, tuna at the time being too expensive. To his knowledge she had never tasted the fish he had bought
to feed to the cat. Neither had the cat. George Blackbird, who
thought of it as surplus, now had it to himself, if it was what
he wanted. Why was it, he wondered, his mind turned to things
with which he couldn't cope?

West of the bridge, he dropped down into the ditch grass
to make sure he wouldn't miss the turnoff to the ranch. It had

never been much: two rutty lanes. More than thirty years of weeds and neglect, allowing for a few vagrants, would have covered it over. He could hardly believe his eyes to come on a path grassless as a schoolyard, almost as wide as a road. The gate he had made in the barbed-wire fence—he had to keep stray sheep off the highway—had disappeared. A few strips of rusty wire indicated where it had hung, but the path was barren as a cattle entrance. What had happened? Would he find poachers on his land? For a moment he thought he should go back for Blackbird, but the Indian would only complicate matters. Had people widened the road to get to the river? It occurred to him that that might explain it. Over the low rise ahead, where the road narrowed, it would dip to a point almost level with the water after the floods. But from the rise he could see that the road continued toward his ranch. Picnickers and fishermen had used it this far, leaving their litter and empty beer cans, but they had built their fires in the river's backwash, a jungle of half-buried timber and driftwood. They had never lacked for wood, but they often lacked for wood that would burn. In search of it they would sometimes follow the path to Warner's ranch. Muriel might give them, or sell them, enough kerosene to start up a fire. Sometimes all they wanted was matches, having come out with no more than what they had in their pockets to light cigarettes. Almost forty years ago Warner had seen the start of what was now taken for granted. Young people who didn't know what to think, or how to act, not having been told, and lacking examples. After a few years of that they would naturally think they were *free* to think, and do, as they wanted: the problem seemed so elementary he could only marvel why it seemed a problem. He had turned to stand with the prevailing wind, the same wind still prevailing, at his back, the last grain of dust blown from the cracked earth at his feet. Gazing in the direction from which he had come, he seemed to see his life mapped out before him, its beginning and its end, its ups and its downs, its reassuring but somewhat monotonous pattern like that of wallpaper he had lived with, soiled with his habits, but never really looked at. A piece of this paper—he couldn't tell you its color, only that it was darker where their hands touched it, lighter behind calendars and under hooks where clothes hung—Muriel had herself put on one wall of the kitchen to make the room brighter dark mornings and evenings, although the rest of the day she drew the blinds at the windows against the light. He thought it queer, himself, to come in from the yard and see the bright colors on one wall only, the rest of the kitchen, and the walls of the bedroom, the natural dark hue of the wood previously used in bridge construction, and available to him without the cost of transport.

In the direction Warner gazed, a truck with a clattering tailgate, the sun glinting on four or five jangling milk cans, approached the bridge so slowly Warner was sure that it meant to stop. The truck looked so old it might be owned by an Indian, or some local rancher who would let an Indian drive it. It dropped from sight crossing the bridge, and Warner just assumed it had stopped for Blackbird. The clatter of the tailgate continued, however, and the truck reappeared on the slope to the west, the sun flaming on the dirty cab window. It puzzled Warner to see local people not bother to stop. Even if the cab was full, or a woman driving, there was room for the Indian at the back with the milk cans. It testified to how suspicious and unneighborly people had become. Warner felt this was largely the doings of hippies, some of whom were known to be crazy, but whether crazy or not, one thing led to another—one thing led as if willed to another—so that little happenings, on reflection, could not be described as accidental. The wind pressed at the small of his back like a hand, almost enough to lean on, to feel the support of, until the sound of it replaced the clatter of the tailgate in his ears.

The path he followed dipped sharply toward the river, then rose to the rim of the bluff where he had once bailed for water when his well dried up. At that point, as if a machine had collapsed, he found an assortment of iron wheels, one of the largest mounted on an axle across two wooden horses, a gulley trenched in the earth beneath it so the wheel would turn freely. To the outside rim of the wheel cans of various sizes had been bolted or wired. What did the builders have in mind? The river was thirty feet below, even during the season, but near the lip of the rim water from a spring darkened the earth. Weeds had sprouted to help hold the crumbling soil. Were there times—*had* there been times—when it formed a stream to drive a water wheel? No, it seemed more likely that the wheel had been used to catch the water and elevate it. Had the project been completed or abandoned? In the brush to one side he saw twisted lengths of roof gutters. Had they planned to irrigate? He recalled pictures in a *National Geographic* showing how it had been done in the Nile Valley and other biblical lands. It had impressed him as both primitive and resourceful, a notch or two above the local Indians. From the look of it, however, the gutters twisted, this irrigation project had been abandoned, but not before it had worked. A piece of the desert had been cleared and a crop of stunted corn marked the furrows that had soaked up the available water. Not much come of that crop, but it had been planted, so he was faced with the problem of squatters, of *squatters' rights*. Whatever the law might say, Warner himself was sympathetic to those who salvaged what others had abandoned, who took over and used what had been vacated. Migrants, more than likely, Mexicans or Indians, or a family of Okies out of the South or Texas; if they had taken it over, could they have it? He hadn't thought that far ahead. He stood, not thinking, listening to a sound like the rustle of grass, but he knew it to be water. As the water in the Pecos lowered, there was a point where the sound dropped to a rustle as it washed over the stones and gravel in the bed. He walked on to where a blowout had widened the trail at the top of the rise, a fine powdering of sand blowing into his face as he approached. Through half-lidded eyes, his gaze partially averted, he peered over the hump into the hollow where the sheep and their ewes often gathered to get out of the wind. It was now grassless, like a play yard, and strewn with the bodies and parts of wrecked cars. The colors of black and rust, in the morning light, made him think of prehistoric monsters, this hollow a place where they came to die. Beyond, just above his eye level, the slope below the house had been terraced in the manner of rice fields. Where water had settled and evaporated, it gleamed like exposed

310

rock. A few shriveled plants were still supported by sticks; others had collapsed to lie in the dust. The house was there, or more accurately the cabin, to which lean-to shelters had been added, open to the yard. These stalls faced the southwest, were roofed with boards and tin, and sheltered parts of car bodies that served as furniture. The door of a sedan provided one room with an up and down cranked window; he could see that it was down. Torn strips of material that once might have served as awnings stirred in the breeze that always followed the sun's rise. The bands of color looked festive, like banners at roadside stands. Where was everybody? Was it so early they had not got up? He peered around for a dog before moving closer. The wind brought him the tinkle of glass chimes. Light glinted on the strips of glass and tin suspended on wires in the open doorway. A cart made of buggy parts, using the tree and the axles, featured old car wheels with tire casings wired to the rims. Lengths of rope, attached to the front axle, were tied to a yoke that could be pulled by men, rather than horses. Directly fronting the house, where the terraces began, large cylindrical objects, like metal jars, were suspended on wires between heavy posts. The jars were graded in size, and put Warner in mind of the pipes of an organ, or something to be hammered. There was every sign of life but life itself, which he felt must be just out of sight somewhere, as if out of mind. At the top of two long tilted poles, reaching into the sun's rays, several gourds were hung from a crossbar, one of them slowly revolving. As it turned to the sun he saw a small bird enter one of the egg-sized holes.

To alert the dog—if there was one—he hallooed. No response. He moved to where he had a frontal view of the house, where the door stood open, loose on its hinge. The flapping of something attached to the roof was audible. He called again, moving slowly forward, but the silence seemed more threatening than the sound of life. He stood as if waiting to be greeted, glancing furtively at the clutter around him. A piece of harrow, consisting of four blades, had been left at the end of the plowed furrows. A board inclined to a log appeared to be a teeter-totter, the two ends polished by sitting. A galvanized tub and two chipped enamel pans sat to the left of the door stoop, one pan powdered with the husks of some sort of seed. Chickens? The dry strip of the yard had the look of a pen picked clean by them. He looked for feathers and saw them in the chicken wire at the base of the house. Had it been used to keep the chickens in, or out? The idea of chickens, however, relaxed him: only reasonably normal people fooled around with chickens. He called, "Anybody home?" in a neighborly voice, then walked forward to stand in the draft of the door. Wind through the boards at the back filled it with the low moaning sound of a gourd. That being a sound with which he was familiar, he was not disturbed. Day and night he had lived with it, but he had never grown accustomed to it. Familiar but not accustomed. "That goddam wind," he would mutter aloud, then come to the door, listening to it. If he feared what he had better sense than to fear, he would fear the wind.

Thinking of the wallpaper, the one wall that had it, he peered across the room, empty of objects, to a scene like fragments of a peeling circus poster, flashes of garish color, parts of bodies, dangling strips of what had once been flags or banners, but at the center of the mess, the words printed on a towel, the towel framed by long-tasseled ears of Indian corn:

WHEN THE GRASS IS PULLED UP
THE SOD COMES WITH IT

Warner stood for some time reflecting on the meaning of what he had read. The style of the printing was remarkably flowery—so much so that it gave him trouble to read it—tendrils and flowers worked into the design in the manner of a piece of framed tatting. Mottoes of this sort, usually of a religious nature, had once been tatted by his sisters and sent to him, framed, on Christmas. THE LORD IS OUR SHEPHERD—having in mind his sheep—was one that he had especially detested. His wife had taken them from the frames to insert calendar views of the heads of horses. She loved horses. On a sheep ranch there was not much to do with a horse.

On the floor of the room, set back against the wall, an assortment of car cushions provided beds, places to sit. He could hear mice scurry in the darkness beneath them. Remnants of clothes, shoes without laces, were scattered about as if left by children. The door to the room at the back had been removed and placed on bricks to provide a low table. Pages from a calendar were strewn about as if torn off in a bunch. The smell of the place was dry and clean, like a cob shed, but the old man hesitated to cross the threshold. His own life here had been displaced by a life, or lives, recently departed. He felt their presence. He knew about, but did not strongly feel, his own. The words printed on the banner seemed to speak to this feeling, but somehow remained elusive. Who had pulled up the grass? What was meant by the sod?

He turned away to see the oil drums at the corner of the house, and one rang dully when rapped with his knuckles. There was water at the bottom. When he kicked the barrel it stirred with life. His boyhood fancy that the white hairs from a mare's tail would turn to snakes if put in a barrel of rain water led him to peer, apprehensively, into the barrel's murky bottom. It stank of slime. Slime always stirred with life. Both the garden to the south and the terraces at the front had been covered with topsoil brought up from the river. Had it proved too shallow? Had they had too long a drought? In the cart made of car wheels and buggy parts there were several flats of seedlings that had never been planted. Had it been nature, or *human* nature, that failed them? In what way were they different? The seeds that crumbled in his hands were some sort of beans. Those big metal jars suspended between the posts proved to be brass shell casings. What was their use? The way they hung there invited Warner to pick up a stick and bang on the large one. Hit sharply, it gave off the sound of a gong. Had it been used for pleasure, or some practical purpose? In his ignorance he felt a curious longing. He wanted to know. In his boyhood, and later, farm hands had been called to dinner by the ringing of school bells, the firing of rifles. Like the motto on the wall, these gongs served a less practical purpose. The boy would have liked it—the boy and his two impractical friends. The old man did not believe, he refused to believe, in the hocus-pocus of the dim-witted, but he would have

313

liked to ask the boy what he thought of this apparatus. Ask him. When he gave it a bang see the look on his face.

He squatted in the morning sun, the boards warm at his back, now and then taking sips of the canteen water. By now, surely, Blackbird would be in Roswell. In a matter of hours the tow truck would come for him. He would hear the honking. He would hear the rattle of the tow truck's chains. Curiously, he had given no thought, once the car would run, where he would drive it.

Only one thing is the same as he left it, and he feels it support him like a hand at his back. If he tilts his head it will moan in his ear like a conch shell. Not so heavy as water, it had proved harder to fight. It seemed wiser to live with it. The wind's invisible will had blown him away, and blown him back. Given time it would work its will on everything it touched, as surely as fire: the works of man disappeared into thin air or went up in smoke. Viola had told him this all her life long, the wind being the invisible will of God, but what she had failed to tell him was that when he came to see this, to know it as the truth, he couldn't care less. God's will and the wind's will were all of one piece.

Back on the plains Viola had gathered around her the ruins and remains of numberless people, some of them believing they would end up in heaven, as she would, or be kept forever in storage, as in a deep-freeze. All of it was now ashes that the first good rain would mix with the earth, and the first strong wind blow away as dust. That he had no earthly use for all that had been lost both pleasantly dazed and amused him. If he had no earthly use, what other use might there be? For Viola there had been no end of the line, since it was on this line she dangled from heaven. In all her long life she had never conceived of a dead end. In all his long life Warner had taken it for granted, but he had never fully grasped its implications. Dead ends are forever. Forever was a thought he could not grasp. The ridiculousness of living forever was not to be equated with being dead forever. No, no. The dead were real in a way the heavenly hosts were not. He could see now that the very presence of the boy had distracted him from Viola's admonitions. He had read these letters to the boy, and through the boy's eyes they were remarkably silly. All of *his* life lay up ahead of him. Nothing lay behind. It was the presence of the boy, tiresome at times, maddening him to a fury at others, that had spared him, until now, the humiliation of the end, of the *dead* end.

He let himself down, out of the wind, on the spring seat of a buckboard. Not his either. Part of a disembodied wagon. His agreeably befuddled state of mind took pleasure in idle fancies. This place was a graveyard. He was one of the many curious objects. Others would be added. The meaning of this escaped him, but he was pleased. From the packet he took one of the Fig Newtons, but found that the cookie coating had crumbled. He didn't really like figs. The boy would eat the cookie crumble by wetting his finger, rolling it in the crumbs, licking it off. Just the thought of that made him thirsty and he took a swallow of the canteen water, the spout shiny with tuna oil and smelling of fish. The smell of the fish brought the Indian closer: why should Warner find that reassuring? It seemed to Warner he could see him licking his fingers, like a raccoon. It was not Warner's nature to be suspicious, or apprehensive, or troubled by darkness like most people, it being what he knew, not what he didn't, that put the fear of God into him. What he knew now should have done that, but it did not. He had given no thought, once the car had stopped, when it might start, or where he might drive it. His thinking had stopped when the car had stopped. It had not started up. One thing led to another. Since morning they had led to where he was, and nowhere else.

Unaware that he had dozed off, he awoke thinking of Pauline Deeter, widow of Arnold Deeter, no children. Lived in the Luau Travel Court in Ojai. Warner himself did the luaus, an expert on the timing of the charcoal fires. The court was near the ocean, and once a week they would gather for a big luau on the beach. Pauline Deeter shared her trailer with an older woman who needed a companion. Warner had felt it a pity a younger woman spent so much of her time with elderly people. She also worked with retarded children in one of the towns neighboring Ojai. On the luau evenings, Mrs. Deeter helped Warner set up the tables and keep things going. He liked her kittenish humor. At the sight of her back he knew she had turned from him to smile to herself. In his letters to Viola he had mentioned Mrs. Deeter, her helpful ways. "You old fox!" she had answered. "Are you looking for someone to take care of you in your old age?" The element of truth in that hurt him. He hadn't thought of it in that way, but perhaps he was. They were so often together, and got along so well, newcomers to the court assumed they were married. This rumor disturbed Warner more than it did her. She called him Floyd soon after their first meeting at a square dance evening in Laguna, but he had only recently been so bold as to call her Pauline. At this particular luau, early in September, they were on the beach early to watch the sunset and sing along with Mitch. After the luau it was their custom to sing a few hymns. It astonished Warner how these grown-up people loved to sing hymns. He had detested hymns from the time he could hear the strident, baying voice of his father singing such favorites as "Brighten the Corner" and "Nearer My God to Thee." He had refused to sing them at that time, or later, but he found it was possible to sing them in the company of Pauline Deeter, on the beach. How did it happen that he knew many hymns the others didn't know? He had a good, if untrained, voice. Pauline so reminded him of Viola—getting so emotional her eyes filmed over—he had felt free to assure Viola that she was just like one of the family, excluding himself. As they were waiting for the moonrise, seated on straw mats, out of the blowing fumes of the charcoal, Mrs. Deeter told them all her story about the blind child with the Seeing Eye dog. It was a sad story, about how the child thought the dog was as blind as he was, and when he found the dog had eyes, he hated the dog. The point of the story was, on reflection, that the child wanted to share the dog's *affliction*, more than the dog's good eyes. Mrs. Deeter frequently told the story because there were often newcomers to the luau. That night they had a fine time, as usual, and Warner was gathering up the coals for toasting marshmallows, which they liked to do over a hollow he had scooped in the sand. He was off to one side, with two of the older ladies, when he heard Pauline ask if they would like to hear a touching story. That was unusual, since she had just the moment before told one. They were anxious to hear another one, however, and gathered around her. "There was this poor blind child," she began, "and his Seeing Eye dog." She then went on to repeat the story she had just told them, but Warner did not stay to hear the last of it. One of the ladies beside him, a Mrs. Wohlheim, whispered to her companion, "My God, Lily, there goes Pauline!"

A dead end? Not the death of his wife, which he accepted, but this death in life that he could not, was the first dead end of Warner's life. There goes Pauline! There—but for the luck of it—might have gone Floyd Warner. How many mornings, or evenings, would he have looked up to see her, her eyes still bright, her face unwrinkled, as she patiently told him, for the umpteenth time, the sad story of the blind child and the Seeing Eye dog. What was left of Pauline, with no sign of going, he understood might go on, and on, and on. One day she would have seen, facing her across the table, this strange old man. In a gesture he had always thought very touching, her small, womanly hand would finger the buttons of her blouse. She had a well-formed figure, enhanced by the smallness of her hands and feet. Fate had spared him, he wrote Viola—which she would interpret as the hand of God—but he did not go on to explain what he had been spared. A man of his age and cranky habits, accustomed to living by himself and resenting intrusions, had no business, he wrote, asking a sweet, gentle woman to share his life. "You wily old thing!" she replied. "I just know it wasn't *your* old age you dreaded sharing—it was hers! Your loving sisters spoiled you. You realize that? I just hope you can make it up to Muriel *later!*" "Later" was Viola's word for heaven, knowing how much he disliked seeing or hearing it mentioned. He knew that she waited to discuss *this* problem, later, with Pauline. "You're such an old *curmudgeon,* you're going to try His mercy—do you realize that?"

Had he come to realize that?

He sat facing mountains he could no longer see, wondering if by now the snow gleamed on them. From this position, gazing westward, he felt at home. Light reflected from the sun-baked yard, but the air was not hot enough to shimmer. He was warm, his body like a potato baked in its skin. In the old days he might stand in the open door, but he seldom sat. He had never been a sitter. Muriel would say, "Now you sit and rest," but he never did. Within the range of his gaze, and his eyes were good, there had always been something that required doing. Was the nearsightedness of old age a cunning way of nature to discourage work, encourage sitting? Out of sight was out of mind. "It would help if you chewed," Muriel once told him, her brothers all being smokers and chewers. How could a woman kiss a man with a chew in his mouth? One thing his father said he had never forgotten, although he had never for a moment believed it. "I was offered a kiss and a chew on the same day of my life, and I chose the kiss." Perhaps he did. No one ever doubted his taste for ladies. In that inherited trait his only son took a certain reluctant pleasure. But he would have liked it better if his taste for ladies had been entirely his own. Muriel had been the first girl he met with an equally responsive taste for men, although her Indian nature was not so responsive as he would have liked. She was willing. His eagerness was something she seldom shared. He felt a drop in her interest when she seemed certain there was nothing much in it for her but pleasure: pleasure being an emotion she accepted, but not one she highly valued. She was willing, he was content, and they shared the durable creature comforts. In the winter one bundle. In the summer apart, on separate cots. He felt rising in him the admission that the warmth of her body was what he remembered, as he now felt the warmth of the sun. Other details—her face and her eyes, the whiteness of her scalp where her black hair parted—like the landscape before him, receded into the receding horizon, a ripple in the thin burning air, up in smoke.

318

8

THE BACKFIRING OF A TRUCK, ON THE grade behind him, cracked as evenly as an automatic rifle. A drying wind but no sun. He felt its warmth on the lids of his eyes. Out with the herd he had carried a rifle with him, on a sling, but within a few weeks the game knew its range. They looked close enough to him, the critters, but they proved to be at more than one hundred paces. He learned to arch his shots, holding his sight down the barrel to note the wavering flick of the bullet. On one occasion he found the lead pellet, blunted by a rock. One day, in its terror, a big jack rabbit bolted toward the flock where the dog had corraled them, leaped into the air, then hopped from back to back as if the flock were a woolly mattress. No one would believe that. Muriel had not believed it. Even the dog had not believed it. But as he wrote Viola, as sure as God made little apples that rabbit had leaped from back to back of the sheep, like a stone skipping on water. Had *she* believed it? "There isn't a day," she wrote, "God doesn't speak to us through His creatures." That meant she did not. The only person who might have believed it was the boy, but he also might have felt the old man was "losing his marbles," as he had heard him comment about the mailman. Where had he heard it? Who had thought it up? A mind rattling like a gourd, losing its marbles. Fear that the boy might jump to such a conclusion kept Warner silent on such stories. He did not want to see in the boy's eyes the equivalent of "There goes Uncle Floyd!" Was he, in fact, losing his marbles? He could not recall what had happened to that rifle. A Winchester automatic. Finest gun he had owned. Gone with the wind.

Traffic he could hear, but not see, bounced the light around like a mirror. His father had used a pocket mirror to signal to farm hands working in the valley. He had pointed out to Floyd, the one time he had listened, how the curve of the earth could be clearly seen in the clouds. On the plains they receded in a series of steps, conforming to the earth. His father had also noted that the flatness of clouds, at the bottom, was due to the heaviness of air at the earth's surface, and the way they billowed into cumulus masses made it clear that the air was lighter in space. He also believed that up *there,* somewhere, he would live happily ever after. Deliberate father of seven children knowing that his wife would die in childbirth. Would George Blackbird say that he had *killed* her? The word "kill" held no terrors for him. What did hold terror for him? Would it be the word "death"? It pleased Warner to think that the word "death" might disturb *him* less than it did the Indian. Recalling Blackbird, thinking about him, he had the curious impression that he was where he had left him, either in the cab of the car or stretched out in the sparse ditch grass, napping, this being the time of day it was foolish to do anything else. Warner needn't trouble to formulate it, but what they had in common, now, was waiting. The day having started, now they waited for it to end. Beyond that, Warner could not push his thought any more than he could push the stalled Maxwell. A dead end.

The tips of his fingers placed on his eyelids resulted in a series of overlapping halos. He could not determine on which side of his eyelids they seemed to be. He reflected on the mystery of seeing on the mind's eye. From exactly where he sat he had fired his rifle at a timber wolf made reckless by hunger. A shift in the wind had blown the smell of sheep and roasting meat into the wolf's face. Warner could sense his torment: how much more he knew than he was able to see! Hunger had brought him so close to the fire Warner could see the graying beard on his long muzzle. An *old* wolf. He understood better what might have made him reckless. Not necessarily hunger. Not necessarily anything he understood.

In the dusk, painfully, after being seated so long, he got to his feet and looked for firewood. This took him to the rise with its view of the highway. The white girders of the bridge appeared ghostly. If there had been the smoke of a fire he would have seen it. He stood there wondering if that reassured him. In the dry bed of the river the rusted body of a car tilted on boulders to provide a shelter. Would Blackbird be there, crouched on his hams in the manner of an Indian? For what was he waiting? Was he waiting for Warner's dead end? It gave him more satisfaction to admit that than it had given him to conceal it. It figured. It had not come to pass by an accident. Somewhere in the shadows, or under the bridge, Blackbird crouched watching Warner, and waiting. Strange that the thought of it aroused in Warner emotions, impulses that were reckless, like those of the wolf. He was tempted to tilt back his head and howl, but he did not: not for an Indian. Blackbird would smile. To himself he would say, "Foolish old man, what do you want?"

What *did* he want? He wanted no more than what he had found.

It pleased him to slowly gather materials for a fire. There were pieces of twisted driftwood in the yard that he knew to be there for some ornamental purpose. Around on the backside of the cabin (why the *back*?) steer horns and skulls found out on the range had been stored on the roof. For what purpose? He had no clue to their purpose. Something Indian in his wife (nothing else seemed to explain it) led her to gather up smooth or colorful rocks and place them, like plants, on the sills of the windows. He sensed in this childish habit some deep inscrutable meaning. The sun shone on them. They soaked up what otherwise might be lost.

In a widening arc, to the north and west, the scrub had been cleaned of anything that would burn. He recalled that some of these long-dried shrubs burned with the colors of Christmas baubles, and gave off a strong scent. As the slopes around him darkened, the sky brightened, providing a softly luminous, indirect lighting. On the highway the westbound cars had turned on their lights. To the east, arching over Texas, the feathery tracings of jets still burned in the sun's rays, but he did not see them, nor the low bank of smog that had drifted or blown here from

321

somewhere, like the exhaust of a grounded rocket. It startled him to see the moon, the lower half illuminated by the setting sun, looking no farther away from him than the horizon. This moon did not seem to arise in space, but to emerge from a slot in the earth behind the mountains, thin as a coin. The haze gave it the glow of a pumpkin, like the harvest moons of his boyhood. He once saw as well by the light of this moon as he did by the sun, perhaps better. There was less glare: he was able to see moving objects quickly, and judge distance. In this light a flock of sheep were like one body, feeding on everything at its circumference. The sound of the cropping, on a windless night, was like that of boots treading crisp snow. The flock itself sometimes moved like a sleeper stirring in sleep. At such moments the stupidity of these creatures seemed less oppressive to Warner, each one being but a small part of the larger, vegetative monster, let out to graze at night. He imagined there might be such vast creatures on the floor of the sea.

In the shelter of one of the tilted car bodies he carefully assembled scrap for a fire. It had been Warner's custom, acquired back when he lived here, to carry kitchen matches in the buttoned-down pocket of his shirt. These matches cast a light bright enough to see by, and a half-burned match, with its charred tip, served as a flame-cured toothpick with a charcoal taste. He now recalled—finding his shirt pocket empty—that he had given his last match to the hippie, and with that match the lamp had been lit that set fire to the house. "You got a match, Pop?" the kid had asked him, and Warner had freely given him his last match. Now he turned from the fire he could not light to think of the one that match had started. Without that fire he would be back in Chapman, curled up asleep in a bunk of the trailer, the boy a lump like a sleeping dog in the bunk overhead. Without that fire all that had happened to Warner would not have happened. The prayer circle of old women (and the spell they cast on him), the grave of Ivy Holtorfer, a white boy killed by Indians, the kitten in the outhouse, George Blackbird in the restaurant, the long day of waiting, and the fire he had built but had no match to light. The meaning of that both intrigued and escaped him. He reflected

322

on it with a puzzling satisfaction. One match had proved enough to leave the present in darkness, illuminate the past. One thing had led to another, and all of it led to where he crouched in the yard, as if he had planned it. Wasn't that what he had wanted? That things should go according to some plan? That however they went, they should not be like ditch weeds fitfully blown in the wind stream of a car. He had been agitated by Blackbird's manner, but he had welcomed the sense of foreboding. He had been free (so it seemed) to choose the white bum, and they would now be as far as Albuquerque, or Gallup, but in point of fact he had not been free to choose one or the other—he had been chosen. Was that so strange? Not so strange as it first seemed. If he went back over his life, as he had been doing, as it seemed to have been planned that he had come here to do, he saw that the crucial decisions, the meaningful choices, had invariably been made by others; his choice had been in conceding that their choice had been right. Viola's will, not his own, had led him to take the boy, and the boy's will, not his own, had led him to pick up the hippies. In these reluctant decisions his own will had been challenged, and lost. In losing he had hoped to hold on to something he valued more highly than his will. The love of Viola; the affection and respect of the boy. George Blackbird, however, challenged his will in a matter that seemed outside of these considerations—outside, in a way that appealed to him, of himself.

Was it true that the black eyes of red men saw better at night? Blackbird approached the house slowly, as if looking for something he had lost. In his right hand he held an object that sometimes glowed like the lens of a lantern. Did he think to see by it? Or to signal? Tilted upward, it reflected the moonlight. He seemed so absorbed in his meandering, Warner appeared to play no part in his calculations. Perhaps it just pleased him to wander by moonlight. At that point where his shadow lengthened he called out, "Old man, where are you?" His tone was familiar. One might have thought that the term "old man" was one of affection.

"I am here," Warner replied. Did Blackbird see him? The

moon shone impartially on the clutter. Blackbird lifted his head in the manner of a man accustomed to smelling better than seeing. When he moved, however, he came along a line that pointed directly at Warner. With each swing of his arms the object in his right hand flashed the light, like a predictable signal. On the baked slope of the yard he cast a shadow so pale it seemed to lie between him and the ground he walked on. The spirit of a man made visible by moonlight. Ten or twelve steps away he stopped abruptly and said, "You no build a fire?"

"I built it," Warner replied, "then found I had no matches. Left my matches in the car." In Blackbird's silence he sensed the judgment that here, too, white and red men differed, the red man not needing a match to start a fire. He said nothing, however, but crossed in front of Warner to the unhinged door of the house. From the pocket of his coat he took Warner's flashlight, directed its beam into the room's corners. He saw it flash dully on the glass at one window, flare briefly at the cracks in the walls.

"Like a war," Blackbird said, "they leave nothing."

"They left it better than they found it," Warner replied. "They did a lot of work. They tried to irrigate it."

"You think war is no work, old man?"

He stepped into the room, kicking at some of the car seats, then crossed it to peer into the room at the back. He was there for some time, returning to the door with what appeared to be part of a fishnet. The dangling strings of the net were tied to strips of tin and glass. "To fish?" he asked.

Warner did not think so. "A piece of fly net," he said. "We used to have a horse."

"Could be yours, could be theirs, could be mine," said Blackbird.

"You can have it if you want it," said Warner. "Help yourself." It amused him to think what Blackbird would consider an object of value. He held the fly net before him, so the glass and tin dangled, rocking the net in such a manner the glass tinkled. "You hang it where the wind blows. It makes a wind chime."

"Not for this you come back," said Blackbird. "Right?"

This word, like the clothes on his back, was something he

had picked up in the Army. It had its use. It was one of the few things he had not left behind. There was a rudeness in the word, a challenge, that Warner clearly sensed, but it did not arouse him. Aloud he said, "Right!" "Right!" the Indian replied. Into Warner's mind popped Viola's comment that it was *his* nature to expect the worst. What was the worst? How did one know it when it occurred? "Now we've had the worst," Viola often said, meaning that whatever it was, they had survived it. So it was something that went from bad to worse, but did not go on forever. The despair that had seized him in Viola's bedroom at the farm had no bottom to it, no name, no handle, but its presence had been so overwhelming it had stopped his breathing, like a weight on his chest. How true it was to speak of being in the grip of death! If there was order in this world, or in Viola's heaven, it was at such a moment Warner should have died, having experienced the worst. It was at such a moment the devil got in his licks, but here he was, a day later, worse off but feeling better. The faintness of this feeling, almost pleasantly giddy, was in part due to the fact that he had not eaten, and the long day in the sun. "The sun's got to you!" Viola would cry, if he said something unusually foolish. He often did to encourage her to say it. What lively times they had had together. Aloud he said, "What's that you got there?" and pointed at the object in Blackbird's right hand.

Blackbird gave it a buff on his coat sleeve, then peered at its surface as if for his own reflection. What he saw led him to sniff it. "Fishy!" he said.

What childish delight, Warner wondered, did the Indian get from the lid of a fish can? A pocket mirror? The ragged edges of the lid were razor sharp.

"Mr. Blackbird," Warner said gravely, "you mind my asking what you plan to do with it?" The Indian seemed to ponder the question, testing the edge with the tip of one finger.

"Razor sharp," he said.

Warner was touched and amused to note this aspect of Blackbird's nature. The lid of a can served him as a mirror, served him as a knife.

"Old man," he said, calmly, "give me your hand."

"I know it's sharp," replied Warner. "Sharp as hell. You think I don't know that?"

Blackbird's hand remained extended toward Warner, the palm up, as if expecting an offering. In contrast to his squat, short-legged figure, his hands were small, the fingers long and slender. A boy's hand, Warner would have judged it, more than a man's. Was this why—against his will, or if not against his will, against his better judgment, against something instinctive in his nature—he put forward his own hand, the palm up, as if Blackbird meant to read it by moonlight. The Indian gripped it gently, his fingers at the back, his thumb firmly pressed into the heel of the palm, and with a gesture so deft Warner scarcely saw it, flashed the lid of the can so that it caught the moonlight. Warner felt nothing but the increased pressure of the thumb in his palm. The blood that flowed into his palm, black in this light, he thought must be from the hand of Blackbird, one of his strange and disturbing Indian customs. He looked up to see why he had cut himself.

"For christ-a-mighty's sake," he said, pulling both hands toward him, where he saw that the blood flowed from his own wrist. It pumped, as if a leak had occurred at his pulse. The Indian continued to grip the hand, firmly, the thumb pressing to the palm as if to slow the bleeding, the dark blood filling, then overflowing the cupped palm. Did Warner cry out? Not to his knowledge. Pain might have aroused or disturbed him, but he felt no pain. The hand that gripped him, the thumb's steady pressure, seemed to bring to one spot all of the life in his body, there for him to observe.

"Mr. Blackbird—" he said, but hardly in protest. Out of wonderment, perhaps, out of clarification.

"Old man," Blackbird replied, "you sit quiet and you live longer."

That amused Warner. Did Blackbird feel that was his concern? As if taking his pulse, his thoughts elsewhere, Blackbird had turned to face the rising moon, stirring Warner to marvel at what might be on his Indian mind? Had he been a good soldier? His cunningly laid plans were well carried out. From Warner's

326

watch pocket he would take the timepiece that had stopped
sometime during the morning, a gold-cased watch with a movement so weary it would run something less than twenty-two hours
a day. Warner had learned to give the stem a twist each time he
looked at the time. In the pocket of his shirt, the flap buttoned,
he would find eighty dollars in ten-dollar bills, and maybe ten
to twelve dollars in his wallet. Otherwise, nothing much of value.
Several clippings sent to him by Viola about the death of people
in and out of the family, at least one of which had encouraged
him—without mentioning names—to outlive the bastards. In
many ways he had. About George Blackbird, who would sur-
vive him, his feelings were more complicated. Step by step, as
if Warner had helped him plan it, all the pieces fitting neatly as
a jigsaw puzzle, the Indian had picked up his scent and tracked
him down to where he was lying, his wound self-inflicted, the
razor-edged can lid lying in his lap. Faintly, due to his weakness,
Warner felt a twinge of admiration. A passer-by, if there had been
one, would have said that the red man had paused to help him,
and stood holding his hand. On Warner's mind's eye he saw this
scene—one of the last he would see—as if clearly painted. It would
bear the somewhat puzzling title "Old man, what do you want?"
From the scene it seemed clear it was help that he wanted, but
he seemed reluctant to ask for it. What help? All his life he had
made it a point never to ask. Everything had happened according to a plan that would prove to be his as much as Blackbird's,
so that what he wanted, strange as it might appear, was what
he had got. That would prove to be even truer of Blackbird, who
now took from Warner such things as he valued: the money from
his wallet, the watch from the bib pocket, a knife with a blade
less sharp than a can lid, and from the canteen, dangling on its
strap, enough of the water to rinse the blood from his fingers.

These movements of the Indian affected Warner like the
ritual of the prayer circle. A presence known to him, outside of
himself, noting his weakness and the slow pulse of his dying, gazed
on him with eyes like those of a creature at the rim of the fire.
A trick of his senses? Were these unseen eyes his own? In a house
near the sea, facing a roaring fire, he had turned to gaze through

the patio doors to see the same fire burning in the space before him, as if over the sea. One of the guests had explained the illusion, but it had not dispelled Warner's vivid impression. He saw it out there, a fire over the sea, as well as in the room behind him. In the same way he could not dispel the impression that he was outside, not inside, his own body. Without reason to question this sensation, he was no longer disturbed by its novelty. One seemed as real to him as the other: to be outside, perhaps, even realer. Was it so unusual for the strange to seem commonplace, or the commonplace miraculous? He thinks, *I have been walking in my sleep, and now I am awake.* As simple as that. As unlikely as that. As irrelevant.

With one of his own paper matches Blackbird lit the fire that Warner could see, but not feel the glow of. By its light, however, Blackbird can see that the blood has drained from his face. The effect has emphasized, as in a carving, the essential elements of his nature: the stubborn will, the self-centered actions, the independent, inflexible cast of his mind, yet curious how in times of crisis his thoughts proved to be on others besides himself. It was not Blackbird's intent to do this for him, but Blackbird, too, has been shaped to this moment, the ceremonial opening of the vein in Warner's wrist. Although the muttering he hears is the voices of women, he can no longer distinguish their faces. The voices hover above him, Viola's among them, and the Indian stands before him gently holding the wrist he has just sliced. It is a painting, the title a motto that somehow escapes him, stamped on the frame of the picture he is within. His eyes watch the Indian, now crouched near the fire, take the last of the Fig Newtons from the carton, then tip it to spill the cookie dust into his palm. This he lapped up with his tongue, like a cautious cat. He did not much like it, but he had learned to live and make do with what he had found. Warner, too, had been young like him, a good hunter, a killer only when necessary, a man who knew his own mind, kept his own counsel, and had lived in the manner he believed he had chosen, not knowing that he had been one of those chosen not merely to grow old, but to grow ripe.

328

Printed November 1993 in Santa Barbara & Ann
Arbor for the Black Sparrow Press by Mackintosh
Typography & Edwards Brothers Inc. Text set in
Sabon by Words Worth. Design by Barbara Martin.
This edition is published in paper wrappers;
there are 250 hardcover trade copies;
150 hardcover copies have been numbered & signed
by the author; & 26 copies handbound in boards
by Earle Gray are lettered & signed by the author.

PHOTO: Barbara Hall

LONG REGARDED as one of the most gifted American writers, Wright Morris received the National Book Award in 1956 for his novel *The Field of Vision*. His most recent novel, *Plains Song*, won the 1981 American Book Award for Fiction. He is the author of seventeen other novels, several collections of short stories, books of criticism and a number of photo-text volumes. He and his wife make their home in Mill Valley, California.

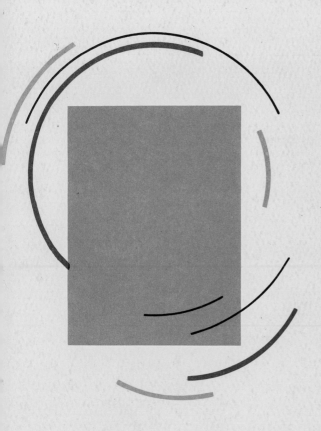